MAHARIA

Book 3

The Kaelandur Series

Thrice Nine Legends

Joshua Robertson

Published by Crimson Edge Press, LLC
www.crimsonedgepress.com

Printed in the United States of America

First Printing, 2017

ISBN-10: 1-945397-96-9
ISBN-13: 978-1-945397-96-7

Cover art by Winter Bayne.

Mapwork by Josephe Vandel.

Acknowledgement

A special thanks to any who have saved faith in life, and in love, despite the tender trials we must endure to seize either.

There once was a time when the gods were gods without question. When men were men without example. When heroes were only the frivolous dreams of lurid mortality. It was a time when truths and untruths were indistinguishable, hatred and love were equally excusable, and life and death regaled all of humanity in the same breath. Myths of old were realized and legends were born from the very dust man was formed of, to be told and retold until the grace of time altered them beyond knowing or forgot them completely. Still, some tales were preserved deep within the hearts of mankind, for reasons that could not be fathomed. Perhaps bearing the fruit of some profound truth or kept alive merely by the strength of the men who lived them. Some tales would never be forgotten.

Table of Contents

Thrice Nine Legends Saga

Additional Works

Published by Crimson Edge
**Forthcoming by Crimson Edge*

MAHARIA

Book 3

The Kaelandur Series

Thrice Nine Legends

Prologue

Dorofej Kaligula angled his eyes to gaze at the iron manacles binding his arms to the stone wall in the lower levels of Melkorka. He shuddered at the sight of his pasty, white flesh, prickled with gooseflesh, hanging exposed against the dry air. His thin legs were also fixed to the floor, keeping him rigidly hooked in place. His brittle bones ached; his strength was ever-fleeting.

He chest tightened with despair—not from the arduous position—but from knowing how *Koldovstvo*, the ancient magic, had once again gifted him with old age. Only weeks ago, he had been young and vivacious; but now, his wrinkled skin hung loose from muscle, and his body twinged as though his insides no longer had the resolve to function another day. His organs were likely as frail as the white hairs dangling over his eyes.

The black mage kept his knees locked to prevent the metal above from digging into his wrists. The blood from past captives staining the metal clasps spoke clearly of the antagonizing pain that would come if he allowed himself to simply hang. He questioned how long any man could hold this position before his wits were broken along with the finite body.

Dorofej did not know how long he had been standing in this irregular position. It may have been days, possibly a week. No light entered Melkorka's dungeon, only shadows. The room changed considerably since he had last been within its confines twelve-hundred-years ago. Where dirt paths and rickety cells once stood, rarely used, Dorofej now saw chiseled red stone, fresh timber, and twice as many chains for prisoners.

With a strained breath, he twisted his neck, where he knew a carved symbol of the eye, scraped with the moon and cross, hung over his head. The magical marking prevented him from touching the craft, *Koldovstvo*. He whispered its ancient name. *"Znaki."*

He dropped his head in defeat. Even if the symbol were erased, Dorofej was not certain he had enough life in him to wield *Koldovstvo*. Another trickle of magic through his fingertips may very well end his life.

He had no interest in dying. Not yet.

He suppressed a cough. The odor of urine and feces clung to the air as closely as a hero might cling to honor and glory. Sadly, his own filth was among the filth beneath his feet. Rats and unmarked pests screeched and scraped across the stone floor. Over and over, the creatures neared him to nibble at his wrinkled toes, checking for decay.

With a shudder, shout, or twitch, Dorofej indicated to the vermin he was not dead. But the rodents were patient, accustomed to the unwritten process of the underground, hollowed chamber. No doubt, in short time, there would be no resistance, no shuffling or screaming, and then they could feast on his flesh.

Across the room, the latch clicked and the oak door creaked open. Air from beyond the dungeon circulated into the room. Dorofej could not hold back his cough this time, and hacked harshly, the ashy dust filtering up to his nostrils and into his throat.

The flickering torchlight danced across the dungeon, nearly blinding him. Twisting his neck, his long white hair fell away from his face, providing a faint image of many shadowed figures slinking into the room.

"Careful," said a man in white robes. "Do not loosen the binds until the giant is chained."

The *Kadari* paid no attention to Dorofej. Their attention stayed on the Ispolini, the giant, who was being dragged across the floor with magical strands of *Koldovstvo*.

Dorofej recognized Tyr Og. The giant had helped kidnap an innocent boy, Bohumir Mager, for the *Kadari* to sacrifice here at Melkorka. Though, none would have guessed the plan would have been thwarted by the red mage, Eisliev Kluk, who slaughtered the boy first.

Tyr growled, having the ability to do nothing more but speak. "For the hundredth time, I did not kill the boy. Eisliev killed him, and the half pint killed Eisliev with a dagger."

"Hold your tongue," Falmagon Sej spouted, following Tyr and the other *Kadari* through the door. The Patrician of the *Kadari*, once known as the Highborn Long-Walker, was easily distinguishable. "We will hear your so-called truth when it is time."

"Listen to me. I helped you," Tyr shouted. "There is no reason to hold me here. Please!"

Falmagon responded to the Ispolini, but lifted his blue eyes to Dorofej, mockingly. "I will be most interested to hear more about this dagger in very, very short time."

Dorofej strained to keep his head elevated to maintain eye contact with the Patrician. The muscles in his neck and upper back ached. He tried to focus on breathing through his nose to forget the pain.

It was a mistake. He coughed harshly again at the rotten smell.

Falmagon maintained the smirk on his face. "Yes, the truth will be revealed soon enough. Won't it, Dorofej? Say, why don't you give up your little charade and tell me what I need to know?"

Dorofej wheezed, desperate for a drink. "Oh, tell me—you must—what needs to be known, yes?"

The demeanor of the Patrician changed as soon as Dorofej opened his mouth. "Do not play your games with me. Where is *kaelandur*? Does Branimir have it?" Falmagon flared his nostrils, blowing air through his thick mustache. He advanced, holding himself inches in front of Dorofej's face.

Dorofej lingered, stone-faced. Indeed, his friend, Branimir Baran held *kaelandur*, the copper dagger, the hourglass of Dorofej's life. Though, he would never tell Falmagon such a thing.

"I say, why do you care?" Dorofej said. "Dead, the boy is. Sacrifice him, you cannot."

"Answer the question," a deep voice demanded from behind Falmagon. The man, called Dagmar, ambled forward from the shadows. Dorofej fought the man on the shores of Folkmar before being imprisoned. At the time, Dagmar lost years of his life casting *Koldovstvo*. But now, the Stuhia regained his youth. He had a head full of red hair and smooth, unmarred skin. Seeing Dagmar reminded Dorofej the Ash Tree and the Waters of Life were just beyond the castle's dungeon. His salvation was less than a hundred feet away.

Dagmar gripped a thick book under his arm, and continued, "Someone has broken the old laws by creating this dagger with *Koldovstvo*. If you are truly Stuhia, you know the maker must be killed to abolish the dagger."

"Know the law of the Stuhia, I do," Dorofej said, eyeing the leather book. He knew its name: the *Varkolak*. "I say, why are you eager to destroy *kaelandur*?"

Falmagon huffed with superiority, seemingly offended by the question. "Because demons have continued to come from the Netherworld and it must be stopped. They are intent on destroying the Ash Tree. This started with the creation of the dagger, and it will end with the dagger's destruction."

"That is why you sent Alyona and Artemiy after the dagger, yes?" Dorofej contemplated. "Want the dagger, you did, to stop the demons?"

"Why else?" Falmagon squinted at Dorofej, likely questioning how he would know of Alyona and Artemiy. Yet he said nothing of the two *Kadari*. Instead, he defended his reason. "It was not until I met Dagmar that I learned you were a Stuhia, and I had to kill you to destroy *kaelandur*. Everything I do is for the saving of this world, Dorofej."

"Misinformed, you are, Falmagon Sej. Proof, you are, there are worst things in this world than demons," Dorofej said, coughing again. He unsuccessfully tried to find saliva in his mouth. "And come, the demons will, whether *kaelandur* exists or not."

"Do not insult me with your lies," Falmagon said haughtily. "You are trying to save your own skin."

"My own skin?" Dorofej said, lifting his eyebrows with as much innocence as he could muster.

Dagmar fell into the façade. "Did you not create *kaelandur*, Stuhia?"

"Of course, he created it!" Falmagon cried, glaring at Dorofej. "Don't bother entertaining this pile of piss with such a question. He is talking in his riddles to buy his time, hoping someone will come and save him. Listen, it was only him and Jhar who crafted the dagger, and Jhar is dead."

The black mage snorted, looking to Dagmar. "The law of the Stuhia, I know."

Dagmar tilted his chin to Falmagon, and then back to Dorofej. "Humor me."

Dorofej swiftly stated, "Familiar with the *Varkolak*, I am." He bobbed his head in acknowledgement of the book under Dagmar's arm.

The redheaded man in front of him stepped backwards in sheer shock, mouth gaping and eyes widening. "How do you know the name of this codex? How does he know this, Falmagon?"

"Because passed it to my son, Mihael, I did, after the fall of the Carian Council?" Dorofej kept his eyes from Falmagon, who he could hear breathing heavier and heavier. He locked eyes with Dagmar. "Scribed it, I did."

"What!" Dagmar roared, his voice echoing in the dungeon. "Mihael? You gave this codex to my father?"

Dorofej lowered his head.

"You are my grandfather?" Dagmar asked shakily.

"He is deceiving us, Dagmar. Let us kill him and be done with this. His death will save Aenar," Falmagon demanded.

Dagmar hurriedly grabbed Falmagon's arm, pulling him away. His eyes never moved off Dorofej hanging from the chains. "No. If he did not create *kaelandur*, killing him will do nothing but have Dahz find disfavor in you."

"One way or another, the world is better without him. I would rather watch him burn than reach Thrice Ten Kingdom," Falmagon proclaimed.

"If he is my grandfather…if he knows the law of the *Varkolak*…"

Falmagon interrupted. "Wouldn't you know if he was your grandfather? He is lying."

"I never knew my father's father," Dagmar sluggishly said. "You do not understand the significance of what this man is saying. Whether he is lying or not—even to know the name of this codex—speaks of the knowledge he holds. We cannot kill him," Dagmar said while Falmagon stared incredulously back, "yet."

"Your logic is the same as my predecessor, Kinhar Sayan," Falmagon whispered, "and he is dead. The *Kadari* cannot fight an endless war against Marheena's demons and lead the people of Aenar to redemption. We can kill him now and end this."

Dagmar shook his head. "The only way to destroy *kaelandur* is to kill its maker *with* the weapon."

"What?" Falmagon sneered.

"You cannot simply kill him. His life is bound by the life of the dagger," Dagmar explained. "And you need the weapon and creator to complete the deed. Without *kaelandur*, you are powerless. You would not be able to kill Dorofej if you tried."

Falmagon bawled in frustration, folding his hands into fists. "Fine, Dagmar. Then we must find Branimir Baran."

Dagmar curled his lip. "I can find him."

"If you won't tell me where *kaelandur* is," Falmagon turned back on Dorofej, staring hard into the black mage's icy eyes, Branimir will. Even if I must tear him limb from limb, he will talk."

Dorofej hung his head in defeat.

Month of Harvest

Fourth of Warmth

1352 CE

Chapter I

"You don't have to watch me," Branimir Baran said, staring blankly across the subtle ripples on the placid lake, absorbing the morning sun's warmth on his back. He overlooked the strands of black, thin hair tickling his eyelids, situated just above his long, crooked nose.

"You keep saying that, and I keep watching," Sulanna Maelthirren replied from a few feet away. He could hear her fingernails scraping against the smooth rock in her hand patiently waiting for him to finish his morning routine. The two stuck to the same, mundane schedule since the warm months had come. Branimir knew her and Adamus Ebordon rightfully worried about his affliction, but their constant concern only deepened his distress.

The breeze shifted, filling his nostrils with a hint of the pollen from the poppy field north of the lake, the *Gnyn Waters*. His stomach tightened with every forced breath, sucking the stale air through his nose and blowing it out from his lips. More than a year passed since fleeing from Falmagon at Melkorka, and he had come no closer to rescuing Dorofej or ridding himself of the cursed copper dagger, *kaelandur*. Moreover, Bran scarcely traveled beyond Gaetana's city walls, remaining under the watchful eye of his trusted friends.

His sigh was long and intentional. "Enough time has passed. I would think if Falmagon wanted me, he would have come by now. We have abandoned Dorofej for too long."

"Adamus and I have told you many times, returning to Melkorka would be a mistake," Sulanna said, her faded, brown hair swirling against her thin cheeks. The number of grey strands on her head had significantly increased this past year. "You have only recently healed from your injuries. A broken arm is never easy to overcome. Give yourself some time."

Branimir instinctively rested his left hand on his right forearm. He rubbed his red skin softly with a frown. Falmagon snapped the bone at Melkorka during the battle on the shoreline. Occasionally, the bones still tingled or ached but he would not admit as much to Sulanna.

"You cannot keep me here forever," Branimir said.

"You speak as though we are holding you captive against your will, Bran." She pushed her flailing hair behind her ear. "We did not flee from Melkorka only to watch you go back and die."

"I wouldn't die," Branimir said.

"You have many talents, my friend, but seeing the future is not among them." Her voice lacked her usual sing-song tone, reiterating the same speech she had given many mornings before. "Falmagon Sej has the Ash Tree in his grasp, promising immortality. He can afford to be patient."

Branimir maintained the frown, sitting motionless. His mind wandered briefly through memory like a melody trapped between the ears. The images of battles won and lost weighed on his heart, remembering what had come to pass and what may have been done instead. He envied old men with weak minds. For all his years, Branimir could not forget.

He finally said, "The *old-dark* are escaping into Aenar and demons flood from the Netherworld." Branimir chewed the inside of his cheek. The entity they encountered at the ruins of *Garain'l*, and now trapped within the copper dagger, still frightened him. The dark, ancient god called itself a Likhyi, intent on annihilating the Ash Tree and the world with it. And now, the malevolent deity somehow became bound to him through *kaelandur*, promising to kill Branimir if the dagger was ever destroyed. He scrunched his face, doom weighing heavy on his heart. "I do not know what *time* Falmagon would think to have."

"True. The Ash Tree withers more and more each day while the *Kadari* defend against demons. Maybe his mages are too spent to search for a single Kras," she said.

"Not when I hold *kaelandur*," Branimir said. "Falmagon would give everything for this dagger."

"He may not know you hold it." Branimir could hear Sulanna's tongue clicking against the roof of her mouth. She did not even believe her own lie. "Whatever the reason," she finished, "he has yet to come for you. He chooses to wait."

Branimir clenched his fists in angst. "But we cannot. We have lingered around this city for fourteen months and have done nothing."

"We have stayed alive."

Branimir punched his fist through the air. "While Dorofej suffers."

"Dorofej is still alive," she returned with softness. The scraping on her rock ceased. He could feel her gaze burning into his back along with the sun's heat. "Whatever he has suffered at the hands of Falmagon would be wasted if you were to return with *kaelandur*."

Pulling his red-colored hands to his lap, Branimir danced his thin fingers along the copper hilt nestled between his belt and stomach. Not long ago, Branimir learned Dorofej had crafted *kaelandur*, and per the magical law of the Stuhia, the dagger could only be destroyed through its creator's death, meaning Dorofej still breathed. While *kaelandur* existed, Dorofej was living.

His eyes glazed, staring at nothingness across the lake. "You and I cannot outlive Falmagon without access to the Ash Tree, and I cannot unbind myself from *kaelandur*. We have remained deadlocked for too long."

Sulanna said, "Dorofej opened the gate for us to come to Gaetana. He must have had his reasons for sending us to the capital. We cannot leave here until an opportunity presents itself."

He remained silent, his shoulders falling. Gaetana was half a world away from Melkorka. He suspected Dorofej had simply sent them as far away from danger as he could with his magic. Branimir doubted any hidden meaning lay in the deed.

Sulanna apparently misread his body language, gliding forward and kneeling to place her wrinkled hand on his drooping shoulder. He often forgot Sulanna was middle-aged for a human. "You have not been the only one struggling this past year. Remember, we also abandoned Alden in Talastein, and I have had to fight the compulsion to rush back south to save him. Every morning, the thought is heavy on my mind. I do not have the comfort he is still alive anymore, but I hope."

"I am sorry, Sulanna." Branimir gave a weak nod, knowing the love Sulanna felt for Alden and the pain she experienced when he was captured by the Lilitu. Branimir long ago considered the old warrior dead; he honestly thought Sulanna did the same, especially with Adamus's insistence that the Lilitu did not keep their prisoners alive.

"Hope is not lost, my friend," she said, "not yet."

"I know what you are saying. But whether we stay here or go, I die at the end of this story," Branimir said.

"The same could be said of any who call themselves mortal. Do not be so eager to rush to your end." Sulanna squeezed his shoulder, hurling the smooth rock into the lake, an indication of the storm brewing inside her. "Come now, Adamus approaches. No more talk of death."

Branimir cleared his throat, watching the ripples expand from the impact. His sensitive ears heard Adamus, the hero-warrior from Ariadne, approaching. The gruff man's heavy footfalls were unmistakable, scraping against the dry ground.

"Who is with him? Wit?" Branimir off-handedly asked. His eyes drifted to the cracking earth. The summer had been scorching, leaving the morning dew to imagination.

Sulanna shifted next to him and hummed in response, indicating the persnickety historian, Witigor Sirska, from the *Highspire* remained attached to Adamus's side, as he had been for the past month. The undernourished man had wedged himself between Adamus and Branimir, openly ridiculing any who were not an Anshedar or male. Branimir considered silencing Wit with a fist in his loud mouth, but Sulanna coached tolerance, reminding him they would be better off not to draw attention in the King's city. King Frantisek was a man closely allied with the *Kadari*.

"Wit and I crossed a runner at the gate. The Uvil sacked Draha the night before last," Adamus informed them, stopping a few feet behind Branimir's back.

Sulanna replied, "I thought King Frantisek was taking back Raybin."

"He tried," Adamus said, "and failed. They were pushed back two weeks ago."

"Gaven Frantisek has no sense for war. He probably never read *Fate Without Duty* by Anthony Janes. He is not like his father." Witigor whistled through his lips.

Branimir could already visualize the dozen or so blonde strands hanging from Wit's scalp, bouncing as he talked about his books. His hair would be clinging to the side of his cheek, held in place by the ridiculous pointed hat he often wore. Half of the man's head had been scarred from a fire long ago, decorating his face with folded skin and red lines, leaving him quite bald and grotesque. Without judgment, Branimir understood why Wit had taken up copying books in the *Highspire*; the capital library was a place where he could escape the disparaging looks of his fellow citizens.

Adamus went on, "No doubt, the cities of Tyrewen and Utulock will form a barrier with their armies; the Ariadneans will send what fighting men are left. But when they fall, nothing will stop the Uvil from sieging Gaetana. With supplies, the King could hide behind the walls for years, but we would be trapped inside with everyone else. We will not be able to stay in the capital."

Branimir's heart jumped at the thought of leaving Gaetana. He spun around and rose to his feet. Adamus faced him, beard hanging to his chest, and blue eyes wild with excitement. Witigor, a head taller than the Ariadnean, joggled his head in agreement, the overhanging flap of his ridiculous brown hat bouncing over his brow.

Sulanna stilled them with her hand. "What about Dorofej? The Stuhia has not survived this long simply to stay captive in a dungeon. Are we to continue to trust that he will find a way to escape?"

"'Tis a thought I hope to be true, Sulanna," Adamus said, "though the odds are not favorable. I am not proposing we attempt to free Dorofej. We simply cannot stay here much longer. Besides, if Dorofej does escape, he can always find us with that *thing* he does."

"*Klukas*," Branimir said. "Yes. He can find us in the shadow world."

"Oh, here we are again, talking of this mysterious, all-knowing man called Dorofej." Wit grimaced, pulling the sleeves up on his shirt. "The man might as well be a god, the way you speak of him." Wit's eye twitched. "Still, you are correct on this matter. The Stuhia can find anyone in *Klukas* if they have come across them before. Their gift of scrying supersedes the skill of the greatest oracle. He would be able to find you no matter your destination, I assure you."

"Oh. Are you suddenly an expert with the Stuhian people, Wit?" Sulanna mocked, twisting her mouth with suspicion. "Funny you have not said a word of them until recently."

"Well...I have read Tom Flitter's *Mystagogical's Forlorn Folio* and Colin Turney's *Unchanted and Unequaled*." Wit crossed his arms, leaned back like he had taken a blow to the bits, and then wobbled his head back and forth in disbelief. "Do you not know I have access to every book in the known world, Sulanna? I would have been reading about the *dragon people* long before now if I had known anyone cared to know about them. But you three keep your tongues wrapped so tight, I would not be surprised if you did not have any tongues at all. I don't know how you expect me to help."

Branimir stuck out his tongue. "No one asked for your help. We asked for one book on ancient religions, and here you still are—"

"Yes, I remember. *The Compendium of Infernal Light* by Emrys Trudgeon. Wit widened his eyes. "No other man could have gotten you that little treasure. If you don't want me, I can be on my way." He stomped the back of his foot against the earth, indicating he had no intention of budging. "You know, it is not everyday someone asks about a text not highlighting the Lightbringer."

"Czern's breath. You mustn't go anywhere," Adamus said, angling an eyebrow at Branimir.

Sulanna flashed her teeth, chiming in, "Indeed. Your input is always welcome, but our business will remain our own."

"Of course, my Lady," Wit said, nodding his head again with enough momentum to bounce his hat. "And I don't mean to pry, but anything you need to know, I can find." He winked, pointing at Branimir. "Don't get me wrong. The Kras have wicked memories, but none are as old as books. None can know how their minds have twisted their words over time."

Branimir clenched his jaw, catching another narrow look from Adamus. "Okay," he murmured, "is it decided? Are we leaving Gaetana?"

"We will discuss it more after breakfast," Adamus answered. "We should have a destination in mind before simply packing up and marching out of the gates."

"South is clearly out of the question," Sulanna said.

"Sulanna…" Adamus opened his hands, repeating himself, "after breakfast, eh? Branimir needs to get back to the tavern. He has work to do. We all have work to do."

Hanging his head, Branimir sighed. He, Adamus, and Sulanna had been trading work for lodging and food for the better part of the year.

She folded her arms. "Very well, Adamus Ebordon. But I hope you have better sense than to give me orders and expect me to simply follow."

Wit peered at Sulanna over his shortened nose.

Adamus's features turned to stone seconds before he threw his head back with a booming laugh, his beard bouncing against his chest. "Never, Sulanna. Never."

Branimir tailed the other three on the dirt path winding back through the gates, beneath the half-raised portcullis, to return to the *Peddlar's Rose*. The road to the inn branched into a hundred twisted routes within the city. According to Wit, the city had been built sporadically over the age with buildings thrown wherever space allowed. Built from both stone and wood, the shops and homes were as intertwined as a briar patch. The *Shielded Boar* sat against the smithy, like a crooked blade against the hilt. The *Poppy Garden*, the apothecary, was positioned so close to the cobbler, the front doors would collide if ever they sprang open at the same time. The hodgepodge of mangled architecture continued from the housing district to the *Highspire* to the looming hold of King Gaven Frantisek.

The *Peddlar's Rose* sat only a few streets south of the King's courtyard, frequently full of patrons from all stations in Gaetana, common and noble alike. Yet mornings typically were slow with only a few guests descending from their rooms for breakfast.

Branimir was the last to enter the *Peddlar's Rose*, closing the oversized, wooden door behind him. He imagined a giant from the western island of Tundris Mor, an Ispolini, could fit through the entryway without straining the neck. He instantly caught the scent of sausage and biscuits, skimming the common room to see a handful of patrons sitting amongst the tables.

"Good morning, Master Branimir," one of the men at the table lifted his hand. Branimir forced a smile at the frequent customer named Jon Goraen, having more greying hairs on his chin than combed over his receding hairline. Although a citizen of Gaetana, he spent ample time at the inn due to marital spats. Branimir only met the wife twice prior, and neither instance was pleasant. She had a shrill whine, matching the fracas of demons.

"Morning," Branimir replied, forcing a serpentine grin.

"Will you be honoring us with your dagger throwing tonight? I came a bit too late last night," Jon said, tearing a biscuit in half.

"I do not know what Lady Gail has intended for evening festivities," Branimir answered.

Jon laughed, pushing the bread into the back of his cheek. "I'll talk to her then, and see that it is *intended*."

Branimir held the smile. Jon likely would persuade Gail, considering the amount of coin he spent at the *Peddlar's Rose*. Branimir care little for the spectacle he provided for the townsfolk, but understood the fascination they had with his ability with a dagger. He once entertained in a similar fashion after leaving the Netherworld while working at *The Oaken Bard* in Gavlok.

"I best get to balancing the books," Sulanna said, scrunching her small nose. "Lady Gail will likely have another stack of letters to be drafted by midafternoon. We all have to earn our stay, right?"

Adamus said, "And I will head to the stables to shuffle hay. Morkanfej plans to come by this morning with a fresh pair of mares, looking for a buyer." He lowered his voice. "If we plan for departure, we would make better with a couple of horses."

"You mean the kingsguard?" Branimir asked. He had not heard Morkanfej's name in weeks. He and Adamus played cards frequently after settling in Gaetana, but the man seemingly disappeared.

Adamus rumbled, "The same. I am hoping to learn more about the Uvil's advancement. We would be wise not to travel in any direction they may be scouting."

"Don't spend all of our coin, Adamus," Sulanna said.

"I know the circumstance," he replied, rubbing his thick beard. "I will only make a deal if 'tis fitting. Besides, Morkanfej owes me a debt, whether he remembers it or not."

"He owes everybody a debt," Branimir mumbled.

"I have an hour until I am needed at the *Highspire*," Wit said. "If it pleases you, Adamus, I will join you. Confronting a man about money should not be done without witness."

The Ariadnean grunted in agreement.

Branimir gave pause as the other three took their leave, Adamus and Wit through the front door again, and Sulanna marching to Lady Gail's study to ruffle through the stacks of papers. With a heavy heart, Branimir turned to the kitchen, snatching an apron from behind the newly furnished bar top on the way.

He swung open the galley door, the clang of a stirring spoon dinging against the pot while Meisher, the scrawny boy, began a soup for midday. Lady Gail supervised nearby, cutting dough for more biscuits.

"Master Branimir," she said, rolling a ball of sticky dough between her old, boney fingers, blue eyes bugging from under her eyelids. "I hope your morning stroll was pleasing. If I had been thinking, I would have asked you to stop for another sack of flour on your way back."

"Would you like me to fetch one now?" Branimir asked.

"No, no," Gail said with a laugh. Her dimples creased under the wrinkles beneath her eyes, nearly hiding her age. "I will have Meisher go once the soup is set. The Lightbringer knows my boy could use some muscle on those skinny legs."

"I spend a lot of time running, Ma," Meisher said. "They are skinny because I am so fast."

Gail rutted her brow, holding back a chuckle. "You run like a ruffled chicken."

Her son cackled at the joke.

Branimir gave a polite smile.

"Does a mood hold you this morning, Branimir?" Gail asked, turning the dough.

Branimir scratched his head. "I must not have slept well last night."

"Maybe your heart will be lifted to know you have a visitor then?" Gail said. "The young lass arrived early this morning while you were out."

"Visitor?"

Gail nodded. "I admit I was surprised. You and your friends have been here for some time and made no mention of friends or family seeking you out. But she did ask for you specifically by name."

"She has the prettiest eyes I have ever seen," Meisher swooned.

Gail giggled at her boy. "You have time yet before you need to be thinking of a wife. You jump into marriage too soon and you will be as miserable as ole' Jon out there."

"Who is it?" Branimir pressed.

"Oh, she may have given her name…I cannot remember. She said she came from the east," Gail said. "Maybe she is one of those *Kadari*." The innkeeper hooted at her own joke. She waved at the door. "I had her wait for you in the study."

"The study?" Branimir stumbled through the swinging door, his mind on fire. The *Kadari* had finally come to kill them. "Sulanna…"

Chapter II

The room blurred while Branimir pondered his few options. He did not have time to rush to his room upstairs to retrieve his daggers. By the time he pulled the chest from under the bed, and returned to Sulanna in the study, she could be dead. From the bar top, Branimir could see the windowless door of Gail's study, situated behind the curved staircase. The thick door remained shut beyond the scattered tables. He had no choice but to go now and discover the danger on the other side. But he needed a weapon.

With uncanny precision, Branimir scoped the room for an alternative blade, resting his eyes on Jon, who scraped absentmindedly at his breakfast plate. Branimir quickened his footfalls until he stood at Jon's table, barely peering over the edge.

The old man turned from his plate of sausage and biscuits to lift his bushy eyebrows with wonder, holding his food at bay in his cheek. The two younger men who shared the table also stopped chewing.

"Master Branimir," Jon began, gritting his teeth, the wrinkles on his face as defined as valleys pitted within the northern hills, "you nearly stop a man's heart sneaking up so fast. What can I do you for?"

"Your knife." Branimir held his hand out expectantly.

"My knife?" Jon repeated.

"The Kras has a dark look about him," one of the other men said.

Jon squinted at Branimir, lastly chewing whatever food remained in the corner of his mouth. He slowly swallowed.

"All of your knives," Branimir forcibly said, "now."

Jon's eyes bugged like a boy who had never seen war, and now faced unmatched bloodshed. "No need to make a fuss, Master Branimir." He grunted. "Go on. Hand them over, boys."

Three serrated blades, fixed in wooden handles, were hastily placed at the edge of the table. Branimir scooped them up in his tiny hands, testing the end with the tip of his finger. They held little sharpness, but would do the trick with enough force.

"Be careful now, Master Branimir," Jon cautioned, dipping his saggy chin to his chest. "Don't be doing anything you would regret come the 'morrow."

Branimir averted his eyes and covered the expanse of the common room to the study door. He ignored the fretful whispers of the three at the table, and listened carefully through the door. The hushed sounds were loud in his sensitive ears.

"Do you think anyone is going to believe such a ridiculous story?" Sulanna questioned in a husky undertone, followed by the sound of a chair dragging along the wooden floorboards. "Why did he not come instead?"

"He cannot move through his own gateway, and few others have the skill to create one," a woman answered.

"Were you not the one who betrayed him?"

"You must believe me…"

He gripped the knives in his hand, sliding one to his left while holding the other two in his right.

A thump of something heavy hit the floor, causing Branimir's heart to jump. He wasted no time, swiftly pulling the latch and pushing the door open.

The dim room, shadowed by lantern light, had no impact on Branimir's eyesight. As a Kras, he could see as clearly in complete darkness as under mid-day sun. Shelves sitting at his eye level sat on either wall, filled with books and loose manuscripts. The walls above them were decorated with amateur paintings and armaments that would be as effective in battle as a quill pen.

His instinct was to throw the blades. Yet, too many times he had killed without thought, whether against the Lilitu, last year, at the Ariadnean port or…the red mage…Branimir was not sure how much more guilt he could stomach.

Branimir's eyes flickered by Sulanna, who raised her head from where she kneeled to pick up a stack of books from the floor. He settled his gaze on the woman with short, dark hair, barely touching her ears, and inimitable, purple irises. She was the same woman he discovered being interrogated in the dungeons of Melkorka a year ago, but the narration of their history seized centuries more.

"Alyona," he croaked, almost dropping the knives. He held them up at waist level instead to appear menacing, if anything, remembering the beating he watched her take at the hand of Falmagon.

She dropped to her knees almost instantly at the sound of her name. The hoary shirt she wore hung loosely on her thin skin, covered partially by the faded, black cloak. "Alyona Gounari, at your service, Branimir Baran. Please, you must believe me. I have been sent by Dorofej to see you safe."

Sulanna clicked her tongue, setting the heavy books on the desk. "Her story is remarkable, and hardly believable, Branimir."

"Did she try to harm you?" Branimir asked.

"No," Sulanna said. "She had the chance, catching me unaware when I first came in here. But she has not so much as lifted a finger."

"I will not hurt you," Alyona said, remaining on her knees. "I may have done wrong many times in my life, but I have no interest in seeing the Likhyi return or Aenar destroyed."

"She claims redemption," Sulanna said. "Yet, is she not the one who followed you and Dorofej into the Netherworld? A spy for Falmagon and the *Kadari*?"

Branimir nodded. "She and her brother, Artemiy. Though, she was nearly slain when held at Melkorka. I watched them torture her."

"And Artemiy?" Sulanna asked.

"Dead," Alyona said, giving Bran a peculiar look, widening her purple eyes. "Dorofej said he had fallen to Marheena shortly after we fled the Netherworld. Her magic withered him away into an old man. He died protecting the Mager bloodline."

Sulanna opened her mouth to respond, and Branimir hurried to shush her.

Alyona uncomfortably shifted on her knees, and added, "I know the boy is dead too. Not only did Dorofej tell me what happened before we escaped, but I heard whispers of the events while in the dungeon."

Branimir's heart swelled in his chest. "Dorofej escaped?"

Alyona dipped her chin to her chest.

"Do not believe everything she says, Branimir," Sulanna again cautioned, moving around the desk with a noble's grace.

Branimir looked at the knives in his hand for a moment and grasped them tighter. He boldly stepped closer to the *Kadari* woman. Her unwashed, pastel skin seemed to pale even more under his gaze. "Tell me what you know. How did you find us?"

"Dorofej said to start asking around Gaetana about you, and well, I cannot say many Kras travel the area. Finding you was not difficult." Branimir gritted his teeth, seeing the simple logic of the explanation. He motioned for her to continue. Alyona nodded, purple eyes still wide. "Three days ago, Melkorka was attacked by Bukavac—"

Branimir interrupted. "Three days? You were at Melkorka three days ago?"

"Yes. Dorofej sent me here through a gateway, the same as he had done for you. His magic does not allow him to pass through himself, or he would be here too," Alyona replied with a steady tone.

"He was nearly dead when we parted ways," said Branimir.

"And he was restored by the Waters of Life before leaving Melkorka," she replied.

"How?"

Her eyes stayed fixed on Branimir as the thoughts poured through her lips. "Melkorka was sieged, and the dungeon walls collapsed around us. I used *Koldovstvo* to free Dorofej, and then Tyr pulled us to safety. The Ash Tree was not far from the castle keep."

"She has rehearsed the story well," Sulanna said.

Branimir scrunched his face, and shook his head in disbelief. He knew the Ash Tree lay within Melkorka's walls, but her story still did not add up. "Not well enough." He crossed his arms. "Why would the Ispolini help you? Why would he rescue Dorofej when he last tried to kill us?"

Alyona folded her hands, and continued, "Tyr was held captive by the *Kadari* too. Falmagon believed him to have killed Eisliev, and..." Alyona continued speaking but Branimir's mind clouded.

The name rang in his ears, a name he wished he could disremember. A year ago, Eisliev Kluk, always drowning in his red robes, helped capture the boy, Bohumir Mager, and took him to Melkorka—the same boy Artemiy, Alyona's brother, supposedly had tried to protect. Eisliev brutally slaughtered the boy to exact his own revenge on Falmagon, and in turn, Branimir gave Eisliev equal punishment.

Branimir could still smell the charred corpse of Bohumir withering in the flames of the cottage fire. He could still feel Eisliev's warm blood gushing around his fingertips.

His thumb picked at his fingers on either hand at the horrid recollection when he struck the thin, silver band on his left forefinger. He frequently forgot he was wearing the piece of simple jewelry, called *Faegrim*, which was not all that simple at all. He stole the magical band from Eisliev after killing him, unable to resist keeping the polished trinket. While the ring held no purpose for Branimir, it gave Eisliev the ability to control the mind of any who did not possess the power of *Koldovstvo*. Branimir did not like to think about how the red mage once forced him to act against his will, causing him to hurt Adamus, Dorofej, and their now deceased friend, Hanna. The thought gave him chills, thinking such a thing existed in the world, to give one being power over another.

Alyona's words pulled him from memory.

"Wait…" Branimir said, perking his pointed ear. "What did you just say?"

Alyona took a breath. "I know it does not sound believable. I know, okay? But Eisliev returned from the dead more powerful than any *Kadari* or Stuhia I have ever seen, with an army of Bukavac at his back. It was like the battle at Shayol Domier with Nedezhda Mager, Branimir." She pulled at her dark hair, shaking her head. "Eisliev marched on Melkorka with such vengeance…he killed so many…and now, he is coming for *kaelandur*…"

Sulanna blinked with an unconvinced frown and cocked her chin. "I told you that her story wasn't anything to be believed."

"No…" Branimir's feet were frozen to the floor. "She is telling the truth."

Sulanna did not remain so fixed, nearly falling where she stood. "What?" She gripped the desk. "You mean the Stuhia *you* killed came back from the dead?"

Branimir tried to keep his hands from shaking. "When I killed him with *kaelandur*, I was so angry. I didn't think. I just…"

"I don't believe it," Sulanna said. "How is it possible?"

"I have seen it before." He nodded at Alyona. "We have both seen it before," Branimir said, pulling *kaelandur* from his waist belt. "The blade's power is dangerous." He gripped the handle, looking at Sulanna. "Keeping this dagger from Eisliev's grasp is the only thing saving the Ash Tree. If he gets *kaelandur*, he will release the Likhyi."

Alyona stared at the dagger, unable to tear her eyes away, as though she was surprised he held the fabled weapon. Yet her words confirmed his fears. "Eisliev said as much. He aims to release the *old-dark* at the behest of Marheena. He says the living had their time on Aenar, and he brings a new age."

Branimir heard the riddle in her words. He was suddenly reminded that Marheena, the Frozen Goddess, was also responsible for telling Dorofej to create the copper dagger. "How did you and Dorofej escape?"

"Eisliev let Tyr, Dorofej, and myself leave freely," she replied in a whisper.

Branimir trembled, returning the dagger to its safe holding. "Why? Do not lie to me."

"I am not," she said, jaw tightening. Her eyes lingered at his waist and then lifted. "Falmagon and Dagmar escaped Melkorka, and Eisliev wants them dead. We promised to kill the two for him, in exchange for…"

"Exchange for what?" Sulanna raised her tone.

Alyona answered, "A place safe from suffering when the *old-dark* are released to reform the world for the dead." She hurried to add. "Listen. We bought our time from death to protect Aenar and the Ash Tree. You must believe me. Dorofej was wily with Eisliev and riddled our way to freedom."

Sulanna sighed. "That much I believe."

Branimir agreed with her. "But where is Dorofej? And Tyr?"

"They come to meet us," Alyona explained, "but we must hurry. Dorofej fears Falmagon and Dagmar have already come for *kaelandur* too, and Dagmar can forever find you in *Klukas.*"

Branimir shivered. "Why have they not come for me sooner?"

"I—I do not know," Alyona said, "but they are not at Melkorka. Dagmar departed weeks before Eisliev returned from the Netherworld, and Falmagon left days ago."

"Where are we to go to escape them?" Branimir asked.

"*Iriy,*" she answered.

Sulanna looked at Branimir incredulously, her eyes larger than he had ever seen. "We are meant to travel to the fabled City of the Gods. For what reason?"

"Dorofej says we must seek the gods to gain their wisdom and end this chaos," Alyona said. "He thinks they might destroy *kaelandur.*"

Branimir clenched his fists, realizing he still held the table knives. He tossed them through the open door behind him. They clattered in the common room, igniting a series of grunts and chairs shuffling from Jon's table. Branimir ignored the din.

"Then we go," he said.

Chapter III

"You cannot simply up and leave in the middle of the day," Gail insisted. Her dimples from this morning were gone. Her small figure held rigid in the doorway of their room, clinging to the frame as though a wind might send her reeling down the hallway. Branimir clipped his green, hooded cloak around his neck, despite her protests. "We have a room full of customers, letters to be sent, and horses to be tended. Our agreement was you would work for your room and board."

"And we have," Sulanna debated, falling back on her feathered bed to slide on her boots. "I understand our going comes as a surprise; believe me, we are all surprised. But you will be better off if we are not here."

Gail's voice cracked, the wrinkles on her face crinkling across her old skin. The innkeeper clearly did not believe her. "Your tab is unsettled."

Sulanna leveled Gail with a hard glare. "By the Nine Lands, who are you trying to bluff? I have been running your books for a year. I know exactly your worth and ours. If anything, you owe us money."

Branimir disregarded the entire conversation, sitting next to Adamus a few feet away. He watched the hero-warrior slide his steel axe into his belt loop. The weapon fit in his hands much more naturally than the reins of a stable horse.

Adamus humored Branimir with a spirited nudge. "Tis far too warm out for your cloak."

"Not enough room in my pack," Branimir said with little enthusiasm. Adamus was joyous after hearing they were leaving the inn, and although Branimir was glad to be gone, Alyona's summary of events repeatedly played through his mind. Dorofej was free. Dagmar and Falmagon were coming for him. And Eisliev had returned from the dead, because of Branimir's past ignorance.

He grazed by *kaelandur* with his hand to fasten his two, well-weighted daggers at his belt. With determination, he gave each blade a firm jerk to ensure they were properly secured. He could not calm his heart from thumping against the inside of his chest. The weight of the world suddenly fell back on his shoulders.

Adamus spoke softly, "We will be fine, Branimir. Tis important to keep faith."

Branimir jumped as Gail struck the frame of the door with her open hand. Her voice stole any response he may have had for Adamus. "You are going to force me to hire those senseless mandrills back. They barely know the quill from the ink!"

"I am sorry, Gail," Sulanna said with an air of grace, once again reminding Branimir of her noble upbringing. "You knew we would leave eventually. None of us belong in an inn."

"What did that *Kadari* woman say to lug the three of you off so quick?" Gail's eyes flashed madly around the room. "Where is she anyhow? She strolled in and ruined everyone's day and then scamper off?"

Branimir replied, "Leave it alone, Gail. You would be better off not knowing the details."

"Don't talk to me all mysteriously, Master Branimir, after your stunt. You stole kitchen knives from patrons just to toss them across the commons!" Gail stretched out her hand to shake a boney finger. "You scared the beard right off ole' Jon's chin."

Branimir tensed his jaw, having no response.

Sulanna redirected Gail. "Alyona is preparing the horses, and Branimir is right. You do not need to be concerned about our business.

Gail clenched her teeth, keeping what words she had left trapped in her throat. Her gaze fell to Adamus. The bearded man quickly turned away from her and went back to rolling a bedroll. With a final grunt, the old woman threw her hands up. "Fine. I'll have Meisher pack up some of the leftover biscuits from breakfast. You could have at least waited until the morning."

"Thank you, Gail," Sulanna said, giving a half-smile and gesturing to the door. "If you would, please."

Gail squinted her beady eyes at Sulanna with ire, pursing her lips. Holding the grimace, she bobbed her head and shut the door. Branimir could hear her feet stomping down the hallway.

Adamus waited until the footsteps faded before saying anything. "'Tis likely we will not find a moment anytime soon to talk without being overheard. What can you say of Alyona? Can we trust her?"

"Of course not," Sulanna said, snagging her leather chest guard from the bed beside her. She continued speaking, slipping the armor over her head and pushing her arm through the already fastened side. "From what I understand, she has lived as long as Branimir or longer. Time surely has given her the upper hand. We cannot know what secrets she holds."

Branimir said, "I agree. When I first met her, she was cruel at Shayol Domier. And then to learn she had tracked Dorofej and me in the Netherworld to retrieve *kaelandur* for Falmagon..." His voice trailed off for a moment. "She has too long been loyal to the *Kadari*. I cannot think she truly wishes to serve those she has forever betrayed."

Sulanna started as soon as he finished. "Mark my words, we will see Alyona telling stories of her torture to justify her reasoning in the coming days," Sulanna added. "She will do what she can to gain our trust, and we cannot be drawn in too closely."

"What do you know?" Adamus asked, meeting Sulanna as she stood and moved to the center of the room. He took the leather strap hanging from her disconnected shoulder piece and pulled it through the adjoining buckle.

Sulanna replied while he tightly clasped the leather. "My family built their name in Eldhaft by persecuting the Crown's enemies."

"Your father is the northern Vornic?" Adamus finished with her armor and stepped back in surprise.

"Hm." She nodded. "Most know the name Maelthirren because of my father's rather vicious pursuits of seeking justice," Sulanna answered. "He bends knee to Count Vlassi in Eldhaft, who historically hungers for violence. The man is nothing like King Frantisek."

"So, your family tortures people?" Branimir concluded.

"My father persecutes those who are deemed to be unlawful, and he *extracts* the truth by whatever means necessary. I watched him torture the young and old alike when I was but a child. In some instances, he tortured the soldiers who failed the directives of Count Vlassi. In no instance did cruelty ever weaken their commitment; if anything, the soldiers became more loyal in fear of any backlash."

Adamus sighed. "Tis then as I thought it to be. You must agree we cannot go traveling across Maharia with the three of us against one *Kadari*. We are formidable fighters," Adamus looked at Sulanna, and then Branimir, "but we can do little against *Koldovstvo* without Dorofej's protection."

Branimir took a breath, his hand resting again on *kaelandur* at his belt. "I do not trust her either, but by happenstance, if she is telling the truth, we cannot risk otherwise. We have no choice but to go with her."

"I think so, too," Adamus said.

"If you are not suggesting we should leave without her, what are you saying?" Branimir asked.

Sulanna sunk her long knife into the sheath at her belt, and eyeballed Adamus in equal suspense. She must have noticed something Branimir had missed. "Out with it, Adamus. What did you do?"

"After you told me what Alyona had said," Adamus cleared his throat and tugged at his beard, murmuring his words as though they were an afterthought, "I asked Wit to ride along."

"Why? Why would you bring Wit? He…he has other duties to attend at the *Highspire*," Branimir moaned.

"I can stomach the man," Sulanna said, "but he offers nothing but another mouth to feed."

Adamus shrugged. "Maybe so, but Alyona does not know as much. Maybe she will be intimidated by our numbers. Besides, Wit has no interest in being in Gaetana if sieged, and he has been talking for some time about needing to go to Lonemere to retrieve a manuscript or two for the library. We can, at least, share the road until Gavlok."

Branimir tensed. He had not realized they would be traveling through Gavlok. The couple years he spent working at *The Oaken Bard* after he and Dorofej had exited the Netherworld left a sour taste in his mouth.

Sulanna crossed her arms. "You told him we would take him to Gavlok?"

"Wit is not that bad," Adamus said, placing his shiny, oval shield across his back against the steel, polished breastplate.

"He only talks about how great he is, and insults the intelligence of anyone he crosses." Branimir pulled his pack over his shoulder. Dealing with the snooty historian for three days and having no escape would contest with a millennium in the Netherworld. "If Alyona is threatened by Wit, we have nothing to fear from her."

"Come on," Adamus said, pulling at his beard. "A few days on the road, at least, until we can have a better understanding of Alyona's motives."

"Fine." Sulanna said.

Branimir raised his hands defensively. "I am not saying he cannot come, but if he says one more thing about how his books hold more knowledge than the Kras, I might kick him."

A soft knock rattled the wooden door of their room.

"Who's there?" Adamus asked, taking a step and reaching for the latch.

"Meisher, Master Adamus," replied the familiar voice of Lady Gail's son. Adamus pulled the door open to reveal the lanky kid balancing waterskins and several wrapped handkerchiefs in his hands. "My ma sent me to give you some food for your travels."

"Come on in, boy," Adamus said.

"I'll take it," Branimir said, opening his pack. "Set it on the bed, Meisher."

The boy did as he was instructed with a half-hearted smile, and Branimir went to work to find room in his pack. He could smell the leftover biscuits and dried sausage.

"Ma said she would have brought it up herself, but she is *too* busy in the kitchen," Meisher said. "She wanted to be sure I tell you as much."

"We appreciate your ma's hospitality, Meisher," Sulanna responded, rolling her eyes at Branimir.

Meisher smiled. "I am sorry to see you go so soon, but I guess there are grander things to see in the world than dust settling on chairs."

"Yes," Branimir said, handing Adamus and Sulanna each a waterskin before pulling the ties to his pack.

"Oh," Meisher said, "I almost forgot. You have another visitor waiting down in the commons." Branimir's heart gave pause. "He said he was an old friend."

"Dorofej," Branimir pushed himself from the floorboards to rush downstairs only to be stopped by the strong arm of Adamus.

"Hold on, Bran," Adamus said. "Did he give a name? What did this *old friend* look like?"

"Uh…he was a younger man, taller than most, with a thick mustache," Meisher replied, scrunching his brow as if trying to recall detail. "He asked for you in a hushed tone like he was trying not to draw attention. He told my ma he was the Patrician. Isn't that a title among the *Kadari?*"

Branimir's heart sank.

"Falmagon," Sulanna hissed. "I told you we could not trust the girl."

"Careful," Adamus said. "'Tis not likely Falmagon would come strolling into an inn asking questions if he was working with Alyona."

"We don't know that," Sulanna said. "Who else would call themselves the Patrician?"

Adamus crumpled his beard to mustache, and grabbed Meisher's shoulder. "What did you tell him, boy?"

"Well…" Meisher's eyes were wide with panic. "I…I told him I would see if you were here. I did not say you were." The boy frantically looked around the room. "Are you in trouble? He is not an *old friend?*"

"Hardly not," Branimir said, yanking a dagger from his waistline.

"Branimir…" Sulanna started from the corner. "The commons is full of innocent people."

Branimir pulled his pack over his shoulder, and stepped out the door. "My aim is true, Sulanna. I can end this right now."

"At what cost?" Sulanna pressed. "What if you find Alyona with him? You are not going to battle two *Kadari* with a couple of daggers. Adamus, tell him."

Adamus let go of Meisher. "I agree this should be ended, but Sulanna is right, Branimir. What if your dagger isn't a deathblow? What if he has flasks of the Waters of Life with him?"

"Waters of Life?" Meisher echoed with wide eyes.

Adamus went on, "Even if you are successful, the kingsguard would take you to the dungeons and remove all weapons from your person, including *kaelandur*. What attention will you draw when the dagger is taken from your hand?"

Branimir frowned, returning his blade to his belt. With the Likhyi embedded in the dagger and bound to him, Branimir could not pull the dagger away from his skin without considerable pain. The feeling was akin to having his flesh burning from the inside out. "I had not considered losing *kaelandur*."

"We would face greater difficulty in destroying the weapon if the King were to take the weapon," Sulanna said.

Meisher paled, blankly staring at the wall between Adamus and Sulanna. "I do not think I should be listening to this. Please…just leave, and see no one is hurt."

Branimir examined the innocent boy, and then jerked his head in response. "You will need to distract Falmagon while we exit from the door."

"Not the front door," Meisher said. "Go down the stairs and through the kitchen. He will not notice you slipping behind the counter from the staircase."

"I will lead the way." Sulanna gripped the neck of her waterskin. "Adamus take the rear."

Branimir rubbed his nose as Sulanna pushed by him in the hallway. She clearly believed he might attack Falmagon, and wanted him bound between her and Adamus. Of course, his two friends could not stop him if he chose to become invisible. Yet he had no desire to risk the lives of the people in the commons, or the fate of the copper dagger he carried.

The hubbub of chatter and mugs clinging echoed as they made their way down the staircase and into the kitchen. Branimir peeked for only an instant to gain sight of the crowded commons. Gail stood over a man in a faded robe, nodding and laughing as though she were hearing a clever tale. Bran struggled to make out any features beyond the back of the head, shorn with brown locks. He could not see enough to discern the man to be Falmagon for certain, and yet he knew. The image was brief as Meisher moved himself in front of the counter to block view of Branimir and the others sneaking away.

The kitchen was empty, save the contents of the evening meal, a venison stew, cooking in an oversized pot. The three of them exited the *Peddlar's Rose* in a few steps with Adamus swinging the thin door closed behind them.

Without a word, Sulanna stayed the lead, heading down the timber staircase and straight to the stables adjacent to the inn. Few people of Gaetana littered the streets, going about their business with little concern of their surroundings. Most of the citizens stayed inside and avoided summer's heat.

Branimir kept his feet forward, despite every muscle in his body wanting to turn around and face Falmagon. He took a hearty breath, glancing at the sky, full of a raging sun and absent a single cloud for shade. Sweat beads lined the base of his neck moments before they walked up to the stables.

The doors were already open with Alyona and Witigor standing inside, ready with the mounts.

Alyona crossed her arms under her breasts as they approached, hugging the light shirt to her torso. Sweat dripped down her cheek, falling to the dark cloak hanging down to her knees. "Am I to expect he will be coming with us?"

Witigor tipped his brown, pointed hat at Alyona. The few strands of his hair were barely discernible against his malformed skin. "I have already answered her question a hundred times. I understand the girl is young yet, but she is the daftest woman I have ever met." The painted horse he held whinnied next to the brown pony he also held at bay. He lifted the pony's reins to Branimir with a snort.

Alyona ignored the three horses standing behind her calmly. She glared at the historian. "I would suspect few women have stomached your company."

Wit twitched his nose, considering the argument. "Few women are worth being in my company," he concluded.

"No one is going to be appreciative of your humor, Wit," Adamus said.

"Wit-less," Branimir muttered.

"He is coming with us, Alyona," Sulanna said over him. The terseness of her tone was unmistakable. Branimir almost expected the noble woman to breach the topic of Falmagon within the inn, but Sulanna gave pause.

Branimir reached out and took the cords to his pony's bridle from Witigor. He then fastened his pack on the saddle, signifying the need for haste. Adamus mirrored him, taking his own from behind Alyona. The *Kadari* stood, unmoving, glowering at Witigor.

"We are losing the light," Adamus said.

"We should have waited until morning," Wit said, "when it would be cooler. We are going to burn in this heat."

Branimir gazed at the sky with the sun directly overhead. The day barely reached its apex. Wit may have been sweating more than any of them, even without wearing armor. He only clothed himself in tan britches and a grey shirt as though he were a commoner.

"We will draw a lot of attention with a large group," Alyona argued. "Every man, woman, and child will remember us from here to Eldhaft."

"And, why would we care about that?" Wit asked, cocking his head. "You trying to get rid of me?" He shook his finger at her. "You are just upset because I asked why your eyes are such a peculiar color, which I may add, you have not given an inkling of an answer. You talk and talk and say nothing at all. Just like a woman." Wit rubbed the back of his head and squinted at the *Kadari* with disdain.

"Mind yourself." Her nostrils flared. "I don't need to be pressed by some wiseacre for the next three days."

Branimir wondered if Alyona was fabricating her scorn toward Wit, but he agreed with her. He did not want to hear Witigor's persistent yammering on the road either. Making his decision, Bran pulled himself up on his pony and wiped the sweat forming on his forehead. "Stop insulting her, Witless."

Wit wrinkled his nose. "My name is Witigor. I have never met a group of people so insistent on holding onto their secrets than you."

"You obviously haven't met many people who understand the function of a secret, then," Alyona said, pointing her finger at him.

"Enough," Sulanna muttered. "We must—"

A loud commotion from the *Peddlar's Rose* interrupted her. Branimir spun around, hearing what may have been shouting and the breaking of glass.

"Nine Lands!" Wit exclaimed, springing back against his mount.

The horses, battle-trained, held stagnant against Wit's sudden shout, but Branimir's pony lurched with the intent to bolt down the twisting road.

"Whoa," Sulanna cried, reaching for the pony, but Alyona was quicker. The *Kadari* stepped in front of the pony and touched its head, calming the animal straightaway.

Wit did not seem to notice, gawking at the inn. "Should we go see if they need help?"

Adamus answered, crumpling his forehead. "No, tis not our problem."

"Nothing directed toward us," Sulanna said evenly, a hint of knowing flickering in her eye, "and not worth investigating. We have other concerns to heed."

Wit twisted his neck, gazing at each of them. The crashing grew louder from in the inn. "Wait a minute. Someone could really be in trouble. What if someone is killed?"

"Czern's breath! Then they are killed," Adamus said. "Get on your horse. We are leaving. Come on."

Alyona stepped away from Branimir's pony as he repositioned himself on the animal. He did his best to keep the suspicion of her use of *Koldovstvo* from his eye, but he guessed she had done something to calm his mount. Knowing *Faegrim* had the power to control the mind, he thought his trinket suddenly felt exceptionally heavy upon his finger. He could not help but check her hand as she neared her mare, but noticed no jewelry.

Witigor lifted his eyebrows at the four of them preparing for leave-taking, and then reconsidered the inn.

Branimir wondered if the historian believed them to be immoral because of their decision. Of course, they would not use Falmagon's presence as an argument to avoid the *Peddlar's Rose*, but even then, Branimir was not certain he or the others would have gone inside. Branimir knew he changed over the years. Bygone battles hardened him. A commoner like Witigor could not understand.

"Are you coming, Wit-less?" Branimir mocked, hoping the historian would return to the *Highspire*.

He answered the question with a question. "Should I expect similar respects if I am to encounter danger on the road? Will I be left for the crows and forgotten?"

Alyona's reply gave Branimir's answer before he could part his lips. "Yes."

Chapter IV

Evening set, darkening the already colorless tufts of the Gaetanean Grasslands. The uniform blades had faded with the lack of rain during the warm months, threatening to soon wilt and wither. Branimir could see above the far-stretching meadow from the top of his saddle, though the grass would stand higher if he were walking along the road.

The frequent traffic between Gaetana and Eldhaft had stripped the road bare of grass, leaving a hardened, cracked, and uneven dirt path. Bran was sure that any wagon wanting to pass between the two cities would leave the passengers with a crick in their neck and a sore bottom. Yet he had not seen a single wagon, and only a handful of travelers since leaving Gaetana. Wit claimed they were the only ones stupid enough to travel in the heat.

Admittedly, Branimir could have refilled his water skin twice over with the sweat secreting from his face. He removed his cloak an hour after leaving the city, thinking it might keep him from passing out in the heat, but the sun only warmed his red skin. Since then, he had been unsticking his shirt from his chest so often he practically fanned himself with the fabric. They stopped plenty to water the horses and huddle in the ditch under the tall grasses for shade, but something about the temperature left them feeling feverish and exhausted.

The dark blue sky contrasted against the dark grey scattered clouds, and soon it would all fade to black. Of course, for Branimir, he could see easily enough, despite the failing light. He rode alongside Alyona in the back with Adamus and Wit leading and Sulanna in the middle.

"We should break for camp soon," Wit suggested, helplessly peering into the fading light.

"No," Adamus said. "We have Branimir to help lead us in the dark if needed, and the road will be cooler at night."

"You all have been in a rush since leaving Gaetana," Wit carped, tilting his hat. "What in the Nine Lands for? You act as though you are being chased."

Branimir bit his tongue while Sulanna answered, "We have our business, Wit. If you need to turn back for Gaetana, we will understand."

Adamus turned his head at the mild proposal, but said nothing.

Wit stubbornly grunted, showing no sign of changing course. He impatiently looked to Adamus. "Are you not going to say anything more?"

The Ariadnean patted his horse. "About what?"

"You are going to leave me in suspense about why you have suddenly left Gaetana and headed north?" Witigor pressed.

"Sulanna answered you," Adamus replied with a shrug.

"My father was silenced by my mother's commanding tone too, until he killed himself, Adamus. She never let him have a say about anything, and it drove him mad," Wit said heatedly, glaring at Sulanna under the brim of his hat. "It is not right for a woman to speak a man's thoughts, or tell him what he should think. Read Campbell Lilliard's *Women and Slaves*, and know the truth. You will fall to ruin."

"Czern's breath! You know you have my deepest sympathies for your loss, but Sulanna will hardly lead any man to ruin." Adamus forced a soft smile. Branimir wondered how long Adamus had known about Wit's loss. He supposed Adamus would feel sorry for Witigor, but Branimir did not see it to be a fitting excuse to treat others poorly.

Branimir watched Sulanna glide her hand from the long knife at her belt to her saddle. She did not share Adamus's sympathy. "Wit, I have overlooked your slights for the better part of a year, but if you continue to insult me, I will run you through."

"You are threatening me?" Wit gawked, looking again to Adamus for help.

"I most certainly am," Sulanna said. "I would threaten anyone who vouched for the written works of Campbell Lilliard. The man was a misogynist and a pig."

Wit moved his jaw back and forth awkwardly, trying to form words. "I was only asking why the hurry."

Branimir filled his lungs. He wanted to give a suitable answer, saying they needed to put more distance between themselves and Falmagon, who had somehow come to Gaetana. Branimir longed to ask Alyona how Falmagon could have skipped across time and space to arrive in Gaetana from Kalamaar. However, where Dorofej had supposedly aided Alyona, Branimir suspected Dagmar had somehow helped Falmagon.

Regardless, Sulanna had not breached the topic of Falmagon with Wit or Alyona, signifying the secret should remain so for now. Wit knew nothing of Falmagon in any sense, and Branimir found no reason to enlighten the historian. Besides—after giving more thought—Falmagon had Dagmar to find Branimir in *Klukus* no matter where or how fast they fled. Therefore, the argument was moot.

For another hour they traveled quietly until Wit broke the silence. "If we are going to travel all night, we could, at least, talk about something. Tell a story or something."

"Talk about the weather," Alyona muttered so fast, Branimir thought she might have been waiting for Witigor to open his mouth so she could shut him up.

Wit scoffed, and then—out of what might have been pure spite toward the woman—he went on a tangent about the weather. "This heat belongs to the desert, not the grasslands. Maharia is known for harsh winters and mild summers. I remember, last year, everyone was talking about the warm weather; it was thick with every conversation. But these Months of Warmth have exceeded anything known to history."

"The written history does not stretch so far, Wit," Adamus said.

"Long have patterns been documented by the Anshedar, whether on animal migrations, the stars, or the seasons, and only a couple generations of study can recognize the design," Wit argued. "We have had scrolls and books detailing the weather much longer: *Moon of Next Year* by Farkas Finn, the *Fine Manual of Fire and Frost* by Saym Green, or Pap Benjamin's *Pamphlet of Lunar History*. I am telling you, something unnatural is happening."

"I agree we have seen many patterns, which have been documented. But do you not think smaller cycles could work inside of larger rotations," Sulanna spoke up, "like the gears and cogs of a water mill?"

"Ah, yes," Adamus nodded in agreement. "'Tis like a story. We know every great tale has minor lessons taught within the overall story."

Branimir could see Wit tapping his saddle in thought. He turned his head to give view of the most deformed side of his face. "What evidence do you have to think the seasons work in such a way?"

Sulanna shrugged. "None. We are but mortal. You cannot think we will have all the knowledge needed to know the truth of something in our lifetime, else we would be called gods. A thousand years ago, those living hardly know what we know now."

"*The Tract of Wonderful Words* by Paul Friar," Wit said with a smile. "You are talking about his works."

"I thought you might recognize it," Sulanna said.

"You know the hour has drawn late when Sulanna begins to speak about gods," Adamus laughed, twisting alongside Wit to watch Sulanna pull back her shoulders. She may have very well flattened Adamus's nose if they had been any closer.

Branimir slowed his pony to keep distance.

Sulanna preserved her unruffled tone, saying, "I am not paying them reverence, Adamus. I am repeating Friar's argument that humans would not offer their lives up to worshipping *gods* if we were *all-knowing*. Sadly, our lifespans are too short to learn all we should." She cleared her throat, nodding her head back at Branimir. "Thus far, the Kras and their knowledge is the closest thing to godly I have found on Aenar."

Wit scoffed. "I doubt any Kras will lead you across the Kalinov Bridge to the next life. Knowledge is not everything."

Adamus roared with laughter. "And the historian betrays his profession for faith."

"Earning the name Wit-less," Branimir said with a scowl.

"I am not a fool. History helps me find my footing while alive, but what knowledge I gain in this life has no bearing on the next," Wit said, hat flopping wildly with his defense.

Adamus responded again, but Branimir cut him out to focus on Alyona riding next to him. He did not want to hear any more of Wit's insults, even if morsels of truth were hidden in his words.

Night had come, and whereas the others squinted their eyes to find the road, Alyona was watchful with wide, purple eyes. Her gaze fluttered in his direction shortly, before turning back to the road.

"Why do you stare?" she asked under her breath.

Branimir watched Sulanna move her horse further from Wit and Adamus as they continued their inquiry on the meaninglessness of their lives, and its connection to the afterlife. Noticing they were not listening, he hurried his words, "How did you calm my pony at Gaetana?"

Alyona pressed her lips together, trying to fight back a smile. She intentionally gazed at Branimir this time. "Many questions I had expected from you while we were on the road, but nothing so slight."

"I am curious," Branimir said.

"Very well," Alyona said, settling in her saddle. "You have been with Dorofej for a long while. What can you tell me about *Koldovstvo*?"

"We did not speak much of it," Branimir said. "I know *Koldovstvo* consumes life when power is spent."

Alyona's lips curved in a smile under her small nose. She assented with a hum in her throat. "The magic originally comes from the Stuhians, gifted by the gods, but has been blended with other races over the centuries as the Stuhians mixed bloodlines. Stuhians themselves do not age unless they wield *Koldovstvo*, whereas mixed bloodlines age at a slower rate. The Highborn, as you knew them in the last age, were not Stuhian, save Dorofej."

Branimir picked at *Faegrim* on his hand nervously. "That does not answer my question."

She smiled all the wider, and went on, "The limits of what a Stuhian can do with *Koldovstvo* is limited by imagination and bloodline." Branimir frowned at the comment, but Alyona did not give him pause to speak. "Our blood reveals the source of *Koldovstvo* for each of us, specifically identifying what kind of magic will steal our life the slowest. Most who manipulate *Koldovstvo* can access any type of elemental magic: sea, sky, fire, or stone; though some, like I said, may be stronger in its design. Other users are skilled in the intangible arts: profane, sacred, primal, or void. We each have our special gifts."

"And you?" Branimir asked.

"Sacred," Alyona finally answered. "Among many other things, I can remove fear, or provide protection, or even mend wounds from living creatures."

Branimir straightened a bit more in his saddle, leaning toward Alyona. "Like Dorofej?"

"No." Alyona pushed her hair from her cheek. "Dorofej is an aberration. He descends from the Kaligula bloodline, giving him greatest strength in void magic, altering space and time, or even thought. Yet he also wields sacred magic with an uncanny ability. He is the only Stuhia, Highborn, or *Kadari*—pick your term—who I have found to practice more than one intangible magic."

"How is that possible?"

"I don't know," she said.

Branimir realized his assumption about Dagmar likely held truth. If Falmagon's mentor held the same blood as Dorofej, he could help Falmagon escape to Gaetana through a gateway like that from which Alyona traveled.

"How do you know so much about Dorofej?" Branimir asked, his words suddenly swallowed by a resonating clamor coming from up the road. He rotated with Alyona to look for the cause.

"Branimir," Adamus directed in a soft voice, stopping his horse, "the road is too dark. What do you see?" Sulanna and Wit halted their mounts on either side of him. Branimir followed Alyona's lead and stopped behind the other three, having no room on either side of the road to fan out.

"Four riders," Branimir began, his heart thumping against his chest in realization of what he was witnessing, "surrounding a male Svet in the road." Branimir looked at his companions with excitement, away from the five torches flickering further up the road. "I have not seen a centaur in so long."

"Savages," Wit said, standing in his stirrups as though it would help him see better in the dark. "He must be their property. No Svet would wander onto the main road unless he was already a slave."

"Slave…" The word hung on the edge of Branimir's tongue. "Anything else, you would like to add Wit-less?"

"Stop calling me that," Wit said. "It is Witigor, and you know it."

"No, the Svet is not a slave." Alyona interjected, soothing her mount with her hand. "He is arguing against being one with the riders. The men are unknown to him."

Wit plopped back into his saddle and rubbernecked at her. "How can you hear them?"

"Because my ears are not filled with the sound of my own rattling tongue," she said.

Wit jerked his head away from the woman, clearing his throat in contempt.

Branimir knew the distance was too great for any of the humans to hear more than muffled conversation, but Branimir, too, could hear the words. He kept his eyes forward, away from Alyona, and abridged the words. "The Svet is called Farthr. He says he is among the Crimson Sun." Bran looked to the old Crimson Sun affiliate. "Sulanna?"

Sulanna noticeably perked in her saddle, an evening breeze suddenly erupting across the highlands and rustling her brown locks. With a subtle nod, she said, "If it is Farthr, the centaur speaks the truth. We would do well to align with him against these men."

"How have you come by this knowledge?" Wit demanded, only to be ignored by the rest.

"To arms then?" Adamus said.

"First, let us see what we can accomplish with words," Sulanna corrected, directing her horse toward the increasing commotion. "I will do the talking."

Sulanna led them ever closer, down the dirt road, with Wit falling back to Branimir's side with noticeable discomfort. The historian's hands shook well enough he could have been riding in a wagon instead of a horse's saddle.

The words between the riders and Farthr were clear as they closed the distance. The man closest to Farthr spoke in a shaky voice, waving a torch in his hand. "He may be telling the truth. Look at his crossbow and the leatherwork of the quiver. Those are not common armaments, and definitely would not be found in Svet settlements."

"He likely stole them from the last human he killed," said another. "I bet a hefty reward is on his head. We should take him back to Eldhaft, or even down to Gaetana."

"I have told you the truth," Farthr said. "I am Farthr of Brennen, retained by the Crimson Sun. Delaying my orders will have you answering to Ivarr Gauthus."

"That is the name of the man leading the Crimson Sun."

"Are you certain?"

"Yes."

"Does it really matter? Anyone north of the Dyndaer could find the name of Ivarr Gauthus. I say, he is an escaped slave who killed his master and stole his weapons."

Farthr growled as the men argued, swelling his burly chest. Branimir could see the Svet's ears twitching near his long, black mane. Farthr said, "I have not survived the face of death to listen to this drivel. Be off or wish you had."

"Something I would expect—"

"Rocher," another cut in, "others approach on the road." The man pointed at Branimir and the other four, who advanced leisurely. Each of the four horsemen shifted, waving torches in their direction for better light.

"Good evening. The Svet is who he says he is," Sulanna said, guiding her horse into the light. She leaned toward them like two old friends chatting over noontide tea, and smiled. "He is free in Maharia."

"And who are you?" the man called Rocher asked.

"Sulanna Maelthirren, also one among the Crimson Sun, and friend to all who are employed by them," Sulanna said, holding the smile, "including Farthr. I understand he may appear a bit brutish, but his services have long protected you and the people of Eldhaft."

"Maelthirren?" One of the men furrowed his brow. Two others murmured the name.

Rocher scooted his horse back, a sudden fear enveloping his eyes. "Your father is Vornic Myrthos Maelthirren?"

"He is," Sulanna said. Farthr rumbled again, air pushing through his wide nostrils, before dipping his head to greet Sulanna. "He and Count Vlassi, who the Crimson Sun has often worked in hand with, would be displeased that you have threatened such an esteemed member. Yet I would guess this is but a misunderstanding. The night is dark, and only words were exchanged."

"Indeed. Only words," Rocher agreed. He signaled the other men with his hand. "We will be on our way. Apologies to you, Farthr. We owe you our thanks to your service."

"You have no idea." Farthr snarled.

"Travel safe, friends," Sulanna said. The men turned their own mounts, heading north on the road.

When they were beyond earshot, the Svet lifted his torch toward the five of them, eyes tempering on Sulanna. "Seeing a familiar face after all this time does me well. Though, last I knew, you had abandoned your station among the Crimson Sun with Alden Forgaff. Ivarr Gauthus has a bounty on both your heads."

Wit spun hard enough in his saddle to glare at Sulanna, he nearly slid off. The historian, of course, knew nothing of Sulanna's misdirection from the renowned group of mercenaries.

Sulanna kept her poise. "Should I expect you to take me to Tamarri then, after I intervened on your behalf?"

"I have never had a quarrel with you, Sulanna." Farthr held out his torch to examine the rest of them, stopping the flame near Branimir. "I long ago rid myself of any notion of pursuing you or Alden, despite what orders were given."

Branimir stared at Farthr through the flame. He saw a glimmer in the Svet's wide eye. Sulanna must have picked up on it too. "You have recently come across another Kras," she said.

"I have," Farthr admitted, stamping a hoof against the dirt, "though not as recent as you may think. A year has now come to pass since, and many dark tidings with it."

"We aim to travel through the night to escape the heat, Farthr. 'Tis a long road ahead to Eldhaft," Adamus said. "If you are traveling the same way, you should share the tale."

Farthr twitched his ears. "I am. Yet I am uncertain the tale would add any light to the darkness. I survived long enough to recite the tale to Ivarr before being sent to see more perilous deeds done." He returned his gaze to Sulanna. "Deeds I have yet to act upon. I, too, have recently been sought by the Crimson Sun for my waywardness."

"So, you do not travel back to Tamarri?" Sulanna asked. "I truly did save you from an ill-fated outcome with those horsemen."

Farthr dipped his head, the horns on either side of his fawn-like ears glimmering in the torchlight. "Yes, you did. I now return to Sorod, to my tribe."

"We are really going to allow this mongrel to travel alongside us? A deserter to the most powerful company in Maharia?" Wit gaped, flinging his hat upright for a better view of the rest in the flickering light.

"Mongrel?" Branimir scrunched his face. "Why would you attack him? You do not even know him."

"I do not need to know him. My father once told me all about his kind, and it is well documented in the history books. Read *Slaves for Men* or *Friends of the Stockades* by Duras Thatcher," Wit said. "His people are all the same. Savages."

Sulanna, an identical defector, pursed her lips at Wit in consideration, as though the man's true colors—the haughty, superior rascal Branimir knew him to be—continued to reveal himself. Adamus, on the other hand, flashed his white teeth between his black beard and mustache as if the historian had just told a great joke.

Branimir could only stare incredulously at the man.

Alyona replied in a dry tone. "We are all guilty of falling from youthful oaths once ripened with wisdom. Such lessons cannot be adequately taught in books."

Wit wrinkled his scarred nose, nostrils flaring. "If I had known traveling alongside the lot of you would have brought such ridicule of knowledge, I would have stayed in the *Highspire*. None of you have any respect for reason."

Branimir scowled at the historian. "Wait until you have to forget what you know to save your friends or yourself. Those who defend reason have never done much more than sit and judge those who were faced with an inescapable fate," Branimir said. "For your sake, I hope you never have to come to learn that the *just* choice is not always the *right* choice."

"Well…" Witigor wiggled his head back and forth, sticking his chin up. "Just who oversees this group anyway? Who has the final say on our decisions? Sulanna? Please…" His face tightened with disapproval. "To lead this party, we need someone intelligent, preferably male, and likely me. But since I have only come along, I suggest Adamus—who obviously is the only one with any sense—makes all definitive decisions."

Branimir directed his horse away to keep himself from punching Wit in the mouth.

Adamus, on the other hand, who suddenly was overwhelmed with amusement, burst into a deep-throated chuckle, which swiftly changed into a howling cackle.

"Oh, Wit," Adamus wiped the tears from his eyes, his entire chest shaking uncontrollably with laughter, "you should really shut up."

Wit's jaw fell. "What?"

Adamus could not keep the grin from his face, distracting from the seriousness of his words. "You are going to find yourself crawling back to Gaetana if you keep at it."

"We make our decisions together," Branimir clarified.

"Clearly," Wit mumbled, drifting his eyes from Adamus to Bran. "All the same, when we reach Eldhaft, I think I will venture to Gavlok alone."

"Whatever suits you," Sulanna said in a flat tone, directing Farthr to follow her down the road. He lifted the torchlight for them to see the path ahead. Adamus and Alyona followed with Branimir close behind, and Wit, finally at the rear, who paled in shock at the sudden dismissal.

Branimir breathed easy. He wished they had left the man at Gaetana.

"Farthr," Sulanna said in harmony with the clopping of the horses' hooves, "tell me about the Kras? What has caused you to drift from the Crimson Sun?"

"I am uncertain you would believe me unless you have crossed such darkness yourself, but I will tell you all I know," the Svet responded. "Seigfeld Brecher and I were sent to explore the ruins of the Dyndaer, directed by Ivarr, but truly by the hand of Falmagon Sej of the *Kadari*. The mages of Melkorka believed the *old-dark* were returning to the world."

Branimir's heart thudded in his chest. Falmagon had knowledge that the depletion of the Ash Tree was releasing the *old-dark*. Yet he continued to kill the source of life of this world, and the prison of the ancient gods. The last thing Branimir wanted to think about was the terrible evil he faced in the catacombs of *Garain'l*. The same evil, called Likhyi, had implanted itself into the Kras, Drak, until Branimir was forced to take his life. Now, the Likhyi lived within *kaelandur* at his belt.

Farthr stopped talking to consider them. "Strange none of you ask what the *old-dark* means."

"I hardly need a history lesson from an illiterate savage," Wit spoke up from the rear, his over-confident tone piercing the ear like a fine blade. "For those learned, who have read Tom Flitter's *Mystagogical's Forlorn Folio*, we know the Likhyi, as they were once called, to be the eight old gods worshipped in Aenar before time had been recorded. I recently found the eight cruxes of the Stuhian magic is also the elements of each god: sky, stone, fire, sea, primal, void, profane, and sacred. Legend tells of the Ash Tree being a prison for the *old-dark*, and upon its withering will come the release of the Likhyi."

Adamus gave a weak smile absent Farthr's gaze, who scowled at the road ahead of them. "'Tis something some of us know without reading a book."

"It's a tale," Wit replied dryly. Branimir twisted to see Wit glowering at Adamus.

"You believe in the modern gods," Branimir said, "but not the old?"

Wit turned to Branimir. "The gods have transformed over time with our understanding of them, but have never changed themselves outside of name."

"Your conjectures are misguided," Alyona said.

"Quite mistaken," Farthr agreed, "or my eyes, my hands, and my memory have deceived me."

"I am among the mad," Wit claimed. "You speak as though you have walked among gods and drank from the very waters surrounding the Ash Tree. You realize you are contesting hundreds of years of written research on the subject?"

"You would be wise enough to know some write history with the intent to misdirect the masses," Sulanna said. "If knowledge is power, as you press, why would anyone share the knowledge and distribute it to the many. Best to keep said information close to heart while pointing others astray."

"You are claiming the histories I read are fiction?" Wit asked, his voice like silk, captivated by the thought.

"None here would argue against the tutelage the *Highspire* has provided you or the other pupils. Many of your references I may agree with, Witigor, but you cannot believe all you read," Sulanna said. "A lesson my father would voice strongly."

"Hm." Wit grunted.

Sulanna refocused her attention on Farthr. "What did you and Seigfeld find?"

Farthr replied, twitching his ears, "While passing through the Dyndaer, we found a Kras and Uvil on a path to find similar answers about the *old-dark*."

"An Uvil?" Adamus scratched his beard.

"Another race of ignorant sods," Witigor muttered.

Farthr growled, continuing, "I know the pairing seems odd. How they came together, I do not know, but the Kras and Uvil woman sought Shayol Domier to find the name of death. I advised Seigfeld for us to go our own way, but he refused, believing our greater numbers gave us the advantage. His thinking gives reason to why I still hold breath today; yet Seigfeld was not so lucky."

Sulanna gasped. "Seigfeld is dead."

"Fallen at Shayol Domier, along with the Uvil." Farthr said. "The Kras and I took separate paths after escape, having no bonds of brotherhood."

"Escape from what?" Branimir asked.

Farthr rested his hand on the crossbow hanging next to the bolts at his side. His hooves echoed against the dirt for several steps before responding. "I fear myself as mad as the scraggy human suggests for even saying the word, but a Likhyi."

Even when guessing what Farthr would say, Branimir's fingers bound around *kaelandur* in his grasp, horrified. The *old-dark* had gained more power over the last year, solidifying into the world of the living as the Ash Tree deteriorated from the *Kadari*.

First at *Garain'l*, and now, Shayol Domier.

Dorofej once told Branimir that Marheena gifted the Stuhia with *Koldovstvo*. Yet the first *Eretik*, Nedezhda Mager, had been sent by Marheena to destroy the Ash Tree, the prison of the Likhyi. Now, if the eight Likhyi were incarnations of the eight cruxes of *Koldovstvo*, what would this mean to the Stuhia whose blood embodied each type of magic? Branimir's mind raced with unanswered questions.

For as long as Branimir could remember, Dorofej said Marheena, and the other gods, had no interest in men and their actions. He said no gods were good or evil, but simply were. However, Marheena's hand guided Dorofej in making *kaelandur*, the Frozen Goddess incited the ruin of the world, seemingly intending to return the magic she gifted to the dragon people back to the *old-dark*.

"A Likhyi?" Wit finally echoed after a minute of silence from the rest. "You expect us to believe you came face-to-face with an *old-dark*? Even if such madness were true, I cannot think you would survive the encounter."

Farthr snorted. "I expect you to believe nothing. I barely believe it myself. Though I was asked to tell the tale as I know it."

"The Kras you were with knows the same?" Alyona asked.

"Better than I," Farthr said. "Wrylyc Titchen, son of Gard, son of Potap, helped lead us from the Likhyi's distortion."

Potap! Branimir nearly fell from his saddle. The name, though old, was familiar, marking a Kras he had known a millennium ago at Shayol Domier. To hear his friend secured a worthy lineage nearly brought a smile to his face.

"What do you mean distortion?" Branimir asked, clinging to the reins.

"After Seigfeld's fall, Wrylyc and I were attacked by demons in the darkness," Farthr said, "and we secured our lives. But a fog fell on our senses, like the haunting of a dream, which we had difficulty in waking. Images of what I had longed for danced in my vision as though reality for days and days."

Sulanna said, "And how did you wake from the dream?"

"I truly do not know, but Wrylyc and I slipped from the madness and escaped into the Dyndaer," Farthr grunted. He then took in a deep breath, waving the torch in his hand. "I have told what I know, the same as I told Ivarr in Tamarri."

Sulanna led her horse forward to touch Farthr's arm. "I am sorry you had to see Seigfeld part from this world. I know what he meant to you. May he and Alden find peace in their passing."

Farthr turned his head sharply. "Alden?"

Sulanna nodded. "I fear he fell some time ago in Talastein."

"No, Sulanna," Farthr shook his head. Sulanna's hand retreated to her chest with the Svet's next words. "The old kook yet lives. I crossed him upon the road two days past."

"This road! Going which direction?" Sulanna asked.

Farthr said, "North toward Eldhaft. He and I spoke for nary a minute, passing pleasantries, before he set off again."

"He is looking for me," Sulanna whispered, a smile forming on her face. She turned to look at Branimir, who responded with a wide grin. "He would search for me in my home city."

Branimir scratched his head in bewilderment, a grin plastered to his face. He looked to Adamus for an answer. "But how did he escape the Lilitu? You said the Lilitu did not keep their prisoners alive?"

Farthr replied before Adamus could form a word. "The Crimson Sun paid for Alden's release. To knowledge, they planned to deliver him to the *Kadari* for questioning. But Alden escaped on the road back to Tamarri."

"Who was sent to retrieve him?" Sulanna's voice quivered with her question.

"I don't know." Farthr shook his head. "But Alden made short work of them."

"He killed them?" Branimir gasped.

Farthr's ears twitched. "I heard the deaths were swift. Merciful."

Branimir could hear Wit mumbling from the saddle behind him.

Adamus grunted, speaking aloud before Wit could say anything substantial. "If we make haste, we may still find him in Eldhaft. Tis not likely he will be welcomed by any who recognize him."

"Alden is well known in these parts…" Sulanna said. "If he is looking for me, he would go to *The Harper and Mug* in Old Town."

"Then," Branimir said, "let us not waste any time in getting there."

Chapter V

Branimir could not help but smile at the thought of Alden traveling on the road ahead, and Sulanna had not stopped grinning since she heard the news. For hours, Branimir enjoyed listening to the high-spirited, idle banter of her and the others. Farthr and Sulanna swapped heroic tales from their days among the Crimson Sun. Adamus soon joined, reliving his tales of battle; and then Alyona matched him with her own mystifying feats against demons rising from the Netherworld. Wit, of course, would not be left out of the haughty bragging, sharing the histories of men—greater than himself—who had fought against powerful foes, as though he had warred against them himself.

"Gebereht was favored by Svathevit," Wit said, referring to the legendary *hero-warrior* from Ariadne, whom the God of War had allegedly blessed. The historian clicked his tongue, followed by a haughty chuckle. "Veselin's *Excursions into the Dyndaer* tells the account of Gebereht's battles fought in *The Second War*. He may have been the greatest warrior among the Ariadneans during the sixth century."

Branimir watched Wit deliberately pause and look to Farthr, who tensed at the mentioning of *The Second War*.

"You know *The Second War* was between the Anshedar and the Svet?" Farthr rumbled at Wit. "For forty years, we killed one another, until the Svet were beaten down by the *Kadari*, not Gebereht."

Wit smiled. "Oh, but Gebereht was a mighty enemy to the Svet—"

"I am not questioning Gebereht's valor." Farthr interrupted Wit. "Gebereht is remembered among the Svet much like he is among the Anshedar. The Svet respect a warrior no matter where he stands on the field of battle. But you knowingly insult me."

"How could I insult a beast?" Wit said, tipping his hat with a sneer. "Have you no control over your primal emotions?"

Farthr snorted. Branimir was certain the centaur heard far worse in his travels across Maharia, especially with his people considered as slaves among the Anshedar.

Branimir, on the other hand, already was curling his fingers into a fist.

Farthr spoke in a low voice. The strain to remain civil with Witigor was evident. "Adamus, Sulanna, and even Alyona have shared their own exploits, none of which have slighted any other here. Yet you crow about ancient wars, which you held no part in—wars that led to centuries of bondage and oppression for my kind."

"Your slavery was blessed by the gods," Witigor said, pointing his finger at the Svet. "Look what has been accomplished by intellectual minds directing those of lesser beings. Cities have been built. Governments have been strengthened. Crops and commerce have considerably expanded."

Farthr's eyes slanted at the historian. "You humans have destroyed the land. You believe your will—your way—gives light to the future. Yet I have also heard how you claim your god—this Svathevit, a mirror of the Svet God of War, Rujan—blessed you in leading my kind to servitude. Funny how your path to the future is borrowed from savages. Somehow, you humans—simple and weak—fail to see that the only reason us *savages* stand as slaves is because of the *Kadari's* vile magic. They won *The Second War.* Not Gebereht. Not any human. And, especially, not you."

"Vile magic?" Alyona raised an eyebrow more with intrigue than offense.

"Yes," Farthr said in a dry tone. "You use your power to strengthen shackles when you could instead shatter them."

Wit shouted in defiance to Farthr, while Alyona slowed her mount. "Not true! The *Kadari* only came in the final years of the war, after the Svet were pushed back to their so-called Holy Lands. Holy lands, I may add, that we were kind enough to allow the free Svet to hold until this very day. Tell him, Alyona!"

Alyona tensed her jaw, staring at the wild-eyed historian, and then simply shook her head. "I was not here during *The Second War.* I know Gebereht played a significant role in the war, as you said, but I also know the *Kadari* have stolen glory from the Svet before in the past."

"The savage insults your magic and you defend him!" Wit said.

"Many do use their magic for immoral reasons," Alyona said.

"Farthr speaks the truth, Wit-less. I have seen how the *Kadari* have robbed life and glory from the Svet," Branimir said, glad for Alyona's remark. He remembered too clearly the first time he had met Alyona, and her brother Artemiy, on the outskirts of Shayol Domier over a millennium ago. The two, and the *Kadari* with them, were quick to slaughter his Svet friends, Melyena Rogov and Asgrim Garoar.

Bran wondered what changed Alyona's position on the *savages.*

"Must my words be refuted by every confounding fool amongst you?" Wit glared, holding his gaze temporarily on Branimir. "Do you have no respect for written history? No! Of course, you do not. I have somehow been tossed into a party of cranks and criminals."

"Claiming Gebereht pushed the Svet back to the Holy Lands is one thing," Branimir said, "but saying the Svet deserved enslavement and death is wrong."

"You are going to lecture me on what is right and wrong?" The man ripped his pointed hat from his head, flinging accusations at each of them with equal disdain. "Two defectors from the Crimson Sun bent on finding a third turncoat, a fugitive from the *Kadari*, and a two-tongued Kras, who should be bending knee as much as this brutish Svet. You all deserve lashings." Witigor spit over his shoulder. "I would not be surprised to find you had absconded from the war, Adamus. How else would you get caught up with this lot of misfits?"

"Wit," Adamus scowled, stopping his horse and turning it around, "you have been warned over and over. We talked about your tongue before we left Gaetana. You go too far."

"Do I?" Wit scoffed. "Or do I speak the truth?"

Sulanna kept an even tone, pushing her brown hair behind her ear. "Wit, go back to Gaetana. Return to the *Highspire*."

"No," Wit said, squaring his shoulders. "I am going to go ride straight to Eldhaft, and tell Count Vlassi what contemptible itinerants approach his gate, so he can take care of you appropriately."

"You will not," Branimir said, easing up in his saddle.

Alyona circled around Wit on her horse. "The historian compromises our journey."

"Where is your sense, Wit?" Adamus moved his horse closer, leaning forward. "We invite you to travel alongside us and you answer with disrespect and threats. You really think tis possible to give insult and then attempt to deliver us into a hang noose?"

Witigor's eyes flashed. "You think you can stop me?"

"Without effort," Adamus said, then swung his leg over his horse to dismount.

Branimir moved quicker than his friend. Climbing up on his saddle, he leaped through the air at Witigor. In a fluid motion, he tackled Wit from his saddle. The historian cried out in surprise, releasing his horse's reins, flailing over the side of the animal with Branimir holding fast to the front of his shirt.

With a groan, Wit hit the rutted road. Branimir crashed into Wit's ribcage with all his weight. With a bawl of passion, Bran ignored the faint shouts of his companions behind him. Staring at the disfigured face, he punched Wit squarely in the teeth. When blood barely surfaced on the upper lip, Branimir hit him again. This time the lip split wide open.

Satisfied, Branimir stood. Adamus grabbed Branimir's shoulder and pulled him back from Wit.

"Keep the red brood away from me," Witigor cried, straining for breath. He scooted away from Branimir across the dirt, fumbling to his feet, grabbing at his bleeding nose and upper lip. "By the gods, you will all be punished for this. I swear it. I have done nothing wrong."

He stumbled, almost falling over.

"And you do not know what we have done to come this far," Branimir said, trying to steady his shaking hands. He had already lost Dorofej; he would not let Witigor endanger the lives of his other friends. "You risk too much."

Adamus let go of his shoulder. "Czern's breath! I don't think you will find any argument from any here, Bran. But what do we do with him?"

"He cannot come with us to Eldhaft," Alyona said, "and he should not be allowed to return to Gaetana."

Witigor's eyes widened.

"We could see if he calms down before reaching Eldhaft," Sulanna said. "For now, take the reins from his horse, and tie him up.

"I'll do it," Farthr said, reaching for Wit's horse.

Witigor gained his balance, eyes whipping up and down the road for any sign of life…or escape. "You cannot—"

Alyona shocked the historian into silence, using *Koldovstvo* to pick up his body and fling him toward Farthr, who caught the scrawny human in a single hand. The centaur snarled with sharpened fangs, causing Witigor to clench his jaw with fear, twisting his head away.

Branimir watched Farthr place Wit back in his horse's saddle. The Svet bit through the reins, using one end to tie together Wit's hands. "You don't mean to set him free, do you?" Branimir asked Sulanna.

"I do not know what *we* will do with him yet," Sulanna answered.

Farthr snagged the remaining cord hanging from the bridle to lead the horse. "I can take him with me to Sorod and give him a proper education." The Svet smiled. "We could slow cook him before feasting."

Branimir twitched, knowing the centaurs had a habit of eating their enemies, as well as their own dead.

Witigor whitened. "Adamus. Sulanna. I have done nothing so grievous as to be treated this way. I thought we were friends."

Adamus shook his head, grimacing. The Ariadnean's muscles flexed, balling his hand into a fist. "'Tis interesting how his tune changes at the thought of filling the belly of the Svet. We suddenly become friends again, where moments ago he wished to call us enemies to the crown."

"No," Wit said. "I would never have called you enemies to the crown. You misunderstood…"

"You would do best to stop talking," Adamus growled. Wit responded by clamping his jaw shut and hanging his head.

"Listen," Alyona said, redirecting attention from the historian, "even if we keep riding for the rest of the day and night, we will not make it to Eldhaft. The sun will be rising any time now, and we are going to need some sleep."

"She is right," Sulanna said, rubbing her sore neck, "but sleeping on the side of the road in the broad daylight will bring unwanted attention, especially with Wit bound up."

"We have put in many miles between here and Gaetana," Branimir said, choosing his words carefully. He did not want to hint anything about Falmagon being in Gaetana. Alyona should not know their late night had been to increase the distance between themselves and the Patrician of the *Kadari*, in case she had not been honest about her allegiances. "We may be able to afford a couple hours off the road for sleep."

Alyona gripped her animal's reins, her purple eyes watering from exhaustion. Branimir imagined the woman was completely fatigued, considering she came from Melkorka after being held prisoner in a dungeon and surviving a siege. "A couple hours would be welcomed."

Adamus said. "Our horses need rest, too. Tis early yet and the road is clear. We can take a couple hours to rest."

Farthr grunted. "I have no need for rest. I will continue my own way and take Witigor with me."

Sulanna shook her head. Branimir noticed that she eyed Alyona from the corner of her eye. "Farthr, I was hopeful you would stay among us for a while."

"I have no interest in traveling too close to Eldhaft." Farthr snorted. "I do not have a family name to keep me safe. I will make for Sorod."

"You think my name will keep me safe?" Sulanna nervously laughed. "My father rejected me from his sight two decades ago. He is the reason I joined the Crimson Sun."

"One can never know how time may heal wounds, and your name holds power still," Farthr said. "I am a Svet in a world of Anshedar. No name. No title. No power. I will be enslaved or killed without my position among the Crimson Sun."

Sulanna rubbed her hands together, looking to Adamus and then Branimir.

Bran knew what she was considering. The protection Adamus sought from Alyona was rapidly dwindling, and none of them would be able to predict whether Falmagon was already in pursuit.

Adamus pulled at his beard, keeping his eyes from Wit, and reluctantly nodded. With a sigh, Branimir dipped his head in agreement too. "What will be his fate, Farthr?" Branimir did not like Witigor, but he also did not want the Anshedar to be eaten by the Svet.

Farthr twitched his ears and looked to Sulanna for direction.

"You remember Ailin Meadhre?" Sulanna crossed her arms, glaring at Wit. A smile formed on Farthr's face as he bounced his head. "Give him the same fate, but let him roast a bit longer."

"What?" Wit screamed as Farthr grabbed the reins and began leading him away into the grasses. The historian rocked in the saddle, fighting against the restraints. "Who is Ailin Meadhre? Who is he? Nooo!"

Branimir twisted his neck for some explanation from his companions. Adamus and Alyona looked equally confused by Sulanna's sentencing. Branimir finally asked her the question. "What happened to Ailin Meadhre?"

Sulanna smiled. "He was stripped naked, tied to a tree, and left to roast in the sun until found. I suspect Wit will be back in Gaetana before the week's end."

Branimir's light chuckle was swiftly drowned out by Adamus's raucous laughter.

Chapter VI

Three and a half days passed before they reached the gates of Eldhaft in the northwest, a city of liars and thieves, as Sulanna once claimed. They lost almost a full day traveling to the city due to the heat. Several times Sulanna advised them to stop and take shelter off the road, hunkering down in the shade. Branimir worried Falmagon would gain on them, but he had seen no signs of the Patrician of the *Kadari*. He did wonder how far Farthr had taken Witigor from the road while traveling northeast; he doubted the historian would survive long under the sun. Despite his feelings for Wit, he hoped he was quickly found.

Eldhaft was nearly the magnitude of Gaetana, lying nestled in the Gaetanain Grasslands. Knolls rose and fell as far as the eye could see—a slight suggestion of the Hyaendi Hills further to the north. Thick grasses covered much of the land, but the locals cleared patches for farms and crops. In the midday light, Branimir could see homesteads reaching to the skyline, chockfull of hard-working men in the field, animals roaming amongst their fenced cages, and children running amuck, diverted from chores by imaginary play.

Branimir wished he had the energy of the children, but the sweltering heat stole all he could muster. He barely could stay aloft on his pony. For what felt like the hundredth time since noon, Branimir wiped the sweat from his cheeks and forehead with the end of his cloak, hanging over the neck of his saddle. He then reached for his waterskin, glancing to the river running alongside the road. They had traveled near the water since the sunrise.

Sulanna must have noticed his gaze. She pointed to the water. "The *Deep Run* flows from the mountains in the north all the way to the ocean in the south, slowed only by the *Gnyn Waters* at Gaetana. You will find, here, in the city walls of Eldhaft, the *Gneveh Rill* merges with the *Deep Run* to give the river enough strength to pierce through the southern lake. The sound of the rushing water can be deafening in some areas of the city. Honestly, the two rivers coming together is breathtaking."

"We should see it while we are here," Branimir said.

Sulanna rubbed the neck of her horse. "You will not be able to miss the sight. The main road through Eldhaft passes by the rivers."

Branimir gazed up to the green and gold banners hanging from the almost perfect, circular stone wall surrounding Eldhaft, and took another drink from his waterskin. The banners displayed a golden horse dancing on its hind legs, wearing a crown of arrows, which Branimir mistook for strands of wheat crop at first glance.

Branimir said, "I once saw an image like that horse on the chest piece of the man we fought at Cavell. Remember, Adamus? He was with the Crimson Sun, too."

Adamus scrunched his beard, peering at the tapestry. "I remember something of it. Tis been a while, and if I recall, I drank more than I should have that night." Adamus returned his eyes to the road, stone-faced. Branimir wondered if he triggered memories of Hanna, Adamus's friend who died in battle last year. She had been with them at Cavell.

"Teodor Bacheva?" Sulanna interjected, raising an eyebrow and slowing her horse. She whispered, "I would not mention anything of it in the city. Teodor's father is stationed among the league of thieves, the *Guardians of Gero*, and as such, gave Teodor a considerable place in the Crimson Sun. He may have been Ivarr's most strategic asset among any in the company. Being involved in Teodor's death would not grant you any favors here."

"Great," Branimir said, remembering something more at the mention of the *Guardians*. "I forgot the league of thieves was in Eldhaft. They were looking for me several years ago when I worked in Gavlok. They were interested in my dagger-throwing."

"Let us hope they have forgotten your name, if they ever knew it," Sulanna said. "The *Guardians* believe themselves to be the very voice of Gero, the so-called god of Fertility, Harvest, and Rebirth. These men and women commit unlawful acts of violence for his *exaltation*. They lose so many of their affiliates to the gallows; they are frequently seeking more capable recruits."

"And why does Count Vlassi allow it?" Branimir asked.

"The *Guardians* do not rob or kill anyone in Eldhaft. At least, not without permission from Vlassi. Instead, they focus on neighboring cities, like Lonmere. You will find *Guardians* bled dry on pikes outside that city," Sulanna replied with a shake of her head. "The *Guardians* preach that Gero was stolen from Perom and delivered to Wolos, and so they steal from those unfaithful to Gero and deliver the goods to Eldhaft."

"Nary has a week passed, and again I hear Sulanna teaching the history of the gods," Adamus said. "Are you feeling well?"

"When you spend half a lifetime with Alden, you pick up a thing or two," Sulanna said with a frown. "I am not saying any of this is true. I am telling you what those fanatics believe. I would prefer we do not spend any more time in this cursed city than we must."

Branimir shook his head with emphasis, his thin hair bouncing against the edge of his eyelashes. "We will stay long enough to find Alden, and be done."

Alyona swept her eyes over them, reaching for her dark hood to pull over her head. She had been quiet most of the morning, watching the road intently, but finally spoke. "I agree. We must hurry to *Iriy* to meet Dorofej. He will be traveling with the wind; and we do not have time to waste."

The sound of flutes and harps permeated outside the walls, reaching Branimir's sensitive ears. Laughter and boisterous voices imbued the sound, as though the whole city may have been a patron-filled tavern. Branimir struggled to hear the faded trickle of the peaceful river flowing away from the city.

"A sprightly bunch, are they not?" Adamus said, steering his horse with a gentle tug, leading them beneath the portcullis. The guards gestured them through, talking loudly to one other about some evening festival. None seemed interested in any who came or left from the gates. Adamus continued, slowing slightly, "Most of the people will be prepping for harvest this time of the year, if the heat has not burnt up all their crops. Still, I suspect these people will laugh their way through starvation. I fought alongside a man from Eldhaft at Raybin. I cannot say I ever caught him without a smile. Even when the Uvil put a hooked sword into his side, he grinned like a fool."

"And yet, Sulanna rarely smiles," Branimir said with a crooked grin, stopping his pony as two girls ran by the road in front of him, laughing and holding half-made wreaths of flowers and ferns over their head. They looked up at Branimir for a half-second, giggled, and continued into the crowded streets.

Sulanna smirked, stopping her own mount. "I was born here, Branimir. I did not stay around long enough to adopt the drivel." The color from Sulanna's face suddenly drained as she examined the roads ahead of her.

"What is it?" Branimir asked, searching the streets for the cause of her distress. The road immediately forked left and right on either side of the gate, leading through buildings nearly built on top of one another. Some of the structures were homes, built behind tall wooden fences, while others were shops or taverns. People encumbered the streets. Young women pranced about with similar wreaths as the first two girls, men ambled by carrying long strips of wood, while handfuls of others laughed, danced, or talked.

Sulanna rotated on her mount to address the first guardsman found, leaning against the stone wall behind them. "What is today?"

The young guardsman smiled with oversized, white teeth filling the space between his lips, standing upright. His hand rested on the hilt of the longsword at his belt, the horse head glimmering on his chest plate in the sunlight. "Why, my lady, it is the Day of Myestera. Join us at sun fall in Old Town for dancing, drinking, and merriment. The fires will burn bright through the night." He dipped his head at Adamus and Alyona, swinging his hand in a wide arc, "Bring your husband, your daughter, and..." he looked at Branimir with hesitation, "your Kras."

Sulanna gripped the reins until her knuckles turned white. "My what and my what?"

"Your daughter may find herself with a gallant husband before the night is through," the guard said, turning his eyes from Bran to Alyona once more. The *Kadari* sunk into her hood, turning her purplish eyes away. The guard's words lingered. "No city can offer better men than Eldhaft."

"Come on," Adamus sniggered, drawing out the next word, "my sweetness. We should find a place to freshen up before the festivities."

Sulanna growled through her teeth, despite the flashes of color on her cheeks. "Do not push me, Adamus. My blade is recently sharpened and your neck is bare."

Adamus only grinned wider, directing his horse down the dirt path. "Where to?"

Branimir coaxed his pony forward, leaving the guardsman behind them. He personally thought she would make an excellent mother someday, but decided against mentioning it.

Sulanna took a moment before answering. "Take the right fork. We will go to Old Town to *The Harper and Mug*."

"We cannot stay long," Alyona pressed with concern.

"Only long enough to find Alden," Branimir repeated.

Adamus did as he was told, leading the way with Sulanna directly behind him, then Branimir, and finally Alyona at the rear. Branimir spotted a second set of walls almost immediately, dividing Old Town from the remainder of the city.

Branimir waited until they navigated through the congested street and passed under the second portcullis before raising another question. "Would anyone like to explain to me what the Day of Myestera is?"

Alyona moved her horse next to Branimir's pony, people flooding on either side of them. "The celebration is also called *Pal'ka*, honoring the marriage of the Mother of the Stars and the Lightbringer. Women yet wedded end the feast by tossing handmade wreaths into a river. They say it will foretell the future of their own marriages by whether the flowers sink or float. The holiday was once sacred, but now, it is really an excuse for excessive drinking and fornication."

"Mother of the Stars…Myestera…" Branimir wondered aloud. "We are talking about the Moon Goddess, a goddess worshipped by the Vucari."

"Yes," Alyona said, turning under her hood to look at Branimir. "The Vucari first worshipped Wolos, and then Myestera. Neither god has been revered among humans in my lifetime." She bent over, hovering above Branimir on her horse, and asked softly, "How have you come to know the skin-switchers of the far north?"

Branimir gazed under the hood into Alyona's purplish eyes. "A long time ago, before we first met, I was friends with a Vucari woman from *Anaerfell*. She told me many things about her people."

"Friends?" Alyona cocked her head.

"I know the *Kadari* believed the Vucari to be wicked creatures, but they were the wardens of the Ash Tree. When they fought you at Shayol Domier, I think they were trying to protect the tree," Branimir explained, "but the *Kadari*…only wanted power."

Alyona sighed heavily. Branimir could see the water forming at the corner of her eyes, unhidden from him despite the dark folds of her hood. "My father would say the Vucari are savage beasts, but I know better."

Branimir gritted his teeth. "I do not know your father, but I would guess he is the same type who would call me a demon." Branimir tugged at his hooked nose irritably, and then laid his hand back in his lap. "Yet I have met demons and devils alike, and I am nothing like them."

"No," Alyona said, "you are not."

Sulanna whipped her head around, hushing them. "Do not draw unwanted attention our way. Need I remind you, we are in Eldhaft. The guards may have their hearts set on dancing and drinking tonight, but the *Guardians* will not be as unconcerned."

"We are not speaking against Gero," Alyona said.

Sulanna's nostrils flared unattractively. "No, you speak of Wolos, who stole Gero, and his long-forgotten, faithful people. May I remind you of the rumors of Wolos being murdered? Those in Eldhaft do not readily forget."

"I do not see what—" Alyona started.

Sulanna growled under her breath. "Do not talk about any gods or goddesses, old or new, real or otherwise! Not until we are a hundred miles outside of Eldhaft, and even then, you best ask me first." She gave a motherly stare, and jerked her head frontward again.

Branimir hardly heard Adamus's muffled jest. "Three times."

"By the Nine Lands, Adamus," Sulanna said. "I am trying to keep our heads. And the three of you seem intent on seeing them severed."

It was nearing dusk by the time they reached *The Harper and Mug*. The road, although long and crowded, was a straight shot to the three-story edifice, sitting three buildings south from the doublewide bridge passing over the *Deep Run*. Branimir stretched on his pony to look at the water. The dark blue, rigorous river surged under the bridge, crashing against either bank, pitching into small waves. The water smelled anything but crisp, likely full of waste from the inhabitants of the city. Yet the river did remind him of the sun's heat. In that moment, he abruptly noticed the fact that Alyona had been sheltered beneath her thick hood, but showed no signs of discomfort, including sweat.

Branimir forfeited his attention on the inn shortly, to confirm Alyona did not seem to be affected by the weather. Whereas the rest of the party—as well as every citizen of Eldhaft who ventured too close—reeked like the rotten mires of the Dyndaer. Alyona held no such smell.

She may be telling the truth about Dorofej, but she was hiding something.

"Afternoon," a middle-age man approached them from the steps leading up into the inn. "If you are looking for a room, I can take your horses to the stables. Chaid Paddley is the barkeep. He can see you to room and board inside."

Sulanna took the lead, dismounting and grabbing her pack. "Our thanks, Master…"

"Ayden Stansfield," the man filled in the blank with a smile, "and just Ayden, if you please. I have done nothing to deserve any title."

"Thank you, Ayden," Sulanna reiterated, handing the man a few silvers. "Please keep the horses well attended. We will speak to Chaid about a room."

Ayden clinked the coins in his hand with a smile. "Well attended, indeed."

Branimir's buttocks and legs were sore as he climbed from the saddle and grabbed his own pack. He purposely held his cloak over his forearm, blocking any view of *kaelandur* at his belt. With a grunt, he took his place behind Adamus and Alyona who followed Sulanna up the solid staircase. Awkwardly, Bran attempted to rub some of the soreness on the back of his thigh. He only now realized they had been riding since the early morning without taking any time to rest.

The Harper and Mug had a worn disposition, complete with faded wood and hung oil paintings to put Lady Gail's artwork at the *Peddlar's Rose* to shame. The commons were half-full of patrons, who started their drinking a few hours early. The design was like the *Peddlar's Rose* with the staircase against the back wall, accompanied by several doors leading into other rooms on the first floor. Tables and chairs were equally spread out through the commons, adjacent to the long bar to the left. Branimir barely took notice of a beaming woman entertaining the gathering, playing a fiddle on a corner stage, before the barkeep stole his attention.

"You have a Kras in your party?" The man known as Chaid leaned over the bar to peer at Branimir. His bushy eyebrows ran together over his nose, forming a single brow, nearly thick enough to cover his beady eyes. "I am not sure we have a bed small enough to accommodate him, but I can check with Master Berkeley. We don't see many Kras in these parts."

"That will not be necessary, Chaid," Sulanna said with a soft smile. "He is perfectly capable of sleeping in a regular-sized bed."

"Now, my Lady, Master Berkeley will want to be assured you are well taken care of while staying at our establishment," he said with a grim smile. "I would hate to be the reason your stay is less than expected."

"We hold no unreasonable expectations," Sulanna began.

"It is no trouble," Chaid insisted. "Go on up to your room. Third door on the left will sleep the four of you comfortably, even with the addition of another bed. I will speak with the Master."

Sulanna frowned. "When is supper served?"

Chaid kept the smile plastered on his face, as though painted on. His eyes fell to Branimir, blinking several times. "As soon as you are ready for it."

"We will take it in our room," Sulanna replied.

Branimir met the man's stare while Adamus thanked Chaid, and ushered Sulanna toward the staircase. He trailed behind, finally turning away from the gawking barkeep.

"What do you think his problem is?" Branimir hissed at Alyona as they climbed the staircase.

"Maybe he has never seen a Kras before," Alyona offered, looking behind them under her hood.

"I do not know I feel right staying here tonight," Bran said. "Something does not feel right. We would do better to stay camping out in the grasslands."

"Let us not start with sinister thoughts already," Sulanna replied, pushing their door open.

Branimir walked behind her, ready to respond, when he bumped into the back of Sulanna's leg. His comment was forgotten when he realized she had unexpectedly stopped.

Peeping around Sulanna, Branimir caught a glimmer of the large, low-lighted room, prepped with a water basin, fresh beds, and readied wine. Yet an aged man with white, braided hair, and a thick, curled mustache, dressed in a green suit with gold buttons, sat in a wooden chair with his legs crossed, already gifting himself with the wine. His blue eyes, sheening a likeness to Sulanna, skimmed over them briefly before he took a slow sip from his golden chalice.

Sulanna rigidly suspended her chin and folded her arms under her breasts. "Father."

Chapter VII

"Quite the muddled mess you have made for yourself, Daughter? I thought the Crimson Sun would have ironed out your rough edges, but even the ways of war and death were incapable of teaching you proper reason." Vornic Myrthos Maelthirren sipped from his chalice again, eyes thick with malice as he watched Sulanna take the seat across from him.

Branimir remained at Sulanna's side, eyeing the old man with uncertainty. Adamus and Alyona piled into the room behind him. The few hanging lights around the room likely made it difficult for Adamus and Sulanna to see. Though, Bran saw the room was clear, save the old man.

Myrthos gulped the mouthful of red wine, catching a droplet on the edge of his lip with a thin finger. "And now, you return to Eldhaft to further blemish the family name, and plague an old man with your foul schemes. Oh, yes…I have a very clear understanding of what plots you have tangled yourself in with this red brood, and," he squinted at Alyona and Adamus, "these indecent coconspirators."

Sulanna moved her hands to her knees, shaking her head slightly. "Whatever you think you know is far-removed from the truth, Father."

"I think not," Myrthos said, his mustache lifting with a sneer. "Ivarr Gauthus has sent for news regarding your whereabouts more times than I can remember. And the Patrician has had a mark on that *red brood* for a year and more. Now, less than a week ago, he sent a message to every major and minor settlement in Maharia to bolster efforts to bring you both to justice. Did you not think the *Guardians* would see you approaching the city? You have broken the law, Sulanna. The very law you swore to uphold. You have shamed this family for the last time."

"Falmagon is the one who cannot be trusted," Branimir said earnestly. "You do not know him. You do not know what he is capable of."

"'Tis the truth," Adamus said with a jerk of his head, exchanging glances with Sulanna and Branimir. "Far more is at stake than the egos of men in position."

"Oh," Myrthos said, unable to mask the mocking tone, "and I should believe an outlaw over a *Kadari* who saved Aenar from itself, not only fending off demons from the Netherworld, but also holding fast to the faith of the Anshedar."

"An outlaw? I bled for Maharia!" Adamus thundered, flexing his arm in restraint from grabbing the steel axe at his belt. "My brothers, my friends, have died to give men the capacity to hold faith."

"Yet you help shroud those who hold precious artifacts to save this world from demons," Myrthos said, casually placing his goblet on the floor.

"You know nothing of the nature of these *artifacts*," Sulanna said.

"I may not," Myrthos said, "but Falmagon has kept men on the righteous path of Dahz the Lightbringer. To truth! I trust he knows what should be done, and the Crimson Sun supports his claim."

"You seek to further yourself," Sulanna scowled.

Branimir spoke over Sulanna. "What are you talking about?" He stood up straight as he had been jerked, staring at Myrthos. "The gods have no interest in how they are worshipped or what we do to honor them. Any *truth* Falmagon told you has been to gain power."

Sulanna looked daggers at her father. "My father seeks the same power, Branimir. He is the Vornic of Eldhaft, remember? He tortures innocent men and women to gain position and privilege. Our words fall on deaf ears."

"You speak blasphemy, as I would expect from your kind. I have dealt with lawbreakers my entire life," Myrthos said. His blue eyes were haunting through the thin slits of his eyelids. "Sulanna should have known I would see through your lies. You are the sort to leave an educated scholar from the *Highspire*, without any account of wrongdoing, bound unclothed to a tree for your own sick enjoyment." Branimir's mouth dried. The Vornic must have noticed his changed expression. "Oh, yes. I have had the pleasure to talk at length with Witigor Sirska this morning. I have learned a great deal about the four of you, and we will find the Svet soon enough."

Branimir folded his arms to keep himself from shaking. The extra time they spent resting had apparently given Witigor time to beat them to Eldhaft. The historian had kept to his promise. "Haven't you tortured people your entire life? I am sure you do far worse than tie them to a tree," he said.

Vornic Myrthos Maelthirren took another sip from his wine with a smile.

"Where is he?" Adamus said under his breath.

"He has been given residence at my estate after your contemptible mistreatment," Myrthos responded. "Not that it matters. You will never be within arm's reach of him again."

Branimir trembled. He could punch Witigor in his scarred face. The historian was keeping him from Dorofej.

Myrthos returned his attention to his daughter. "I am sickened, Sulanna, that you have aligned yourself with these types…but you clearly have chosen your own way, despite having a father who did all he could to place you on a better path."

Sulanna shuddered, turning eyes away from him. "You discarded me with my mother."

"Your mother chose to leave," Myrthos retorted.

The tears streamed down her cheeks, stealing her strength. Her words were drawn out. "What choice did she have after what you did to Hegedus?"

Myrthos's voice seethed with anger. "You moan like a sheep, Sulanna. Your brother was a heathen, and enemy to the crown."

"You…publicly gutted him in the streets…like a swine."

Adamus roared at the revelation, pushing past Branimir to stand between Sulanna and Myrthos, protecting her like a shield. "You murdered your own son!"

Myrthos did not as much as flinch, standing to face the Ariadnean. His words dripped venom. "A fate each of you will share when I have finished recovering what information you have locked inside those insignificant skulls."

In an instant, the room became a flurry of movement. Adamus's hefty fist plowed into the under jaw of Sulanna's father, knocking him back into the rear wall, flipping the chair and dumping the goblet of wine. Behind them, the doors of other rooms in the hallway sprung open, and out poured more men than Branimir could count, all dressed in similar dark green, hooded cloaks, stitched with golden embroidery.

"No," Sulanna shouted, seeing her father crumple against the wall. Adamus moved to strike the man again, before becoming aware of the countless men rushing into their room. He spun around Sulanna's chair, pulling his axe free and swinging it at the first coming through the door.

The lithe invader rolled under the swing, springing to the side, and elbowing Alyona under the chin. She flailed back into the bed, her hood falling back, revealing her purple eyes and dark hair.

Branimir faded from view, releasing his pack, and pulling the two daggers from his belt. He dove for the first invader, stabbing a dagger into the man's leg, and then his knee. The attacker bawled for a moment, before Alyona was back on her feet. With a wave of her hand, she flung the injured man back through the door, causing several more to collapse in attempt to catch the airborne body.

"Who are they?" Adamus shouted as more rushed into the room, pulling knives from their belts. The men moved quick, rushing around the room, surrounding them.

"*Guardians of Gero*," Sulanna said, pulling herself from the chair. Her hand hung over the long dagger at her belt, but she did not pull it free. "We will not be able to overpower them."

"We can try!" Adamus growled. "Come on, Bran." The Ariadnean crashed into the circle of *Guardians*, his shield moved to his left arm, mid-jump, crushing a smaller, unaware man into the wine jugs sitting in the room. Adamus belted a second *Guardian* in the side of the head with his axe. He dropped to the floor with a gravelly groan.

Branimir reacted straightaway. He threw his dagger with deadly intent into a *Guardian*'s chest, who was raising a dagger at Adamus's side. The man dropped his own dagger, gripping the handle of Branimir's lodged weapon. Bran skittered across the floorboards, stabbing another man in the leg, before picking up the dropped dagger and flinging it into another *Guardian*'s eye socket.

Adamus cleaved off a man's arm, and smashed another with the shield, roaring as though he stood among thousands on the battlefield. More *Guardians* entered from the hall replacing their fallen brethren.

"Alyona, come on," Adamus cried, pivoting on his foot to dodge the blade of a *Guardian*. Branimir shadowed Adamus, looking to the bed where Alyona had tumbled moments ago. "Nine Lands…She tricked us." Adamus inhaled, his jaw falling.

Alyona Gounari had vanished. Her white shirt, dark trousers, riding boots, and faded black cloak were scattered over the bed and floor, and she was gone.

Before Branimir could process what had taken place, Adamus snarled with pain. Branimir whipped his head around to see a dagger buried into Adamus's leg. Dark, red blood already seeped through his trousers from the wound.

The *Guardian* who threw the weapon still had his hand extended, standing near the doorway. Branimir dashed forward, using his single dagger to slice the tendons in the back of the *Guardian*'s legs. The man screamed and collapsed to the floorboards, only to be speedily silenced by Branimir's blade cutting through his neck.

Branimir ignored the warm blood splattering on his face, hearing Adamus cry out once more. Another blade plunged into the Ariadnean's back, causing him to sink to one knee.

"Stop this, Father!" Sulanna screeched. "Adamus! Branimir! Stop it."

"Enough." Myrthos keened with a gasping breath, grabbing at the wall behind him. Slowly, he pulled himself to his feet and cupped his jawbone. A bluish-black bump swelled beneath the lip. Myrthos's beady eyes locked on Adamus, raising his other hand to stop the *Guardians*. "Take him and my daughter to *Harrowhal*."

A *Guardian* behind Adamus slipped a rope around the *hero-warrior*'s thick neck, rigidly jerking his head back. Adamus strained against the lesser might of the *Guardian* as the other thieves removed his weapons and bound his hands and feet.

"Run, Branimir," Adamus grated, dropping his axe to the floor. "'Tis over. Get out of here. Wherever you are. Get out of here."

More *Guardians* advanced on Sulanna, who looked pleadingly at her father. The wrinkles of her own aged face were suddenly evident in her distress. "You truly mean to rid this world of all your children."

Myrthos scowled. "If only the gods had blessed me with children worth saving." He stomped by her, addressing the *Guardians*. "Someone get downstairs and block the front door. No one leaves or comes without our knowing." One of the *Guardians* rushed to do as bid, while Myrthos went on, calling out, "Master Bacheva?"

Branimir slipped into the corner of the room, staying cloaked with his invisibility. From the hallway, a middle-aged man with a salt-and-pepper goatee hurriedly emerged, wearing the same attire as the other *Guardians of Gero*. He dipped his head in respect to Myrthos. "Yes, Vornic Maelthirren?"

He recognized the name of Master Bacheva, marking this as the father of Teodor, who they fought at Cavell last year. He was the very man Sulanna had said to avoid while in Eldhaft.

Myrthos wiped his hand on his clothing as though there were something of note on his skin needing removed. "Find the *Kadari* woman and the Kras; they could not have gotten too far. Once found, you can bring them to *Harrowhal*."

"Of course," Master Bacheva said, "but I must warn you that finding the Kras will prove difficult. Their kind can stay invisible indefinitely, and can only be seen by another of their kind. And, unless we bring the *Kadari* down unaware, she could topple half the city on itself."

Myrthos frowned at the man, taking a moment to glance at Sulanna and Adamus having their mouths gagged. He finally said, "Are there any more Kras in Eldhaft?"

Master Bacheva paused for a moment before responding, perhaps realizing he overstepped. "I will check, Vornic."

"Good," Myrthos said. "You will also send word to Patrician Falmagon Sej. He was heading east from Gaetana. Tell him we have found what he has been looking for."

Master Bacheva hesitated. "As you command, Vornic Maelthirren."

Branimir's blood boiled at the mention of Falmagon. If he came to Eldhaft, Branimir would make sure to kill him for good, as he should have at the *Peddlar's Rose*.

The *Guardians* hauled Sulanna and Adamus from the room, Master Bacheva traipsing behind them out the door. A few more thieves fell in behind him, taking the dead from the room.

Branimir tiptoed a couple steps forward as the room emptied, suddenly halted by Vornic Myrthos Maelthirren who filled the frame of the doorway. Sulanna's father scanned the room with vigilant eyes. His voice boomed, "If you are here, Kras, you should know your friends will be dead by morning."

Branimir clutched the dagger in his hand, itching to take the man's life, pausing only with the knowledge that the Vornic was Sulanna's kin.

With a smirk, Myrthos departed, shutting the door behind him, and leaving Branimir alone in the room.

Branimir gazed at the wooden door, turning the dagger in his hand in contemplation. The *Guardians* would be lurking in the hallway and in the commons, and they surely would be guarding the exit leading outside. Invisible or not, Branimir could not run around the inn opening doors and remain undetected. A *Guardian* would notice, and then Branimir would be forced to kill someone else.

His hand reached for the doorknob, and paused. He would kill hundreds to save Adamus and Sulanna, but maybe he could find another way out of the inn.

Rubbing his chin, Branimir examined the room with the flipped chairs, spilt wine, and pools of blood on the faded floorboards. Eventually, the innkeeper would send someone up the stairs to clean the mess and he would be able to exit the room. However, by then, Sulanna and Adamus would be long gone, taken to this place the Vornic had called *Harrowhal*. Certainly, the whereabouts of *Harrowhal* was in Eldhaft, but the city was massive. It could take weeks to find *Harrowhal* without directly following Adamus and Sulanna.

He glowered, suddenly recognizing the room did not have a single window.

Sulanna's father had been wise in devising a scheme to capture them. Of course, Branimir placed full blame on the assiduous historian. Witigor, of course, had earwigged Sulanna's intention to stay at *The Harper and Mug* to start looking for Alden. Branimir speculated that Witigor had told Myrthos everything he needed to hear—having the information sought by both the *Kadari* and the Crimson Sun—and they ignorantly let Witigor walk right into the Vornic's hands.

From what Myrthos said, Farthr remained safe for the time being. If the centaur made his way back to Sorod, the *Guardians* would be unlikely to follow. They could not survive in a city of Svet.

Branimir cleaned his dagger off on his pant leg, and returned the weapon to his belt. He could not risk staying in the inn until morning. He had to rescue Adamus and Sulanna. He moved for the door again.

The creaking of a floorboard caused Branimir to freeze his movements. He heard a rustling near the bed, and slowly peered over his shoulder. To his astonishment, Alyona bowed over the bed, naked to the world, retrieving her clothes from where they had fallen.

Completely oblivious of Branimir standing invisible behind her, the pale-skinned girl hastily yanked the trousers over her thin legs, and then slipped on her boots as quietly as she could. As Alyona reached for her shabby shirt, Branimir rematerialized.

"Where did you run to?" he murmured. "Was this part of your plan all along?"

Alyona spun around into a crouch, with her shirt halfway pulled over her neck, just above her breasts. Her purple irises swelled at the sight of Branimir. She blinked and then yanked her shirt down over her torso, pushing her arms through the sleeves. "No, Branimir. My plan is to get you to *Iriy* as I said in the beginning. I had no idea Myrthos was looking for you, or that Falmagon was in Gaetana. Nor did I know Witigor was a fickle rat!"

"Why did you not fight with us?" Branimir accused, crossed his arms. "You could have ripped the *Guardians* to pieces with *Koldovstvo*."

"For what reason? To have my life drain away in the musty room of an old inn while thieves rained down upon us? They would have eventually killed me, or subdued me and taken me prisoner, too," Alyona scoffed.

"Subdued a *Kadari*?" Branimir wrinkled his brow.

"The *Guardians of Gero* are thick in Eldhaft. The *Guardians* would not have been defeated here. Why do you think Sulanna did not raise her own weapon against them?"

"Because her father was here," Branimir said. "She could reason with him."

"Sulanna doesn't care about her father, and Myrthos is beyond reason," Alyona hissed, standing upright and snagging her cloak from the bed. "The man slaughtered her brother. Believe me, she has no love for him."

"Then why wouldn't she fight to the death? Why wouldn't you? Isn't that a better fate than being tortured and killed?" Branimir protested.

"I am not going to die in a tavern bedroom, Branimir," Alyona said, pushing her short dark hair behind her ear. "My quest is to take you and *kaelandur* to *Iriy*. We are trying to save Aenar, remember?"

"If you are going to suggest we leave Sulanna and Adamus with the Vornic—"

Alyona grimaced. "I would not even attempt to convince you."

Branimir twitched his nose, and finally kicked at the floorboards. "Tell me what happened to you. How did you disappear like that? I have never met a *Kadari* who can do what a Kras can."

Alyona winced. "I did not disappear…I…"

"You what?"

"I transformed," Alyona lingered, "into a bat. And I hid up there on the ceiling. In the corner."

Branimir followed her eyes to the shadowy corner of the room, barely discernible in the lowlight of the windowless room. "A bat? How?"

Alyona fastened her cloak around her neck, and then fell back to sit on the bed. "My mother was a Vucari, and my father a Stuhia. She died giving birth to me and my brother, but her blood runs through me as strongly as the Stuhian."

Branimir peered at Alyona as though he was seeing her for the first time. "So, when we were traveling on the road, you could see in the dark as well as I can?"

"I can do much like the Vucari, but not everything. I never had a…guide." Alyona turned her gaze from Branimir.

"But you killed the Vucari at Shayol Domier. You were bent on slaughtering every skin-switcher in the Dyndaer."

"I did as I was commanded. My father believed in the *Kadari* and Patrician Moreth, and I favored my father's teachings," Alyona said. "While they did not do everything right, Falmagon has further warped the *Kadari* and their doctrine." She crossed her arms, giving the indication she was growing tired of defending herself. "I told you in Gaetana, I am trying to make things right."

"I cannot believe you have the power of the Vucari and the Stuhia. You are not human at all…" Branimir's mind reeled with the possibilities.

"We all have our secrets, Branimir," Alyona said, her eyes drifting to *kaelandur* at Branimir's belt, "and our burdens." She ran her hand through her dark hair again, considering Branimir. "We don't have time to chit-chat. If you want to rescue your friends, we must get out of here."

"The *Guardians* are still waiting out there," Branimir said, reaching for his pack and slinging it over his shoulder.

"If they are truly calling for Falmagon," Alyona said, running her hand down her face in thought, "I would prefer not to use *Koldovstvo*. If we should fight the Patrician, I will need every ounce of life in me to have a chance at defeating him."

"I guess burning a hole through the wall is out of the question," Branimir said.

"Okay," Alyona said, pulling her shirt off again.

Branimir stared at her naked chest. "Why are you taking your clothes off?"

Alyona pulled off her boots, and then her pants. "I am going to turn back into a bat. You will keep me inside your cloak and get out of here." She shoved her clothes inside her small pack and handed it to him.

Branimir took the pack and slung it over his other shoulder, balancing the weight. He stood toe-to-toe with Alyona, barely reaching her belly button. "They will see the doors opening and closing. Even the blind may occasionally hit targets they cannot see."

Alyona, having no shame, put her hands on her hips and cocked her chin. "You walked amongst demons for a thousand years in the Netherworld, Branimir Baran. By the Nine Lands, you can slink by a throng of thieves and down a flight of stairs."

Branimir blinked a couple times, his hands twisting incessantly around the straps of the bags hanging over his shoulder. He replied stiffly, "Very well. I guess there is no other way." The packs suddenly felt heavy. Heavier than a mountain.

Branimir stepped away as the stark-naked woman standing before him swiftly warped and wound her body—bones cracking and skin shriveling—until all that remained was a woolly, leaf-nosed bat.

Alyona flapped her wings in a circular motion, hovering expectantly in the air. Branimir watched her at the end of his hooked nose for a moment, and then he spread open his green cloak. Alonya pulsated forward and clung onto his shirt with her trifling fingers. He took a slow breath, feeling her weight suspended from his attire.

"This is weird," Branimir said, adjusting the pack on his shoulder again. Alyona squeaked in response, and Branimir could only think she directed him to get on with it.

Fading from sight, Branimir moved to the door and listened, his hand resting on the latch. Footsteps passed by the door and were moving away from him toward the staircase. Taking the chance, he sprung the latch and pulled the door open, peeking into the hallway. A *Guardian*, as expected, paced away from him facing the stairwell. The green and gold cloak flapped behind the man with every swish of his feet.

No others were in sight.

He eased into the hallway, and firmly closed the door behind him. The bang of the wood hitting the frame clacked loudly in the hallway. Branimir sneaked away and the *Guardian*, who hastily flipped around rushed to where he had been standing. The light-eyed man pulled a dagger from his belt and pressed his ear to the door.

Branimir held his breath as the *Guardian* gently opened the door to investigate the sound, and stepped inside the empty room. Branimir crept down the hallway, ignoring the *Guardian*, and began his descent down the staircase. With the packs on his back, he could not share much space with any other, especially in a close-knit hallway or on the stairwell.

Chaid Paddley disappeared from behind the bar, leaving the commons to the many *Guardians* who hounded around like hunting dogs rapt on startling the fox from its hole. Branimir counted close to twenty of the thieves traipsing in and out of the back rooms, a couple purposefully stationed at the exit door. Branimir would be unable to swing the door open without being stopped by the boot of either guard. Yet if he could break the large window next to the front door, he may be able to spring to the streets without being grabbed.

Alyona's hind claws scratched at his chest through his shirt as she clung to him. He resisted the urge to let go of either pack and respond to the subtle sting.

Footsteps echoed from behind him as the *Guardian* from upstairs approached the staircase. He twisted his neck to see the blue-eyed man start down the stairs.

"I had a door slam upstairs," he shouted into the commons. "Have you seen anything odd down there?"

Branimir scooted off the stairs to avoid the man from colliding into him, clinging to the wall that led to the back rooms. Several *Guardians* met the blue-eyed thief as he reached the bottom step.

"Nothing."

"What do you mean a door slammed?"

The *Guardian* said, "I mean the door opened and then shut without reason. My guess is the Kras snuck down there."

"We don't even know if he is still here," said another.

"Fan out," the first one called out. "Do not leave any space between you. Not so much as a child should be able to squeeze through."

Branimir shirked back further as the *Guardians* throughout the commons hurried to follow the hastened command. The thieves leapt over tables and chairs, exiting the back rooms, forming a line that blocked the staircase, the barkeep, and extended across the front door and promising window.

"Draw weapons and advance," said the first. "Two of you remain by the door." In unison, the thieves jerked the daggers from their belt and took a step forward.

The *Guardians* kicked chairs out of the way and flipped tables. The line remained firm.

Bran scooted back along the wall. Again, the *Guardians* advanced, clearing anything in their path. A chair turned, landing close to Branimir's feet.

The thieves ignored the barkeep, continuing forward, closing the empty space.

Unable to find an opening in the line, Branimir turn toward the back rooms to find the thieves had left both doors standing wide open. He darted to the first doorway on his light feet, discovering what appeared to be an office. He looked for anything of use in the room. A desk, bookshelves, chairs, and…a window.

Nightfall had come.

Grabbing a paperweight from the desk, he rushed to the windowpane. As he prepared to break the glass, he noticed the simple latch. The window opened sideways. With a smile, he ignored the clashing of furniture being flung in the commons behind him. He flipped the clasp and sprung the window open.

He was free.

Chapter VIII

Branimir scuttled along the western road, veering in and out of the swarms of people—dancing and singing around bonfires blazing in the streets—who were already immersed in the celebration of *Pal'ka*. He snaked between the thin and fat, ducked under flailing arms, and dodged the drunk and sober alike, while darting around mindless children who senselessly changed their trajectory, heedlessly stumbling into his path. The multiple melodies from many musical instruments rebounded through the streets, especially alongside the river, where young girls tossed their handcrafted wreaths into the water, and then giggled with unrivalled delight. Branimir had not the time to gawk at the flowers floating in the water to see which floated or sank.

He remained hidden from sight, clinging to the packs over either shoulder, while Alyona, in her bat-like form, clung to his shirt beneath his cloak. He rushed for the wall and gate, marking the exit to Old Town, and away from the *Guardians of Gero*.

To his left were rows of shops and houses, and to his right roared the *Deep Run*, crashing against the shores of Old Town and whatever lay on the other side. Branimir could make out the castle keep sitting on a small rise overseeing the city, where he presumed the Count held residence. The sight told him he had exited *The Harper and Mug* and fled in an unfamiliar direction, but his only concern was placing distance between himself and the thieves. And then, he needed to find this place where Adamus and Sulanna had been taken, *Harrowhal.*

Branimir glanced to the moon, hanging like a silver coin in the sky, emitting a hoary light bright enough to dim the twinkle of the stars. Yet, as he made his way through the streets, Branimir's eyes witnessed wonders, including men forcing themselves on women—who tittered in pleasure—in alleyways and on street corners without shame. After a thousand years and more, Branimir could not understand the minds of the Anshedar, who meant to give reverence to the gods through debauchery, dancing, and fornication.

He could only guess humans believed the gods to be more of fleshly desires than anything divine. Though, as Dorofej often expounded, the gods had little care about the whims of humans.

The open gateway, leading from Old Town, pulled Branimir from his brief musing. Branimir almost expected the *Guardians* to be nipping at his heel, shouting to all guardsmen to close the gates, but no guards were found. Those who should have been standing watch had joined in the festival.

Branimir soon withdrew from Old Town without any taking notice of the pitter-patter of his invisible footfalls.

He sprung onto a dirt road, reaching a statue that he did not bother to examine. A bridge on his right led across the *Deep Run*, while his left led back to the entrance to the city gate, where he and the others entered that afternoon; and ahead lay more houses and merchant buildings than he could stomach.

Several common-folk ambled by Branimir toward Old Town. He took the moment to catch his breath, pulling his green cloak open to check on Alyona. Her nostrils flared on her triangular nose, suggestive of her anticipation, but he could read nothing of her thoughts as to what they should do next.

He whispered so only she could hear. "I don't know what direction to go. Any way could lead us further from them."

Alyona scratched at his chest again and then let go of his shirt, flapping out from beneath his cloak. He watched, as she stayed suspended in front of his nose for a few moments before taking off into the air.

"What now?" he muttered, keeping an eye on the brownish bat fluttering above him.

To the Anshedar, Alyona likely blended into the night, unseen, but for Branimir she was clear as day swooping up and down along the city street. He raced after her down the road, staying clear from any humans heading to the festival, which seemed centralized in Old Town. Recurrently, Branimir could hear Alyona squeaking loudly into the night, causing a bothersome ringing in his ears. The humans around him did not seem to notice the riling sound, but for him, the echoing peep was maddening.

Alyona lunged back and forth for several blocks before she decisively darted into an alley on Branimir's left. He pursued her, until she finally stopped where the backstreet ended. The alleyway ran perpendicular into a stone wall; he guessed it was the opposite side of the same inner wall circling Old Town.

Alyona landed and transformed back into her human form, stifling a groan as her body snapped back into place, leaving her crouching on all fours in the dirt. Branimir surfaced from the shadows in front of her.

"Are you okay?" he murmured.

"Hm," she hummed. "You followed me. Good."

"Of course, I followed you."

She reached her hand out for her pack. He swiftly passed the bag into her hand, peering over his shoulder to look at the main road while she slipped on her clothes.

"Where are we?" Branimir asked after a moment.

"*Harrowhal,*" Alyona replied, her feet scuffing against the ground as she stood up. "Adamus and Sulanna are being held somewhere in this building."

Branimir turned around as Alyona lifted her hood back over her head. She repositioned her dark cloak to cover her bag. "How did you find it?"

Alyona approached a wooden door in the brick wall on their left. With a flip of her hand, the door unlocked and opened. "Bats cannot see well, but they have exceptional hearing, even better than a Kras. The *Guardian* out front said something of the Vornic's daughter being inside. I can only assume this is *Harrowhal.*"

Branimir pulled at his nose, wondering why he had not heard the men. Maybe he was too focused on following Alyona to pay much attention, or maybe bats did hear better than Kras.

"I hope you are right," Branimir said.

He followed Alyona through the wooden door into the horseshoe-shaped courtyard surrounding the oversized brick building that towered stories above them. He examined the several balconies suspended from the second and third levels of the building. Each window had the curtains drawn, outlined with yellow light.

In the courtyard, Branimir could hear the voices of the many *Guardians* walking the perimeter. "We cannot stay out here," he said softly.

"This way." Alyona grabbed his arm and pulled him along the walkway to an iron door almost directly in front of them. Again, with the wave of her hand, the door unlocked and opened, yellow light flooding the path. She crept inside with him lightly following at her heels.

The immediate hallway stretched before them for about twenty feet before venturing right. Branimir could see lanterns every ten feet on both sides of the hall, giving more than enough light for any patrolling *Guardians*. Alyona would not find any shadows to cling to for concealment.

Branimir was glad he would not need shadows.

He could see a set of double-doors on their left and another door directly ahead of him. He could only imagine how many twists and turns, and other doors, would be found in this massive manor.

"It is quiet," Branimir said.

"I do not hear anything either," Alyona said in a hushed tone, inching down the hallway, her feet clicking on the wooden beams of the floor. They turned the corner to find another long corridor, without any end in sight. It stretched to the far right, leading to a small incline of stairs, and then another hallway.

"This is going to take a while," Branimir said, hopelessly looking back and forth. "Can you use *Klukas*?"

"I cannot go into the shadow world, Branimir. My bloodline is diluted with Vucari blood." She rubbed her hands together in thought. "We only need to think about where they would hold prisoners. Likely they are being detained in a dungeon, which means they would be on a lower-level."

"That is heartening to hear," Branimir said. "That means there is probably only one way in and one way out."

"A staircase," Alyona said.

"Or a secret passage."

Alyona frowned at him. "They would want to place the entrance to the dungeon far away from any door to the outside to slow down any who might escape." She looked behind them at the door they had come through, and then to the west. "Meaning if we entered here, and the front door is that way…" she pointed down the long hallway, "our best option is to search down this way."

Branimir raised an eyebrow. "Unless…a door leading outside is also located on that side of the building."

"Then maybe we will find the door somewhere in the middle." Alyona peered at him from beneath her hood. "Do you have a better place to start?"

Branimir shrugged. "I don't."

The *Kadari* led them halfway down the long corridor when the left wall suddenly disappeared to an open wide foyer. Alyona stopped walking at the sound of voices echoing somewhere beyond the foyer. Branimir pressed his body against the left side of the wall and peered around the corner edge.

A candlelit chandelier hung from an elevated ceiling between two spiraling staircases on either side of the sweeping room, decorated with sitting chairs and small tables. A wide, decorative rug covered the floorboards, and along the walls stood several suits of armor on embellished stands. Beyond the staircases, Branimir could make out broad double-doors leading back outside.

As incredible as the architecture may have been, the men standing beneath the chandelier was what caused Branimir to catch his breath. The first was Master Bacheva from *The Harper and Mug*, the father of Teodor Bacheva, pulling nervously at his salt-and-pepper goatee. And the other was none other than Dagmar Kaligula, Dorofej's unkind grandson, who had been advising Falmagon at Melkorka. Dagmar stood a head taller than Master Bacheva, dressed in a red button-coat, black trousers, and a blood-red cloak. He was dressed as though he were a powerful noble.

"What is he doing here?" Branimir grimaced as though he might spit.

He could see Alyona only shaking her head from the corner of his eye.

"Lord Kaligula," Master Bacheva trembled, "the Vornic retired to the dungeons some time ago to begin questioning the prisoners. He is determined to discover whatever information he can before their passing."

"You should have sent for me sooner, Gaspar," Dagmar said, running his hand through his scraggily red hair and placing a hand on his waist. Branimir could see several flasks hanging from leather cords around his midsection; Dagmar carried bottles of the Water of Life. Branimir loosened the dagger at his belt, eyeing Teodor's father warily.

The liquid would do nothing for Dagmar if Branimir buried a blade in the man's skull. "Does Myrthos have the *Kras*?" Dagmar asked.

"Not yet," Gaspar replied, moving his hands to his sides awkwardly, settling his thumbs in his belt loops. "The *Guardians* are tracking his trail as we speak. He has been confined to *The Harper and Mug* in Old Town. The *Kras* cannot stay hidden forever."

Dagmar smirked. "He has found the means to stay hidden from me for the past year. I would not underestimate the red brood."

The Stuhian should have been capable of finding Branimir in *Klukas*. He wrinkled his brow with confusion, turning to face Alyona. The *Kadari* was wide-eyed and biting her lip. He asked, "How exactly have I stayed hidden?"

She shrugged, but said, "If we wait, they may lead us to the dungeon."

He replied softly, "I would prefer to get Adamus and Sulanna free first..."

"We don't have the time," she said.

Heavy footsteps echoed as Dagmar and Gaspar neared them, making way for the corridor. Alyona grabbed Branimir's shirt, pulling him back down the hall from where they had come, pulling him around the corner and out of sight.

"Falmagon will not be pleased you have sent for him and do not have Branimir. He was specific in what he wanted," Dagmar said. "Tell me, who does Myrthos hold?"

"I...thought to suggest as much to the Vornic, but my position does not give the voice to question him." Gaspar cleared his throat. "I hope the Patrician will be pleased that we have captured Adamus Ebordon and the Vornic's daughter, Sulanna Maelthirren."

"The Ariadnean…" Dagmar rubbed his neck as they turned the opposite way down the corridor. "I owe him a debt of pain. Does the Crimson Sun know Sulanna is being held here?"

"I do not think the Vornic has elected to share his daughter's discovery with them," answered Gaspar.

"And what of Alden Forgaaf?"

"No," Gaspar said. Branimir's heart skipped a beat, moving back into the hallway to follow the two men. Alden was alive and being held in the dungeon too! "We have not told the Crimson Sun of his capture either. I apologize, Lord Kaligula, I am not certain of the Vornic's purpose in withholding the knowledge from Master Gauthus."

Branimir had never met Ivarr Gauthus, but he heard his name often enough from Dorofej. The man headed the Crimson Sun, but supposedly answered to Falmagon.

Dagmar murmured offhandedly. "Do not worry about it, Gaspar. Ivarr paid a large sum of coin to the Lilitu for Alden's release. The matter is no longer a concern, but I would guess the man would be displeased to discover Myrthos hiding him in Eldhaft. If the plan is to keep it secret, be certain it stays buried."

"Alden's stay here has not been pleasant." Gaspar stopped to lead them down a narrow staircase on the eastern wall.

Branimir hurried to catch them, stopping at the top of the stairs. Looking back the way he had come, he realized Alyona was no longer following him.

Gaspar and Dagmar descended from sight, reaching the bottom of the stairs and turning right.

"Alyona," Branimir hissed down the hallway. When she did not respond, he tried once more, louder, "Alyona!"

Again, silence.

Pulling his dagger from his belt, Branimir balanced the weight in his hand. The *Kadari* woman vanished at the first sign of danger as she had before at the inn. Branimir did not have the time to look for her. He had no choice but to move forward and rescue his friends in the dungeon. He would start by weakening Falmagon by taking the life of Dagmar Kaligula.

He only wished he brought more daggers.

His footsteps were silent as he made his way down the staircase, though the foreboding trek downward caused his heart to feel as though it would beat from his chest. The walls of the narrow corridor were lofty, yet uninviting. He finally made it to the last step and took a slow, shallow breath.

He listened. Nothing.

He hoped Dagmar and Gaspar had not gone behind a locked door.

At a snail's pace, Branimir turned the corner and inhaled in fear as Dagmar Kaligula stood in waiting with Gaspar several feet behind. Dagmar growled, seizing a hold of Bran's shirt, cloak, and straps of his pack in one burly grasp and hurled him into the stone wall opposite of the stairs.

Branimir's bones rattled and stung on impact, the knife in his hand skittering out of his reach. Before he could think of grabbing *kaelandur* at his belt, Dagmar used *Koldovstvo* to lift Branimir from the wooden floorboards and back to his hand.

"Gaspar," Dagmar gleamed with a sinister glare, "you can now tell Falmagon we have the Kras."

Chapter IX

Branimir awoke with a spasm, suspended from a vertical, iron table in the corner of a rectangular room. The cold metal prickled at his bare flesh. He wore nothing, save a belt tightened just above his waist with a sheathe holding *kaelandur.* He remembered Vornic Maelthirren repeatedly attempting to remove the cursed, copper dagger, only to return it to Bran to stop his curdling screams.

He told the Vornic all that he knew, but what he knew was not enough. Sulanna's father wanted to know where Dorofej was located, so *kaelandur* could be destroyed.

Many times, Branimir explained he knew nothing about Dorofej's whereabouts, except he was somewhere between Melkorka and Eldhaft. The answer had consistently been less than satisfactory.

The room spun, out-of-focus, but Branimir finally caught a glimmer of his red skin, goose-fleshed and bruised, trembling against the slab. In desperation, he lurched against the thick, pigskin straps clasping his wrists and ankles. He twisted his neck up and down to see the leather strung through slits in the iron on either side of his limbs, buckled on the other side of the table. Escape was impossible.

The soreness in his head pulsated, reminding him of the beating he received from Sulanna's father before losing consciousness. He licked the dried blood from his swollen, bottom lip. He could not even recall the questions he refused to answer.

His finger nicked at the silver ring, *Faegrim*, still on his finger. The Vornic had not taken the trinket when preparing him for the torture chamber.

His eyes fluttered, hanging his head helplessly. He could not have been in *Harrowhal* for more than two weeks. If Alyona had not betrayed him, she may come yet. Or perhaps Dorofej if he did not meet him in *Iriy*, but that could be weeks or months.

"Bran-i-mir," Adamus strained from somewhere within the room.

Branimir lifted his head once more, seeing the room for what felt like the first time. His mouth felt too dry to make a response.

To his left lay Sulanna naked and destitute on a table, tied in a similar way as Branimir. Her eyes were closed with her mouth corded. She looked to be unscathed from blade or flame, but he could not remember seeing her awake since being dragged to the dungeon. Her skin had paled considerably, the flesh clinging to her ribcage. They had been given water once a day to wet their throats, but no food.

Next to her lay a table with cogs and wheels and ropes, which Branimir had grown to understand was meant to pull bones from the sockets of his victims. He tried not to look at the device for too long.

Adjacent to the rack was a large wooden basin of water, large enough to fit a human if they kept their knees tucked to their chest. And then, a barrel full of what sounded like rats shrilling and squeaking, while running over one another in attempts to escape. Further yet burned a fire pit, flashing blue, orange, and red, with metal bars deeply sunk into the fiery coals. And, only a few feet more, extended a table with hooked blades, and knives, and other torture devices Branimir had no interest in remembering.

He shivered as his eyes fell on a metal cage hanging from the ceiling. The bald, old man, who Branimir never thought to see again, powerlessly stared back at him before turning to gaze at Sulanna on the table. Alden Forgaaf flexed his muscles against the sturdy cage, whispering prayers fervently under his breath.

"Bran-i-mir," Adamus echoed with less air.

"Adamus," Branimir finally forced the word from his throat, twisting his neck past Alden to see the Ariadnean, hanging with his hands bound from a chain above the ceiling. The iron cut into his wrists as he struggled to hold himself upright, feet dangling inches above the stone flooring. Affixed around Adamus's neck was a belt enfolding a bi-pronged metal fork with one end pushed under his chin and the other firmly pressed to his sternum. Adamus strained to keep his chin to the ceiling—his exposed body shivering with little control—to avoid dropping his head and letting the prongs pierce the soft flesh beneath his chin and chest simultaneously.

The Ariadnean could not have slept since the Vornic attached the device to him, or he would already be dead.

Adamus gulped, his Adam's apple recoiling against the sharpened points at his neck. Sweat dripped from his dark beard and mustache. "I…will be dead before long," Adamus said, quivering again, the chains rattling over his head. "'Tis been an honor…to call you…friend, Bran-i-mir."

"No!" Branimir rasped, pulling uselessly against the restraints. "You must keep fighting, Adamus. Dorofej will come. Alyona will come."

"Czern's breath! She deceived us," Adamus groaned, "as Sulanna said."

"Listen to him," Alden said from the cage, peering at Adamus from over his bent nose. "You cannot lose faith. We can still survive this. The gods have delivered us from worse fates."

"My leg burns…" Adamus groaned in torment. "Even if I live…I will not…*survive* this."

Branimir cringed at the sight of Adamus's mangled leg, wholly skinned from the knee down, the muscle and sinew filleted—the rind slacking and dangling—with his blood seeping to stain the stone beneath. It was a wonder the hero-warrior had not lost consciousness.

"Dagmar will pay for what he has done to you," Alden said between gritted teeth. The old man pathetically pulled at the metal bars on his cage with a muffled roar. "Svarog will show us a way."

"The…gods…will not help us…" Adamus sighed, tears forming at the corners of his eyes and falling from his cheeks. The salty droplets soaked into his beard.

Branimir was inclined to agree with Adamus. Marheena was the one who had bid for Dorofej to make *kaelandur* and wrought this evil upon them. If the other gods were of like mind, none would save them.

He wanted to know *why*? But, more than anything, he wanted to see Dorofej again.

A clang of a metal door opening recoiled through the stone room, followed by the commanding voice of Vornic Myrthos Maelthirren. "Are we awake?" Multiple footsteps clicked down the staircase from somewhere behind Branimir. "Or are we dead? Let us properly inspect our guests."

Branimir stiffened as the Vornic noisily passed by him and approached Adamus to survey the hanging body as though he were a butcher examining meat. Myrthos wore the same simple, black trousers, white shirt, and boots that Branimir had seen him dress in for the past couple weeks. But today, his hair was unkempt and unbraided, wildly hanging on either side of his sunken cheeks.

"You lasted through the night without impaling yourself," Myrthos said, running his finger down Adamus's chest admirably, "or bleeding out. No wonder they call the

Ariadneans, hero-warriors. I have seen *Guardians* die in half the time with fewer injuries. Those thieves always think they are craftier than any other." Myrthos laughed to himself, looking over his shoulder at Branimir. "Plainly not craftier than a little Kras, eh? I suspect your *friend's* stunt at the inn will keep the *Guardians* questioning their ability for months to come."

Myrthos tapped Adamus on the chest a couple times, eliciting a groan from the Ariadnean. "You know," Myrthos went on, reaching for the pronged instrument at Adamus's neck, "I could remove this if you would only tell me what I want to know. You would have at least a few more hours left before you…bleed out…"

Adamus peered down at Sulanna's father for only a moment before twisting his eyes back to the ceiling.

The Vornic leered for a moment, pulling at his white mustache, and then poked Adamus again. "Lucky for you, I am feeling kind today." He reached up and slanted the metal fork, giving Adamus the ability to drop his chin without inflicting a wound. "I would hate for you to die before allowing you time to consider my offer."

Alden rumbled from his cage, glaring at the Vornic hatefully. "The gods will see you punished. You rob men of their charge for your own gain. You rob them from Thrice Ten Kingdom." Alden's eyes lifted to look to the man beyond Branimir. "You will both be punished."

"Why do you not torture the old man?" Dagmar's voice lifted from the door. "He may have something useful to share with us besides menacing premonitions concerning the will of the gods. Falmagon had the Crimson Sun pay a hefty sum to pull him from Talastein. I doubt Ivarr would like his money spent without purpose."

Branimir twitched at the sound of Dagmar behind him. This was the first time Dagmar had come to the dungeon, which likely meant either the Vornic was not satisfying him, or Falmagon was close to Eldhaft.

Alden spoke from the cage in wonderment, as though the information was new to him. "The *Kadari* ordered my release from Talastein? Not Ivarr?" He frowned squeezing his hands around the bars of his cage. His escape from the Lilitu had been a ruse to have him captured for questioning.

"The Crimson Sun will acquire more coin." Myrthos waved off Alden, approaching Branimir. "Besides, I have no interest in a man who is compelled to commit penance for the *blessing of gods*. He knows pain in equal measure with breath. My daughter, however, will tell us many things by watching him suffer." Myrthos stopped in front of Branimir as Dagmar approached from behind. "That is, unless the Kras wishes to save his friends from such unpleasantries. He could simply tell us what you need to hear."

"Don't...Bran-i-mir..." Adamus coughed.

Myrthos and Dagmar ignored Adamus.

Branimir snarled at Myrthos. "What more could I tell you? You will not listen to me."

Dagmar grabbed Branimir's jaw, wrenching his head sideways to look at him. His bedraggled, red hair curled in every direction placing a shadow over his face. "You will tell us where we can find Dorofej, so we can rid the world of this..." he flicked *kaelandur* hanging at Branimir's waist, "...cursed dagger."

Branimir tensed under the hard gaze of the Stuhia, but he still found his voice. "I will tell you what I have told him." He shifted his eyes toward Myrthos. "Kinhar ordered *kaelandur* to be made. He brought the first *Eretik* back from the Netherworld with its power," Branimir said, returning his gaze to Dagmar's cold, blue eyes. "Kinhar wanted the dagger to fulfill his prophecy, to give power to the *Kadari*."

"I do not care about any of that," Dagmar said. "I do not care about the *Kadari* or their ridiculous adoration for the Lightbringer. I want this dagger destroyed."

"You held Dorofej prisoner, and you did not kill him," Branimir said. "Why now? You must have known he created *kaelandur*."

"I may have." Dagmar sneered, clenching his jaw. "But Dorofej cannot be simply killed and the dagger be destroyed. He must be killed *with* the weapon he created. Otherwise, he would continue to *linger*." The word rolled off his tongue, leaving Branimir stunned.

He had been terrified this whole past year of Dorofej dying, while the threat was empty while he held *kaelandur*. Did Dorofej know he was safe while Branimir remained hidden? What more did Dorofej hope to accomplish at *Iriy*?

Dagmar suddenly hit the iron table next to Branimir's head. "And I did not yet have Eisliev Kluk return from the Netherworld in pursuit of my head."

Branimir held his mouth closed. Alyona had been telling the truth about everything. Eisliev returned from the Netherworld, and sought to exact his revenge on Dagmar Kaligula. Bran did not know what blood feud bound the two Stuhian families, but Dagmar looked *afraid*.

"Now tell me where Dorofej has gone?" Dagmar asked in a raspy whisper.

"Why are you doing this? Why are you listening to Falmagon and not your own kin?" Branimir snapped back.

"You mean listen to Dorofej?" Dagmar shook his head as though the question made little sense. "Grandfather or not, he has threatened the world by making this weapon. I will not die by his hand or any other," Dagmar winced. "And if you think I grovel at Falmagon's feet, you are mistaken, Kras. Now tell me where he is, so I can rid myself of Eisliev Kluk."

"Destroying *kaelandur* will not rid you of Eisliev," Branimir said, peering at the Stuhian. Dagmar had no more interest in dying than Dorofej did. Branimir hoped he could use the insight to say something smart. Yet, he struggled to find the words to persuade Dagmar. "Eisliev can only be ended by luring him back to the Netherworld, and killing him there. The same happened with Nedezhda Mager twelve-hundred-years ago. Dorofej killed her in the Netherworld to stop her from attacking the Ash Tree."

"He created a weapon that would destroy the world, but killed the demon who returned to destroy the world? Why?" Dagmar asked.

"I don't know," Branimir said. Dagmar squinted at Branimir as though he were trying to assess the truth of his words. At least, he seemed to listen more intently than Vornic Maelthirren.

"But, I am telling the truth," Branimir insisted. He hoped Dagmar would understand the futility of Falmagon's quest. He repeated what Erzebeth Navenka had told him at *Garain'l* last year. "The god, Wolos, was killed, leaving none to lead men after their deaths. The Netherworld cannot house all the dead." Branimir was almost shouting, hoping Dorofej's grandson was listening to him. He had to understand. "It was two men at *Anaerfell*. They are the ones who did this to us."

"What do you know about my sons? How have you come to learn this?" Dagmar twisted his face with fury, spit flinging into Branimir's eyes.

Branimir struggled against the restraints, having no way to escape Dagmar's quickened temper. "I didn't know they were your sons."

"Answer me!" Dagmar screamed. The Stuhia grabbed *kaelandur* from Branimir's belt and tore it away, holding it in the air away from him.

Rocking against the table, Branimir screamed until his throat burned and his ears ached. A few seconds lasted an eternity.

"Stop it!" Alden yelled at Dagmar. "You will kill him!"

Branimir's bones cracked, the feeling of flames seared through his insides. He needed to reclaim *kaelandur*. His body thrashed, his head repeatedly slamming into the iron.

With *kaelandur* away from his flesh, Branimir would rather have been pierced by a hundred arrows, and trampled by a thousand horses.

"Stop…" Adamus tried.

Dagmar pressed the dagger flatly into Branimir's left hand. Feeling the weapon back on his flesh was like having his heart restored to his chest. He wrapped his fingers around the hilt, chest heaving.

With a deep breath, Branimir said, "The death of Wolos brought demons from the Netherworld…not the dagger. *Kaelandur* is only a tool to destroy the Ash Tree."

Dagmar gasped, seemingly forgetting about his sons, considering Branimir's frantic words.

"The Ash Tree…is dying, regardless of *kaelandur*. The *Kadari* have wasted it away," Branimir heaved, locking his eyes onto Dagmar. "The *old-dark* are being released from their prison."

"The *old-dark*?" Myrthos looked to Dagmar for an explanation. "What is he talking about?"

Alden rumbled from his cage, giving hint of his knowledge. "Svarog will not allow it."

Branimir went on, "Falmagon doesn't know what he is doing. His efforts are wasted."

Myrthos stepped forward. "How is he bound to this dagger, Lord Kaligula? Why does he continue to scream when it is taken from him? What madness have you brought to *Harrowhal*?"

"Some ancient evil has bound it to him, and possibly abundant knowledge in the melding," Dagmar said.

"Knowledge we can extract," Myrthos said. "Falmagon will be here soon enough. He will be pleased."

"We will see. Falmagon has little appreciation for knowledge," Dagmar muttered, standing upright to study Branimir. He straightened his grey shirt, loosening the strings around his collar. "But we would be wise to discover all the Kras knows…especially if *kaelandur's* destruction truly will do nothing to save us from the demons. You will help me convince Falmagon that finding Dorofej is no longer a concern…we have wasted our efforts." Dagmar suddenly tensed his jaw, and reached for Branimir's hand almost dislodging *kaelandur* from his grasp. With an exasperated breath, Dagmar ripped off the simple, silver ring from his finger. "What is this? Where did you get *Faegrim*?"

"I found it," Branimir forced the lie, clinging to *kaelandur* in his hand. Dagmar could use *Faegrim* to control the minds of any who did not wield *Koldovstvo* like Eisliev had done to Branimir at Cavell. "I do not know what it is."

"*Faegrim!*" Dagmar shouted, moving away from Branimir, and pulling a strange book from his pocket. The book quadrupled in size at the command of *Koldovstvo*, and Dagmar flipped through the pages.

"What is that?" Myrthos asked, clearly confused by most of the conversation and now this strange revelation.

"This is the *Varkolak*," Dagmar said, "and this ring is how the Kras has avoided me this past year." Branimir juddered at the sight of the *Varkolak*, a book Dorofej had transcribed ages ago, holding the mysteries of *Koldovstvo* and the gods knew what else. Dagmar nodded to himself as he read through a faded page in the codex. "As I thought, *Faegrim* keeps the wearer blocked from being found in *Klukas*."

"I didn't know," Branimir cried.

Dagmar shook his head, speaking through his teeth at Myrthos. "Come; let us see if Falmagon has arrived."

Chapter X

The door slammed at the top of the stairs, echoing back into the dungeon.

Sulanna stirred on the table near him, moaning softly, but still not awake. Branimir turned his neck to see Adamus had also lost consciousness. Blood persistently oozed from his battered leg.

"They will likely kill us now," Alden said, fine-tuning his position in the metal cage. He crossed his legs for comfort and folded his hands in his lap. "Fight in any way you are able, Branimir. Die with honor. For glory."

"Why? Why do you say that?" Branimir asked.

Alden angled a bushy eyebrow as if the answer was clear and Branimir were too dense to see it. "Because you have given them no reason to keep us alive. We were being interrogated to give away Dorofej's position."

Branimir squeezed his eyes shut with frustration. "And I told them the truth," he muttered, hitting his head against the iron table. "Now that Dagmar sees destroying *kaelandur* will not save him, he has no reason to kill Dorofej."

Alden lifted his shoulders to his ears. "Besides keeping Dorofej from being a pain in the ass for Falmagon? No," Alden took an exasperated breath, "I see no reason they will pursue Dorofej. You have magnificently removed the target from Dorofej's back while identifying the rest of us as loose ends."

"But what should I have done? Keeping the ruse would have only left us to be tortured without reason," Branimir said.

Alden remained surprisingly calm given his words, a knowing curve of a smile dimpling his old cheeks. "We had reason before, Branimir. We were holding ourselves alive until a chance for escape or rescue presented itself. I am less certain now. Adamus is dying. Sulanna and I will be quick to follow when Falmagon comes. But you," he rubbed his brow, the fake smile disappearing, "you have the knowledge of a lifetime upon a lifetime. You have traveled the Netherworld. You have fought monsters that most believe to be only from fairy tales. Dagmar can keep you alive, picking you apart piece by piece as he unearths what you know."

Branimir shivered, his stomach tightening in fear. "Why would he do that?"

Alden answered with a rhetorical question. "Why did he leave Dorofej alive at Melkorka for the past year?"

"You heard him say he needed *kaelandur* to kill Dorofej," Branimir said hesitantly.

"Whether true or not, Dagmar hungers for knowledge. For power," Alden said. "You have already proven your intelligence with *Faegrim*."

"No," Branimir argued. "I did not know *Faegrim* would keep me hidden from *Klukas*. I only knew…" Branimir stopped, jerking his head to Alden with excitement. "I am no longer wearing *Faegrim*. I…I am no longer wearing the ring."

"I know," Alden sighed.

Branimir kicked his feet as much as the binding would allow him. "No. You don't understand. I wondered why Dorofej had not come for me—why he had not sought me in *Klukas*. I *was* wearing *Faegrim*; he could not find me in *Klukas*, but now, he can!"

Alden spun onto his knees, eyes widening. The cage clanged, swaying from its perch in the ceiling. "Where was Dorofej? How far does he travel?"

"You have heard me answer the question many times. He was at Melkorka," Branimir answered. "If Alyona told the truth, he would have been at Melkorka only a few weeks ago. He would have to pass near Eldhaft to go to *Iriy* in the Shade Fells."

Alden scratched his bald head in confusion. "This Alyona woman? How did she come to find you so soon?"

"Dorofej can make these gateways that create an opening between two places, but he cannot travel through them himself. She said Dorofej made her one to travel from Melkorka to Gaetana. It is the same as how we had escaped from Melkorka last year," Branimir said.

Alden arched his eyebrows in surprise.

Branimir answered the unasked question, or what he thought Alden may have been thinking. "Of course, the Ash Tree at Melkorka would have allowed him to return to his youth right after sending her to us."

"But, if you wore *Faegrim*, how did he know you were in Gaetana?" Alden asked

Branimir began to give the same reasoning Sulanna had clung to for the past year, considering Dorofej sent them to Gaetana so he could find them when needed, but a more evident truth struck him. "Dorofej still could have found Sulanna or Adamus in *Klukas*, even if he could not see me?"

"With that thought, he would then know we are here…and he has not come…" Alden sunk back onto his bare haunches, defeat filling his eyes.

The hard truth stung Branimir's chest. He shouted in defiance. "He will come for us!"

He grimaced, scratching his bald head. His words were soft. "He may come for you eventually. The rest of us will be long dead."

Branimir's heart sunk.

Alden went on, "I am not concerned for myself. I have lived a long life serving Svarog well. For a thousand years, humans have rumored that the God of the Dead was killed, but I scarcely believed it. Yet, if Wolos has been killed as you say, I will have no guide across Thrice Nine Lands to reach Thrice Ten Kingdom in the afterlife. I will forever be perverted by Marheena's death magic, becoming one of her devils in the Netherworld." Alden's shoulders shuddered, blinking away his tears. This time was the first Branimir saw any weakness from the old warrior. Alden lifted his eyes to Sulanna. "You cannot let her die here. Not by her father's hand. Not by our enemies."

Branimir's fingers curled with determination. The hilt of *kaelandur* weighted his hand. He had nearly forgotten that Dagmar left it in his palm instead of returning it to the sheath at his waist.

"I will not. We are leaving," Branimir said. "Now."

Branimir turned the copper dagger in his hands, rotating the blade downward along his forearm, gripping the sleek hilt in his long fingers. Ever so carefully, he inched the dagger up, balancing its weight above his hand, transferring his fingers from the hilt to the blade.

"You can do it," Alden encouraged, moving in his cage again to gain a better view.

Straining his neck to peer at the blade in his hand, Branimir manipulated *kaelandur* further and further until the tip of the blade hung over the pigskin strapping that held his hand suspended on the table. Then, with the utmost care, Branimir kept the dagger flat against his skin, slipping it between his wrist and the leather strip. He did not stop until the blade hung passed his wrist and the hilt was back in his hand.

Alden was elated from his hanging prison. "You did it, Branimir. You did it. Quickly now."

Branimir used what muscle he had to slide the copper dagger up and down against the leather bindings. In little time, the magical blade—holding a honed edge unlike any weapon of its kind—soon began to split the strip around his wrist.

Time seemed to stand still as Branimir cut at his bindings. Soreness seared through his body, from his wrist to his stomach to his knees. The world was pain and fire. He pushed through the agony. Slicing. Cutting. Until the last thread fell away.

"Yes," Alden praised.

The strap fell to the ground, and with its release, the buckle on the opposite side of the iron table clinging to the ground. The sound echoed, and with the echo came the clang of the door opening once more at the height of the staircase.

Branimir froze.

Alden rattled in his cage, hearing the noise. His eyes locked on Branimir with intensity. He pressed himself up against the bars of his cage, his nostrils flaring. "Flee!" he hissed.

In a half-breath, Branimir twisted sawing at the leather around his left ankle, and then the right. *Kaelandur* tore through the pigskin like flame through flesh. Footsteps thundered down the steps like an impending storm.

"Hurry!" Alden balked.

Branimir held his breath, hanging suspended from the table by a single arm, his bare legs slipping and sliding in desperation for something to grip. He wildly slashed at the final restraint on his right hand, while keeping the blade clear of his own flesh.

"Destroying *kaelandur* will not end this." Branimir listened to Sulanna's father speaking from the stairs. "Dagmar believes the Kras is telling the truth."

Falmagon's recognizable tone boomed. "By *Mulafell*, Branimir will say anything to keep Dorofej alive. A malady I fear Dagmar also suffers from. One that has cost us dearly."

Bran did not hear the response, slicing through the final strand of his shackles. He dropped to the floor without making a sound, and vanished from sight, clutching *kaelandur* in his hand.

Branimir stayed on his toes, springing across the floor, and ducking behind the water basin. He gripped *kaelandur* in his hand, knowing he could not kill either of the two with the magical dagger, lest they would return like Eisliev from the Netherworld.

Myrthos was the first to exit the staircase, running a hand through his white, ragged hair. The old man paused as though he had taken a blow to the gut, gawking at the empty table where Branimir had been moments before. Like clockwork, he sifted the room to ensure the other three prisoners were untouched.

"The Kras is gone," Myrthos said, "but not far."

Branimir gulped, taking a step closer to the fire pit in the center of the room. The rods sticking from the coals glowed with intense heat, too hot for him to grip and use as a weapon.

Falmagon bounded over the last couple steps with the spoken revelation, his brown cloak flapping behind him. He dashed to the iron slab, his long, crumpled, brown hair whirling around his face. A year passed since Branimir had last seen Falmagon, and before that, an eternity. Even now, Branimir's nerves were shattered upon seeing his old Highborn master.

Falmagon struck the flat surface of the table with an open hand as though the action might make Branimir magically appear. The sudden movement caused Branimir to jump away, almost falling to his haunches.

"What is this?" Falmagon roared, balling up his fist. His other hand clawed at the stubble along his cheek and chin, his eyes maddening with rage. "Is this supposed to impress me, Myrthos?"

Myrthos stepped behind Falmagon as though the man were a shield. "The Kras must be in this room. Not only is the door above locked and guarded, but I doubt he would have left his friends. We likely caught him in the act of escape."

Branimir finally slid *kaelandur* into the sheathe hanging from the belt, the only garb on his naked body. He would not be able to use the dagger against his enemies. Instead, his eyes locked on the table with the hooked blades and knives.

Of course!

"He did have the dagger on him," Myrthos warned.

"He still has *kaelandur*," Falmagon glowered, whipping around to look at the room.

"Something binds him to it," Myrthos said. "He cannot be parted from the blade."

Falmagon relaxed his fist, facing the room. He directed Myrthos to block the staircase with a wave of his hand. The man once known as the Highborn Long-Walker soothed his voice to what may have been a stern father suddenly trying to comfort a disobedient child. "Branimir, you cannot win this fight. Show yourself."

Branimir shuffled to the table. Two of the torture knives were possibly throwable. He grabbed them and then a hooked blade about the size of his forearm. They clinked slightly as he shuffled one knife and the awkward blade to his left hand. Expecting Myrthos and Falmagon to react to the faint noise, Branimir nosedived into a somersault toward Alden's hanging cage, clasping the weapons to his chest, and then springing back to his feet.

While Falmagon seemed oblivious to the sound, Myrthos waved a boney finger at the table, shouting, "Over there! Several of my tools just disappeared."

"What tools?" Falmagon asked.

"Knives," Myrthos stuttered. "A couple knives, I think."

"I am not playing this game, Branimir!" Falmagon screamed, his face reddening. Using *Koldovstvo*, he blasted energy at the table of torture tools, flipping it over. The remaining objects scattered across the floor. Falmagon moved around the table, staring beyond the fire. "Show yourself now!"

A gurgled, muffled scream across the room followed the clinging iron as Sulanna abruptly awoke. Branimir watched as she strained against the binds holding her feet and hands, her naked body arching off the table. She whipped her head sideways, her brown and grey hair clinging to her face. She glared at her father and Falmagon.

Branimir used the distraction, slinging the blade from his hand at Falmagon's head.

Falmagon howled unintelligibly, jerking to the side as the blade materialized mid-flight. The knife missed the Patrician, grazing by his ear, and unpredictably speared into Vornic Myrthos Maelthirren's eye.

Myrthos's other eye wobbled in the socket until it rested on Sulanna, who stared at him with her head reared back, suddenly frozen in silent confusion. A bloodied tear dripped from the corner of Myrthos's eye, sliding down the length of his nose. And then his body convulsed. He dropped to the dungeon floor.

Sulanna lay captivated by her dead father.

"Kill him, Branimir," Alden shouted, his head pressed against the bars.

Branimir darted back toward Sulanna, moving the other knife to his throwing hand, while gripping the hooked blade in his left. Falmagon steadied himself, pulling his eyes away from the fallen Vornic.

He did not wait for Falmagon to stand fully, throwing the other blade. Branimir gritted his teeth in anticipation for the deadly blow to fell his enemy. But Falmagon was quicker, using *Koldovstvo* to pull the weapon as it appeared from its route to his outstretched hand.

Falmagon whipped his head, staring at the direction from which the blade had been thrown. "You cannot win,

Branimir." Falmagon raised his hand to the fire, lifting one of the heated rods from the pit. The metal glowed with immeasurable heat.

Branimir crouched, moving from his position, prepared to dodge the flying projectile. The metal bar spun in the air over the fire as Falmagon glared into the corners of the room. Branimir inched closer, promising himself that he would finally kill Falmagon. He could not be found unless Dagmar came and ventured into *Klukas*. He would not let Falmagon make it back up the stairs.

"You will lose," Falmagon said, his voice eerily soft.

With a wave of his hand, the sizzling metal bar flashed like light into Adamus's stomach to remain lodged in the pit of his gut. The Ariadnean, ripped from his comatose torpor, threw his head back to the ceiling and cried out until his voice cracked into a pitiful scream. Branimir covered his ears, aghast, unable to look away from his friend. Adamus's skin singed and smoldered away, eaten by the flaming, metal rod, his insides emptying out until the makeshift weapon clattered with them to the stone floor. Completely catatonic, with a slobbering sob, Adamus convulsed mindlessly in his chains with spit and mucus staining his dark beard, until his life fled from his body.

"No!" Sulanna choked on her own scream, her muscles flexing and fists clenching in attempts to burst from her bindings. She thrashed about on the table in desperation.

Alden kicked at the door of his cage.

Tears welled in Branimir's eyes, blurring the image of Adamus hanging dead from the linked chains. He felt his face tighten, his hand hurting from squeezing the remaining hooked blade in his hand.

"Who will be next, Branimir?" Falmagon yelled, pulling another burning rod from the fire with *Koldovstvo*. "The old man or the woman? Who else would you have die for your foolishness?" He dwelled in the moment. "Show yourself!"

Branimir howled from the depths of his drying throat, the sound echoing from every wall, as he raced across the short expanse with his weapon held to his side. Falmagon rotated half a step before Branimir was on him.

With another cry, he swung the blade, catching the hook into the meaty flesh at Falmagon's side, just below the ribcage. Falmagon roared, losing his control over the heated, metal rod. It clanged against the ground harmlessly behind Branimir. Mechanically, Falmagon reached for the wound with his right hand while swinging his left at Branimir.

Branimir ducked under the hand with ease and jerked the weapon free before Falmagon could cling to it, ripping a chunk of skin and fat from the Patrician's belly.

Ignoring the blood spraying his face, Bran carried the arc of the pull, rotating the blade around his head to land for a second blow. This time, the hooked blade tore into Falmagon's thigh.

Branimir barely heard the spine-chilling scream as Falmagon reached out his hand. A gust of wind struck Branimir in his chest and flung him into Sulanna's iron table. The back of his skull cracked against the corner surface, and the dungeon of *Harrowhal* faded black.

Chapter XI

A hand pressed firmly against the back of Branimir's aching head. He flinched, attempting to pull away, but a secondary hand grasped his forehead to hold him in place.

"Hold steady, Branimir." His eyelids fluttered while Alden shushed him. His vision was distorted, but the interior of Alden's cage was unmistakable. "I think the cut has stopped bleeding but you are going to tear it open again if you keep thrashing."

Branimir sank into Alden's arms, with no mind that the man was also unclothed. He relaxed, letting Alden support his weight. The hot coals crackled from across the room.

"Will he live, Alden?" Sulanna's voice pierced the hollow room from the table where she remained bound.

"I think he will," Alden said, easing his hand from Branimir's head, "for a while yet. Once Falmagon's wounds have been stitched, he will return with a mind for punishment." Alden physically tensed under Branimir. "I suspect he will take out his wrath on you and me, Sulanna, and force Branimir to watch."

Sulanna's words barely masked her low whimper. "Why must you say such things? Have we not already suffered enough?"

"It is the truth of it, and we must prepare for what will come," Alden said. "I have known the minds of men like Falmagon before. He will not stop until he feels as though he has extracted justice, and righted the wrongs against him."

Branimir futilely tried to sit up from Alden's lap only to fall back and press his eyes shut. It did not stop the aching. He could feel his heartbeat pounding in the back of his skull. "Where did he go?" Branimir said hoarsely.

"Falmagon used *Koldovstvo* to move you in here," Alden said, "and then returned upstairs. Soon after, a couple of *Guardians* came and took the Vornic's body."

"Nine Lands." Branimir forced his eyes back open. He could not see Sulanna. He intoned, raising his voice so that she could, at least, hear him. "I…I am sorry about your father, Sulanna."

"Myrthos's death warrants no apology," Alden said gruffly. "You leveled the scales by ridding him from this place."

"At what cost?" Branimir shivered, thinking of Adamus's atrocious death. The Ariadnean's last moments were filled with pain and suffering.

"Adamus was already dying," Alden barked with authority, reading his thoughts.

Branimir gazed into nothingness. "I did not mean to kill him."

"You did *not* kill Adamus," Alden growled, hovering over Branimir.

"Stop." The bite in Sulanna's tone completely tore away the sobbing undertone she had moments before. "Adamus died a hero, and my father deserved much worse than a quick death. He only brought suffering to this world," Branimir heard her shifting on the iron slab, "suffering which will not soon be forgotten."

"No," Alden agreed, looking past the confines of the cage, "it will not."

Alden's words added a heaviness to Branimir's heart. In another attempt, Branimir reached for the bars to pull himself off his back. "Help me up." Alden reluctantly nodded, his flimsy white beard swaying. As Bran wrapped his fingers around the bars, Alden steadied him, holding his thin, narrow shoulders.

Branimir instinctively covered his mouth at the sight of Adamus's ruined, naked body. The skin lost its color; the blood was dark and a viscous consistency, sitting like syrup on his leg and from the wide hole in his stomach. The mutilation of his friend's body made his stomach churn; though, with two weeks from food, Branimir would have nothing to spew. Only Adamus's closed eyelids gave him a sense of serenity.

"I only wish he would be able to go to a better place," Branimir finally said, sliding his eyes to Sulanna. She, too, stared at Adamus with watered, blue eyes. Knowing the afterlife only held more pain gave them more than enough reason to weep Adamus's passing.

"We need to leave this place," Sulanna choked.

The clang of the doorway at the top of the stairs sounded as it opened and shut. Branimir reached for a dagger at his waist to find *kaelandur* secured back in the leather holding on his belt.

"They did not take *kaelandur*," Branimir said, gripping the hilt of the cursed weapon.

"No, Branimir." Sulanna arched her back off the table, twisting to face him and Alden in the cage. She behaved as though she might fling herself from the table if she were able. Her whisper was demanding. "Leave the dagger alone."

Branimir removed his hand, and dipped his head. He understood the danger of taking someone's life with *kaelandur*. The victim would not only return from the Netherworld, but they would be more powerful and more dangerous than before. Like Nedezhda. Like Eisliev. And even if the person did not die, who knew what the Likhyi now bound in the dagger could do.

He watched the staircase, holding his breath, hearing only the descent of a single set of scraping footsteps. No voices chattered this time to give away the potential harm awaiting them. Branimir's shoulders tensed; nausea and pain fleeing from his body. In fact, he abruptly felt very aware of the reality of the dungeon. As Alden anticipated, Branimir was certain graver consequences were coming for them. In this moment, he could not help but wonder if Adamus's death was a blessing.

Yet the emergence of the purple-eyed woman from the cliff of the stairs was unexpected. She looked to have been wearing the same white shirt and black cloak from when Branimir last saw her, but now—in addition to the pack on her back—she carried an armful of gear and bags.

"Alyona," Branimir sighed in relief, pulling his face to the bars.

"Alyona?" Sulanna disparaged, arching her neck to see the woman behind her. Alyona lay all she carried to the floor, her eyes falling on Adamus at her right. She stifled a gasp, and turned her head away. Sulanna whispered with doubt, "I thought you betrayed us."

"Never." Alyona covered her mouth, her eyes daring to look at Adamus's hanging corpse once more. "I should have come sooner...I tried. I had little chance with the *Guardians* and *Kadari* combing the halls."

"*Kadari?*" Branimir coughed. His stomach pined from hunger. "You mean Falmagon and Dagmar?"

Alyona sniffed. "Several who survived at Melkorka came with Falmagon. A couple dozen, I think."

"How did he and Dagmar travel so fast to Eldhaft with so many *Kadari* when Dorofej has not yet come? Where is he?" Branimir asked.

Alyona shook her head. "Dagmar left long before Eisliev attacked Melkorka. How Falmagon came to be here…" Alyona swallowed, reaching into one of the packs and pulling out Sulanna's long knife. She made her way to the iron slab with Sulanna, purposely keeping her gaze away from Adamus. "I don't know. We can ask these questions another time. Right now, we need to move."

Alden stirred behind Branimir, moving the cage. "How do we know this is not another one of Falmagon's schemes? Branimir just killed the Vornic, you know?"

"And I killed the guards at the top of the stairs," Alyona said, raising her eyes and scoffing at the old man. She gestured her hand at the cage, popping the lock with *Koldovstvo*. "You must be the man called Alden, who they came here to find. Well, Alden, it will not be long before someone notices what I did, and if we are still down here, we will be dead."

Branimir creaked open the cage door, pulling at Alden's arm. "Let's go."

Alden grumbled in agreement, grabbing Branimir's arm to help lower him to the ground. Bran welcomed the support considering the surroundings of the dungeon continued to blur in and out of his vision.

Across the way, he could hear Sulanna ardently speaking to Alyona as she cut away the leather bindings. "I should not have disbelieved you." As she freed her hands, Sulanna gripped at Alyona's black cloak. "Forgive me. Please."

"Think nothing of it, and do not thank me yet," Alyona said. She cut away the last strip, handing Sulanna her long knife. She gestured to the gear and bags. "I found your things stored not too far from here, but I—" her voice trailed, turning to Alden. "I have Adamus's gear. Alden, I did not know you were down here."

Alden shuffled by the body of Adamus, steering Branimir to the bags at the base of the stairs. "It will make do. Thank you."

Weakly, the three of them rummaged desperately while Alyona peered up the stairs. Clothes and weapons were scattered as they pulled on trousers and shirts, and fastened blades and shields. Sulanna's breaths were the heftiest as she slipped on her shirt, and then the leather breastplate, which Alden soon helped her fasten much like Adamus had in the past.

Branimir felt like a stranger in his own green cloak and wooly garments. However, holding the balanced dagger in his hand returned some strength to his muscles.

"We have to leave him here," Sulanna's shaky tone pulled Branimir's attention. She stared across the room at Adamus. "I am getting tired of leaving friends behind."

Branimir placed his hand on her back. "He will not be forgotten. We have more to do if we are going to bring his spirit peace."

"He is right," Alyona said. "And you will need to be at full strength. Hold steady." She approached Branimir first, cupping his head in her hands. A familiar glow of reds and yellows swirled and swelled in her palms, sinking beneath the skin of Branimir. The gash on the back of his head mended, the strands of skin reconnecting, sealing the wound. The soreness in his muscles absconded with the hunger cramps in his stomach, and soon the dizziness and exhaustion disappeared too.

Branimir huffed in a breath of air like he had awoken from a long night's rest. "Alyona, what have you done?"

"I told you," Alyona said. "I have the sacred bloodline."

She reached for Sulanna next, and then Alden, stealing away their minor aches and fatigue.

Alden clasped the axe in his hand. "I admit, I did not think we would be able to escape *Harrowhal*, but you have given us a fighting chance. I knew the gods would send for aid. How will we repay this kindness?"

"Survive, and escape Eldhaft," Alyona said, leading the way up the staircase. "Let us ensure Adamus did not die for nothing."

Sulanna hurried to follow Alyona. The color returned to her face, her cheekbones tight with determination. "Let us escape this foul city."

Branimir's hand quavered around the handle of his knife, following Sulanna with Alden at his back. "Falmagon will die."

Alyona stopped at the door. "If you think you can kill him, Branimir, I will not stop you. Though our priority is to reunite you with Dorofej and Tyr at *Iriy*." Her purple eyes dug into Branimir. He stared back at her. He had almost forgotten the Ispolini was traveling with Dorofej. She added, "The fate of the world and the gods rests on you delivering *kaelandur*. The dagger will be safe among them."

He gazed back, having no desire to argue with the *Kadari*, who saved them. "I understand."

Alyona cracked open the upstairs door, the familiar clang of the door echoing down the staircase into the dungeon behind them.

Sulanna whispered. "By the gods, if I never should hear that sound again."

Her voice was drowned out by the sounds of screams and the din of battle filling the halls of *Harrowhal*. Alyona swung the door open to give full view of the dead littering the corridors. Dead *Guardians*, as well as men not wearing the distinct cloaks, were strewn in all directions. Some had blood seeping from beneath their garments, and others had their skin wrinkled and blackened by flame. None gave any sign of life.

"What did you do?" Branimir asked.

Alyona's jaw tightened, listening to the roar of battle echoing in the distance. "I did not do this."

"Dorofej?" Branimir wondered, starting left down the hallway.

"No." Alyona grabbed his shoulder. "Dorofej could not have made it here yet. The distance from Melkorka is too far."

"Dagmar did. Falmagon did," Sulanna said, her weapon drawn and held at the ready. She stood on her toes, waiting for anything to barrel into the hall.

"Dagmar may have created a gateway like Dorofej to send Falmagon here," Alyona explained in haste. "Another *Kadari* must have been able to do the same for Dagmar; yet, the effort would have likely killed him."

"I thought you said Dorofej was the only one who could create gateways," Branimir said.

Alyona scrunched her face as though remembering her words. "I said he was one of few. Dagmar and Dorofej have the same bloodline. Their power is great, and they both touch *Koldovstvo* in a way unlike any I have ever known."

"As much as I am enjoying the lesson in magic and Stuhian bloodlines," Alden interjected gruffly, his hardiness returned, "We should move our asses."

Sulanna agreed. "Even if Dorofej found a way here, he will do well enough to find his own escape. If he escaped Melkorka, *Harrowhal* would not be difficult."

Alyona led them only a few paces down the corridor when they reached the corner leading into the oversized foyer. For Branimir, the time since he laid eyes on the extended room with the double staircases, leading to the second floor, felt eternal.

Branimir sprang back as a *Guardian* blasted through the opening; feet lifted off the ground, and slammed into the wall opposite of the foyer. His head cracked against the wall, and he fell to the ground. The expressionless gaze on his face clearly told of his fate.

"Where are you, Dagmar Kaligula? Will you continue to hide behind the weak?" a gurgled, male voice shouted from the foyer. "I did not travel from Melkorka to slaughter these swine."

"No, no, no," Branimir said, whispering to the other three. He stepped back, clutching the hilt of *kaelandur* at his belt. "I know that voice. It is Eisliev. He has come to

Eldhaft." Branimir remembered what Dorofej said about Nedezhda when she returned from the Netherworld. "He is drawn to *kaelandur*. I cannot hide from him. I cannot outrun him."

Alyona replied in a hushed tone. "He is more interested in his revenge on Dagmar than the dagger. But, he is bound by the magic of the blade to destroy the Ash Tree. He cannot be distracted by his selfishness for long."

Alden tightened his hold on Adamus's axe.

"What do we do?" Sulanna followed Branimir's lead and stepped away from the archway leading into the foyer. "Can we fight him? Should we?"

"He is limitless with his magic," Alyona said, hearing Eisliev scream for Dagmar again. His voice rebounded through *Harrowhal*, lifted by the power of *Koldovstvo*. Branimir could hear the chandelier hanging from the ceiling shake from the reverberation. "We could not win."

From behind them, toward the dungeon, Branimir barely heard the strained words being spoken. The syllables were broken apart; the tenor uneven and grating. His vision blurred while sourness laced the inside of his cheeks. He gagged on the taste, and try as he might, Branimir mentally fought against whatever foul magic swept over him.

Yet he was powerless.

Harrowhal vanished from his sight to be replaced with the grand hallways of *Heshayol* in the depths of the frozen Netherworld. The memories buried in his mind swiftly resurfaced, taking hold of his senses. From somewhere in the far distance, beyond this world, he could hear Dorofej's screams.

Ososcica.

The monstrous, white snake guarding *Heshayol* emerged from nothingness in front of him like a nightmare, coiling and looping, a hundred times greater than his size. The snake's body must have been twice as wide as he was tall. Branimir was swift to disappear, hiding from the slimy forked tongue, slipping between its encrusted lips. The glowing black and yellow eyes searched for him, hungered for his flesh. He screamed, slashing his knife at the thick scales of the beast.

A bawl of pain pealed at his ear drums; blood colored the end of the blade. He could not see the cut on *Ososcica*, but he must have hurt it.

"Branimir!" someone called his name.

The snake whipped its head with incredible speed and lifted its triangular head to strike, baring fangs dripping with glistening venom. Branimir choked with fear, clinging to the dagger in his hand. In desperation, he sprang into a roll to escape the lurching attack.

A decorative rug suddenly appeared under Branimir's hands and feet as he sprung back to his toes. The sitting tables and chairs of the foyer magically reappeared before him; the staircases spiraled before him and in front of him stood the red mage, Eisliev.

Dead bodies of *Guardians, Kadari,* and the gods knew who else had been torn to pieces. Eisliev stood among them victoriously, his arms folded and attention on the hallway behind Branimir.

Branimir maintained his invisibility, but he could not immediately recall how he had come into the foyer. The hallucination remained fresh in his mind. He jerked around to look for *Ososcica* only to see Alden flail into the room by some unseen magic. The old warrior tumbled to the floor, refusing to release the steel axe in his hand. The bloodied cut on his forearm was unmistakable.

Branimir looked back to the dagger clutched in his hand, painted with crimson.

"Branimir," Sulanna cried, rushing around the corner of the hallway to join Alden. She skidded to his side to help him up. "Where are you?"

"Eisliev!" Alyona cried out, backing into the foyer with her hands crossed and extended pass her chest. A blue orb of magical protection crystalized in front of her; flames licked at the gelled barrier from a concealed castor further down the corridor. Alyona dropped the protective wall to spring after Sulanna. "Dagmar is here."

Dagmar!

Branimir did not have to think long to put together what happened. Dagmar had used *Faegrim* on him and controlled his mind. Leaving his line of sight must have broken the connection.

He jerked his gaze to Eisliev dreadfully.

Eisliev's blue eyes glowed, causing his grey, rotting skin to fade more in comparison to his black veins. He twisted his bloodstained lips into a smile at Alyona, running a hand through his long, red locks. Branimir shuddered at the sight of the undead red mage who he had slain at Melkorka last year.

"You have obeyed well, Alyona," Eisliev crooned. "As promised, you will have a place among the Likhyi." Eisliev's eyes dropped to Branimir, who stayed invisible. "You brought me the Kras with the dagger, too."

Branimir shuddered, stepping back from the red mage, remaining hidden.

Eisliev leered, leaning over Branimir. Red streaks of blood pulsed through the whites of his eyes. "You cannot hide while you hold *kaelandur*, little murderer."

Bran's blood ran cold. He tried to ignore the fear, remembering how Eisliev had slit Bohumir Mager's throat, and tossed him into the fireplace. "You earned your death after what you did to that boy."

The evil grin did not leave Eisliev's face. "As you have earned yours—"

Sulanna's knife plunged into the red mage's belly, thrown from a distance across the room. Eisliev stumbled in surprise, gripping the hilt of the blade lodged inside his tainted flesh.

Branimir whipped around to Sulanna, who ogled at her outstretched hand from which the dagger had been thrown. Alden groaned from beneath her knee, pressed against his chest.

"Wha—" Sulanna could barely utter the word, eyes clouded in confusion. She pulled herself back from Alden to allow him to breathe.

Looking for the obvious explanation, Branimir spotted Dagmar gliding through the archway. As expected, the silver band, *Faegrim*, encircled the small finger on his left hand. He was using mind-control to have them attack Eisliev.

Time and space warped with Dagmar's precipitous use of *Koldovstvo*, a magic Branimir had often seen displayed by Dorofej. Branimir's thoughts flowed at regular speed, but the material world around him slowed with Dagmar's sway over reality.

Dagmar fluttered through the room—ignoring Alyona, Sulanna, and Alden—like a bird flying through the treetops, flickering in and out of view. Hundreds of particles of light bent around his body as he zipped from space to space across the room, advancing on Eisliev. The red mage's moldy face was chiseled in horror as his archenemy assailed without restraint.

Inch by inch, Branimir lifted his blade in preparation, knowing Dagmar would reach Eisliev long before he could raise the weapon at his creeping pace.

Dagmar ripped Sulanna's dagger from Eisliev's stomach, tearing it from his fingers with ease. With unmatched speed, Dagmar rotated the weapon in his hand and knifed the red mage in the chest twice, and then the neck, where it remained.

Branimir could only watch, frozen in time.

Eisliev gurgled, blood sloshing out of his mouth. And yet, the red mage feebly twisted his hands to release a fiery inferno at Dagmar. The flames carved through the air like clouds grazing the heavens, struggling to take shape against

Dagmar's time-altering magic. The blaze distended like distorted fingers, ever eager to melt away Dagmar's sneer.

The spell abruptly dispersed as Dagmar attempted to dodge Eisliev's weaving of *Koldovstvo*. He dove toward Branimir—yet invisible—and Eisliev shadowed him maliciously with the fully forming fireball. Branimir acted fast, leaping into Dagmar, and plunging his dagger into the Stuhia's chest. He hung onto the handle while Dagmar thundered in agony; Eisliev's fire blistered the Stuhia's back, melding cloth to skin, the flames whipping around Branimir as he shielded himself with the torso.

Dagmar's fingers dug into Branimir's back like iron in attempts to rip him away. When he was unsuccessful, he clutched Bran closer to his chest under his surprising strength. Dagmar's howling twisted into a roar pivoting his feet with intent to pull Branimir into the unyielding flames. Branimir could do naught but gape at the hateful man's gritted teeth.

The sputtering fire snapped at Branimir. His yelps drowned out by a war cry from Alyona. From his peripheral, Branimir saw Eisliev's blood-spattered body zip across the room, tugged by invisible strands of air. The flames dispersed.

The red mage smashed into the rug next to Sulanna, who pounced on him, ripping her dagger from his neck to finish what Dagmar had started.

As soon as the blade was free, Eisliev flung Sulanna away from him with *Koldovstvo*, slamming her into a wall across the room. Branimir could hear her breath leave her lungs; while Eisliev pressed his hand over the bloody wound in his neck and attempted to rise to his feet.

Branimir yelled, booting Dagmar in the bits. With a grunt, Dagmar freed him and toppled back, thrashing his head around to make sense of what happened at the same moment that Alden tackled Eisliev back to the floor again.

Branimir landed on his back, scrambling to stand up with Dagmar feet away, and Eisliev another twenty paces behind him.

"Kill him!" Dagmar growled at Alden, gripping the dagger still lodged in his chest with his right hand, leaving it entombed in his chest. He hugged to it in despair. Baring his teeth, he lifted his left hand toward Eisliev to lash out with *Koldovstvo*.

Alyona was quicker, slinging a fireball into Dagmar's mid-section. He intermittently howled, his lung failing from being pierced by Branimir's blade. The fire scorched the front of his torso, the flames tearing into his belly. He grabbed at his stomach with his hand, lessening the flame with his own magic. His wild eyes, now darkened with wrinkles from his use of *Koldovstvo*, were tinted with unmistakable fear.

Branimir searched for another weapon, only to find *kaelandur*, before Alden's body crashed into him, pitched across the room by Eisliev. Alden's legs smacked Branimir in the head, taking him off his feet again, and leaving the two of them entangled on the floor in a heap. Branimir instinctively grabbed at his skull to protect himself, the weight of the human partially pinning him to the ground.

He reappeared, trying to push Alden's leg off of him.

"You cannot defeat me. None of you can," Eisliev gurgled, speaking to Dagmar more than any other. "You do not have the power. I am immortal with *kaelandur's* magic. I will kill you…and then the Ash Tree."

"Immortal?" Dagmar repeated at a whisper, already nearing death. He shielded his stomach, turning his eyes to Branimir with wonder. Branimir winced under the gaze. He examined the room, seeing Sulanna crawling across the floor attempting to gain her breath, and Alyona not far away, retrieving a sword from a dead *Guardian*.

Suddenly, Dagmar ripped *kaelandur* from its leather holding with *Koldovstvo* and plunged it into his own chest.

"No!" Branimir cried out, the pain instantly searing through his body with the separation from the copper dagger. His body ached from his head to his toes; the taste of metal stung the tip of his tongue. His mind swirled, stinging from temple to temple. He reached in despair for the dagger sticking from Dagmar's chest cavity.

"No!" Eisliev echoed, flinging his own arm upward and using his magic in attempt to pull the dagger to him. Dagmar grasped hold of the hilt to keep it in his heart, fighting to hold back his own yell. Eisliev's force lifted Dagmar off his feet, pulling him across the carpet.

"I…will have the…power now." Dagmar forced the words with his last breath. His hands slipped from the blade at the same moment his limp body fell to the carpet. Dead.

Branimir cringed, fire burning his insides. The room faded, threatening to leave him blind without the *kaelandur*. The last he saw was Alden leaping over him toward Dagmar. If Eisliev had said anything more, they were lost as Branimir's hearing was replaced with a loud ringing. He quailed, hitting his head against the ground.

What felt like an eternity passed, and then the familiar hilt was pressed into Branimir's open palm.

He gasped, sucking air into his lungs, and wrapped his fingers around *kaelandur*. Alden hung over him, his thick eyebrows arched in concern. Feeling his strength return almost immediately, Branimir rolled away from the old warrior to face Eisliev Kluk.

To his surprise, the red mage's face was fastened with shock, a curved blade erupting through his mouth from the back of his head. Alyona let go of the hilt, and pushed Eisliev to the side.

"Our odds have worsened," Alyona muttered. Her use of magic had added extra wrinkles around her eyes, but concern lining her eyes caused her to look all the older. "*Kaelandur's* magic will bind both Dagmar and Eisliev to destroy the Ash Tree, giving them unlimited power."

Sulanna replied, "More the reason to get to *Iriy* and have the gods destroy this dagger."

"Yes. However, the dagger will not end Eisliev's and Dagmar's desire to destroy the Ash Tree and free the Likhyi," Alyona said. "It will only steal away their immediate means."

Alden grumbled. "What do you mean?"

Alyona faced the old warrior. "The two will continue to seek a way to release the *old-dark*, even if we convince the gods to rid the world of *kaelandur*."

Branimir coughed, his throat dry. He spoke with a strangled breath. "Why would Dagmar kill himself with *kaelandur*?"

"Power…knowledge…immortality…" Alden speculated with a shake of his head.

"We can hope their blood feud will keep them at each other's throats, even in death," Branimir said, collapsing to his knees next to Dagmar's corpse. He pulled *Faegrim* free from the finger to put on his own.

Sulanna huffed, eyeing Branimir warily. "Keep the ring close. I do not know its power, or what Dagmar did to me. But it is best no one who can touch *Koldovstvo* touches it, or we might kill each other."

"I will keep it safe," Branimir replied. Although he spoke of the ring, his hand rested on the hilt of *kaelandur*, wondering how he could keep anything safe against the power of *Koldovstvo*.

"What about her?" Alden said, pointing at Alyona. "She did save us from the dungeon, but for what purpose? She did not know Eisliev had come here. And we all heard what Eisliev said about her working for him? How long would it have been before you betrayed us?"

"I would never deceive you." Alyona frowned. "At Melkorka—"

"We can trust her," Sulanna interjected. "The story was a ruse crafted by Dorofej for them to escape Melkorka."

Sulanna stood next to Alyona, almost protectively. "We can trust her."

Branimir agreed, turning his eyes from Dorofej's dead grandson. He combed the room laden with the dead. "But where is Falmagon?"

Chapter XII

Branimir avoided the blood pooling under Dagmar, and searched the body until he found the ancient codex, the *Varkolak*. Dagmar had kept the tome magically folded with Koldovstvo to fit snuggly in his pocket. Branimir did not have the power to undo the leather casing holding the faded vellum. He pushed the small-scale book into his pocket. Dorofej would want it; he was certain.

Alyona rummaged next to him. She watched him put the ageless text away, pressing her lips together as though she were holding back her words. Returning to her work, she unbuckled the belt holding the vials of Water of Life from Dagmar and carefully slipped it off. Three glass containers shattered when Dagmar had fallen to the ground, but there were three remaining for her use.

Considering the few age lines on Alyona, Branimir guessed she would have some time before needing to restore her youth.

"Eisliev does not have anything on him." Sulanna said, cleaning her knife on his clothes.

"I found some silver on the *Guardians* and *Kadari*. And these," Alden said, handing two daggers to Branimir. He took the blades with a nod, and carefully tucked them into his belt, along with the blade from Dagmar's chest. He slipped the sheath with *kaelandur* to the far side, grazing the handle uneasily. Alden added, "We should have enough coin to get us by until we reach Gavlok."

"We should get moving," Alyona said. "More *Guardians* will eventually arrive, and we do not need to be here. Not to mention, I have little interest in facing whatever *Kadari* remain with Falmagon."

"What about Falmagon?" Branimir asked, again, for what felt like the hundredth time. "With Dagmar removed, the *Kadari* are weakened. Falmagon was injured when he left the dungeon. We can end this right now."

Alden was the first to respond, hooking Adamus's shield over his back. "*Harrowhal* has a lot of space to track, but I agree with Branimir. If we do not kill Falmagon now, we will be looking over our shoulder for him and whatever *Kadari* remain all the way to *Iriy*."

"Why press our luck?" Sulanna asked. Despite Alyona's healing, Sulanna looked exhausted once more with the color fading from her skin. Branimir suspected the undue amount of death, including her father, was weighing on her. Her words clarified his suspicion. "We have already lost so many, Alden. Please…we should leave."

Alyona neared Sulanna, wrapping a hand around her shoulders like a mother comforting a child. Her purple eyes rested on Branimir and Alden. "I agree. Eisliev cleared the path but the lack of hindrance will not last. The *Guardians* will come. We may not be able to call this a victory, but it is something."

Branimir shook his head. "We cannot leave. We already made the mistake of leaving Falmagon alive in Gaetana, and look where it led us."

Alyona angled her brows. "I should have been told he was in Gaetana. Why did no one tell me?"

"We saw him at the inn before we left, waiting for us in the commons," Branimir tried to explain.

"But why was I not told?" Alyona asked, removing her arm from Sulanna. Only a moment passed before she answered her own question. "Because you did not trust me." She dipped her head, running a hand through her hair. "I understand."

Sulanna meekly shrugged at the *Kadari*.

Alden cleared his throat, gripping a spear he found among the bodies. "It doesn't matter. Alyona and Sulanna are right. We cannot be sure Falmagon is here anyway. He may be dead already. If we go traipsing about, we are likely to become trapped."

Branimir ran his hand through his thin hair. "Fine," he finally muttered. "How will we leave Eldhaft?"

Alden scanned the room with a knowing look. "The gods have blessed us, providing a proper means to walk right out the city gates. Search the bodies for clothes unblemished with blood."

"No," Sulanna argued. "Wearing the *Guardians's* garb would only bring more attention when trying to leave the gates. If Branimir stays hidden, we should be able to leave."

Alyona agreed. "We have wasted enough time already. We need to go."

As Sulanna and Alyona led them from the foyer, Alden turned to Branimir, who had already vanished. "I know you want to find Falmagon, but stay with us, Branimir."

"I do not plan on sneaking off, Alden," Branimir said sternly. He added in a soft undertone. "Just promise to keep Sulanna safe. She cares about you."

The old warrior lifted an eyebrow with interest, turning his granular chin to the woman, who had traveled and fought with him among the Crimson Sun for so many decades. "I would give everything for her."

Branimir considered his words as they plodded through the bodies lining the hallway. He wondered if Alden's fondness for Sulanna matched her own toward him.

Branimir had not forgotten Sulanna's confession about her love for Alden.

Eventually, the four of them reached the rear door that first brought them into *Harrowhal.* Alden and Sulanna recoiled at the midday sun, while Alyona and Branimir's vision adjusted to the fluctuating light. Holding his breath, Branimir glided behind Alden, who followed the women, up the alleyway to the main road.

The southern gate, which they entered when coming into Eldhaft, sat but a half mile down the road, whilst the northern gate would have been much further in the opposite direction. Sulanna, being the wiser, vouched for the southern gate with the intent to walk around the city instead of through it. Grunts from Alden and Alyona suggested they agreed with her quick decision.

The four made a left and briskly walked toward the towers marking the portcullis. They only traversed half the distance when Branimir spotted the hated historian from the *Highspire,* Witigor Sirska, slinking into a side shop. His ugly, pointed hat bounced with as much vigor as Branimir remembered. He heard him speaking to someone in front of him as he went inside.

"I saved Eldhaft from the worst kind, I tell you. I bet they are all dead now," he scoffed. "By the gods, I am a hero." The door to the shop closed behind him.

"Sulanna," Branimir hissed from behind them. "Wit went—"

"I saw," she whispered back. "He is no longer our concern. Come on."

Branimir's blood boiled, but he followed behind his friends. Moments later, Wit fled from his thoughts and his attention was drawn to the front gate. A handful of *Guardians* gathered around the gate, encircling the too-familiar Ispolini.

"Tyr Og," Branimir identified the Ispolini with incredulity, turning to Alyona who stood next to him. He swallowed, drawing back. After speaking with Alyona at

Eldhaft, he expected to come across the giant again, but not here in Eldhaft. The last time he saw Tyr was at Melkorka when the Ispolini had tried to kill him. Of course, the attempt was moments after Branimir had put a dagger in Eisliev's skull. "Dorofej must be close, right? You said they were traveling together."

Before Alyona could answer, Branimir heard one of the *Guardian's* ask, "What is your business here, Ispolini?"

"I heard the Patrician talking about his kind," another said. "I bet he would be interested in seeing this one."

Tyr raised his hands, taking a step back, gazing to the road ahead—the same direction from which they were coming. "I do not want any trouble. I came looking for my friends is all," Tyr said. His blue eyes were darker than Branimir remembered under his dark red strands of hair.

"I do not see Dorofej," Alyona said plainly.

Branimir grabbed *kaelandur* at his belt again, wrapping his fingers around the handle. At least he knew Dorofej was not dead. Dagmar said he had to be killed by the copper dagger.

"Come on," Alyona directed. "Tyr must have brought a message from Dorofej."

"You expect us to fight the *Guardians* in the open road?" Sulanna asked.

"If it comes to it," Alyona replied. "We cannot let him be taken."

"It will come to that…" Branimir started. "The moment the *Guardians* see us, we will be in danger. We would do better to catch them unaware."

Alden spoke gruffly under his breath. "You said to trust her, Sulanna, but this seems too much the coincidence."

Sulanna loosened her belt knife and shushed him. "I know, Alden." Her face twisted in absolute disgust, her chin shaking with immeasurable wrath. She yanked the blade loose from her scabbard and set the pace toward the gates.

"Put some faith in the *gods*. I am not leaving anyone else behind. If she says Tyr is with us, we will keep him safe."

Alden matched Sulanna's step, gripping the spear in his hand.

"We should make a plan, before…" Alyona started, watching them down the street. She rattled in a frenzy. "Branimir? Where are you, Branimir?"

His words were loud enough to reach Alyona's ears as he hustled by her. "Two steps behind them."

Branimir disregarded Alyona's curses, pulling two of the daggers from his belt, leaving an extra blade plus *kaelandur*. He did not have to study Alden or Sulanna to know the two were not going to wait for an invitation to the battle. Tyr, unaware, lifted his hand as though he might be waving to Alyona—the massive axe in the leather strapping on his bare back swinging with the motion—and then dropped his six-fingered hands to his skin trousers, realizing what was about to happen.

With less than ten paces, Alden and Sulanna attacked without as much as a shout.

Alden's spear ripped through the back of a *Guardian's* neck as Sulanna wrapped her arm around another and sliced his neck open. Branimir bounded by her onto the back of a third, stabbing the two knives into chest. The man tumbled backward with a pained cry. Branimir ignored the sound, dodging Alden, who stepped over his invisible body to thrust his spear into a *Guardian's* gut.

The other *Guardian's* yelled in surprise, moving to counter. Yet, before any could pull their swords free from their scabbards, three more had fallen dead.

Tyr, backed away further, crying out. "What has happened? Alyona!"

The *Guardians* ignored him to respond to the immediate threat.

Sulanna scowled, shouting to the Ispolini. "Tyr!" She ducked under the high arc of a sword, and then stepped over an adjacent attack as a blade swung for her ankle. Branimir rolled behind her first attacker, cutting the sinew behind his knees. The guard barely made a sound before the Kras stuck him in the jugular. "Stand with us!" She deflected another blow from the second guard.

The Ispolini, his bare skin glistening in the summer's heat, looked up to Alyona in the distance, nodding with a hearty growl. He jerked the axe from his back. His roar resounded through the city street as he lurched forward and grabbed a man half his size. He hurled him back into the stone tower to the right of the gate.

"For Svarog, the Kingdom and victory!" Alden bellowed loudly, thrusting the spear into the brains of the enemy.

"We need to go," Branimir shouted among the din of battle. Sulanna and Alden did not seem to hear him. He slashed his blade against the tender skin of Sulanna's attacker, distracting the man enough for Sulanna to scoop in close with her own blade. Branimir did not see the death blow. "Come on," he started.

"Branimir!" Alyona shouted from behind him. He rotated back the way they had come to see ten to fifteen *Kadari* marching at them with Falmagon walking unsteadily behind them, gripping his side, and masking the pain.

"Kill them all!" Falmagon decreed, directing his small legion with a free hand. The citizens of Eldhaft, who had not already fled indoors or in-between buildings, raised the alarm, fleeing in all directions. In the distance, Branimir could hear more men marching through the streets. He suspected them to be more of the *Guardians of Gero*.

Alyona flung up a wide shield of *Koldovstvo* to defend against the lightning and fire that quickly rained down from the *Kadari*. The vitality of the blue field wavered against their power. Alyona's desperate voice called out for him again, carried by *Koldovstvo*. "Branimir!"

Tyr, Sulanna, and Alden held the battle in balance. The *Guardians* would not last against them.

He had to help Alyona.

With persistence, he bolted for the *Kadari* opposite side of the blue shield, remembering the battle on the shores of Melkorka. The mages were not like Eisliev with eyes set on *kaelandur*, seeing between worlds. No, the *Kadari* could not see him; he could lessen their numbers with little effort if he were quick. He could save them all; he could kill Falmagon.

"Stay here," he shouted to Alyona sprinting by her. His feet were light against the dirt, kicking up dust behind him.

Her purple eyes darted where he had been in a failed attempt to see him. "We must flee," she begged over the sound of combat.

His eyes locked on Falmagon, ignoring her. Part of him knew she was being wise, but what Branimir said at *Harrowhal* held true. He wanted his old master to taste the bitter air of the Netherworld as he and Dorofej were forced to twelve-hundred-years ago. Falmagon single-handedly turned the world upside down, robbing free choice from its inhabitants with the *Kadari*, binding the living to his chosen god—his vision—his corrupt concept of perfection. Any who did not bend knee to his will were judged. And for what? The world would burn all the same with the return of the *old-dark*.

Branimir barely recognized the low, guttural growl rumbling in his gullet. He was several paces from the swarm of *Kadari* when he let the first dagger fly at the front-line. The weapon pierced the eye socket of a middle-aged man with short, dark hair, felling him to the dirt. His *Kadari* brethren adjacent to him jumped at the sudden death, hardly noticing the dagger materialize in the air before slaying the unaware man.

Yet Falmagon kept them steadfast, counseling with commanding authority. "Split the ground; spill lightening; rain fire. Kill the red brood before he reaches you."

At the Patrician's command, the ground quaked and split—like a tidal wave—rolling sediment over sand. A stupefied expletive could be heard from behind Branimir, indicating Alyona had lost her balance. He did not have time to look over his shoulder; instead, Branimir had to scrabble and clamber over the roiling dirt wobbling under his feet. The buildings on either side of the city street rocked; the glass in the windows shattered.

The screams of the frightened citizens would have given Branimir pause if he would have had the luxury to dawdle. But Falmagon was resolved to slaying Branimir, even if he should destroy all Eldhaft in the effort.

Branimir jerked the remaining dagger from his waist— leaving *kaelandur* in its sheath—and hurdled over the fissure forming under his feet. He glided by the first—a woman— stabbing her mid-thigh, tearing the blade free at a downward angle; in the same breath, he impaled the man to her right in the groin with his second dagger. The harmonious squawking from the two coalesced with the other *Kadari*, like a tuneless choir, frightfully wailing with panic.

"Kill him!" Falmagon bawled the loudest, slinking away from the *Kadari*, who stopped molding their magic to fan away from the two who collapsed.

"Where is he?" one screamed.

"Nine Lands," muttered another.

Branimir slipped behind another *Kadari* making his way to Falmagon, who slowly continued to retreat. Lightning sizzled and popped from the cloudless sky, tearing through a woman opposite side of the circle. She was dead before she struck the earth.

Branimir twisted to see Alyona back on her feet, casting *Koldovstvo* from a distance. Another bolt struck a man twenty feet ahead of him, ripping a fiery hole from his back to chest.

Defensive blue shields erupted around several of the *Kadari*.

"Run!" a man hollered, pushing a woman out of his way. "We cannot win here." The *Kadari* nearest to Falmagon began the excursion back down the main road, and soon the *Kadari* closest to Branimir started after them.

Falmagon jogged his head with anger, pulling at the corner of his mustache as his small army retreated behind him. Unable to see Branimir, he glared at Alyona across the upturned street. He lifted his hand to cast a spell.

Branimir responded without thought, hurling his dagger forty feet at Falmagon. Although he aimed for the man's head, the distance was too great. Falmagon's eyes bulged as the dagger appeared before him. He swung his hand to defend the attack only to catch the edge of the knife in his palm.

He yelled in agony, blistering with fury. Pulling his injured hand to his chest, he took one final look at the street before fleeing with the *Kadari*.

The echo of the marching guard on the adjacent road grew louder, halting Branimir from racing after Falmagon. He raked through the streets to see *Guardians of Gero* also advancing, ducking in and out behind buildings, measuring their best path to the gates. Without a doubt, Branimir knew he could catch Falmagon, but the cost would be his friends being captured and imprisoned, or even killed.

Near the gate, he could see Alden and Sulanna directing Tyr back out the gate.

He squeezed the handle of his dagger and backed away from the approaching thieves. He stepped around the two *Kadari* he had left injured on the ground, crawling at a snail's pace after their brethren. Bran did not stop until he reached Alyona's side.

"Branimir," Alyona yelled about the time he reached her. "We have to go."

Branimir appeared at the *Kadari's* side. "I know. Come on."

Chapter XIII

The sinuous river, the *Gneveh Rill,* trickled over the patchy rocks scattered beneath the flowing surface. The vibrant water was cool on Branimir's lips, briefly abating the hunger spasms in his stomach. Alyona's revitalizing magic at *Harrowhal* faded over the evening hours while they bolted north toward Gavlok. And, unfortunately, whatever food had remained in their packs spoiled while they had been in the dungeon.

Hunger and discomfort resurfaced tenfold within Branimir's body. Alden and Sulanna did not appear to be faring much better. Luckily, the injuries they each suffered did not return as the hunger did.

"Finally," Sulanna sighed, sinking to her knees in the water. She cupped her hands and slurped the liquid from her palms. Eagerly, she fished for more water.

Branimir hummed in agreement, swooping handfuls to his mouth. Any other time, he may have found the water bitter; but, in this moment, he could not have asked for anything more refreshing. His stomach gurgled in response.

Alden collapsed on the other side of Sulanna, resting on the bank. He followed suit, taking a drink, mumbling between gulps. "The regular guard will stay in Eldhaft unless given a directive by Count Vlassi, but the *Guardians* will not turn so easily from pursuit."

"Neither will Falmagon," Branimir added, struggling to keep his eyes open. He blinked several times, splashing some of the water on his face to help keep himself awake. The sun setting in the west, behind the distant mountains of the Shade Fells, did not help the drowsiness. He looked at the faint peaks. Somewhere in their vastness held their destination, *Iriy*, the City of the Gods.

"No, he won't," Sulanna carped, hitting at the water with frustration. Her short, grey hair clung to her cheeks from the heat. "Maybe we should have pursued him like you suggested, Branimir."

Branimir jumped back, startled by Sulanna's sudden movement. An image of Adamus having his head dunked in the basin of water in the dungeon at *Harrowhal* played through in his mind. He had been helpless watching while strapped to the table.

"He could have killed us," Branimir said, shaking the sound of Adamus gasping for breath from his ears. His hand was trembling from the memory. He tried to steady it, continuing, "I am certain he would have. We should have killed Wit when we had the chance. He is the reason we were held captive in *Harrowhal*, and the reason Adamus was killed."

"I do not care for him anymore than you, Branimir, but Wit acted as I would have suspected him to," Sulanna said with a shake of her head. "He is no longer a threat to us."

Alyona joined them as Sulanna finished her sentence, scanning the landscape warily, crossing the road at Branimir's back. Tyr's heavy footfalls were close behind her. She had asked them to wait another hour before risking the much-needed drink from the river; but Sulanna and Alden refused to stay hidden in the tall grasses any longer. Regardless, the hour had grown late enough to sift most of the traffic from the road's breadth.

"We were right to leave. You would have been either dead or back in a dungeon if we would have stayed," Alyona said. "Right now, our purpose is to get Branimir to *Iriy*, no matter Falmagon's fate. The gods will set our feet on the right path to end this madness."

"I hope so," Sulanna said. "I do not know how much more madness I can stomach. I have seen enough death to last me a lifetime."

Alyona sighed, addressing Tyr, "You should know Eisliev will be returning from the Netherworld—again—for *kaelandur*." She paused, biting her lip. "And Dagmar, too."

"Wait. Dagmar was killed with *kaelandur*?" Tyr asked with a shiver, the suggestive tone in his voice was nearly insolent.

"No one is at fault," Alyona said. "He killed himself with *kaelandur*."

Tyr scratched his scraggily red hair. "We will need to get to *Iriy* before we cross paths with either of the murderers."

Branimir snappily cut him off. The sound of Eisliev calling him a murderer rang in his ears. The color of blood filled his vision. "You are as guilty of murder as Eisliev is! You let that child be killed."

Tyr tensed, his chest flexing in restraint. He wrapped his six fingers into a fist at his side. "You do not know anything about Eisliev and I, or what we have done. I cannot say he was the most honorable, but he was my friend."

Branimir was taken back from the biting response, searching Tyr's blue eyes. His words cut deeper than he expected; he had not expected the Ispolini to attack him. Bran stumbled to find the words to ask forgiveness for his brashness. "I—"

Tyr glowered at Branimir, continuing, "Understand, I did not want Bohumir dead, but I will not be held responsible for the boy's death. Maybe I could have stopped Eisliev from slaughtering him, but from what I can tell, you could have done the same."

"You knew what he intended." Branimir's jaw trembled, smelling the burnt flesh of Bohumir. He could not shake the memory. "You did not see the violent way he slaughtered that innocent child and flung him into the flames."

"No, I did not," Tyr admitted. "But I did not throw him to the flames. What I have done is travel halfway across the world to take you into the Shade Fells." He shook his head at Branimir in disgust. The look on Tyr's face nearly made Branimir apologize, but he held his tongue. "You have the right to be angry. Believe me, no one knows anger more than me, but you best direct it to someone more deserving."

Branimir clenched his teeth, looking for a rebuttal, but his mind was mush. He attempted to distract himself by looking up and down the wide road. Of course, the path was not *completely* empty. Carts continued to rumble in the distance, identifying the coming travelers. They could not stay on the road much longer.

Alyona opened her mouth to intervene, while Alden and Sulanna stared at them with concern.

He kept her from speaking, finding the words to attack Tyr once more. "Where is Dorofej? Alyona said he was with you?"

Tyr rumbled, looking to Alyona uneasily "He was; but he was insistent on getting to *Iriy*."

Branimir searched the giant's face for any hint of deceit. "Instead of coming for us in Eldhaft? Why would he leave us to suffer at the end of Dagmar's and Falmagon's hand?"

"He did not know." Tyr's angled his brow. "When Dorofej and I split outside of Sorod, he said he found Sulanna, Alyona, and Adamus outside of Eldhaft. He never saw you, half pint." Tyr scratched at his head, his eyes falling to Branimir's hand where *Faegrim* rested. "I honestly thought you would be halfway to *Iriy* by now. It was a surprise that you were held up in Eldhaft."

"We had complications," Alyona said.

"I can see that," Tyr said with a frown, directing his eyes away from Branimir. He looked at Alden suspiciously. "I expect you to have more questions for me, half pint. But I, too, have questions. I recognize Sulanna by her description, but this is not Adamus Ebordon."

"Alden Forgaaf," Alden introduced himself. "Adamus is dead."

"I am sorry," Tyr said with heavy eyes. Though, he sounded almost relieved to change the topic. "I do recognize your name from the Crimson Sun." Tyr rubbed his chin. "You and Sulanna were frequently spoken of among many, including Seigfeld and Farthr."

"You are with the Crimson Sun?" Alden narrowed his gaze.

"I joined them with Eisliev after you had long been gone. We worked under Teodor Bacheva," he gestured at Branimir, "until they killed him in Cavell. You may have met his father in Eldhaft. My plan was to find Master Bacheva before the *Guardians* stopped me at the gate."

"You are lucky you did not," Alyona said.

An awkward exchange of disorderly facial features and unsystematic murmurs resounded as Alden, Sulanna, and Tyr jammed the pieces of their mixed histories together. Their roads were nearly as entangled as a tumbleweed.

Branimir tensed with frustration, realizing the topic split away from Dorofej. His heart raced with anticipation.

He remembered the Ispolini to be rough around the edges when they crossed paths before, but he did not plan to back down from the giant. If Tyr believed Eisliev to be a friend, he may betray them, even if Alyona were honest.

After several minutes, when none of them rerouted the conversation back to Dorofej, Branimir broke up the muddled fuss. "Tyr, would you like to explain *why* Dorofej is not with you?"

"I don't have a reason, Branimir. Dorofej asked me to attempt to reach you before you reached the Shade Fells in hopes of being of some help through the mountains. He did not say why he chose a different path. Though, from your brief recount, Eldhaft does not seem the safest place for Dorofej to travel," Tyr said. "If he had crossed Falmagon, while they held you captive…"

"You mean he was saving his own skin by leaving me to die?" Branimir fumed. "That cannot be the reason."

Tyr scrunched his face with irritation. "I would be glad to tell you more of what I know once we make camp. Not all of us hide as well as others, and the road will not remain safe."

Alyona sided with him. "We need to move on anyway and find a place to rest. I am not restoring you four with *Koldovstvo* for the next month until we reach *Iriy*."

Branimir took a final drink, watching Tyr. He hoped he was not buying time to make up a better story. He hated to think Tyr to be untruthful, because, conclusively, it meant Alyona could be lying as well. The Ispolini returned the gaze, and rubbed his jawbone as though it pained him to keep his mouth clenched.

Alden heaved Sulanna up from the riverbank, and minutes later they headed west into the tall grasses outlining the road. Covering their tracks in the Gaetana Grasslands would have been impossible if it were not for Alyona. For almost a quarter mile, she weaved *Koldovstvo* to realign the trampled greensward, including the wildflowers. Her hair continued to grey from the effort, but when Branimir showed concern, she claimed the magic was necessary to keep them safe. The path behind looked completely untouched.

For several miles, they walked.

Branimir's memory was overwhelmed in the silence. He thought of the Netherworld and the demons walking across the frozen wasteland. At the time, their grating and groaning was a constant ambiance that nearly drove him and Dorofej mad. As he thought of the bone-chilling sound, the noise distorted in his head, matching Adamus's screams from when the Ariadnean's leg was skinned at *Harrowhal.* The thought brought tears to Branimir's eyes. He had turned his head when Adamus had been tortured, unable to watch, but the pained cries could not have been ignored.

"Branimir!" Sulanna shouted. "Where are you?"

He blinked the memory away, turning around in the grassy fields to face Alden and Sulanna behind him. He must have accidently disappeared while they were walking with Tyr and Alyona. He rematerialized. "I am here."

"You scared me," Sulanna weakly said. "Don't do that."

Branimir rubbed the back of his neck in confusion, unsure of how he had unintentionally vanished.

Alden raised an eyebrow at Branimir, and scratched his bald head. However, instead of commenting on his strange behavior, Alden changed the topic. "Once my belly is filled, I will be more than keen to travel to *Iriy.* I have wanted to stand before those I have given reverence; and I would like to know what path will lead me to Thrice Ten Kingdom if Wolos is truly dead. I want to know why we should serve gods if they can be slain by mortal men." Alden took the edge of the green cloak he wore and rubbed the sweat from his brow. "Is that not the story as we understand? Two Stuhian asses slaughtered Wolos in a battle at *Anaerfell?*"

"Ye—yes. Dagmar's sons, so it seems," Branimir said. He found himself having difficulty staying calm since leaving Eldhaft; his heart was thudding in his chest. Still, he could recall what Dagmar said at *Harrowhal.* "He confirmed what Erzebeth told me at *Garain'l.*" He jumped suddenly at the memory of the Likhyi at the old ruins.

"Are you okay?" Alden asked.

Branimir bobbed his head, taking a deep breath. "We must keep *kaelandur* from the Ash Tree."

He decided not to expand on the story. Though, he knew the undead Vucari did plan to release those same brothers from their northern prison with the aid of *Lahmia,* a three-headed white dragon. He could not be certain on the full scheme, but the dragon had appropriated Branimir's shiny stone, *Ojenek*, for the quest. Erzebeth believed the brothers could be sent into the Netherworld to see the God of the Dead reborn.

Branimir understood the plot to be the only real hope of saving Aenar. Without Wolos born-again, the dead would continue to walk on Aenar, regardless if the *old-dark* were freed from the Ash Tree.

Alden scratched at his scalp, and would have likely pulled at his hair if he had any worth tugging. "What would lead these men to such folly?"

"I would imagine the same vices leading all men to recklessness," Tyr offered, stamping at the ground. "Power, greed, envy…love."

"Love is not evil," Branimir said.

"Nothing is evil on its own, but, in excess," Tyr said, hovering over Branimir, "all things can lead us to do what we never thought we could. I know as well as any other."

Branimir cowered under the brutal gaze of Tyr, his light, oval eyes widening. His lips parted as though he might add something more, but Alden interjected with a grumble. "Seeking to physically kill a god is not something anyone with any decency would *think* of doing."

Sulanna groaned. "Can we please not dissect the minds of gods tonight? I do not have the energy to listen to it."

Alden hummed in agreement.

In time, the tall grasses did lessen, the road between Eldhaft and Gavloc completely disappeared, and Branimir saw distant trees on the horizon. Branimir's legs ached around the time Alyona finally gave the signal to break for camp.

Alden was the first to sprawl out on the grass, laying out on his back, and sucking in the cooling night air so noisily Branimir could hear it whistling through his teeth. Sulanna crumpled in a heap next to him; her hand reposing over his chest. Alden tilted his head to look at her with a questioning look, but she had closed her eyes.

He turned to Branimir instead for an explanation.

Branimir did not even have the strength to shrug at the old warrior. Instead, he sat at the bottom of the hill they just passed over, and settled against the incline. Clouds blanketed out the moon with coming night, but the weather stayed as timid as it had hours earlier.

"We can build a fire once we have something to cook, but we should otherwise douse it for the night," Alyona said, removing her cloak, and then slipping off her boots. She unloosed the strings on her pants next, letting them fall to the ground. She sniffed the air. "I will go see what is stirring in the brush; I should be able to find a couple rabbits out here."

Tyr's eyes crossed, turning his head from the half-naked *Kadari*. "Why you must remove your clothes to hunt?"

Alden jolted his head off the ground to gawk at the nude woman, almost stirring Sulanna, who already drifted into a deep sleep. His blue eyes broadened until they could not stretch any further.

Alyona scarcely noticed, pulling her shirt off over her head. She then tilted her head at Tyr, and folded her hands under her breasts. "Really?"

"You are no more a savage than I am," he said plainly.

"Nor am I human," she said with a wry smile. "Keep them safe. I will return soon."

Alyona briskly changed from human to animal, holding their attention. Her bones broke and folded, while black, silk fur waved across her skin like a breeze rippling over water. She slumped to all fours, maintaining her balance—her hands and feet erupting into oversized paws paired with retractable claws; and then, she suddenly sprouted a long, thick tail from her back, inches above her waistline. Her neck thickened and cracked; her pale face lost its color, restructuring to parallel the visage of an oversized cat, budding the same black coat as her skin. Alyona had become a panther.

Branimir sat up to meet her brown eyes, widening beneath her cup-shaped ears. Her tongue licked at the air, and then she was gone, dashing into the tall grasses.

"By the gods," Alden said weakly, resting his head back against the dry grass. "What is she?"

Tyr replied, swallowing hard. "A skin-switcher. I thought her kind had all died ages ago."

"She does have Vucari blood," Branimir explained, eyeing Tyr with concern, "but she is also Stuhian. I do not think she holds any commitment to the Vucari or the old ways besides the skin-switching."

Tyr shook his head, blankly staring off into the darkness. He seemed to notice Branimir's concern. "My father said the Vucari were a plague to the Stuhians for a long time, but they never threatened my people. I have rarely heard stories where a Vucari could be trusted."

Alden delicately moved Sulanna from his chest. She curled into a ball, turning away from him. Her breaths were deep as she dreamed. Alden forced himself to sit up and folded his legs. "How do you know her, Branimir? Can she be trusted?" he asked.

Branimir scrunched his nose at the complexity of the question, and finally rubbed his hooked nose as though it itched. After a moment, he nodded his head, answering partially to spite Tyr's concern. "I think we can trust her, Alden."

"How long have you known her?" Alden asked.

Folding his hands in his lap, Branimir realized he never told Alden about his adventures with Dorofej in the Netherworld, his old life at Melkorka, or given him any real indication of his age. Branimir trusted Alden but did not see the need to share the over-told story, especially with Tyr in their company. "A long, long time," he smiled.

Alden accepted the answer with a simple nod. He pulled Adamus's steel axe from his belt and sat it in front of his crossed legs. Rubbing his lips with the back of his hand, he said, "I suppose we should talk about what we do next. I do not know where to find *Iriy* in the Shade, but Alyona said earlier the journey would take about a month. We do not have the supplies or the coin to gain the supplies to survive a month."

"We could get supplies at Gavlok," Branimir suggested.

"Gavlok is closest. Any other place would add weeks if not more to our journey," Alden replied. "We would have to backtrack and the risk of being found by the *Guardians* or Falmagon would only increase."

Tyr grunted. "Gavlok will not be safe. It would be the first place any of them would search for you."

Alden scratched the wrinkled skin of his scalp. "You are right, but what other choice do we have?"

"There must be another settlement between here and the Shade?" Branimir asked.

Tyr met Alden's eyes as though he were debating whether to share a secret, and then sighed. "Out there, Branimir, you will only find the whispers of myth. Most would not dare risk travel under the shadow of the Shade Fells. The woods are unexplored, the terrain is barren, and the closer you roam, the more likely you will come across demons fleeing from the Deep. Not to mention, we will be facing wyrms gliding above the mountain peaks, large enough to blot the skies."

Branimir looked at Tyr with curiosity. "What is the Deep?"

Tyr answered, "The underearth. Paths upon paths of underground tunnels twist and turn, leading to the Netherworld and beyond. And, among other demons, the very enemies to my people, the Witiko, pack its paths like a plague."

"You have seen the dragons and Witiko? You have been to the Shade before?" he asked. Branimir did not remember seeing anything called a Witiko when traipsing through the Netherworld with Dorofej, but the two had not exactly sat around recording every species of demon either.

"I am from Tundris Mor, an island south of the Shade Fells," Tyr paused to take a breath. He rubbed at his red hair. "My people have fought dragons for eons. And yes, I have been within the Deep of the Shade and I have battled the demons therein."

"I am not afraid of demons," Branimir said, "or dragons."

Alden cleared his throat, folding his hands back over his knees. "You have courage lost to most men."

Tyr's pitched gaze sang of admiration. "I have not come across many half pints in my life, but I must agree. I admit your steadfastness is honor-worthy."

Branimir grimaced, waving off the compliments. The Ispolini had not answered his questions regarding Dorofej, and he had not forgotten. "Can we speak of Dorofej now?" Branimir asked. "I think we are far enough from the road for you to give us an explanation."

"Certainly," Tyr said. "Dorofej and I traveled as far as Sorod when he sent me to find you."

"Why?" Branimir almost shouted, fumbling to sit up straighter against the hill.

"Wha—" Sulanna stirred with a gasp, turning over on her side in a rush.

She did not have the chance to say any more with Branimir's words flooding from his mouth. "Why did he stay at Sorod? Is he still there?"

Tyr frowned, shaking his head.

Sulanna's heavy eyes revealed her exhaustion. "Hold on. Are we supposed to head to *Iriy* or not? I thought Alyona said Dorofej would make it there before us." She half-heartedly eyed the area, pushing her hair behind her ear. "Where is Alyona anyway?"

"Hunting," Tyr said off-handedly to Sulanna, and then continued. "Alyona did not lie to you. Dorofej would have reached *Iriy* by now and will be waiting for us."

"You are making no sense," Alden muttered, running his hands down his cheeks. "You just said he was at Sorod. That is almost two weeks in the opposite direction."

The Ispolini snorted impatiently. "Sorod has a temple with a secret gate leading to Rujan. The High Priest has used this passage for thousands of years to travel to *Iriy* and speak to their god. Dorofej said he would use the gate to reach *Iriy*."

"Rujan?" Branimir jarred his memory. He completely missed the end of Farthr's sentence, recalling when Dorofej had told him about the Svet's Four-Faced, God of War. But, more importantly, he remembered when he traveled through Sorod during his first trip to Maharia—a memory he often regretted—and the High Priest who consulted with the Oracle by walking through the magical, underground door. "Remember when we were on the boat to Talastein, Alden? Sulanna? One of the shipmates said Rujan is called Svathevit the Red. They say the God of War has the power to call back Gebereht from Thrice Ten Kingdom to save Aenar. Has Gebereht come back from the dead, too?"

"I do not know anything about any human named Gebereht," Tyr said.

"He was from Ariadne," Alden said, intently shaking his head as he spoke. "At least, he took the name of Gebereht during Ariadne's greatest victories. Some believe he is truly Kowin the Deathless, detained by Svarog in Thrice Ten Kingdom. He cannot be killed by any regular means; his soul is kept separate from his body in a needle, hidden somewhere on this earth."

"Are we talking about the gods again? I cannot believe I was woken up for this rubbish," Sulanna mumbled, rubbing her eyes. She turned on the three of them. "By the Nine Lands, have you three been this tangential the entire time I have been asleep? Stay focused, or I swear, by the gods, I will run each of you through."

"I thought you did not believe in the gods?" Alden's mouth twisted into a smile.

"And I thought you cut your arms whenever you displeased your illusory puppeteers," Sulanna shot back with a whimsical lift of a single eyebrow.

Alden held the grin on his face. "I thought I would try something else…at least, until I know whether I have a guide to cross the Thrice Nine Lands."

Sulanna held her jaw tight to keep from smiling. "Alden Forgaaf, I said to stay on topic."

"So Dorofej fled to *Iriy* and left us at Eldhaft," Branimir concluded. From the time he had known Dorofej at Melkorka to their time in the Netherworld to their journey last year, Dorofej always pledged to stay alive. If the black mage feared anything, it was his own death. But Branimir would never have guessed Dorofej to leave him in a dungeon to be tortured.

"I told you, he did not know you were in danger, Branimir," Tyr said. "He was eager to speak with the gods."

Turning his gaze to the field, bright as day to his peculiar eyes, Branimir noticed movement in the field. He awkwardly recoiled, startling himself, before realizing it was Alyona. He was not sure what he expected, but quickly calmed, meeting her flat expression. She tossed a handful of dead rabbits and a fox to the dirt, and then reached for her garments still lying in the grass.

"Or, he was saving his own skin," Alyona said, echoing Branimir's thoughts, while she clothed herself again. "He would be safe at *Iriy* from Eisliev. It is holy ground."

Sulanna squinted at the naked woman, moving her mouth with an unspoken question before snapping her lips closed.

"Listen," Tyr said, "Dorofej is at *Iriy*. He will be waiting among the gods. He and I spoke, at length, about the *old-dark* and what you had seen at *Garain'l*." Tyr gave a throaty growl, organizing his thoughts. "You have been urged to make haste."

"Then we should travel back to Sorod through the gate that he used. The way is half the distance," Branimir said.

"The Svet would rip us to pieces coming into their Holy Lands," Tyr argued.

Sulanna blinked, pulling her long knife from her belt and reaching for Alyona's catch with the intent to skin their supper. "I don't understand. Dorofej made it through the gate, right?"

"If you think you can reason with the centaurs?" Tyr said.

Alden shook his head. "I don't think that would be wise."

"If we found Farthr, maybe," Sulanna muttered.

Alyona reached for her boots after adorning her other clothes. "Traveling east will only lead us into the hands of the *Guardians*, or Falmagon and the other *Kadari*. I think we stand a better chance going into the Shade."

Branimir did not see how demons and dragons were a better alternative to thieves and the *Kadari*.

"We still need coin. We need supplies," Alden said definitively. "We will not make it far without horses and food."

Branimir clasped his hands together until his fingers hurt, and exhaled. "We will go to the Shade. Tomorrow, we will start for Gavlok to get what we need. I have buried silver we can use for supplies."

Chapter XIV

Branimir was certain they traveled two or three times slower through the tall grasses than they might on the main road and taking the extra time to rest had not helped them cover much ground. But Alyona and Tyr insisted the extra rest would do Branimir, Alden, and Sulanna some good. In the meantime, Alyona led them, snaking back and forth in case they were being followed. The entire process had been dully slow.

Alden and Sulanna's soft tones were comforting to Branimir's ears as he marched ahead of them, and behind Tyr and Alyona. Branimir peeked over his shoulder, unnoticed by the two humans behind him, caught up in their own musings.

"I am surprised by your change of view of the Svet. At one time, every conversation about them was filled with scorn," Sulanna said, her fingers woven between Alden's as they walked. "Remember how quick you were to denounce the Svet and their Holy Lands? Now, I suspect you might even be eager to rescue the heathens."

"Farthr was a brother-in-arms. That is all that I said," Alden claimed, clearly surprised at her prodding.

Sulanna lifted her eyebrow. "Was that all? I heard a lot more in that simple statement."

"Do all women from Eldhaft woo their men by labeling their failings, or have I been furtively blessed? I promise you I have spent more time than most listing my many shortcomings," Alden forced a chuckle. Sulanna impishly glanced up at him before elbowing him in the ribs. Alden grunted, stumbling to the side, but refusing to release his grasp on her hand. He drew close again. "Alright," he said in defeat, returning the earnest gaze. "While imprisoned by the Lilitu, I had time to reflect on my limited understanding of the world. And when I was reunited with you in *Harrowhal*," he shifted his eyes to the horizon, speaking with a hint of humility, "I confirmed what I had considered..."

Alden drifted off, wrinkling his forehead in deep thought. Sulanna nudged him to continue, her features suddenly solemn at mention of *Harrowhal*. The torturous scenes of the dungeon would forever linger with them. "Tell me."

The older warrior shrugged. "I realized that we are all caged in this life. We are destined to live and die, but nothing else is truly guaranteed. Sure, faith may promise something more, but faith is not as tangible as the people who suffer alongside us. Many have suffered next to me," Alden said.

"Isn't that why it is called faith?" she said, her voice cracking. Her face flushed upon seeing Alden being honest with her. His words were counter to the theology he had defended for generations. Sulanna pulled him closer to her.

Alden went on, "You must hear me. The Lilitu do not understand the gods of Maharia; the Uvil have no account of them. The Svet worship their own, and I am not even certain the Kras would know what gods were if humans had not enslaved them centuries ago. And what about the other races of the world—living or dead—what do they believe? How about the more ancient pantheons, like the *old-dark*?"

"I don't know," Sulanna admitted.

Alden rattled on as though she had not said a word. "I believe in the gods. I can't *not* believe in them." Alden took a breath. "But I do not know the nature of gods outside of what men have preached. I have spent my entire life following the *trusted* words of men, who I presumed to be wiser." Alden took a deep breath, sucking in the morning air to calm his nerves. "It is okay. I know you don't believe in them, Sulanna."

Branimir felt the urge to join them, and slowed his pace so they may gain on his position. He watched Alyona tilt her ear with interest from the far-front, but she kept her nose facing forward.

"I believe in the gods," Sulanna replied, clasping his hand between her own. "I just don't think they have done anything worth praising."

"What about your life?" Alden asked.

"A violent father, an executed brother, and with so many friends now dead…" Sulanna's voice wavered, her gaze steady on the warrior beside her. "I am not sure what good can be found in the torment."

Alden responded after a moment. "Svarog has given me too much strength in my life to turn away from him, as they might to any who suffer. But we know many routes lead to unearthing courage. The promise of glory. An oath of loyalty. The blessing of friendship. A vow of love."

An unintentional grin split Sulanna's face. She looked for an explanation for her sudden release. She turned to her crude humor. "In another life, you might tell me all *those* things are meaningless without your gods."

"And today," Alden shrugged, "In absence of any of these things, the gods do not exist; in fact, the gods may very well be *those* things."

Alyona flipped her short, greying hair over her thin shoulder, calling out to them as she skirted through the greens and yellows of the tall grasses. "Yes, we all live and die for the same truths; only the names by which we call them divide us." She yanked a strand of grass from the dirt as she cut her own path for them to follow. Her next words were mumbled, "Sad to think humans spend their entire lives trying to grasp the concept of unity, if they ever figure it out at all."

"Branimir!" Sulanna suddenly shouted. "Branimir, where are you?"

He spun around to face her, realizing he was invisible again. He rematerialized.

"I am right here," Bran said, pulling at his nose with irritation. When he had journeyed with Dorofej in the Netherworld, he spent most of his time hidden from sight. He wondered if that had anything to do with his sudden disappearing when his mind wandered. He knew he was struggling to keep his thoughts from bad memories. "I am sorry."

"How many times is that now, today? Three?" Alden asked. "Are you sure you are feeling alright?"

"I am just having a hard time focusing." Branimir bit the inside of his cheek, and nodded. "Let's keep going."

The next several hours were quiet. The five of them rested midday about two miles from a cluster of trees to the west, an equal distance from the main road to the east. Branimir could not see or hear anything in the distance to suggest danger, and Alyona, too, said nothing.

Yet with the silhouettes of the Shade Fells increasing in height since morning, the blotches of grass had become more sporadic, scattered across the bumpy terrain in uneven clumps. If needed, Branimir doubted they would be able to find concealment.

A few hours later, their trudging rustled up a covey of quail for an afternoon meal. Before long, they were kicking dirt over the fire and picking the greasy meat off bones. After the meal, Branimir could finally claim his strength had fully returned since *Harrowhal*.

Alden and Sulanna also acquired an undeniable, youthful vigor; though, Branimir doubted it had anything to do with the rest or sustenance. The two, separated by maybe fifteen years, intrigued him. They each talked to Branimir with affection toward the other, but he only recently began to understand how deeply they felt.

Never knowing love, or even affection, in his own life, Branimir had difficulty keeping his eyes from the blossoming relationship. Alden and Sulanna fought and journeyed together for years, always bound by their duty and their undying ideologies. And now, with the world slipping from existence, they had torn down the fictitious shade of rigidity in hopes of finding something more binding.

Branimir wondered why so many looked to the horizon for some lofty meaning in their life when the answer stood so near. Life was not about discovering something new, but molding what was already had.

They were nearing Gavlok near nightfall when a sense of uneasiness churned in Branimir's stomach. He caught up with Alyona. The woman changed since Gaetana from casting *Koldovstvo*. She had extra lines around her eyes, and her hair had faded; still, she appeared healthier than most *Kadari* who he had seen cast magic. He quickly thought of a question to ask her, even though he already knew the answer. "How many vials of the Water of Life were you able to pull off Dagmar?"

Alonya pulled her hooded, black cloak to the side to reveal the belt with the three vials hanging from the leather strappings. "I am saving them for the journey ahead."

"You think you will need them in the Shade? Tyr said we might cross demons and dragons," Branimir said, looking over his shoulder. The Ispolini made his way back to Alden and Sulanna about an hour ago.

She lifted her shoulders, moving the cloak back across her waist. "I have not been to the Shade since before Shayol Domier. We will not find anything worse there than what was found in the Netherworld."

"But your magic was limitless in the Netherworld," said Branimir.

"It was," Alyona said, "but I am not helpless. Dorofej asked for me to lead you to *Iriy* for more than one reason, Branimir." He waited in silence for her to explain. She shifted her purple eyes in his direction, and sighed, noticing his silent anticipation. "You did not know my father. His name was Meimer Gounari, a Stuhian from Lairhein. My mother was Erzebeth Navenka."

"Erzebeth?" Branimir squinted at her in disbelief. "How is that possible?"

"The story of the Stuhians and Vucari would take me more than a month to explain to you, Bran," Alyona said softly. "When my mother and father met, the two races were not warring as they have for past centuries; in fact, they had a similar task as Wardens of the Ash Tree. Birthed by Wolos, the Vucari and Stuhia kept each other balanced, having access to eternal life through the Waters of Life as long as they kept the Ash Tree protected.

"When I was nine-years-old, the Stuhians splintered away from the Vucari to gain the power we know as *Koldovstvo* by revering Marheena. Wolos was furious that his *dragon men* betrayed his blessings, and called for a gathering. I attended with my mother and father to *Iriy*," she continued while Branimir listened intently. "Wolos's will was absolute. Stuhians were cursed; those who wielded *Koldovstvo* had their life drained, and their station as Warden was stripped. The Vucari, who remained Wardens, were also punished for not maintaining the balance with the Stuhians. The Vucari who disagreed with Wolos's will were perverted by twisted magic and turned to Vulkodlak."

"The wolf-men and wolf-women," Branimir said, recalling the monstrous beasts he once faced in the Hyaendi Hills. He blinked a couple times, trying to make sense of Alyona's tale. "It has been a long time, but I do remember Erzebeth telling me about when she became a Warden and learned of the Ash Tree. I cannot say yours and her story are the same."

"Did she tell you these stories before or after her death?" Alyona asked the rhetorical question with a knowing look. "Dorofej told me you met my mother's ghost in the tombs of *Garain'l*, and even then, she aimed to correct some of what she had told you while living."

"I don't understand," Branimir said. "Why would she lie?"

Alyona kicked at the ground. "She did not know she was lying in life. Death brings knowledge of the world, and magic, and the gods which is hard to understand while living."

"How has she lived on after death?" Branimir asked.

Alyona hummed in response. "She is a Warden, protecting the Ash Tree in life and death." Alyona tilted her head, and added, "She held to her onus, abandoning my brother and me with my father after the divide between the two races. It doesn't matter. I would have chosen to stay with my father anyway."

Branimir gritted his teeth at the thought.

"My father was a good man. He is the reason I went to Shayol Domier and followed Moreth," Alyona said banally. The two passed over another hill with Alden, Tyr, and Sulanna following somewhere behind. Alyona went on, "Anyway, the Ninth Council was created among the Stuhians to fabricate a lie to keep their civilization functioning. Even today, I imagine most still think they are blessed by Wolos, even though they are the very ones who betrayed him. When the Ninth Council was created, the Carian Council preceding them was slaughtered, save one."

"Dorofej. He was on the Carian Council." Branimir filled in the blank. "How old is he?"

"Old," she laughed. "At least, a thousand years older than me. That book you pulled from Dagmar at *Harrowhal* is his tome, dictating the ancient magics and history of the Vucari and Stuhian races. From what I can tell, Dagmar distorted much of what was written for his own benefit. I am assuming you plan to return it to Dorofej?"

Branimir nodded. "Of course. He told me he had written it. I thought the best thing to do would be to give it to him."

Alyona looked off into the grasses for a moment, not responding to the statement. Branimir wondered if she thought otherwise.

"So, why did Dorofej want you to lead me to *Iriy*?" he asked. "Because you have been there before?"

"Yes, and," Alyona lingered for a moment, "Besides having a sacred bloodline, I can also handle more *Koldovstvo* than most Stuhians. Like Dorofej, I drank the blood of a dragon to gain more power."

Branimir bit his inner lip, nearly crossing his eyes at Alyona in shock.

"You surely have noticed Dorofej can do *things* other mages could never attempt?" Alyona lifted an eyebrow with a taunting smile.

"I thought maybe the flow of *Koldovstvo* had been diluted over time, or repetitive uses of the Ash Tree kept him from aging as much," Branimir said wondrously, running his hands through his hair. "But drinking the blood of a dragon. Nine Lands." He could not believe the secrets Dorofej kept from him. "Do you even need the vials at your belt?"

Alyona moved her cloak to the side again to reveal the Water of Life containers. "These may be the only thing saving any of us from a final death."

Branimir caught his breath. For some reason, he thought Alyona would use the Water of Life to replenish her own life, to help her funnel additional *Koldovstvo* during battle. He never considered that she might use the liquid on someone else.

Branimir stammered over his question as she moved the cloak back across her waist. "Would one of those flasks have brought Adamus back?"

"Not unless his spirit miraculously stayed in his body," she answered. Her purplish eyes met his. "I am sorry you lost your friend, Branimir."

The itch in Branimir's throat came quicker than he had anticipated. He may have been suffering from gaining too much knowledge at once.

He coughed and sputtered to keep himself from breaking down. "Like you, I have watched a lot of people die in my life, but nothing like what happened to Adamus…" he trailed off to find his words. He gulped, blinking back the salty water in corner of his eyes. "You don't often find a friend like him."

"He seemed like a good man," Alyona conceded. "I would have liked to know him better."

"He had family in Ariadne. A sister," Branimir said suddenly, pulling at his nose. "I think I will return to them when this is over and…I don't know…maybe help them if I can."

Alyona placed her hand on his shoulder. "You have a good heart, Branimir Baran. But we may not survive the ending to this tale either."

Chapter XV

The hour was well past dusk when they reached the edge of Gavlok, silhouetted along the winding river. The mediocre town did not have fortifying walls; but it was not completely unguarded, defended with numerous, wooden watchtowers on the outskirts. Branimir scanned the base of the towers and what he could of the streets from their vantage point. Nothing appeared out of the ordinary.

At two-hundred paces, he kneeled, picking at the edge of his chin in thought. Alden, Tyr, and Sulanna, of course, could not see anything in the moonless night, but Alyona squatted beside him staring at the town with equal interest. Branimir talked in a shushed tone, "I hoped we would have come earlier in the day. Nothing is going to be open this late."

Alden jerked his head up and down, but did not seem to be listening to Branimir. "Do you see any of the *Guardians* or sign of the *Kadari*," he asked, gesturing to the watchtowers. "And what about the guards?"

"They have men in the towers as they should," Alyona answered for Branimir. She ran her hand through her hair, addressing Alden. "We do not have any reason to sneak into town."

"Unless the *Guardians* or *Kadari* are close, waiting to ambush us," Tyr said gruffly. "We gave them plenty of time to reach Gavlok."

Alyona scrunched her nose. "Why would either of them be waiting here? We have spent nearly five days walking through the grasslands without any sign of life. I imagine if they came to Gavlok, and saw we were not there, they would have returned to Eldhaft or even to Vucan."

"They may have thought we were going into the lands of the Svet," Sulanna said, reflecting on Alyona's argument. She rocked her head back and forth like she was physically bouncing the idea around. "Falmagon might even think we were aiming to meet Dorofej."

Branimir rubbed his brow. Even at *Harrowhal*, they had not mentioned anything to Dagmar, Falmagon, or Myrthos about going to *Iriy*. So, if Falmagon did not know they were traveling to the City of the Gods, he would not think of Dorofej using the secret gateway to the Svet's Oracle. "They have a point, Tyr."

"What tavern did you say you stayed at?" Sulanna asked.

"*The Oaken Bard*," Branimir said, scratching at the thin hair hanging to his eyes. "The owner is Deak Armin. His father died a year or so before I arrived, and Deak inherited the place. I never knew him to keep the doors open too late."

"What type of inn has a closing time?" Alden muttered, gripping the long spear lying next to him. "People are known to pass through at all hours."

"Gavlok has never been known for heavy foot-traffic, Alden," Branimir replied.

"He is right," Sulanna said. "Remember when we were sent to Lonmere to quell that uprising five years ago? When we passed through Gavlok, we ended up sleeping outside in the mud due to everything being closed."

Alden grunted in response.

Alyona pulled her hood over her head, sliding back behind the hill. "Staying out here for the night may be the smartest move for us, too. We will not gain anything by approaching the city this late besides suspicion."

"I agree," Sulanna said, siding with the *Kadari*. "We will be able to see more at morning's light when the people begin to wake."

"But they will be able to see us better, too, and Tyr isn't going to blend in with the crowd," Branimir replied with a scowl. "If anybody has come looking for us, they have likely defined us in detail. I can hide, but the rest of you cannot. If we are recognized, it will be a fight to get out of Gavlok."

"The same could be said if we go into town tonight, Branimir. We are taking the chance by being here," Alyona claimed. Branimir gave her a wayward look, suggesting he was scheming something better. She took the bait. "What are you suggesting?"

Three years ago, when he emerged from the frozen Netherworld with Dorofej, he brought a bag brimming with coins, shiny stones, and other trinkets he gathered from *Heshayol* and the *Tower of Eresh*. The hoards of treasure he had seen were grander than anything he could have carried in a thousand lifetimes. He could not be sure how long he sifted through the troves before Dorofej could finally pull him away. But the goods Branimir lifted from the Netherworld were special to him. Every single curio, bauble, and gewgaw. Knowing they would have to trade his riches made his chest ache; yet he had no choice if they were going to meet Dorofej.

"I have coin buried here. I will go into Gavlok tonight—alone—and get the buried silver," he began.

"How much do you have?" Alden asked.

"Enough," Branimir answered.

"What are you doing with silver buried halfway across the world from your homeland?" Alden muttered, half under his breath.

"I will get the silver," Branimir repeated, ignoring him and speaking with authority. "You know I can make it and back again without any trouble. I will come right back." He rubbed his fingers together, clicking his thumb against *Faegrim*. "Early tomorrow, we will send Alden and Sulanna to purchase our supplies and horses."

"And what would keep us from being discovered by the guard?" Sulanna asked, adjusting the cloak on her shoulder. "These will not hide our faces well enough."

Branimir revealed his plan with a smile. "Alyona will give each of you one of the vials to restore your youth." Alyona opened her mouth and then closed it, almost appearing wounded. She gazed at Branimir with her half-opened eyes; her concern was only outstripped by Alden and Sulanna's mutual bewilderment. Branimir breathed through his crooked teeth. "This will work," he coaxed. "No one would know them."

"I...I don't know," Sulanna hesitated.

"We may need these vials," Alyona finally said.

Tyr finally spoke up from where he ducked down. "I agree. Using the vials now is not a good idea."

Alden's voice drifted behind her. "To be young again..."

Branimir lifted his hands. "Dorofej must be bringing more vials with him. He would not have left Melkorka without ensuring he had a way to keep his youth."

"We have to make it to *Iriy*," Alyona replied sourly. She probably would have put her hands to her hips if she were not kneeling in the dirt.

Branimir nodded with as much seriousness as he could muster. "I know. And that means we have to get these supplies."

"Okay." Sulanna was the first to hesitantly dip her head in agreement. A second later, Alden followed suit. Alyona conclusively pulled the vials from her belt and handed them to the humans. "We will do it your way, Branimir, but if you are going into Gavlok tonight, I am coming with you."

Moments later, Branimir vanished and was skittering across the heath toward Gavlok with Alyona tucked inside his cloak in her bat-like form. Her little claws hooked into his shirt, scraping lightly against his chest. He almost did not feel it.

With any luck, the short jaunt to grab his hidden treasure and return to the hill where the other three waited would be swift. He abstained from sharing the full account of how he had come by the coins, and besides, Alden, Tyr, and the two women did not seem to care much. All in all, he hoped to leave some of the treasure planted in the dirt.

He did not see a reason why they would have to use everything he brought back from the Netherworld.

Branimir hardly paid attention to the guards he snuck around. From those tarrying at the base of the watchtowers to those ambling down the lone street paths, not a single guard seemed concerned. They waved their torches in the dark aimlessly; their blank faces fully indicating they did not anticipate finding anything out of the ordinary.

If the guards were not tense, it could very well be that Falmagon or the *Guardians* had never come to Gavlok to search for them.

The Oaken Bard was not difficult to find. The long, two-story building stretched off the main road near the center of town by the blacksmith and armor shop. Interlaced logs constructed the mainframe of the inn with two large, paned windows carved into the front of the building like watchful eyes. Similar windows were spaced equally along either side of the building to give patrons a clear view outside, and natural light when the establishment was open. As of now, the lights had been turned dim outside of a fireplace burning in the commons near the back wall. Branimir had forgotten about the oversized fireplace, mirrored after the old hearth fires of past days.

Branimir did not have to creep up to the windows to see inside with his sharp vision. Several bodies were moving around the fire; their voices were faint outside the building, but not so much that Branimir could not hear them.

"Holding all the power in the world, ran out of our home, and now chasing a Kras across the countryside blindly," one of the men muttered before tilting a mug to his lips. "We would be an embarrassment to our forefathers. The *Kadari* are supposed to be ruling this world."

"We are not without power yet, Beryl," said a woman sitting adjacent to him. "Rulers across Maharia, including Kings, still turn to us for counsel while trembling in our wake.

"No," Beryl said, coughing against the liquid in his throat, and pulling at a yellow sash around his waist. "They tremble for Falmagon Sej. Not the *Kadari*. If they had known what we sacrificed at Melkorka to keep them safe, to keep them alive in their *precious*, *little* fantasies, we each would have been given lands. We would all hold the esteem of the Patrician."

"You speak dangerous words," another woman said, wrapping a fresh bandage around her thigh. Branimir recognized her as the *Kadari* he stabbed at Eldhaft. Although invisible, he hunched back from the window as she continued, "The Patrician will be downstairs soon enough; it would be wise for you to change your tune."

"Falmagon is here," Branimir murmured to Alyona inside of his cloak. She squeaked in response as though he would understand the rickety noise.

Beryl harrumphed loudly from inside the building, taking another swig. "The time of the *Kadari* is coming to an end. We can all see that. The world is crumbling with the demons bleeding from the Crags. Dagmar is dead, and we are only a few."

"The *Kadari* have always battled against demons, even when our numbers were trivial," the first woman said. "And Dagmar was not always among our number."

"Kerra is right," Falmagon's voice carried into the commons room from the middle of the stairs. Branimir peered through the window pane at the Patrician. He slipped down the stairs carefully, undoubtedly favoring his many injuries. He cringed, holding his left side with his right hand, while clutching his bandaged, left hand to his stomach. "Our numbers will grow again, and we will push the Bukavac back to the Netherworld. We must only first destroy *kaelandur*, which means we must rid this world of Dorofej Kaligula."

"Then why are we chasing the Kras?" growled Beryl.

"By *Mulafell*," Falmagon cursed, maneuvering off the staircase. "Branimir will lead us to Dorofej."

"Not if we cannot find him," Beryl said. "You had Dorofej in your grasp and he escaped. We could have put an end to this nightmare a long time ago."

Falmagon looked exhausted, dragging himself across the floor to the fireplace. "You know full well why we did not kill Dorofej at Melkorka. We needed *kaelandur*, and none could have predicted Eisliev returning from the Netherworld. None could have predicted his power." Beryl only frowned at the Patrician, before turning back to the fire. Falmagon growled to gain the fellow *Kadari's* attention. "Dagmar is dead. We will now do what is right."

Beryl took another drink and then spit the liquid into the fire. The flames flashed higher, illuminating his face. "Too late. Branimir could be well on his way back to Melkorka by now."

Kerra scoffed, standing from her chair. She moved it to the opposite side of the fire for Falmagon to take a seat. He nodded appreciation, falling into the wooden chair while she talked. "He was seen heading north from Eldhaft. Where else would he have gone?"

Alyona suddenly scratched at Branimir's chest, stealing his attention away from the window. He peeled back his cloak to look at her brown eyes peeking back at him, taking the concealed meaning. Eavesdropping on Falmagon and the

Kadari was not telling him anything he did not already know. And the longer he stayed away from Alden and Sulanna, the greater chance of them coming to look for him, leading them all to being discovered.

He hastened his steps around the side of the building, naturally ducking beneath the windows even when he had no need for the extra precautions. Before long, he reached the rear of *The Oaken Board*, and scanned the area. Sadly, the buildings in Gavlok were not built like those in Eldhaft or Gaetana. The spacing between each structure was wide enough that Branimir would have difficulty hiding his actions from any patrolling guards. Naturally, he was invisible to the naked eye, but anybody passing by would notice a hole being *magically* dug in the hardened dirt.

He pulled his cloak to the side again to remove Alyona from his shirt, cupping her small frame in his hand. She peeped by surprise as he whispered, "Keep watch." He then boosted her into the air with his hands, and watched her flap into the air above him. She circled overhead repeatedly disappearing over the inn only to return again and again.

Branimir ignored her, effortlessly remembering where he buried his treasure. He darted to the edge of the building, faced north, and stepped heel-to-toe twelve steps. Straightaway, he dropped to his knees and started digging at the dirt with his bare fingers. The Season of Warmth kept the ground stiff, but tough skin and nails gave him the leverage to tear into the dirt with minimal difficulty. Although he did not have claws like the demons he faced, Branimir had been born to quarry stones and rocks from the underearth like any Kras. He might as well have been a child sinking their hands into a pie.

Trifling mounds of dirt piled on either side of the hole as he dug. He sank his hands deeper until he was elbow-deep and the dirt had softened, and nothing. Worry crawled into the pit of his stomach about the time his hand grasped hold of the moistened fabric.

He smiled, hearing Alyona's excited squeaks over his head. He looked up to her with a crooked grin, forgetting she could not see him. She flapped over the edge of the building out of sight, about the time he realized he had stopped concentrating and reappeared again.

The thought was fleeting as he wrenched the backpack out of the hole, hearing the clinking of his coins and gems inside. He remembered first collecting them from the *Tower of Eresh* and *Heshayol*. He had not been able to grab all he wanted, and even now, he considered how difficult it would be to go back and collect more.

"Gah!" he groaned. He barely felt the gust of wind that flung him from the ground into the side of the inn. His head cracked against the wooden planks, rattling his head. With a stifled cough, he struggled to gaze up at Falmagon, and several more *Kadari*, who stood triumphantly behind him.

"Branimir Baran," Falmagon said with a deep-rooted laugh, gripping his side. "The Lightbringer does answer prayers."

Chapter XVI

Branimir only had seconds to comb the sky for Alyona's bat-like form before he was dragged inside *The Oaken Bard*. He had been too excited about his shiny stones and lost his concentration. He could not believe he had been so stupid. The door slammed behind him before he saw any sign of Alyona. She could not have fought all the *Kadari* alone. He could only hope she rushed to get Alden, Tyr, and Sulanna to free him.

He frantically eyed the room, counting almost a dozen and a half of *Kadari*. Some bounded down the stairs while others were waiting around the fireplace. The men and women watched him with frozen grins foul enough to drain the color from Branimir's skin.

Beryl, and an equally large man with a greying beard, held his arms in iron fists, hauling him to the center of the room. The lithe woman with the dark hair, called Kerra, pushed chairs and tables out of the way to make room. A few other *Kadari*, who had not been in the commons room earlier, hurried to help her.

Branimir could hear Falmagon's boots smacking against the floorboards behind him; the Patrician maintained a flamboyant recoil to his step, despite his injuries. He whistled between his teeth with delight. Branimir twisted to glare at his old master, but could not see beyond the humans on either side of him.

"Marla," Falmagon clucked, "go reset the wards before we have any other unexpected company. I suspect Branimir's friends are not far away."

A grey-haired woman separated from the crowd. Depending on her use of *Koldovstvo*, she could have been any age. "Patrician, my apologies, but I told you I am not proficient with sacred magic."

"We are aware," Beryl barked, "or half of us wouldn't be limping around here like old geezers."

"I may have the bloodline, Beryl, but I never had a mentor," she barked, pushing around the mouthy *Kadari*. She shifted her eyes to Falmagon. "We do not have any more vials left to restore my life. We do not have vials to restore any of us," she said.

"I appreciate your sacrifice," Falmagon said from behind Branimir. He could hear the Patrician's voice shake, but whether from the fury of being questioned or frustration for their predicament, Branimir could not be sure.

The woman physically tensed, her eyes holding over Beryl's shoulder. "I can maintain them for another hour or two, but we should simply take turns keeping watch."

"We must risk it," Falmagon replied steadily. "Whether Branimir's friends are in waiting, or Eisliev returns for *kaelandur*, we will need forewarning. Men will fail and the magic will not. Go set the wards again."

Branimir frowned, watching Marla circle around.

The door of the tavern banged shut with Marla's exit.

He turned his attention to the scraping chair near the fireplace as the dark-haired lady he stabbed in the leg several days ago pulled herself to her feet. Her blue eyes examined him like butchered meat in the marketplace. "So, this is the red brood who attacked us in Eldhaft?"

"Yes, Kveta," Falmagon grunted. The Patrician hobbled around the left side of Beryl, his hand pressed against the side of his stomach. The two men holding him tightened their grip as though they had divine knowledge of Branimir's imminent misfortune. His mouth dried as he met Falmagon's iced eyes, twinkling under his tangled, brown locks of hair.

Branimir's chin already ached from clasping his mouth closed. His heart rapidly thumped against the inside of his chest, blood pulsating through his veins. He did his best to appear brave—to mask his fear—but Falmagon held no kindness in his eyes. And Branimir did not know the words to entreat the man to reason, to forgiveness, to understanding.

Despite the few passing seconds, the time Branimir spent in the shadow of Falmagon's unblinking scowl felt like an eternity. He unmistakably wanted Branimir to grasp his power in this room with *his Kadari*. He coveted Branimir's subjugation to his will; he intended for Branimir to abandon his hope—to believe Falmagon held absolute control over his insignificant fate.

And, although panic coursed through Branimir like a drunken man's liquor, Falmagon's effort was wasted. For whether Branimir was believed or doubted, hated or loved, or caught and tortured—even to the extent of having his heart carved from his chest—he would never again be a slave.

Kveta emerged next to Falmagon, stooping over so low that Branimir could feel her hot breath on his face. "You think you are smart, knifing folks when they cannot see you? Using your devilish magic in battle? I bet you think you are a brave warrior." She sneered. "You are a coward."

"Kveta…" Falmagon started, as though he might be hurrying her along instead of silencing her.

She cut him off. "Dalibor bled out from the bits because of this little, red brood. Vladan had to be buried with a dagger still lodged in his eye socket," she growled, her thin lips trembling. "And how many of ours did he kill outside Melkorka last year?"

Again, the bearded *Kadari* and Beryl tightened their hold on his arms.

With a flash in her eye, Kveta pulled aside Branimir's cloak and pulled the dagger from the belt. *Kaelandur* stayed hanging from its sheathe around his waist. She barely looked at the copper blade, twisting the iron dagger in her hand. The sharpness of the weapon gleamed in the firelight.

Her free hand grabbed his shoulder roughly, balancing her weight to keep pressure off her bandaged leg. "Should I wedge this in your leg, your eye, or your *dear*, little bits?"

Beryl's blithe snigger robbed the air from Branimir's lungs. "Why choose only one?"

Disbelief and horror seized Bran, his timorous lip quaking with realization. He twisted against the *Kadari* holding him, hardly budging.

He dared to break from Kveta's ghastly expression to look at Falmagon. The twisted smile under the Patrician's mustache screamed of gratification. After *Harrowhal*, he realized how far gone Falmagon truly was. He once thought Falmagon, at least, considered himself decent, but nothing was left of the Highborn Long-Walker.

Nothing could have readied Branimir for the shockwave of pain riddling through his body as Kveta speared him with the dagger. He reacted at instinct, thrashing violently against the two *Kadari* holding him hostage, his wail causing the very flames of the distant fire to waft. He could not pinpoint where she struck him at first, only knowing the pain surged from beneath his belly. The heat of the immediate wound was only diluted by the warmth of the thick blood flowing down his slender leg.

He moaned. Tears descended from his cheeks with heaved sniffles, snorting his slick snot back into his nose and off his upper lip.

Kveta twisted the blade, grating the sharp edge against his femur, isolating the dagger's location. Branimir blubbered softly, catching the saliva on the edge of his tongue, hatefully glaring at the *Kadari* woman.

He gagged in effort to keep his throat from closing, gasping for oxygen. He needed to breathe. He had to shake away the abysmal pain. Inhaling the metallic odor of his own blood, Branimir gazed to Falmagon and exhaled the bitter thoughts flooding his mind. "I *will* kill you! I swear it! Marheena will leave you broken and deformed!"

"I have done all I can to protect Aenar," Falmagon shouted, spit flinging from his lips. Any joviality he may have held left him. "You and Dorofej have enticed demons to plague us for giving glory to the Lightbringer instead of your pathetic, Frozen Witch. We know how you survived the Netherworld. We know how her magic even twisted Alyona and Artemiy from the path of righteousness." Falmagon's faced reddened. "I am the chosen leader of the *Kadari*. Kinhar chose me! Do you think you can rid me from this world? Rid me from record like the thief you are? I will be remembered as a god!"

Branimir puffed his chest, holding himself up on his one good leg, despite Kveta's bulk remaining heavy on his shoulder. He crowed with his reprisal. "I would not steal your name from history. I would tell your story to every ear. History should know you, so the hearts of men are never again rapt by such selfish delusions."

Falmagon shoved himself in front of Kveta, knocking her to the side where another *Kadari* quickly caught her before she fell over. Branimir rocked back with surprise only to be straightened like a sword stabbed in stone. The ire in Falmagon's eye suggested that he noticed nothing, smashing his good fist into Branimir's nose with all his strength.

Branimir's head popped back, the cartilage cracking on the bridge of his hooked nose, spurting crimson from his nostrils. He gasped, snapping his head forward as a second blow connected with his cheekbone.

Falmagon's fury was everything Branimir remembered from his subjugated days at Melkorka. "I will bleed the lies from your lips until all left to be spilt is truth!"

"You are cursed," Branimir faltered, blood dribbling from his lips.

Falmagon screamed between his grinding teeth. The *Kadari* around him stepped away as the tables and chairs lifted from the ground with the power of *Koldovstvo*, only to be smashed to the ground again. The clangor echoed in the commons room as wood splintered and cracked.

"Patrician Sej," a weak voice whispered from the top of the staircase. "Patrician Sej, what is going on down there? My customers are—"

"Master Armin," Falmagon bellowed, fastening his gaze to Branimir, "stay upstairs and remain quiet."

Branimir turned to the staircase.

Frightened whispers reached his ears, listening to his old employer, Deak Armin, urging his patrons back to his rooms while crouching beyond view. The pitter-patter of footsteps could be heard as the customers were shooed back to their rooms.

A moment later, Deak half-heartedly tried to speak to Falmagon again. "Patrician Sej, my Lord, if you could be careful while—"

"Be gone, Master Armin," Falmagon snapped, "or by *Mulafell*, I will have you feeding yourself the embers from your fireplace."

"Ye—yes, my Lord," Deak replied. Briefly, Branimir considered calling out to Deak for help, but the thought was lost when Falmagon brusquely closed the space between them.

Branimir recoiled as Falmagon grabbed his sore chin, wrenching his neck to a curve to force him to look at his insufferable eyes. Branimir squeezed his words through swelling lips. "What do you want?"

His head grew light from the blood endlessly leaking from his leg, making it difficult to hear Falmagon's demands. "Tell me where Dorofej has gone? Is he with you?"

Branimir faintly shook his head in Falmagon's grip.

"We can hang his feet over the fire until there is nothing left but stubs," Beryl said in Branimir's ear. "He will talk to you, Falmagon. He will remember his place."

Kveta sneered over Falmagon's shoulder. "Move aside, my Lord, and I will twist the dagger in his leg. He will know what it means to be enemy to the *Kadari*."

The room buzzed in agreement. Falmagon tore his hand off Branimir's face, snapping his head sideways. He leaned closer until Branimir's bloodied nose touched him. "Maybe I should let Kveta and the others finish you," Falmagon said, holding his injured hand to his stomach. "But I know how to make you talk. You will tell me where to find Dorofej. I will cut his throat. I will destroy…" he moved Branimir's cloak to the side, "*kaelandur*."

Falmagon wrapped his fingers around the copper hilt of *kaelandur*. Acidity touched the edge of Branimir's tongue, his stomach churned. "One more chance. Where is Dorofej?" He could do naught but shake his head. Falmagon scoffed, "Have it your way. Hold him."

He withdrew with *kaelandur* in his hand, turning to face the cackling flames.

The room gyrated. The aching in Branimir's body was tenfold compared to what he suffered at *Harrowhal* when Dagmar removed *kaelandur* from his being. Although he could move his eyes back and forth, and his vision was clear, Branimir's body became as rigid as a gravestone.

He cried out as his inner skeleton pulsated against his muscles. Lashing out at the *Kadari* on either side, Branimir snapped his teeth and slung his head, yearning to be free. His chest burned as though an inferno streamed through his veins.

With palms spread open, his howl quickly turned to a death-chilling scream; the taste of blood lined the glands of this mouth. He felt like he was being torn apart from the inside. The Likhyi was tearing him to pieces without *kaelandur* near his skin.

Shadows formed at the corners of his eyes, clouding the edges of his vision; yet his other senses were heightened. He twisted his neck in time to see Kveta collapse to her knees. Her gurgling buzzed in his eardrums. It sounded as though the Likhyi was ripping her apart, too.

Despite his feverish thrashing, the bearded *Kadari* and Beryl dragged Branimir from Kveta's body to the front door of the inn. Although they pressed solidly against the timber, he swore he could feel the sting of lashes striking against his back.

He screeched like a diseased animal.

Falmagon sprang from Kveta, collapsing to his knee, while clinging to *kaelandur*. He caught himself on his injured hand and wailed in pain. Biting his tongue, his blue eyes locked on Kveta scraping at the floorboards with her fingernails while the life drained from her.

"Patrician!" Kerra skidded next to him. "We need to get you away from here. Eisliev may be out there." She grabbed him under his arm to help him to his feet.

He grappled with her and a table to stand. "No. We need to protect ourselves," he said, barking orders. "Frang and Morgan, move away from the windows. Ailis and Sine, douse the fire." He finally hobbled up to his feet. "Beryl and Seoc, do not let go of Branimir."

Bran kicked, his fingers reaching for *kaelandur* across the room, dangling in Falmagon's fingers. His throat burned from shouting; his chest may as well have been crushed by boulders. He felt himself slipping from their grasp. Without the dagger, he would die.

"Falmagon, his flesh is cracking and peeling," Seoc shouted. "We cannot hold him much longer."

"What?" Falmagon asked.

Branimir cricked his neck, tears swelling, to see pin drops of blood trickling through the pores of his red skin. Seoc and Beryl's grasp skated over Branimir's arm, his body becoming lathered in blood.

"No," Branimir cried, feeling his body judder. His vision turned pitch.

"This is not Eisliev," Kerra cried.

Screams rebounded in the commons, increasing his overwhelming nausea. The *Kadari* fell on either side of him, releasing his arms from their iron grips. He could not see what happened, but their death cries were nauseating. Without their support, his legs buckled from underneath him, unable to hold his weight. Branimir dropped to the ground in a throbbing heap.

From somewhere, light flared on the opposite side of the blanketed darkness like the sun radiating behind the thickest of fogs.

A voice emulating the dying song of a demon rumbled like relentless thunder. Frenzied, foul laughter followed— arcane and abysmal—cackling inside Branimir's head.

He could only believe the Likhyi trapped within *kaelandur* surfaced from the copper blade with timeless hatred.

The veil was lifted from Branimir's eyes, but the pain was anything but fleeting. The unyielding sting surged through him. He writhed against the inn's wooden floorboards, his own hands mechanically etching over his body like frantic maggots on a corpse. His voice had become hoarse; the smell of sulfur pricked at the inside of his nostrils. His blood dripped off his flesh.

In front of Branimir lay Seoc with his head hanging limply, neck broken, blood oozing into his beard. His dead gaze stared pass Branimir to Beryl, who sat dead against the frame of the door. Branimir could not see what killed him.

"Help." A woman's voice whispered from the base of the fireplace. With great effort, Branimir tilted his head to see Kerra sprawled among a dozen dead *Kadari*. Limbs were broken. Bodies were torched.

Yet his questions fled his mind, witnessing the murky mass swirling over Kerra like a storm cloud. The Likhyi.

The *old-dark's* vehement undertones sprang about inside Branimir's skull. He cried out, slamming his head into the floor to knock away the vexing sound.

"Branimir!" He heard Alyona shout from outside.

"Branimir!"

"Branimir!"

Those yelling his name seemed so far away. He tried to scoot over to the window. The *old-dark's* unintelligible words grew louder. From the corner of his eye, he saw Kerra's body lift into the air by an unseen magic. She scarcely wriggled before being flung through an adjacent window, her head cracking against the wooden beams of *The Oaken Bard*.

"By *Mulafell*," Falmagon cowered on his knees beneath the *old-dark* with *kaelandur* clutched in his hand. He pressed his head to the floor in prayer, his brown locks hanging over his face, shielding his fear. He was the last of the *Kadari* in the commons. He averted his eyes from the blackness, fervently pleading to the Lightbringer, "My God, Dahz the White-Clad, Protector of Man, ride swift on *Mioengi* wielding *Mulafell*, the Hammer of Righteousness and protect us from the wicked. Do not let us drift into the night without your righteous light."

The Likhyi susurrated like a pit of vipers, grating like a whetstone against a sword's edge. The shade swirled and swelled above Falmagon.

The Patrician cried out louder to Dahz for protection but to no avail. In its place, Falmagon's pleas to the Lightbringer twisted into garbled, blood-curdling yells. Time bent around Falmagon, aging him decades in seconds. His hair greyed, whitened, and fell from his scalp, while his skin dehydrated and clung to his bones. The smell of rot—Falmagon's body decaying from the inside out—caused Branimir to retch, and, all the while, Falmagon continued to huskily scream for help.

No gods would come to save him. The gods would not save any of them.

The door leading outside suddenly opened. Branimir's sight was teeming by the visage of a young, dark-haired man and an equally young, light-haired woman. The man gripped Bran's cloak to pull him outside the inn. "Come on," he said. "We need to get you out of here."

He swung at the stranger's clasped fingers, feeling the heat swell in his gut, suggestive of his insides boiling. He uttered the single word, "*kaelandur.*"

Branimir did not see Alyona step over him and pass into the *The Oaken Bard.* Nor did he see her use *Koldovstvo* to whip *kaelandur* through the air from Falmagon's degenerating hand to her own. But Branimir did feel her slip it into his shaky fingers.

The grisly *old-dark* faded from being the moment the dagger connected with Branimir's skin as though it never existed. Branimir wheezed like he had never known breath, the pain from the Likhyi's separation softening. The shadow in the corners of his eyes drifted, and his body relaxed against the inn's floor. Yet he could not keep the tears from flooding.

Agony crept across his body from the gaping hole in his leg to his broken nose to his aching heart. Blood oozed from every cavity of his body, seeping from his skin as though he had been stabbed a hundred times.

"Thank you," he blubbered, looking to Alyona and then the other two, quickly recognizing them as the younger versions of Alden and Sulanna. "You…you drank the vials of the Water of Life. You are young."

"And we have one left for you," Alyona said, gripping the back of his head.

"Hurry," Alden urged. "The guard will come and Tyr cannot stay hidden in the hills for long."

Branimir did not argue with the *Kadari*, sipping the renewing water. As swiftly as he downed the water, his body mended his muscles and settled his bones, stitched his skin and restored his vigor.

"Branimir," Sulanna said in kindness, placing her hand on his forehead. "We thought we had lost you."

Branimir could hear the rustling of movement in the inn beyond his gaze. The low rumble of Falmagon's tenor slipped across the commons like a final breath.

"He is still alive," Alden said, lifting his strong jaw. "What should we do with him?"

Branimir did not think the question really required a response, but he felt better saying the words. "Kill him."

Month of Sickle

Sixth of Warmth

1352 CE

Chapter XVII

Falmagon was dead.

"Less than a week and we will be at *Iriy*," Alyona said from the top of her pale horse, a few steps ahead of Branimir. *Koldovstvo* drained enough of her life that, absent her youth, she reminded him of her mother, Erzebeth. She definitely spoke with the same authority.

He forced a half-smile at the thought of seeing Dorofej again. He was eager to have the black mage give reason to why he hurried ahead to the City of the Gods alone.

Alyona returned the smile, continuing, "We have done the impossible, but we are not done. We should expect Eisliev and Dagmar to come for *kaelandur* to finish what Nedezhda started with the Ash Tree. Remember the magic binds them to release the Likhyi."

"It has been almost a month since Eldhaft," Tyr said, plodding alongside her, his axe swinging from the strapping of his back with every step. He lifted an eyebrow under his long bangs, suggesting they had little to worry over. "And we have not seen any sign of life since Gavlok."

Branimir listened, slanting the waterskin and wetting his lips. He was careful not to drink much of the liquid. The heat had lessened since leaving Gavlok weeks ago, partly because the rapid approach of the Months of Frost, but also due to their increased elevation in the mountains. They had abandoned an unnamed, multi-forking river yesterday, which led them hundreds of miles from *The Oaken Bard* and Falmagon Sej's wan corpse. Now the five of them delved deeper into the spiraling Shade Fells with the supplies they purchased with Branimir's silver; none could be certain when they would come upon water again.

He adjusted in the saddle of his pony. "Of course, Dagmar and Eisliev will return for *kaelandur*, but Melkorka is on the opposite side of the world. We will reach *Iriy* long before either find us."

"We *hope* to reach *Iriy* first," Alyona knowingly said with a dip in her voice. "There are many exits from the Netherworld across Aenar. The Shade Fells are riddled with rumors of demons bleeding from these very mountains, crawling to the surface from their frozen pit. Nothing promises Dagmar or Eisliev will choose to exit from the Crags of Kazimir."

"We can hope they would," Branimir said. "Or, with any luck, they are locked in an eternal battle with one another."

"Have some faith, Alyona," Tyr said. He was daunting, his height stretching over seven-foot-tall, standing above the horse she rode. His large, six-fingered hands swung on either side of his bulky body as he walked bare-footed next to them. "The Bukavac may be chipping away at the Ash Tree, but they cannot completely destroy it without *kaelandur*. We will have real dangers to face in the Shade. The demons are more than rumors. We cannot be worrying about ghosts chasing us down."

"We need to be prepared for anything," Sulanna murmured, twisting to look back the way they had come. Her olive skin was smooth, and flushed from the slight chill on the wind. Her grey horse strayed a hair behind Alden. Branimir looked to them. Whatever started between Sulanna and Alden after Eldhaft had been further strengthened after Gavlok. The two were practically inseparable. For many nights, Branimir had caught them slinking back and forth across camp to share blankets, but after a couple nights of forgetting to drift back to their own bedrolls, they gave up on hiding their affections.

Branimir did not think it was worth hiding anyway. He was happy for them.

"Where is the nearest exit?" Alden asked. After drinking the Waters of Life, he was hardly recognizable to Branimir outside of his angular nose and blue eyes. He may have had a receding hairline to give promise to the baldness to come, but his thick, curled hair hid most of the evidence. The *old* warrior did not have a wrinkle on him anymore; instead, his skin was taut against his youthful strength.

Alyona pointed to the southwest, specifically to a towering peak rising far above the rest in the distance. "I do not know the closest exit, but see Mount Zyem," Alyona said marvelously. "Legends say the tunnels within the hollow of Mount Zyem leads to the Kalinov Bridge, defended by Zyem. Many demons are known to spread from that mountain."

"Zyem, Marheena's serpent, the Lord of Dragons," Alden mused, gazing at the mountain in the distance.

Alyona replied, "None can pass to Thrice Nine Lands without passing by Zyem. "The balance of life and death would be chaos if living men frequented the world of the dead to bring back their lost loved ones."

"More chaotic than now?" Sulanna smiled, blue eyes sparkling. With a month now gone since Adamus's death, or even her father's—which she would not mention—Branimir was surprised by Sulanna's attitude. Whether credit was given to her newfound youth or Alden's company, she had seemingly found solace.

Alyona snickered with amusement, keeping her head on the landscape ahead.

Branimir bit the inside of his cheek. "If we suspect Eisliev or Dagmar will come by the Kalinov Bridge, we will not have any chance of defending against them here."

"No, we could not defeat them in open battle," Tyr said, as he walked, rubbing Alyona's horse with care. "We would run and hide."

"I cannot hide from them while holding *kaelandur*," Branimir said softly. Most days, he kept himself from speaking to Tyr. Although, he had come to believe the giant was genuine in his effort to help, like Alyona. Branimir remembered the Ispolini to be an ignorant brute, but he could not ignore Tyr's loyalty—considering how he defended Eisliev, despite the red mage's clearly evil motives.

Still, he hoped Tyr had changed his allegiances. Branimir suspected they all changed in some way since starting this adventure, whether for the good or worse.

For instance, what they had gone through at *Harrowhal* and at Gavlok should have been enough to break Branimir, to leave his mind as bruised and bloodied as he had been himself. His nerves had undoubtedly been rattled, leaving him with a pounding heart, racing thoughts, or suddenly vanishing or reappearing without thought. Yet, in the past week, he found some comfort. Surely, he should have been looking over his shoulder for Dagmar or Eisliev. He should be terrified.

But Falmagon was dead.

Since reuniting with Tyr, Branimir had undoubtedly wondered why the giant supported the red mage. The two clearly were not cut from the same cloth. Unable to satiate his curiosity, he turned toward Tyr, and asked, "How did you meet Eisliev Kluk?"

Tyr grimaced, the large axe on his back bouncing in rhythm with his footsteps. "My father and Eisliev had been in an alliance together for some time, scheming against the *Kadari*." Tyr scratched at his head, swelling his chest with a breath. "I trusted my father. He had always been a bit mad, you know? But I trusted him."

"So, he led you into an alliance with Eisliev?" Branimir concluded. "He had you scheme against the *Kadari*?"

Tyr rocked his head in agreement. "He believed the God of the Dead had been killed and we needed the Stuhians to be safe from the demons. Eisliev's price was Dagmar's head. I agreed to go with Eisliev to kill Dagmar to maintain my father's alliance."

"And now, Dagmar and Eisliev are both dead-ish," Alyona said, interrupting Branimir's interrogation, "and we need to be ready for them. I would expect them to come from Lonmere, where Branimir and I slipped from the Netherworld several years ago. The path is less known, especially by the demons, but he would find it. He would have a better chance of closing the distance on *kaelandur* than trying to cut us off."

Alden gasped with sudden clarity, reaching over his horse and tugging on Branimir's cloak. "Your courage makes sense, now. You were with Dorofej in the Netherworld for all those years. No wonder you fear so little." He looked to Sulanna as he leaned back; lifting an eyebrow as though he had discovered a great secret. She simply shook her head at him.

Branimir tried to smile. He was terrified of losing Dorofej, who would die with *kaelandur's* destruction. His only comfort was that he would die too, and accompany Dorofej in the life hereafter, even if they were warped into demons.

For another half mile, the clopping of hooves against the softened, unkempt grasses and uneven rock were all to be heard. The size of the mountains expanded on either side of them.

They journeyed through a natural crook in the mountain, which may have been a wide river at some time in history, stretching miles wide. The Shade Fells showed no sign of retreating from the heavens, obscuring the horizon as though they were a boundary to the edge of the world. Signs of vegetation dwindled considerably as the number of broken boulders and smooth rocks lined the uneven path.

Branimir reached for *kaelandur* at his belt, unable to erase the grimace from his face. He had no understanding of why or how the Likhyi escaped from the copper dagger and attacked Falmagon. He remembered the fear and the pain, but he could not place how such a thing was possible. He carried *kaelandur* on him for a year without any display of such godly power.

Now, with the understanding that Eisliev could come around any bend in the road, he wondered if the Likhyi would abscond from the dagger once more. His heart told him the *old-dark* waged war against Falmagon, because the Patrician had aimed to destroy the *kaelandur*.

Eisliev Kluk, on the other hand, intended to unshackle the old gods from their eternal chains. Branimir would bet having *kaelandur* taken by the red mage would be a welcomed notion by the Likhyi.

And if Bran were parted from *kaelandur*, he would die.

He pressed Alyona to tell him more. "Will we be safe at *Iriy*?"

Her silence gave his heart reason to quicken, and he nearly repeated the question. But before he was able, Alyona replied, "*Iriy* is holy ground, meaning the dead would be kept from treading there, but I cannot pretend to know the will of the gods."

"But you have been among the gods," Branimir said. He noticed Alden sitting up straighter in his saddle at Branimir's comment. Sulanna also seemed intrigued by this information, pushing her mare a step closer. Neither must have been listening to him and Alyona's conversation when traveling to Gavlok.

"I was a child," Alyona said distantly. "I barely knew who I was; let alone who the gods were."

"But are they magnificent?" Alden asked.

"The word does not quite live up to the feeling you have when standing with them," Alyona said.

"Real gods?" Sulanna questioned.

"Yes." Alyona said simply.

Alden turned and grinned at Sulanna. His boyish grin nearly cut his face in two. "I told you they were real, Sulanna."

The clacking of the pony's hooves melded with those of the other horses as they ventured in the shadow of the mountains. Tyr tirelessly stomped along beside them. The dim sun from the morning faded to overcast, as it had been the night before, with an occasional light drizzle.

After a while, they stopped to let the horses rest and eat, and then set off again.

It was not long before Alden was tugging at the small curls on his dark beard in thought. "Something has been bothering me. I understand Dorofej hopes the gods will help us. But what more can be done?"

Alyona petted the mist from her brown horse's mane with her fingertips, swaying back and forth in her saddle. "The gods will give us counsel on *kaelandur* and the Likhyi," she said.

"What does that mean?" Sulanna asked. "We require more than simple words. Will they destroy *kaelandur*?"

"I believe that is what Dorofej intends for them to do," Tyr said. "Why else would we come all this way?"

"No." Branimir pulled at his long nose. "That cannot be it. Marheena told Dorofej to make *kaelandur*. I cannot see why she would direct him to create something only to destroy it when asked."

Alden practically threw his hands in the air. "I don't understand why Marheena would have him make the dagger to begin with. What did she hope to accomplish?"

"I have asked the same question," Branimir admitted.

"Maybe it is a test of faith," Tyr said.

"I could believe that, maybe. But I don't see the gods killing Dorofej, or Branimir," Alden responded to Tyr, adjusting the long spear at the side of his saddle. "If Dorofej was commanded by the gods to make something, and he did, why would he be punished? Why would they let Branimir die when he has done so much to save this world?"

"Well, I am comforted that I have *not* died yet. But I have this feeling in my stomach telling me the gods have little concern whether any of us do or not," Branimir said.

"That is terrible," Sulanna said.

"Maybe they don't, but they surely don't want to die any more than we do. The Likhyi would destroy everything, including them, right?" Tyr asked with a grunt. "Are they not all-powerful and all-knowing?"

Alden ruffled his beard. "Again, Tyr is right. That has to weigh on their minds."

"Assuming they are mindful of anything," Sulanna said. "Dorofej may want them to bring Wolos back from the dead? Can they do that? I mean, they are gods."

Branimir frowned. If Wolos returned, the dead would no longer flood from the Netherworld, meaning *kaelandur* would no longer be needed to destroy the Ash Tree. But Erzebeth planned to have the two men at Anaerfell bring Wolos back to life. If the gods returned the God of the Dead, Branimir would have given his shiny stone, *Ojenek*, away for nothing. "No, I don't think they would do that either."

Alyona snickered from the front. "No, they would not bring Wolos back. They may have the power to restore him, but the gods cannot be responsible for the mistakes of men."

"They created us to be capable of making mistakes to begin with," Sulanna muttered, seemingly frustrated for having her idea so easily rejected. "I would think they are partially responsible."

Branimir scratched his head, repeating the question to Alyona. "So, what is Dorofej hoping to achieve at *Iriy*?"

"Maybe he hopes they will destroy *kaelandur*," Alyona said. "I cannot be certain, but I know the gods will tell us how we can stop the Likhyi."

Tyr suddenly stopped Alyona's horse with his hand, pointing in the distance at the rock-strewn terrain. "Did you see the movement up ahead?"

Branimir edged his pony forward, along with Sulanna and Alden on their horses, eyeing the distance. He did not see anything, but his pony stepped back nervously as Alden jerked loose the spear from its holding.

"What is it?" Branimir asked.

Tyr rubbed his hands against his skin trousers, and then removed his large axe from the leather strapping against his bare back. His dark-blue eyes narrowed. "Witiko."

"Demons?" Sulanna reached for her long knife. "How many? Where?"

"I do not see it now," Tyr said, looking to the sky and squinting. Branimir followed his gaze. Twilight had come quicker in the shadow of the Shade Fells. "We should find higher ground and make camp. Who knows how many roam these parts of the mountains?"

"Does that mean there is an exit from the Netherworld nearby?" Branimir asked.

"Not necessarily," Alyona answered, continuing to peer across the landscape ahead.

"The Deep runs through the Shade Fells," Tyr said, referencing the many tunnels of the underearth he had told Branimir about. "The Witiko call them home, and they are numerous."

"But the dragons keep guard over the mountains, usually lessening their numbers on the surface," Alyona added. "From here on out, we will need to be watching for either, and take equal precaution."

Branimir trembled with the onslaught of another gust of wind, unmoved by Alyona's dire warning. Nothing would stop him from reuniting with Dorofej.

The clouds dispatched and a full moon had risen before they settled around the fire. The evening was cool enough that the flickering flames were a surprising blessing. Branimir pulled his green cloak up around his shoulders and scooted closer. Tyr sat on his left, while Alyona scanned the darkness for the Witiko to his right. Alden and Sulanna huddled under a blanket together on the opposite side of the fire, blocked by the roiling smoke.

Tyr's voice came without invitation, diving into his tale again as though he had onus to share the full of it until their ears bled. "After Melkorka, Dorofej and I moved with haste, thinking you would reach *Iriy* long before we could. We expected to fight the *Kadari*, demons, or even the Crimson Sun. Yet nothing deterred us from Melkorka to the edge of Sorod. He went to *Klukas* many times to see how far you had gone, but he never could see the half pint."

Branimir could feel Tyr's eyes on his skull, but did not meet his gaze.

"I remember you mentioning as much before," Sulanna said. "He would not be able to see Branimir while he wore *Faegrim*."

"Ah," Tyr said. "I thought as much."

"But he could see the rest of us, and therefore, he could gaze on Branimir?" she added.

"No," Tyr replied. "Branimir always remained hidden with *Faegrim* on his finger, even when Dorofej found the rest of you. Luckily, I knew something about *Faegrim* from the time Eisliev carried it in his possession. It did not take long for us to think Branimir picked it up, but I was not certain." Tyr paused for a moment. "Do you still have the ring?"

Branimir nodded, watching the fire.

"Were you wearing it when you were being held at Eldhaft?" Tyr pressed.

"For a time," Branimir replied, eyeing the Ispolini curiously. "Why?"

Tyr explained gruffly. "As I said, I separated from Dorofej before you reached Eldhaft; but even if he did not see you, he should have found everyone else in *Harrowhal.*"

"Unless Dagmar used *Koldovstvo* to block any of us from being found in *Klukas,*" Alyona reasoned, scraping her foot against the dirt. "I heard him and Falmagon talk about the ability many times."

"I see," Tyr swallowed. Branimir glanced at him from his peripheral. Tyr clenched his chin as though he were expecting an explanation of how they may have escaped Dagmar's schemes. When none elaborated, Tyr said, "I suppose that explains it then. I thought Dorofej would meet us on the road."

"He seems to have chosen to stay at *Iriy.* We would have crossed paths long before now," Alden said.

Branimir gritted his teeth, remembering how Dorofej originally fought with Falmagon about going to the Netherworld, fearful of dying, or the many times he escaped death, whether using Moreth's skull or the Ash Tree. In all their time together, Branimir repeatedly heard Dorofej's confession about how he sought to live more than anything else. For all his bravery, Dorofej was a coward when facing the grave.

"The thought baffles me," Tyr said. "He undoubtedly cares about each of you. You can see it in his eyes."

Branimir stared into the fire. And, although his words sounded unforgiving, he could not say he was angry with Dorofej. "Yet he fears death more."

The smell of rot stung Branimir's nostrils an instant before a gangly, ash-grey monster, howled and rushed into the camp behind Alden and Sulanna. Branimir cried out as the demon sprinted on two legs, jumping with outstretched, clawed hands. He had no time to respond, reaching for his weapon while attempting to spring to his feet.

Tyr similarly struggled next to him.

Alyona shouted spinning around, to face the beast bounding for Alden; her hands were already rising defensively. She hastily weaved *Koldovstvo*, whipping the flames from the campfire around the demon like ghostly hands, and pulled the monster through the air to the searing fire.

The movement was so quick, Branimir had barely jerked his dagger from the sheath at his belt.

Branimir fumbled, scooting away from the thrashing Witiko, while acknowledging the massive size of the demon, its length as long as Tyr was tall. The lanky beast floundered in the flames, screeching, until the color faded from its bulbous eyes. The death-howl of the beast echoed against the mountain sides.

"By the gods," Alden pulled Sulanna close to him, skimming the darkness around them. "I barely heard it until it was on top of us."

"We will be alright," Alyona said, taking a breath. "The Ispolini have fought these demons for ages. Tell them, Tyr."

Tyr growled under his breath, kicking the rotting limbs hanging beyond the campfire's edge. "I know the Witiko well. One or two are easy to defend against. They are mindless beasts, attacking anything they can eat." Tyr covered his nose from the smell, his dark-blue eyes filled with fury. "But, out here, I would not be surprised if we cross larger droves."

Branimir returned his dagger to his belt, shaking his head at the giant and his so-called soothing words. "Tyr, you should take first watch."

Chapter XVIII

Branimir often heard the demons from the Deep at night, howling and screeching against the frigid wind; but, for the next two days, none of them saw any sign of the Witiko.

The path leading to *Iriy* had become arduous. Their mounts fought to keep footing on the loose rocks, which had long since rolled down from the enfolding crags. Even now, Branimir clung to the saddle as his pony lost its foothold, scrambling its hooves to keep pace with the larger horses.

He huffed in surprise, eyes fixated on Alyona ahead of the company leading them up the mountain. He tightened his thighs so he would not topple off the animal.

Tyr, who walked next to him, reached out and snagged the bridal of the animal, holding it steady with his incredible strength. "Careful there, girl," he whispered, calming the animal. "We will find a break up ahead."

The pony whinnied as Branimir repositioned himself, leaning his weight forward. "Thanks, Tyr."

Tyr's blue eyes met Branimir's. "The trail will level out once in a while, but it will not get any easier."

Alden grunted behind them as he, too, steered his horse up the difficult incline. Sulanna encouraged him to push through.

Tyr added, "The longer the mounts can carry you along, the better. You would exhaust your legs trying to keep balance. You do not want to be tumbling back down the mountain."

Branimir was sure Tyr had less difficulty than most climbing alongside of them with his thick legs.

He cricked his neck to look behind them, quickly realizing how far *up* they traveled after leaving Gavlok. His perception had been skewed by focusing on the road ahead, seeing little except the wall of the Shade Fells. Yet gazing across the expanse of Maharia articulated the truth of how far they had come.

He could see no signs of civilization from where they were positioned. The landscape was painted with yellows, oranges, and greens, coupled by the blue and white sky. He did not see any signs of plowed fields, or cropped woods. Yet he could see the wild grasslands nestled between the scattered forests; he could see the rocky knolls they journeyed beyond, dwarfed at a distance.

"That is beautiful," Branimir said.

"Very," Sulanna said, swaying on her horse. "I imagine few in the world ever have the chance to see a sight like this. Maybe fewer would fight amongst themselves if they could."

"Bah! If you think that is something, you should see Tundris Mor," Tyr pointed over Mount Zyem, ever-expanding to the south. "You cannot reach the islands of the Ispolini without going around the Shade, but the venture is worth the labor. Our isles are as much a part of the Shade as the crags we are crawling through. And when you climb to the tops to see the world," Try breathed, shaking his head in memory, "you really see Aenar. The ocean. Maharia, Haemus Mons. The land stretches for thousands of miles in all directions."

"I have never been to Tundris Mor," Alden said, "but you must be stretching the truth. No offense, but look at the size of Mount Zyem. If you can see anything beyond that mountain, you would be soaring across the sky with Dahz in his chariot."

Tyr grinned. "I may exaggerate, but not to boast. Lofty memories keep my hopes high and my mood mended, much in the same way parents speak about their children."

Sulanna said, "Alden and I traveled through most of the North and never met an Ispolini. The fact you journeyed across the continent and joined the Crimson Sun is beyond strange."

"I imagine before you crossed over, most the world thought giants to be legends," Alden chuckled.

"Some continue to think so," Tyr laughed, keeping his hand firm on the bridle of Branimir's pony. Branimir noticed Tyr stealing a glance at him. "Others think the Ispolini are monsters or demons. It is a difficult thing to live in a world where others are afraid of you for looking different."

"Why did you leave your home?" Branimir asked.

"Bah!" Tyr hesitated, shuffling his bare feet over the rocks awkwardly. He did not give any sign that the rocks were hurting the soles of his feet, but then again, the Ispolini did not seem to be affected by much. In fact, the cold mountain air hardly made his bare skin pimple gooseflesh, whereas the rest of them kept adjusting their cloaks to keep warm. Branimir saw the muscles in his neck and back noticeably tense before he answered the question. "The story is complicated. My home is the heart of Mount Dvargen, the city of Almdalir. The law of the Ispolini works similarly to those in Stuhian lands." He nodded at Alyona near the front, who had not bothered to engage them. "You are familiar with the Stuhia?"

Branimir shook his head. "Not really."

"Oh," Tyr said, angling his brow. "Well, the government is made up of a Council of Elders who lead the people and enforce laws. My father, Enlil, was an Elder until…" Tyr fidgeted, making a six-fingered fist in his right hand. "…until I was banished from my home after the death of my mother and sister."

"You killed them?" Branimir asked with shock.

"No, no," Tyr said, forcibly shaking his head. "Nothing like that. But I did kill someone who insulted their honor. It is not something I like to talk about."

"You did right by them," Alden said from the rear.

"I like to think I did, but that day I became an outcast to my own kind," Tyr said. "I should have been cast into the lava pits and left to burn. Instead, I was sent to the Deep."

"To wander with the Witiko?" Branimir asked, directing his mind off the idea of being thrown into scorching lava.

"Yes," Tyr replied. "I crossed a few Witiko while in the tunnels. Some I killed, and others I avoided. We would be blessed by the gods to not cross them again before reaching *Iriy*."

Eventually, as Tyr promised, the path straightened and flattened between towering escarpments. Alyona directed them to give the horses a rest, and they gathered to eat what dried food they had in their packs. Branimir was discouraged at the scarcity found in his own, but even more frustrated with how light his waterskin had become.

He sat down next to Alden, who hurried to move his spear to the side and make room. The warrior bit into a piece of dried meat, and scratched at his head of black hair.

"You would not believe how ridiculous you look to me, Alden," Branimir said, crossing his legs.

"I can imagine." Alden beamed his white teeth, chewing steadily in the corner of his mouth. "Sulanna has poked at me many times regarding my beard and hair. Ha! You know I had been bald so long, I almost forgot I ever had hair."

The thought made Branimir giggle.

Alden gestured to Sulanna unsaddling her mare. "I will not argue that I have changed how I think over the past month, but people hear you differently when you aren't as wrinkled as a rotten prune," Alden said, holding the smile.

Branimir unwrapped his dried bread, shaking his head at the warrior. "I could drink the full of the Waters of Life and I would look no prettier."

Alden flattened his gaze, leaning over to study Branimir's face, knowing he had drunk the last vial. "Your skin looks…smoother," he offered.

Branimir pushed him away with a laugh. "Save your compliments for when I have lived to be five-hundred and have need of it."

Alden lifted his bushy eyebrows. "Do the Kras really live to be so old? Naturally, I mean?"

Branimir nodded, taking a bite of his food.

Sulanna approached, digging in her own bag for rations, her dark hair whipping about in the swirling winds. She paused her rummaging to pull the fabric of her cloak around her. "I remember the cold of the mountain in Lonmere," she said, "but it has been so long. And to think we still have a couple weeks until the Season of Frost."

Alyona and Tyr were not far behind. Neither seemed concerned by the cold chill as though their bodies had been built specifically to withstand the frigid weather. Alyona checked over her shoulder at the horses tied together as she spoke. "We will be marching into snow by tomorrow, if not tonight. I would suspect the weather is going to drop considerably by nightfall."

Branimir widened his eyes at the prospect of sleeping among the brushless terrain. "We would freeze to death."

"I will create a fire with *Koldovstvo* to keep us warm," Alyona offered. "We will not need much to keep the magic aflame."

Tyr grunted. "We should find a cave for shelter. I hope we can find one hollowed enough to hold the fire, but without any deeper paths."

"No, we do not need the Witiko coming upon us in the night," Alyona said. "Then again, we must keep watch for Eisliev or Dagmar. With limitless magic, they could gain on us, and we do not want to be caught in a cave only to have it come crashing down on our heads."

Alden frowned. "Maybe we should just travel through the night and continue to *Iriy*."

"Maybe," Alyona said, biting her lip. "Branimir and I may do well enough if we abandoned the horses, but the rest of you would struggle on the path."

"We should not abandon the horses," Tyr said. "If you plan on leaving *Iriy*, you are going to want them. We have hundreds of miles stretching between us and civilization."

"And the gateway to Sorod?" Branimir asked.

Tyr shook his head. "Bah! I do not think the centaurs would be favorable of us appearing in their underground temples. We would be disemboweled and roasted."

"Well, that is pleasant," Sulanna muttered. "Sounds like we have the choice to risk the road or holing up. Considering we know the road is a hazard even in the light, and we have not seen any warning of Dagmar or Eisliev, we fortify ourselves in the rock."

Alden dipped his head, chewing the dried meat.

Alyona bit her lip, glancing in a circle for objections and found none. "Our days are growing shorter in the shadow of the mountain. We may have a few more hours. Let's see how far we can make it until dusk."

Soon, they were winding through the mountain path sliding and slipping across the rocks. The slope of the mountain tilted, and although the path was wide, Alyona had to lead them in a zigzag to give the horses enough traction to stay afoot.

Tyr maintained his hold on Branimir's mount, helping guide the pony. The giant breathed heavily as though he may have been physically lugging the pony up the side of the mountain. His muscles bulged from his chest to his back with sweat layering his skin despite the damp cold.

Branimir opened his mouth a few times to caution the Ispolini, but chose to refrain. He did not get the impression Tyr was going to back away from aiding him.

The sun faded into the west about the time the path leveled again. A valley appeared to the north with what promised water and vegetation, but the drop-off was so steep, they would have killed themselves going down or never would have found a way back up. Branimir could hear Alden and Sulanna murmuring similar realizations behind him.

Alyona heaved with exhaustion at the front of the line, but continued forward on her horse, muttering something about a few more miles.

"We should…" The smell of decay stopped Branimir from finishing his sentence. He jerked his head to the mountain ridge opposite of the valley, catching sight of Alyona already swinging off her horse with a warning shout.

From the shadows, bursting from an oblique fissure in the side in the rock, rushed the too-familiar, ash-grey monster. Standing as tall as Tyr, the long-limbed beast had blue, bulbous eyes with skin dried across the length of its frame like a rind splitting over rotten fruit. Bone and muscle surfaced along the body where the flesh had decomposed.

Tyr sneered, unstrapping his two-handed axe to intercept the demon. But Alden was the quickest to respond, flinging his spear over Branimir's head with deadly accuracy. The perfected point tore through the temple of the monster, knocking it sideways off its feet, and leaving it dead, skidding over the rocks.

"Witiko," Tyr growled stomping toward the mountain as though he might tear it down with his hands.

His voice was met with the ringing howls erupting from the opening. The demons from the Deep burst through the crags with gurgling growls and rippling snarls. Alyona extended the first's blood-hungry roar, lifting it in the air with *Koldovstvo* and flinging it behind them into the valley below.

A second, third, and fourth fled from the hole.

Branimir swung off the pony about the time it twisted to bolt from the impending battle. Branimir vanished from sight and pulled his dagger from his belt.

In two large leaps, Tyr reached the next Witiko in line, swinging his axe to slice the demon across the chest. Bluish blood spurted, but the beast hardly noticed. The Witiko swung clawed hands at Tyr, baring sharpened fangs.

Branimir twisted around the Witiko, barely standing above the knee, and jabbed his iron dagger into the back of the knee. The Witiko kicked wildly with a howl, but did not fall. Sulanna ran on the opposite side, slicing her long knife across its belly and releasing its innards.

The smell was as horrid as the tombs of *Garain'l.*

Tyr roared in the face of the Witiko, hitting it with the handle of his weapon and felling it to the dirt.

Branimir turned from Tyr and followed Sulanna into the midst of the Witiko horde. Alden's heavy footsteps thundered close behind him.

"For Svarog, the Kingdom and victory!" he cried.

Sulanna ducked the wild swing of the giant monster, stabbing the creature on the inside of the thigh. Branimir slid on the rocks beside her, attacking the knee ligaments once more. The Witiko screeched in pain, spraying spit with its furious roar. Sulanna ignored the sound with the tenacity of a seasoned warrior, jamming her knife into the under jaw and through the brain.

Alden, armed with Adamus's steel axe, threw his weight into the next Witiko, lifting the beast off the ground and hurling it into the rock. The warrior then flurried his attacks with a deafening roar, hacking and slashing the refined blade into the monster's meaty flesh.

Rasping cries rang, against the rigid rocks, and across the lowly vale. Branimir whirled between the many Witiko, sieving between his friends, lending his service where he could. He felt crippled, equipped with the single dagger, but the demons were dwindling and none of them had dropped.

Tyr noticed Alyona aging behind them. He shouted to the rest of them. "Give Alyona some relief." She flung fire and frost from the edge of the drop-off behind them, her hair greying in patches and skin wrinkling from the use of *Koldovstvo*. Without a weapon, she was limited in her fighting power against the Witiko. Branimir was certain that changing into the panther would leave her more vulnerable against the quick demons.

Alden and Tyr retreated to form a barrier in front of Alyona. Before Sulanna could join them, a Witiko emerged from the drove, striking her in the chest with the back of its oversized hand.

"No!" Alden shouted as she slammed against the rocks with a hollowed groan.

The Witiko advanced on her with outstretched claws and incalculable speed, saliva dripping from its pointed fangs. Not worrying about the aftermath, Branimir slung his dagger and struck true. The blade cut through the back of the Witiko's head. Yet, where the one fell, three more rushed to overcome Sulanna.

Branimir darted to Sulanna, materializing halfway across the distance. She attempted to scramble to her feet, gasping for breath.

Tyr took off from the opposite direction, abandoning Alyona, noisily shouting at the Witiko as though it might draw their attention. He held his axe in front of him like a battering ram, his face wretched in fury. The Witiko's raucous roars out-pitched those of the Ispolini as they closed the distance.

"Get up!" Alden shouted. He flung his axe, splitting the face of one of the demons. The Witiko crumpled to the rocks, and Alden sprang for the spear still sticking from the first Witiko's skull. "Get up!"

The ear-splitting roar at Alyona's back sounded seconds before the black-scaled dragon swooped up from the depths of the vale, colliding against the cliff's edge. Alyona dove from the space, rolling shoulder over shoulder to escape the wyrm.

Rocks crumbled and cracked under the beast's mass. Its long tail swished like a snake over the expanse.

Branimir did not have time to lay eyes on Tyr or Alden, hardly capable of processing the sight of the dragon, as he slipped in the loose rock, falling to his knees at Sulanna's side. The dragon had three crescent-shaped heads swaying forebodingly, its massive, weather-beaten wings flapping strongly as it balanced on two of its hind legs. The two muscular, front legs were tucked near the wings. The screech released by a single head was enough to make Branimir grab his sensitive ears. When the second two heads echoed the sound, Branimir's heart threatened to stop beating.

He would never forget the white dragon, *Lahmia*, but the black dragon before him made her seem a molehill compared to a mountain.

In desperation, Alden's renewed command came as a faint, frantic wail. "Stay down." From the corner of his eye, Branimir saw the warrior jerk the spear free from the Witiko's corpse. He barely lifted it to his waist before fire fell from the dragon's gullet.

The flames pierced through the darkness, igniting the two Witiko in mid-step. More demons rushing from the rock turned to retreat, shrieking in pain. Their howls were cut short in the sudden fiery death. Branimir could only watch with Sulanna in wonder as the horde of demons burned. His face heated, stealing away the ice in his veins.

"Keep to the ground," Alyona screamed at them through the crackling flames. "It is Torn'ash, the Father of Serpents. He is protecting us."

The skin of the Witiko sizzled and frothed, melting away with the cold of the mountainside.

The dragon brought down its front legs, smashing a demon beneath its massive foot, the claws digging into the earth. One of the heads whipped around to release fire breath again on the host of Witiko. Their decayed skin liquefied against their bones; the dragon fire was all-consuming.

Branimir twisted his neck to see Tyr holding firmly to the ground like Alyona commanded. Alden, too, had chosen to lay down his weapon and cling to the rocks.

A rumble from the black wyrm's throat ended the second spectacle of dragon breath, leaving the route littered with burnt corpses. The dragon then kicked off the rock, flapping its wings all the harder to soar into the sky.

As it lifted, a fleeing Witiko was snatched up in the strong jaws of one of the heads. Torn'ash snapped the body in half, raining the bluish blood down over them, and then turned away from the mountain side. The remaining pieces of the final Witiko crashed against the ground around them.

Branimir dared to stand, covering his head protectively, watching the beast ascend over the valley. "I don't even know what question I should be asking."

Alden rushed to Sulanna, pulling her to her feet. They held on to one another, shadowing the wyrm with their eyes.

"Bah!" Tyr stated, pulling himself to his feet. "I never thought I would see the day a dragon swooped in to protect a mortal."

"I told you the dragons protected these mountains from the demons. Wolos may be dead," Alyona said. "But his servants are not."

Chapter XIX

The elevation of the Shade reached the clouds. The silvery vapor relentlessly eddied across the frost-covered rock for the next three days. The mountain pass widened once more with the disappearance of the low-cut valley, leaving boulders and rocks with few scattered bushes. Alyona dispersed the few edible snowberries when found, but for the most part, little food was unearthed.

The sky was almost constant smoke, reeling from white to grey to black. Flurries flounced with few actual snowfalls, leaving drifts of snow as tall as Branimir accumulating on either side of the road. He had taken note that Alyona stopped them more frequently to rest the horses, feeding them what little grain remained in the saddlebags. The mounts thinned significantly since purchasing them at Gavlok; Branimir hoped none would die before reaching *Iriy*.

Branimir pondered over whether they would slaughter his pony for meat when Tyr announced, "At last, we have arrived."

"Nine Lands," Sulanna said breathlessly to his left. Her mare snickered, its nose aligning with Branimir's pony.

Wordless, Branimir beheld *Iriy*, the City of the Gods. The mountain path had all but evaporated, splitting open into a wide-reaching dale. In the center erupted a rock-strewn summit, stretching hundreds of feet into the air. *Iriy* covered the entire mount, built in nine layers, crowning in a circular, archaic fortress. Branimir could see the vertical, white-stone columns erected at the zenith of the stronghold.

He could identify the ramparts sectioning off each area of the city, glimmering majestically. Spherical domes of hundreds of buildings and rectangular towers with triangular overhangs were proportionally ranged at each level. Being hundreds of feet beneath *Iriy* meant Branimir could not fully gauge the size of the archways, cloisters, and walkways, but he suspected a wyrm as large as *Lahmia* could saunter through in comfort.

The heavens miraculously cleared from all signs of storm, the sun almost seeming close enough to touch; the warmness sinking into Branimir, stealing away his hunger and fatigue. He dared to think of removing his cloak and sopping up the sunlight. But before he could act on the thought, he was distracted by the red stags and hares, partridges and wildcats, and foxes promenading through the fields. Trees with low-hanging fruit and bushes laden with berries and nuts crowded the gorge.

"Do not eat or drink anything without invitation," Alyona said, climbing down from her horse. She unfastened her cloak and tucked it into the straps near the saddle. She then turned to the others expectantly, purple irises flashing, running her hands through her hair. "Let your horses roam and replenish their energy. The saddles will not be a burden to them here. And leave your weapons." She considered Branimir with concern. "Bring *kaelandur*."

He bit at the inside of his cheek, but Branimir did as instructed. In tune with the others, Branimir swung off his pony, removed his cloak, and tucked his dagger into the saddlebags. *Kaelandur* remained sheathed, dangling from the leather belt around his waist in full view.

Tyr handed his two-handed axe to Alyona with his leather bindings. She hooked the weapon to her own horse so it would not become lost.

The mounts wandered into the grasses and trees with the other animals. They moved as though they had freshly awoken, and had not just journeyed halfway across the world.

"How far is it to the top?" Alden asked, stepping away from his horse. Sulanna found her way to his side, interlocking her fingers in his hand.

"Half a day," Alyona said. "But we have to be allowed through the front gate first."

"Allowed?" Branimir wrinkled his brow.

Before Alyona had a chance to respond, a light flashed in the dale so bright and brilliant, Branimir may have thought they had been staring into pitch a moment before, even under the vivid sun.

"Bow," Alyona commanded, dropping to a knee, and hanging her head. Tyr followed suit beside her, crumbling to both knees and placing his head to the softened earth. Alden released Sulanna's hand, taking a large step and pressing a fist to his chest.

Sulanna delayed her kneeling, along with Branimir, but decidedly stooped next to Alden while mumbling unintelligible words of wonder under her breath.

Branimir, on the other hand, shielded his eyes from the brightness perforating his senses. Dawning from the pure light, painted in whites and yellows, emerged a golden-haired goddess of immaculate splendor. Although she had the features of a human, she stood as tall as an Ispolini. Her light-blue eyes penetrated through him, ignoring his kneeling friends. Immediately, his heart swelled with infinite love and kindness, as though every sorrow ever known had been washed away from the abysmal pit of his very soul. Grief and regret and mourning fled from his mind like frost from flame.

She divinely touched his very essence with an absolute love he had never known; in this moment, Branimir deliberated if he had never known real love. The rareness of her expression dimmed all other notions—lust, appreciation, and even friendly adoration—which mortals pretended to know. He was dazed; engrossed to the degree that he did not notice when she skated across the greenward to loom over him.

Her white gown, festooned with golden flowers, flowed at her heel. With each footstep, Branimir swore he could hear bells playing like a distant song. She advanced, unnoticed by the others, and hovered in front of Branimir. Her thin lips arched into a smile, and although he heard her melodic intonation in his head, he knew she did not outwardly speak.

'Waiting for you, we have been, Branimir Baran, son of Hrani. I am Lada, the Mother.'

She dipped down giving full view of the ears of grain braided in her long, golden hair. Never had he felt so full of peace. As though she could read his every thought, she gave comfort.

'Here, you are safe. Here, you walk where mortals fear to tread, in the footpath of the gods. Here, you endure til the end of your tale."

Lada delicately handed Branimir a rose, red as an angry sunset. From whence she had drawn the flower, Branimir could not say. He took the stem with a trembling hand.

'Go forth into Iriy and be at peace.'

Branimir hugged the rose, watching as Lada faded from sight. With her withdrawal, a sudden weight fell onto his heart; he pined to return to her presence. He could only think she resided somewhere within the white walls on the summit.

Tyr gasped in response as if he had just taken his first breath of life, gripping the grasses under his fingers. He pulled himself to his knees, staring wondrously at the magnificent city above them.

Alden spoke in bewilderment. "Lada, the Lady of Flowers, and the Mother of the Gods. I cannot believe it."

"It is real," Sulanna said, her buttocks falling to rest on the heels of her feet. Her hands slid from her sides to her belly, shaking her head. The water surfacing glittered against the sunlight.

"We must go into *Iriy*," Branimir said with a shaking voice.

The other four were slow to return to their feet, each stricken with different emotions.

Alyona was the first to look to Branimir, tears flooding the ducts of her eyes. She used the back of her hand to wipe her face. Branimir believed the tears were from gladness, considering what he experienced with Lada. Yet Alyona's frown did not bespeak of any joy.

She dipped her head at the rose in his hand. "You have received Lada's blessing, and the key to the front gate. We have been permitted to enter *Iriy*."

"Not all of us," Sulanna said with a shaking voice. She stumbled to her feet with Alden rushing to her side. His action suggested he understood her words better than any, squeezing her with as much strength as he could muster. His muscles flexed as though he were wielding his weapons in battle, fighting for every delicate breath.

The two fell into a silent embrace for several seconds while the other three gazed in question.

"What do you mean?" Branimir asked. "Why could you not come after all you have done to bring us here? If anything, you have sacrificed the most."

Sulanna gazed into Alden's eyes longingly, and when he finally nodded his head, she answered, "Lada told me that I am with child, Bran. Alden and I have helped bring you to *Iriy* but we must go start a new journey."

She turned to Branimir, eyes riddled with torment.

Branimir broke into a smile. "No apologies from either of you. I wouldn't ask you to come any further."

Alden squeezed Sulanna in his hands, his own tears falling to his thick, black beard. He pulled back and turned to Branimir to make words, but stumbled trying to keep his lip from quivering.

"I know," Sulanna said to him, wrapping her arms under his and pulling him close.

Branimir said what he could only imagine was on Alden's mind. "You have spent your whole life living for the gods, and now, upon arrival, you are given another path." Branimir gritted his teeth, looking up at the *old* warrior. "Few men are committed to their beliefs. Few, if any, ever get the chance to question the gods and be presented an opportunity to be given answers."

"No," Alden interjected, gathering his strength. "Too many men are unbent in their thinking. They question gods because they have no sense to question themselves; and when replied to, they alter the answer to fit their foolish delusions." Alden steadily looked at Branimir. "Their narrow *beliefs* bring dishonor to their *life*. I will no longer be the man who saw my life a burden and dishonored it."

"Alden," Sulanna said, touching his cheek with her hand.

Her soft tone did not quiet him. Alden finished, "*Few* men have the heart to *father* their children. They rush to war, or into politics, or to seek some other misfound glory, forgetting their legacy lies in their blood." He tensed his jaw, shaking his head with purpose. "My child will know their father. My child will know life is a gift."

Branimir flew forward and wrapped hands around Sulanna and Alden. He felt their hands on his back to return the embrace.

"You will forever be missed," he said.

Sulanna replied, "We will remain here in the dale for a while, Branimir. We may still travel together on the journey back to the east."

Branimir let go, looking back to Alyona and Tyr. "I do not know where my road will go from here."

"We will wait for an answer," Alden said in kindness. "For now, the City of the Gods awaits Branimir Baran."

"I hope to see you when we are done." Tyr said, clasping Alden's smaller hand in his own. "If not, take care of one another."

"We will." Sulanna returned his hearty smile.

Bran's fingers grazed across *kaelandur* at his belt like a shadow, seeing his friends for what felt like the last time.

"Come, Branimir," Alyona said, placing her hand on his shoulder to pull him away. "We need to go."

Alden and Sulanna stayed behind to settle in the dale while Bran and the others trudged to the base of the center peak. No road marked a path to the entryway to *Iriy*, but Branimir did notice the grass they traipsed across appeared untouched after they passed. Alyona led them around the side of the rock to the entrance.

Around the side of the mountain, they soon came upon the great gate. Twenty-foot pillars topped with stone effigies first caught Branimir's attention. The sculptures were chiseled from stone resembling men and women wielding swords and staves, mallets and axes, and crossbows and spears. Branimir could see reflections of many races in the depictions: Stuhians and Anshedar, Ispolini and Lilitu, Vucari and Svet, and, finally, the Kras.

At the edge of the final two columns, the grass disappeared and a stone pathway, wide enough for twenty horses to march down, led to an incline of nearly sixty stone steps. The double-doors at the top of the staircase were almost forty-foot tall, made from iron and steel. The doors were firmly placed in a stone archway fixated into the side of the mountain. Whatever walls were built for *Iriy* remained on the summit beyond these doors. Branimir was almost afraid to think how many steps they would find on the opposite end.

"Nine Lands," he mumbled, tilting his neck as far as it would go. "Who built this?"

Tyr answered. "I imagine the gods."

"No one knows for certain," Alyona said. "Though, I have often wondered if *Iriy* is this magnificent, what more could Thrice Ten Kingdom have to offer."

Branimir licked his lips in admiration. "After Lada, I am starting to think our ability to dream is trifling to what really exists."

"We are lucky to be limited in our thinking," Tyr said with wide eyes. "We do worse enough with what we know."

Alyona ran her hand through her greying hair, studying the door.

A ghastly, womanly form with shimmering green eyes, like emeralds, materialized on the steps without warning. She floated in mid-air, solemnly gazing at them as though she were making sense of where she had come, or how she had gotten there.

"Erzebeth!" Branimir recognized her immediately from the last he had seen her at *Garain'l*. "Why are you here?"

The skin-switching Vucari, Erzebeth Navenka, blinked away the glossed-over look, focusing on Branimir first with a knowing smile. The pale green light emitting from under her skin dimmed as she floated down to the bottom run of the stairs to meet them.

"Branimir," she acknowledged in a flat tone, "you have come to *Iriy*. Yet you still carry *kaelandur*. Who have you brought with you? I do not see Dorofej Kaligula in your company any longer."

"He is inside," Branimir explained.

Erzebeth nodded, half listening. She turned her neck first to Tyr, who slowly introduced himself with a look of confusion. He clearly knew Erzebeth was not a goddess. "Tyr Og, son of Enlil, from Almdalir."

Her face stayed like stone until turning to Alyona. Even as a ghost, the look of dread swept over Erzebeth's face. Her faint memory seemed to rush back to her, even without Alyona's words.

"Alyona Gounari, daughter of Meimer, from Lairhein," the *Kadari* said, squaring her shoulders.

Erzebeth swooped down to Alyona, reaching to touch her face. Alyona pulled away from the embrace, leaving Erzebeth's hand to fall back to her side. "My daughter," Erzebeth said, "you should never have been a part of this terrible tale. Meimer and I never wanted this for you. You were meant to stay safe in Lairhein."

"I know what you intended," Alyona said bitingly. "You sought to live forever to serve Wolos. You left Artemiy and me alone to find our own way."

Branimir remained frozen, watching the two. Tyr, also, seemed uncertain how to respond. He shuffled at Branimir's side.

Erzebeth backed away from her daughter, though her tone stayed defensive. "The Ash Tree *needed* protection. It still does."

"We *needed* a mother. You do not know how father ridiculed our Vucari blood. You will never know the heartache of a daughter abandoned…" Alyona blenched with a shake of her head. She snuffled, staring Erzebeth in the eye before finally turning away. "It does not matter anymore. My father is dead. Artemiy is dead. You are dead. And I am left behind to do what must be done."

Erzebeth tensed. "I am sorry, Alyona. I thought I was doing the right thing." Erzebeth blinked, searching for whatever words would bring her daughter comfort. She looked to Branimir, and sighed. "No matter how we elect to live our lives, we always seem to be burdened by the choices we did not make."

"Tell us why you are here, and then be gone," Alyona demanded, her voice cracking.

"Very well," Erzebeth said grimly, turning back to face Branimir. "I hoped you found a way to rid yourself of *kaelandur*. It must be destroyed so the brothers at Anaerfell can begin their quest. The threat of their saga being undone by *kaelandur* is too great. Destroy it so this world may still be saved."

"What are you talking about?" Tyr growled at her riddlesome words.

"I have done as I promised Branimir in *Garain'l*," Erzebeth said. "Wolos is dead and waits in the Netherworld to be rescued. *Lahmia* has set free Tyran and Drast Kaligula from *Anaerfell* to see the deed finished. They will undo their mistake and re-birth Wolos."

"They have *Ojenek*?" Branimir asked.

Erzebeth nodded. "They need your stone to see the task done. I will be joining them soon on the Kalinov Bridge to help guide them to Wolos's prison."

"Can it be done?" Tyr asked, looking to Alyona for answers. "Can two mortal men march into the Netherworld and resurrect a god?"

"They are not ordinary men," Erzebeth said. "They are dragon-men."

Tyr ran his hand through his red locks. "If Wolos were to be brought back to life, he would be able to lead the dead from the Netherworld. Aenar would be safe again."

"Zyem will tear the Kaligula brothers to pieces," Alyona said, turning back to face her mother. "They will not be allowed to pass over the bridge. Marheena would not allow it."

Erzebeth said. "We will see. Though, Tyran and Drast will undoubtedly fail if *kaelandur* is plunged into the Ash Tree and the Likhyi are released."

Branimir gripped the hilt at his belt, and began making his way up the staircase. He gripped the rose given to him by Lada in his other hand. An orange light seared between the double-doors as they opened on their own. Branimir gulped. "Then let's go ask the gods how to destroy *kaelandur*."

Chapter XX

Branimir could not guess how much time had come and gone since they entered the gate and started up the never-ending staircase. Not only did the sun stay at its apex over the City of the Gods, giving constant warmth and light in every crevice, but also something kept his stomach from hunger and his body from exhaustion. Every time his foot lifted and fell, his body seemingly had forgotten he repeated the same movement a hundred times before. In the beginning, the mundane climbing had been a game; but after a couple hours, he lost interest in playing. He stopped counting the stairs after reaching the thousands. Yet he felt no aching in his back, legs, or feet. Bran supposed he should be thankful for being away from the snow and wind on the mountain pass, but the monotony was wearing on him.

"You would think," he said, after several hours, "with all the magic in this place they would find a quicker way to the top. I bet the Svet's gateway takes them straight to the top of the peak."

Alyona ambled along behind him, responding with a dull tone. "Close. You arrive on the seventh tier, near the temple."

"Nine Lands. And no one thought to put one of those gateways at the bottom of these stairs?" Branimir asked, gazing at the rocky wall on either side of them. He was certain a dragon could fit on the staircase without discomfort. Which did not matter much, considering the dragon could fly to the peak of the mount.

Tyr held the smile on his face, climbing besides Branimir on the right. "Bah! Can you imagine when we go back down to leave? I bet we will lose our minds going back down these stairs." Tyr swung is giant arms back and forth as he climbed. Branimir hardly noticed he had six fingers anymore. "How about if we were to arrive through the doorway up there? And then, when we went to leave, we were faced with *this*? At least, we know, right?" Tyr rumbled, peering over his shoulder for an instant. The bottom of the winding staircase could no longer be seen. "I might consider flinging myself down the steps, or simply lying down and rolling. Maybe the gods will spare me if I crack my head."

Alyona's dry tone answered the unasked question. "No, they will not."

The smile faded from Tyr's face. "Well, I will not try to sprout wings and fly then."

Branimir looked at Alyona worriedly as she tread beside him on the left. Her mood had been sour since meeting her mother. She kept quiet for the most part, except when she had a stinging remark aimed to steal away their mirth.

He tried to rationalize Alyona's anger. He remembered, early on, when he first met Erzebeth in Arkaim. She always presented herself as having a mind for survival. From what Bran knew of Alyona, she likely shared this same trait with her mother.

"If you would like to turn into a bat, or something, and fly to the top, I could hold onto your clothes. You don't have to climb all these stairs with us," he offered.

"Yes, I do," she muttered, rubbing at her small nose. "I am not able to change forms here. Not only is it forbidden, but it is also impossible. We cannot wield any type of magic, even *Koldovstvo*."

"Really?" Branimir rubbed his chin in thought. The silver band of *Faegrim* touched the edge of his cheek.

Alyona pressed on. "Climbing the steps is supposed to show your resolve. Demonstrate your dedication to the gods."

"Because traveling a thousand miles through wind and snow, and facing demons along the way, is not enough," Tyr joked.

Branimir smiled, pulling at the edge of his nose. "Wait a second. If it is to test your will, why do the Svet get a gateway leading to the top?" he asked.

"Have you ever seen a centaur try to meander up a flight of stairs?" Tyr hooted with laughter. The image danced in Branimir's head, forcing him into a fit of laughter. One wrong footing and they would be sliding and stumbling back to the bottom. He imagined the effort of snaking up the stairs would be tenfold for a Svet.

Alyona smirked, walking on by them.

Tears touched the corners of Branimir's eyes. He leaned down to hold onto a step to keep from falling, doing the best to stifle his giggles. "Oh, it was funny, Alyona," he said. She ignored him. Shaking his head, Branimir cleared his throat to be more serious. "So, if Eisliev were to attack the City of the Gods, he would not be able to use *Koldovstvo*?"

Alyona shrugged. She clenched her fists, caught up in her own thoughts. Branimir noticed Tyr put a bit more space between them. Alyona did not seem to notice. Her tone was grave. "Eisliev cannot come here, Branimir. He has significant power because of *kaelandur*. But *kaelandur* was made by *Koldovstvo*, and *Koldovstvo* is controlled by Marheena."

Branimir piped up with excitement. "So, the gods would kill Eisliev if he came to *Iriy*? We should have led him here."

Alyona raised an eyebrow in confusion. He was, at least, glad to see a different emotion from the woman. "No. The gods would not do anything of the sort. This is sacred ground." She lastly relaxed her face, trying to find a way to explain. "He simply could not come to *Iriy*. You may never see Eisliev again if the gods can rid us of *kaelandur*."

Tyr dared to open his mouth again. Though, his tenor had lost its joviality. "What do you mean?"

She replied, "Eisliev does not have any purpose on Aenar without *kaelandur*. He was sent here by Marheena to release the *old-dark* from the Ash Tree by using the dagger. If he cannot break the chains, I would hope he would return to the Netherworld."

"Hope?" Tyr questioned. "From what I can gather, there is no place in the Netherworld for him. He will more than likely terrorize Aenar with his unchecked power."

Alyona frowned. "Pray it does not come to that."

Hours came and went before the three of them reached the top of the stone stairs and the second gate, which only stood a hair shorter than the first. As before, the rose in Branimir's hand proved to be the key to *Iriy*. An auburn light illuminated through the center crack, and soon, the massive iron doors creaked open to allow them entrance.

Alyona steered the way, unwavering in her task to take them to the top of the summit. Tyr, who had never been to *Iriy*, ogled alongside Branimir, examining the splendor of the city.

He could not steal away his gaze from the exhibition of exaltation.

The double-doors opened to a three-tiered, stone fountain sitting in the center of an extended walkway. Branimir could not help but stare at the craftsmanship. The stone had been chiseled to reflect a man wearing a crown, tipped with nine flames, kneeling in the swirling pool. The crystal, blue water sprouting from the top of the fountain dropped forty feet to sift through the man's hands before returning to the rippling water. He did not see a single chip or scratch in the fountain, nor a single flake of dirt or dust.

"What is this?" Branimir asked in awe.

Alyona stopped for a moment, twisting her head. "The gods in all their *glory* are no strangers to vanity. This is Perom, the Thunder-Bearer, the Creator. He rules here on *Iriy* while Svarog remains in the Kingdom. Naturally, he would be certain the first image seen in *Iriy* is one of himself."

"The Creator? I had always wondered who made the Kras," Branimir said.

"Perom made every race, Branimir. Did your people never teach you your origins?" Tyr asked. Branimir shook his head, thinking of how his people had their history stripped from them by the Highborn in centuries past. Tyr gestured at Perom's crown. "Nine flames for the nine races on Aenar: Anshedar, Vucari, Stuhia, Ispolini, Svet, Uvil, Lilitu, Arkono, and the Kras."

"By the Nine Lands," Branimir muttered, gawking at the bold chin and fiery gaze of Perom. "I do not even know all of those different people." His rotated around to gaze at the city from the top of the spiraling mountain down to his feet.

Branimir nearly jumped when he realized the paved stone under his feet had been hewn with as much care as the fountainhead. Portrayals of animals running among forests and fields had been carved the length of the path in all directions.

Alyona ambled off to the left. "This way. These gates are staggered out along each wall on each level. It should not take long to reach the top, and then we can speak with Perom."

Tyr rolled his eyes, grunting, "Bah! You act as though rushing through *Iriy* might grant us an audience quicker. The gods will surely do things in their own time, as they always have. Let us relish in this place. It will be a story we will want to tell someday."

Branimir did not miss the heavy look in Alyona's eyes as she looked over her shoulder. She half-nodded, but started walking.

His gut told him that Alyona was holding back from saying something more. Chewing the inside of his lip nervously, he followed her, determined to not disrupt their walk anymore.

Alyona ignored the ivory temples and stone shrines built into the rock. Multiple archways had been cut out, laden with peculiar vines growing from the stone. Under them were entranceways leading into the rock, beckoning Branimir to explore. His tongue quivered with wanting to ask what lay beyond each ingress; yet he said nothing and kept his feet behind Alyona.

The three of them trudged along through five more iron gates. Each rise gave way to what may have been grander sculptures of the gods and goddesses in their many known triumphs. Branimir begged to ask questions of the tales told through the sculptures, but again, he stayed quiet and simply marveled. He knew of a few select deities in the pantheon from those he journeyed alongside, but rarely had the time to hear the tales in their entirety.

But here, in *Iriy*, the history of the cycles and creation were mesmerizingly displayed to withstand the test of time, forever to be speculated upon. Walking along the streets was like strolling through antiquity.

As the orangish light seared through the seventh gate and the doors swung open, the red rose given to him from Lada dispelled from his fingers into ashes. He looked at his empty hand in bewilderment. "I thought we had two more gates to pass through before reaching the top."

Alyona guided them through the door. "We have reached the echelon of the lesser gods. I suspect we must wait here until Perom gives us permission to advance beyond the next gate." She cleared her throat in annoyance. "I thought he would be more eager to see us, considering the fate of the world is at stake."

"I am telling you, the gods do things in their own time, Alyona," Tyr said plainly.

"I know that, Tyr," Alyona snapped. "But this is not a normal instance."

Branimir precipitously turned about, looking through the wide streets and chiseled structures. Everything they crossed by had been beautifully created, but none filled the streets to know the greatness. "You are right. Where is everyone? Why has all this been created if none are here to appreciate it?"

Alyona swallowed her irritation. Her tone suddenly held as much awe as regret. "Many Stuhians and Vucari once lived here together in days long past, but after the Stuhians sought the power of *Koldovstvo*, everything changed. You may consider the divide to be the first breaking of the world, when mortals and immortals were no longer welcome in each other's company." Her eyes filtered down to *kaelandur* at Branimir's belt, despondently shaking her head. "Aenar will not survive a second breaking."

Movement in the road caught Branimir's eye. Based on Alyona's abrupt silence and Tyr's sudden kneeling, he knew they also saw the same sights. Though, Branimir had no inclination of falling to his knees.

A hundred paces away approached three figures. The first was a beautiful woman, taller than Alyona, with high cheek bones and long, red flowing hair. Her gown of gold and purple flowed across her frosty skin. The second, standing as tall as Tyr, had the body of a man, dressed in greens with gold lining, but had the head of a stallion. Branimir hardly had time to gawk at the strange being before he noticed the angled horse ears flip against the brown, stringy mane hanging down his back; the creature's black eyes reflected at Branimir. The horse-man reached out to touch the other man, clouded in black robes, with tufts of blood-red hair bursting from the edges of the hood. His icy eyes attuned to his surroundings along with the redheaded woman.

The three stopped in whatever conversation they may have been sharing along with their casual footfalls down the street.

"Dorofej," Branimir whispered, hardly recognizing the young, black mage, standing between the unnamed god and goddess. Branimir, in his excitement, scarcely noticed the divine light emanating from beneath the woman and horse-man's skin. He ran to embrace him, leaving Alyona and Tyr stooping on the paved stone. "Dorofej!"

A foolhardy grin split Dorofej's face as Branimir wrapped his arms around the waist of his old friend, almost knocking him off-balance. Dorofej patted Branimir on the back lightly, speaking in soft undertones. "Welcome to *Iriy*, the City of the Gods, Branimir Baran. At last, you have come; and *kaelandur*, you have brought."

"I am so sorry we did not come to save you at Melkorka. I wanted to," Branimir said with batted breath. "I cannot believe you lived."

"Give it any more thought, you should not," Dorofej said, pulling back to study Branimir. "I say, we have both had exceedingly difficult circumstances, yes? But, to the future, we must keep our attention. More difficult decisions are yet to come, I am afraid."

The horse-man whickered behind Dorofej, stealing away Branimir's long-winded response, and his question as to why Dorofej had come without him.

"I know," Dorofej said in response to the creature, a hint of sadness in his tone. He folded his arms from beneath his robes.

The redheaded woman folded her colorful gowns and glided closer to gaze at Branimir. Her long, pale fingers reached for him from under her wide sleeves; her touch was as cold as icicles against his cheek. Time slowed as she traced a fingernail from his chin to his eye, her emotionless eyes locking onto him. Branimir was spellbound, transfixed on the center pitch of her iris. He braced himself against a lucid vision dancing in front of him like images in a fire. Beyond her eye, he thought he saw the warped Ash Tree, its roots severed and limbs burnt black. The tree's color faded, sitting in gurgling waters under grey clouds. The luscious vines and fruits once ornamenting the Ash Tree had decayed, oozing slime and death. The stench of its rot clung to Branimir's nose. The familiar screeching of demons echoed.

And then, the image was gone, and only the woman lingered. She withdrew her finger, but a thought surfaced in Branimir's head.

'Speak again, we will, Branimir Baran. Learn, we will, if a world broken by the spirit of men may be saved by those thought the slighter.'

A burst of flashing light like the sun whipping through a crown of treetops pronounced the woman's sudden exit. The horse-man disappeared with her.

Branimir dizzily grabbed his head, hearing Alyona and Tyr whispering behind him. He looked to Dorofej for an explanation. "Who was that?"

"Ah," Dorofej said, seemingly unaware of the revelations that had been dancing in Branimir's head, "that was the honored Marheena, Goddess of the Netherworld, and her brother, Gero, the God of Trickery, Harvest, and a number of equally dreary titles."

Branimir's chest tightened at the thought of the Frozen Witch, the Goddess of Nightmares, touching him. She may have cursed him. "Marheena?" he gulped. "Being in her presence was nothing like when we met Lada."

"You would have seen Lada in the dale, yes?" Dorofej smiled with amusement. "A sweet thing, she is, but she does like to enchant mortals with her charm and beauty."

"Next time you see Gero," Branimir added, "you should tell him what evils the thieves guild in Eldhaft does in his name. They killed Adamus, Dorofej."

Dorofej rested his hand on Branimir's shoulder. "Care what men do in their name, the gods do not, Branimir. Told you this many times, I have, yes?"

"But they dishonor the gods," Bran said. "The thieves kill for Gero, the *Kadari* for Dahz, the Svet for Rujan, the Ariadneans for Czern, the Vucari for Wolos…" Branimir ran out of breath.

"Only themselves do they dishonor," Dorofej replied, cutting him off, "and whether their actions are fated, or not, will be determined when death comes to them, yes? I say, death has its purpose but only if we restore balance."

"What do you mean?" Branimir asked.

Dorofej did not answer. Tyr spoke aloud, approaching first with Alyona at his rear. "Branimir, you ought to show respect when you are in the attendance of the gods. Not all will take kindly to you running amuck."

The black mage grinned at the sight of the Ispolini and the *Kadari*. Branimir did not need any other sign to finally give peace to the thought that Alyona had been truthful with him about her purpose.

"Done the deeds you both have, I could not," Dorofej said, his blue eyes swelling with gratitude. "Not only do I give my many thanks, but through your actions, I hope the world will, too."

"We will see," Alyona said dryly, her purplish eyes meeting Dorofej's with strain. Branimir noticed Dorofej wrinkle his wide nose in consideration, noticing Alyona's disagreeable mood. Certainly, Dorofej could see she withheld words from slipping her tongue.

"I say," Dorofej reached for his beard to tug only to find his clean-shaven chin, "what news do you bring from the road?"

Alyona answered, placing her hands on her hips, "The *Kadari* have been cleansed from Aenar. Falmagon fell at Gavlok. Any remnants are scattered like dust in the sand, but the worship of Dahz will fade less eagerly in the lands of men."

"Told me of their defeat, Marheena did," Dorofej said, blinking. "Roaming the Netherworld, Falmagon is, already being twisted into a devilish wraith, bound to death." He pressed his thin lips together in certainty.

Branimir's throat tightened at the thought. "That is horrible. I cannot say I wish that fate on any man, no matter how evil."

"Wish it on him, too, I would not," Dorofej shockingly claimed. "And, an afterlife Falmagon eternally deserved, it is not." The black mage shook his head. "I fear Dagmar's fate was not so grand, yes?"

"Dagmar fell at Eldhaft, by his own hand…" Branimir said. "He used *kaelandur*."

Dorofej did not appear surprised. "I say, his wrath will be greater than Eisliev's. Fortunately, according to Marheena, drifting through the Netherworld, Dagmar still is." He slowly uncrossed his arms. "But what of Eisliev Kluk? Somewhere on Aenar, he is."

"We sent him back to the Netherworld when we escaped *Harrowhal*," Branimir replied. "We have not seen him again."

"Strange, indeed," Dorofej said. "Expected him to pursue the dagger tenfold, I would have."

"As did I," Alyona said. "Is he not in the Netherworld with Dagmar?"

Dorofej shook his head. "No."

Tyr frowned. "What reason would keep him from chasing Branimir and *kaelandur*? His desire for Dagmar's blood shadowed him into the afterlife, but with his enemy dead, nothing should hold him back."

"Would he return to torment Dagmar in the Netherworld?" Branimir asked. "He never did exact his revenge with Dagmar taking his own life."

"For certain, I cannot be." Dorofej rubbed his chin as though he missed his beard. "The pact made with Eisliev at Melkorka was inexplicably upheld by Alyona, yes? Agreed to help slay Dagmar and Falmagon, the three of us did; and done, it has been."

Branimir rattled his memory, recalling what Alyona said about Dorofej talking their way out of being killed at Melkorka. "Does that mean if the *old-dark* are released and destroy Aenar, the three of you will be spared?"

"Hm," Dorofej grunted.

"Only if Eisliev holds up to his end of the bargain," Tyr muttered.

"I do not understand why you would make such a deal with him, Dorofej," Branimir said. "He could not have killed you anyway. Dagmar told me you could only be killed with *kaelandur.*"

Dorofej scratched his nose, looking to Alyona and Tyr with sympathy. "Yet, killing these two, he would." As though a thought unexpectedly gripped his senses, Dorofej pulled back his robe and revealed a vial hanging from a leather loop on his belt. Branimir caught sight of several other vials too. "I say, Alyona, you have aged considerably since last we met. A vial, saved for you, I did."

The black mage handed the *Kadari* the flask of the Water of Life. She reached out and took it with an appreciative smile, clutching it to her chest. "Thank you, Dorofej."

"Now," Dorofej shooed them with his hands, "go wander about and find a place to rest, yes? Branimir and I have much to say before we speak with the Thunder-Bearer."

Dorofej tapped his lips with an anxious tick while Tyr and Alyona gracelessly accepted their forced dismissal and continued down the road. Branimir watched them only for a second before turning back to Dorofej, who watched him with enough intensity to shatter the ground at his feet.

"Will they come with us when we talk to the gods?" Branimir looked for a place to tuck his hands, and finally hooked his thumbs on his pants.

Dorofej hummed in his throat, suggesting he did not care if they did or not. "Searched for you many times in *Klukas,* I did, and always hidden from me, you were. Whilst in Melkorka or traveling to *Iriy*, discover your whereabouts, I could not." He raised his red eyebrows knowingly, stepping closer. "*Even* when I walked along Sulanna or Farthr on the opposite side of the veil, see you among them, I could not."

Branimir pulled the silver band from his finger, and handed it to Dorofej's already reaching hand. "The ring is called *Faegrim*. I took it from Eisliev after his death at Melkorka. He used it to control my mind when we were in Cavell before they took Bohumir from us." Branimir let go of the piece of jewelry, feeling a sense of loss. The ring had not been with him as long as *Ojenek*, but it unknowingly kept him safe for the past year. "It was not until Dagmar found us at Eldhaft that I learned *Faegrim* also kept me hidden from *Klukas*."

"A blessing that you had it, yes? Right about this trinket, Tyr had been," Dorofej said, rolling the circlet in his finger in wonder. "I say, many artifacts were made in the ageless days before the Stuhia learned of the dangers of mixing magic with the mundane. Unaccounted and forgotten, many still are."

"You mean that you do not know all of them?" Branimir asked with a half-smile. He supposed part of him believed that Dorofej knew everything.

"Know of *Faegrim*, I did not," Dorofej said. "Knowing what more may lie in the folds of time, I cannot say. Yet a shield to ultimately defend against our fates would be welcomed, yes?"

Branimir nodded, not missing the unnerving tone. "I also have brought you something more," Branimir said, reaching into his pocket. "I took this from Dagmar after he had fallen. Your book, the *Varkolak*." He presented the magically folded book, currently the size of his hand. With *Koldovstvo*, the book could be unfolded to be a weighty tome, brimming with Dorofej's recorded secrets.

He reached to touch the book and then withdrew with a satisfied smile. He curled his fingers into a fist, pulling his hands behind his back to keep himself from taking the volume. "A thief, you should have been, Branimir. Ever clever and wise, you truly are." Dorofej grinned, taking a breath. He scanned the statues and chiseled stone walls that surrounded them momentarily before continuing. "You keep the *Varkolak* until there is need, yes?"

Branimir crumpled his brow. He did not understand why Dorofej would cling to the newly acquired *Faegrim* while discarding his sacred text. Though, he had been around Dorofej long enough to know one question would only lead the black mage into riddles which would rarely lead to a sensible answer.

Bit by bit, Branimir tucked the *Varkolak* back into his pocket.

With a self-assured smile, Dorofej motioned for him to follow. His red hair bounced with each footfall as they headed toward the eighth gate.

"Will Perom see us so soon?" Branimir asked.

"Perom?" Dorofej repeated. "Oh yes, we will go see the Thunder-Bearer straightway. But eventually meeting with Svarog, the Grandfather of the Gods, we will be. From Thrice Ten Kingdom, he has come, to grant you audience, Branimir."

"The gods must be concerned about the *old-dark* if Svarog is coming all the way to *Iriy*, right? Alyona told me that Perom usually rules of *Iriy*, and oversees Aenar," Branimir said.

Dorofej hummed in his throat, not giving a clear answer to Branimir's question. "Keeper of Kowin the Deathless, Svarog is, and whether to release Kowin back into the world of the living, he must decide. I say, the Likhyi give him reason to consider doing so."

"Alden spoke of Kowin," Branimir said. "He said that the God of War had the power to call back Kowin to fight."

"He does," Dorofej said, "but bless the request, Svarog must. An easy decision, freeing Kowin, it is not."

"You are telling me that the God of War has already asked for Kowin's release then," Branimir said.

"Indeed, Svathevit has," Dorofej confirmed, "and your witness to Svarog will weigh heavily on his final decision, yes?"

"Why mine?" Branimir asked in shock. "Why should I give balance to the mind of a god?"

Dorofej looked down at Branimir with reverence. "I say, a fair question to ask. But even when asking, a humble heart, you have exposed; and the answer to the question, too, we have found."

Branimir breathed deep and scratched at his thin hair. He did not think he was so kind that he should sway gods in their thinking. Any mortal, by definition, did not have the wisdom of gods; and thus, they were ill-equipped to make godly decisions.

"Ah." Dorofej scratched at his head, seeing the eighth gate ahead of them on the path. "Time, we are wasting. I say, the tale of Kowin the Deathless, you must know, yes?" The black mage hurried his speech before Bran could reply. "Alive, he is not; yet, neither is he dead. The magic Kowin wields is effortless and eternal like that of the *old-dark*, yes?"

"He wields *Koldovstvo*?" Branimir asked.

Dorofej moved his mouth without words for a moment, searching for the best way to explain. "Kowin the Deathless *is Koldovstvo*. If the Likhyi were one, he would be the deadly amalgamation, yes?"

Branimir worked a finger in his ear. He must have misheard. His mouth dried. "Then why would Svarog consider releasing him on Aenar?"

The black mage went on, "The capacity to trap the Likhyi back into the Ash Tree, should they escape, or another prison, he has. Yet..." Dorofej gritted his teeth, his voice like ice, "if the Ash Tree dies, the Likhyi escape, and our gods die. Rule absolutely over Aenar, to forge the world however he would see fit, Kowin could, yes?"

"That is terrible!" Branimir finished. "How could we defeat such power?"

Dorofej tilted his chin, arriving at his point. "Neither blade, nor fire, nor anything natural can kill Kowin. Hidden is his soul, inside a needle, which is in an egg, which is in a duck, which is in a hare, which is in a chest, which Svarog has buried somewhere in this world," Dorofej said. Branimir scrunched his nose at the babbled explanation. Dorofej said, "Control over Kowin, Svarog has, as long as he holds power over the soul; but, if ever Kowin must know death, the needle must be broken."

Branimir grabbed Dorofej's robes, stopping him outside the eighth gate. The Stuhia turned to face him, holding more fear than Branimir had ever seen in his old master. "Why are you telling me this, Dorofej?"

The black mage clenched his jaw, pulling a red rose free from beneath his robes and holding it to the gates. The magical light separated the double-doors. As they opened, his voice trembled, "Remember, you must. Promise me, you will remember."

Branimir hesitated, letting go of Dorofej. "I promise."

Chapter XXI

The streets of *Iriy* remained empty. Branimir's chest swelled with sorrow considering the size and beauty of The City of the gods, and then comparing it to the haunting silence that inhabited the place. Nowhere could he find yelling merchants, laughter or conversation, or even the sound of shuffling feet. *Iriy* was dead.

Dorofej guided them to the Great Hall of the Gods, *Koranitsa*, sitting on the edge of the zenith. Branimir turned from the sanctuary to look at the peak of *Iriy*. Branimir could see the final gate and the utmost level beyond the circular black wall, separating them from the top sphere of the summit. Somewhere beyond the wall awaited Svarog, the Lord of Lords.

Dorofej's words stuck with Branimir, suggesting the High God of Wisdom sought his counsel. Though, Branimir could not imagine what he might say. He simply wanted *kaelandur* destroyed and the world saved. He supposed the gods had the power to make Aenar right again. Branimir wished he knew why they had not already; they surely did not need his permission.

Dorofej promised he would speak to Svarog soon. But first he was to be presented before Perom in *Koranitsa*. The enclosed sanctuary was positioned just east of the eighth gate, towering over all other edifices on this sphere. Branimir was certain he could have seen the magnificence of *Koranitsa* while standing at the base of the mount, but nothing could compare to standing so close.

Koranitsa had twenty-seven, ivory columns, standing thirty-foot tall, around the building, with a single, stone archway leading directly into the building. Sculptures of five gods were built at equal height of the columns, guarding the front of the temple. Branimir had seen similar images of the statues before in other places in the world to know who the figures represented.

From left to right, in a row, he first recognized Dahz the Lightbringer, with his pointed beard, grasping his hammer, *Mulafell.* Second in line, crouched Czern, the Grey-Clad, wearing his stone crown, *Maelifell,* and carrying his scythe, much like the statues found at the catacombs in *Garain'l.* And then, Perom stood with his thunder-axe held above the nine-pointed crown, depicting the races of his creation. The fourth was a beast with horns, three times thicker than the hilt of sword, balanced on hooves, and holding a spear like a shepherd's stick. Branimir could only guess the god to be Wolos, God of the Dead, and Protector of the Eternal Spring.

The final god, he could not place with the long, curling beard reaching his knees. Wings sprouted from the god's back, and, in his hands, he carried a long horn and trident.

"Who is that, Dorofej?" Branimir asked as they approached the effigies.

"Strega the Powerful, Ancestor of the Nine Winds, and Defeater of Marheena," Dorofej said, folding his arms inside his black robes.

"Strega's Deep," Branimir said with a smile, referring to the waters surround Maharia. "He is the god who governs the sea."

Dorofej dipped his head. "Mm. Seafarers would say his might is vaster than the other four, yes? But the measure of one god against another is but another way mortals divide each other, listening little to simple reason, even when told otherwise time and time again." Dorofej expounded on the thought. "Without each part working to be whole, the body cannot function. In the patterned skein, a thread each mortal is, and unraveled they have always been. I say, mortals are untiring in their effort to pursue war instead of peace, disagreement instead of harmony, hate instead of love, or opposition instead of friendship. Fearful, I am, that the world was never meant to be mended while mortals inhabit it."

Branimir swallowed. "If our flaws lead us to the breaking of the world, why would Perom create us to be imperfect?"

Dorofej ascended the steps to the temple. "I say, you cannot know real love without first loving imperfection. The appreciation of beauty may be fleeting, but never will you grasp a greater sense of meaning in this life, whether mortal or otherwise, yes?"

"I think I understand," Branimir said.

Dorofej smiled, gesturing for him to follow. "Come."

Whereas the sun shined endlessly over *Iriy*, giving light to the streets, the inside of *Koranitsa* did not have any such lighting. Of course, Branimir, barely noticed the change, examining the room without difficulty.

The room was as large as he imagined, capable of holding hundreds of people. More columns were positioned equally around the edges of the grand room, much like the twenty-seven outside the temple, to hold up the vaulted ceiling. He almost expected the ceiling and walls to be painted with grand colors and images of the gods, but they had been left completely blank, colored a whitish grey. The center of the floor, however, was decorated with patterned colors that did not make any sense to Branimir. The purples and reds, blues and greys, and yellows swirled and overlapped in exhausting complexity. Time did not seem to wear on anything in *Iriy*.

"Wait much longer, we should not," he said.

Branimir took Dorofej's word and followed him to the center of the room.

Five hours later, he and Dorofej retired to sitting positions on the floor. Branimir walked the inside perimeter of *Koranitsa* several dozen times until the mind-numbing task had worn on him to the point he thought he might cry from absolute boredom. He spent the last hour tracing the colors on the floor with his fingers, while Dorofej sat cross-legged against one of the far columns with his eyes glazed. He could only assume Dorofej entered *Klukas*, but what he had gone to observe, Branimir could not guess.

If time were a weapon, the gods wielded it with perfection. Branimir had no rational defense against time. Due to the enchantment of *Iriy*, he was kept from knowing tiredness, or hunger, or any bodily ailment. Instead, he had been abandoned in silence with his rootless, banal musings. His mind wandered, thinking of Alden, Sulanna, Adamus, and so many others. Many traveled with him over the ages, and now, most had been lost or forgotten. He did not want to remember any longer; he did not want to be waiting in this abandoned temple. At this point, he would have welcomed a headache to add a bit of zest to this sapping reality. Yet he had no choice but to endure.

"By the Nine Lands, it must be dull to be a god," Branimir muttered. Even at a whisper, his voice rebounded off the stone walls of *Koranitsa*.

Dorofej stirred with a grunt. "I say, what is that? Come, have they?"

Branimir poked aimlessly at the painted colors under his stretched-out feet. "No, Dorofej. My apologies for waking you."

"Quite alright," Dorofej said, adjusting his robes around himself. "Perhaps, something of import, I can share with you to pass the time."

"Tell me why you did not come to meet me on the road, and you rushed to *Iriy* without me," Branimir said finally, his hands shaking with anticipation. "Why did you send Alyona and Tyr, but never come yourself?"

"Clear, I thought the answer was," Dorofej said, folding his hands in his lap. "I say, it was too dangerous to be near you with Eisliev, Dagmar, or Falmagon in pursuit."

"You were afraid of dying?" Branimir accused.

Dorofej's blue eyes widened with surprise. "Afraid of death, I no longer am, Branimir. For a long while, I have been, but we all must die, yes?" He swallowed, attempting to form his next words. "Rightly fastened to *kaelandur's* fate, my life is, but yours is not. I say, if I had come for you, and was struck down, you would have fallen with me."

"You stayed away from me to protect me?" Branimir asked in disbelief. "I could have still died apart from what happens to *kaelandur.*"

"True," Dorofej conceded. "Yet, another threat on your life, I would have been."

Branimir wrung his hands together, watching Dorofej carefully. The black mage had been eager to share knowledge with Branimir since they reunited only hours ago, whereas before, Dorofej always kept his secrets well hidden. Either he had an awakening at Melkorka, or he believed he was going to die. Branimir hoped it was the former. "What would have happened if Falmagon would have won? What if he destroyed *kaelandur* and killed us?"

Dorofej sighed, readjusting himself against the hard flooring. "Many things, I am afraid. Erzebeth may still have my great-grandsons attempt to resurrect Wolos, yes? But, continue to weaken the Ash Tree, Falmagon and his *Kadari* would have, which would have strengthened the *old-dark* until the success or failure of Wolos's re-birthing."

"But the *old-dark* could not have been granted their full freedom," Branimir said.

"No. Not unless another means of destroying the Ash Tree came into existence, yes?" Dorofej replied. "But Falmagon's closed-minded teachings would have continued to infect the hearts and minds of men, ridding them of free will for his own gain. Some may consider the *Kadari* to be righteous in solely aligning mortals under the Lightbringer; but, inhumane, I believe it to be." The black mage gestured to the temple they sat inside. "Many other paths exist for mortals to explore, yes?" Dorofej returned his hands to his lap. "Come, what else?"

"Um," Branimir scratched his head. "Tell me about the *old-dark*."

"Ah, yes," Dorofej said. "A topic worth exploring in more detail, yes? Eight Likhyi, there are, who were long ago trapped in the Ash Tree by Kowin the Deathless at the direction of the gods found in the modern world."

"The *old-dark* are gods, too?" Branimir asked.

"What the Likhyi are precisely, I cannot say, but believe them to be ancient gods, some do," Dorofej said. "I say, the same could be said of Kowin the Deathless; though, what he is exactly, I also do not know."

Branimir pressed. "What do you know about the Likhyi?"

"Remember Kowin is *Koldovstvo*, yes? Still, a manifestation of each of the eight cruxes of *Koldovstvo*, the *old-dark* are: void, primal, profane, sacred, fire, sky, stone, and sea. Elements of the world, these are," the black mage said, rubbing his pointed chin. "Profane, the Likhyi was, who we encountered at *Garain'l*, and void, the Likhyi was, who Farthr had said to have found at Shayol Domier."

Branimir hesitantly touched *kaelandur* at his belt. The Likhyi who ruled over profane magic was trapped within the blade.

Dorofej continued, "Where the others may be emerging, I wish I knew; though, no defense do I know to shield humanity from their wrath. Know the extent of their strength, I do. For, fed by one of these elements, each Stuhian man or woman's bloodline is, giving them a taste of the power of the Likhyi."

"From Marheena?" Branimir concluded with a raised eyebrow. "Marheena took the power of *Koldovstvo* from the Likhyi, and gave it to the Stuhians."

"Hm. Well, different traits of the Likhyi, each of the prevailing gods possess. I say, whether it be creation, or magic, or the turn of seasons, the gods see the phases of life completed," Dorofej paused, finally nodding, "but yes, through Marheena, the Stuhia spring their magic. All Stuhians can touch the primary elements of fire, sky, stone, and sea; but, allotted only one of the secondary elements, we are. The strength of our blood determines the amount of life drained from our being, yes?"

Branimir narrowed his eyes at Dorofej. "Alyona told me the Kaligula bloodline is bound to void magic, and yet, you also use sacred magic. Are those both not secondary elements?"

"Yes, they are," Dorofej said, a smile forming at the corner of his mouth. "I say, when I still sat on the Carian Council—when I had begun transcribing the *Varkolak*—I sought to complete the dragon-blood ritual to heighten my power. Though, seek an ordinary dragon, as many might, I did not. In secret, *Zywey*, the gold-plated dragon, I slaughtered, and her sacred blood, I consumed." Branimir stared in amazement at the black mage. Dorofej returned the gaze with endless interest, and then rolled his eyes. "Pleased by the slaughter of his precious *Zywey*, Wolos was not."

"I would think not." Branimir frowned.

Dorofej closed his icy blue eyes, leaning his head back against the column. "Young and restless, I was. If I had known about the *Alatir Stone* before, I would have sought it instead, yes? Forever, it keeps you safe from disease and injury and aging."

Branimir's jaw dropped at the prospect of another shiny stone, brimming with magic. "Do you have the *Alatir Stone* now, Dorofej?"

He kept his eyes closed, despondently shaking his head, speaking mellifluously, "Located somewhere in the Netherworld, it is. Searched for the stone, I did, while we trekked about the frozen wasteland, but never was it revealed to me. Perchance, Zyem holds it at the Kalinov Bridge, yes?"

A crack of lightning near the entranceway knocked Branimir back on his buttocks in fright, and even sent Dorofej scuttling away from the door leading outside.

Suddenly, none other than Perom, the Lord of Aenar, appeared from the thunderbolt, standing nearly twenty-foot tall with his thunder-axe held over his head at an arc. His eyes crackled like thunderclouds, his face like stone; even his pointed, copper beard beneath his silvery hair appeared unyielding. He shielded the exit to the outside street, his dark skin rippling with muscle, scrutinizing Branimir and Dorofej beneath him. The nine-pointed flamed crown on his head fervently burned. Branimir could do little but stare in awe, his skin prickling.

The moment should have remained staggering, but Branimir's attention was drawn from Perom. Dahz, the Lightbringer, emerged from a gateway forming from the stone wall, riding on his sun chariot, *Mioengi*, pulled by the oversized goat-stag with flaming feet and fiery eyes. In a fluid motion, he bounded from the back, clutching *Mulafell*, while sending the chariot flying across the temple through a gateway arising suddenly on the other wall. Flames rippled from the corners of his eyes, standing at equal height of Perom.

Branimir cowered away from the celebrated god of the *Kadari* only to bump into Dorofej.

From the opposing wall, where the chariot exited, materialized Strega, God of Wind and Water, from bristling smoke and cloud. His long, white beard rolled across the floor in front of him, running the length of the floor, causing Branimir to briskly scoot the other way. He flipped the trident in his hand, the ethereal weapon's ends emerging and disappearing through the walls of the sanctuary without making physical contact. He, too, reached the towering heights of *Koranitsa*—standing thirty-feet tall—bespeaking of his divine presence.

And then came Czern, the God of Darkness, hobbling through the door, maintaining the appearance of an old man with a wrinkled face. He outwardly ignored the other gods' intimidating stances, locking his eyes on Branimir. He hobbled forward with his scythe, using it as a walking stick, remaining wrapped in his bulky, grey robes. His stone crown, *Maelifell*, sat crooked over his brow as though it had been placed there in haste.

Czern opened his mouth as though he might speak first, but stopped, and wrinkled his nose. He blinked several times, raising a single white eyebrow with a sense of confusion. He seemed to have forgotten how to form words with his tongue.

In the next breath, the other gods and goddesses rallied in a circle behind Branimir. Dorofej eased to his knees next to Branimir, identifying them as they appeared.

"Myestera, the Mother of the Stars," he said, as a dark-haired woman emerged next to Dahz, yet standing at equal height as Czern. Next to Perom materialized another woman, older and in simple clothing. She, too, appeared as a human might, standing humbly before him. "Mokosh, the Weaver," Dorofej identified her, while motioning for Branimir to respectfully stay at his knees. "They have nearly all come, yes?"

Behind them surfaced Marheena, the Frozen Witch, and Gero, the God of Harvest, tilting his stallion head to better see Branimir. Neither needed an introduction. Branimir balanced himself on his shaking knees, turning his eyes away from Marheena. The vision of the dying Ash Tree she placed in his mind left a lasting image.

Lastly came Lada, the Lady of Flowers, in a flash of white glory. Her golden hair flowed behind her with every step she took, bouncing delicately against her white, floral-patterned gown.

The room vibrated with divine power, a low hum ringing in Branimir's pointed ears.

Lada, standing at the height of an Ispolini, glanced over the room at the other deities. The gods did not speak as mortals might, but imprinted their thoughts on Branimir's mind. Sometimes more than one thought would fill his mind at a single time. Strangely, Branimir inherently could identify who spoke, even though not everyone made a signifying gesture.

First spoke Lada, her voice like ringing bells, *'Grievously pressed, we have become. Let us speak plainly as to not confuse the mortals. Be certain your words are known in their tongue.'*

'Present, some still are not,' Perom rustled, his authoritative disposition clear among the other gods. He peered down at Lada. *'Ever late, grows the hour. How much longer should we wait?'*

'Easy, Thunder-Bearer,' mocked the Lightbringer, his voice booming in Branimir's head like horse's hooves. *'Cleansing the mortal does not require Svarog to be here.'*

Perom's face did not reflect his annoyance, but his voice was biting. *'I speak not of Svarog, but of Svathevit the Red. The judgment must be undisputed.'*

Dorofej kept Branimir hunched over with his right hand, peeking through his red locks at the gods. Branimir stayed stooped, while trying to make sense of the conversation.

'Svathevit has given his sanction,' Marheena said, her voice cracking like breaking ice, *else he would not have brought Kowin to be birthed back into the mortal world.'*

'*A mistake,*' Strega mumbled, his white beard waving over his chest as though a breeze blew beneath the stringy, white hairs. Several of the other gods murmured in agreement, while others simply mumbled nonsense.

Marheena spoke louder, *'We must hurry. The wards protecting Iriy are failing.'*

What 'of the Protector of the Eternal Fallows?' Czern blinked several times, clasping his lips together in a pout. *'Should we not postpone til his homecoming?'*

'Wolos is dead, Czern.' Dahz growled, the fire in his eyes igniting. He began speaking before Czern had time to finish the thought. *'Time for your games, we do not have, brother.'*

Czern adjusted the stone crown on his head. *'He may not be pleased to return and find we made a judgment before his rebirthing.'*

'We cannot give pause and see whether the mortals will resurrect him,' Perom said definitively. He folded his arms across his chest, the thunder-axe held firmly in his hand. *'You steer the dialogue away from the dispute, Czern. Let us find unanimity quickly and be done.'*

Dahz addressed the gods and goddess, *'I remind you, a ruling on Branimir Baran, son of Hrani, and his unnatural bond to the Likhyi, we give. Be swayed by the fate of the forged weapon, you should not be.'*

Marheena neared closer behind Branimir. *'We need no reminder, Protector of Men. We are not moved by mortal desires. We have not the capacity.'*

Lada's voice purred, pressing them to conclusion, *'The old-dark has fated Branimir Baran to an untimely, mortal death for his nobility. All in favor of overruling this mortal's bound fate, and re-weaving his life-thread to foster further goodness, speak now.'*

'The Likhyi yet have the power to command fate,' Strega said. *'No argument is there to be had.'*

'Bound to the old-dark, Branimir Baran, son of Hrani, should never have been,' said Mokosh.

'Remember the grace of the prevailing gods, he should, until death touches him naturally, or comes for us all,' spoke the Lightbringer.

Branimir's mind swirled with the resounded consonance of additional statements, speaking positively of saving him from *kaelandur's* fate. He rose slowly on his knees in confusion. Only now did he begin to understand what was happening. He looked to Dorofej for an explanation, but the black mage stayed on his knees, eagerly nodding his head.

This was the real reason Dorofej had come early to *Iriy*; he had pleaded for Branimir's life.

"You will not destroy *kaelandur*?" Branimir spoke aloud, regarding the many gods in their magnificence. "I came to *Iriy* so you might rid us of this cursed dagger destined to break the world. My life means little in comparison!"

'Kaelandur is not for the gods to remedy,' Perom thundered from above him.

Branimir's mind reeled, dumbfounded. He had come all this way and the gods would do nothing to help them. They would let the world crumble.

'Decided, it has been,' Dahz, the Protector of Men, said with a boom. *'Myestera, purge Branimir Baran of his burden, so we may leave. Kaelandur's magic has weakened the city. The red mage breaches the gates.'*

Branimir twisted in fear, making sense of their words.

The dark-haired Moon Goddess, who Branimir heard much about from Erzebeth in ancient days, glided across the stone flooring and then kneeled at Branimir's side. Her wide eyes met his, filling him with a sense of tranquility that he was unsure he had ever felt before. Perhaps, a long time ago, in the arms of his mother he had felt so serene. Branimir could not be for certain. But he knew the agitation that tightened his chest only moments ago lifted from his body, and quickly drifted to a distant memory.

She hummed a song as elegant as an evening's breeze, soothing him until he wanted nothing more than to lay his head down to sleep. Yet as he peacefully slouched over and closed his eyes, her hand caught his chin, holding him against her lap. Myestera leaned into him, caressing his cheek. Her hand was as soft as a mother's kiss. Without rhyme or reason, Branimir nuzzled into her embrace.

The throbbing began in the back of his skull, trailed down his spine, and churned in his stomach. Surprisingly, he was unflustered by the sharpness burrowing somewhere inside of his skin. The pain was genuine—as real as what he had went through in *Harrowhal* or *The Oaken Bard*—and he held no concern.

When the primordial scream tore from his gullet, he believed the sound to have come from a dream. He may have juddered in Myestera's arms; he may have thrashed. He may have bled.

When he opened his eyes again, the recollection regarding the Likhyi being peeled from his essence was a waning thought. Myestera returned him to his knees, and rose to her feet. Her singsong voice echoed inside his skull.

'No longer will you share the fortune of kaelandur, Branimir Baran, son of Hrani.'

Chapter XXII

Golden light flashed. The Great Hall of the Gods was emptied as swiftly as it had been occupied, save Branimir, Dorofej, and Marheena. The Goddess of the Netherworld lingered, without a word, in the dimness of the temple, watching and waiting, like a looming storm.

Branimir looked at her from the corner of his eye, his hand shaking against the hilt of *kaelandur*. He could not understand why the Frozen Witch would stay behind, unless she wanted to kill him now that he had been saved. Warily, he twisted around searching for Perom, or Dahz, or even Strega to demand answers to his questions, but no, the only uncouth deity left was Marheena.

In truth, he feared the Seamstress of Nightmares; she simply touched him and forced him to see the decaying Ash Tree. He did not want to think about what other terrible images she could force into his head. Yet the thought of her holding such power over him only added wood to the fire burning inside of him.

If anything, she was the most blameworthy for all that had befallen him and Dorofej.

Since Melkorka, her schemes left the world on the brink of destruction. Branimir fought Nedezhda and Eisliev, who she sent back; he battled against her hordes of undead, and her battalions of demons. He survived the frozen Netherworld, and he would survive her in this moment, too.

Despite her divinity, and her reputation for malice amongst mortals, Branimir's fury beat against the inside of his chest. He quivered with untamed anger. His vision turned crimson, as blood red as Marheena's flattened hair, clinging to her pale cheeks.

Yet, before he could say a word, her thoughts became his own. She whispered to him as sweetly as a thief might before stealing a coin purse. *'Promised you we would speak, I did, Branimir Baran. Make haste, for time is fleeting.'*

Branimir fumed. "You have made a mistake. You all have made a mistake!" he screamed. "Call back the Thunder-Bearer and the Lightbringer! Bring back those who can make this right. You must destroy *kaelandur* before the Ash Tree falls."

"Branimir…" Dorofej started, rising from the stone flooring with a lenient smile. "I say, no mistake has been made."

He did not listen to Dorofej. He could not listen to Dorofej. "The gods must take *kaelandur*. Take it and shatter it into a thousand pieces. Save us!"

'Take kaelandur, I cannot. The dagger is from the world of mortals, crafted by mortals. No more can I touch the dagger than the dagger can touch me.'

"Take it," he repeated. "Please. You are a goddess." He could not believe what she was saying. He blinked the water from his eyes. "You must destroy the dagger."

Marheena flowed tranquilly, closing the distance between herself and Branimir. The gold and purple gown rippled with her rapid movement. She tensed her cheek bones and entered Branimir's mind again.

'Branimir Baran, eliminating the peril of kaelandur, and giving shape to this world, rests with you and Dorofej Kaligula. The gods script the pages of history; never do we give precedence to what has not yet come to pass.'

"Nine Lands, you don't!" Branimir barked, his inflection demeaning, staring up at the Frozen Witch. He twisted his sadness into further ire. He jerked *kaelandur* from his belt, holding it daringly close to Marheena's chest, despite her warning that it could not touch her. "*You* commanded Dorofej to craft this dagger. *You* guided the world to its death! And now, *you* refuse to make amends with those you have wronged with your devilish plots!" Branimir screamed, his voice echoing off the stone walls. Marheena only watched him with utter serenity. He howled, "My friends died because of you!"

Dorofej began to say something to Branimir, but he could not hear it over Marheena's reverberating tone. In fact, he was sure Dorofej stopped talking mid-sentence as though Marheena hushed him partially through whatever he might have been saying.

Mistake the gods, you do, Branimir Baran. Preserve the wax and wane of the finite, we do: the succession of time, and seasons, and life and death. The Kaligula bloodline unbalanced the scales, and parallel again, they must become.'

"You think the Likhyi will return balance to the world again?" Branimir curled his lip in disgust. Marheena's expression was emotionless. Branimir shook his head. "The *old-dark* will cleanse the world of everything you have created."

'As we once cleansed it of all they had created. Sacrifice must be made to keep balance.'

Branimir slowly lowered the dagger to his side, gazing into Marheena's blue irises. His words were more of realizations than questions. "You do not care if you die. Being forgotten means nothing to you. You…you are not truly a part of this world."

To die is to be bound by time, and therefore, to be mortal. The gods cannot die; the gods are time.' Marheena echoed her reason. *'Either Wolos should be unbound or the Likhyi released.'*

"You rule the Netherworld!" Branimir shouted. "You could release Wolos at any time."

'Imprison him in death, I did not. Mortals made their choice, and now, they must decide if they deserve to stay upon Aenar.'

"You mean Dorofej and I must make a choice," Branimir said, gritting his teeth. "I understand Dorofej's kin have upset the balance of the world, but why must the burden be put on the two of us?"

"I say," Dorofej said, clearing his throat, "one of us must make a choice, Branimir. *Kaelandur* must be ended, yes?"

"No," Branimir said, turning to Dorofej, "you cannot die." His nose twitched, fighting back tears.

Dorofej's blue eyes watered as well, nodding his head so that his shaggy, red hair bobbed against his ears. His thin lips struggled to form the words. Although Dorofej looked young, Branimir could see the old man with a tasseled beard sadly looking back at him. His icy blue eyes reflected the hearth fire's flame that had long ago given heat to forge *kaelandur*. Dorofej never quailed as he now did. His accented tenor quaked with dread. "I have never loved death, but a mistress I must still lay with, she is."

Branimir grabbed his head as though it might withhold his sorrow. He shouted at Marheena. "He cannot die! You cannot keep me from *kaelandur's* fate, and forsake Dorofej to share it."

Marheena leaned forward, the chill from her body prickling at his skin. *'At Dorofej Kaligula's behest you were shielded from this fate, Branimir Baran. The gods have elected to award his appeal; do not be wasteful of his faith in you.'*

He could not speak at the confirmation of the revelation. Dorofej brought him to *Iriy* to have the gods heal him from the curse of the Likhyi.

"Branimir," Dorofej said pleadingly, "trust in Erzebeth, we must. She goes to *Anaerfell* to lead my kin to the Netherworld to give rise to Wolos once again, yes? I say, our tale ends with the destruction of *kaelandur*. Saved, the Ash Tree will be.”

“Unless they fail, and Marheena entices another to make a weapon to set the *old-dark* free,” Branimir said. “You would have ended your life for nothing.”

“A chance, we must take,” Dorofej said. “Without balance, the world will forever be inundated with demons.”

“You do not have to die, and *kaelandur* does not have to be destroyed. We are safe from Eisliev in *Iriy*,” Branimir argued. “We could stay here indefinitely, or, at least, we could wait to see if Wolos is reborn. Alyona said he could not step foot inside of these walls—”

The temple flashed with a fiery, blue light, illuminating a path to the door leading outside. Immediately, Branimir was forced to his knees by an unseen power pulling him down by the shoulders. At first, he thought Marheena or Dorofej had grabbed ahold of him, but they, too, had dropped to their knees by the same force. With a startled cry, Branimir covered his eyes from the sudden brightness, peering between his fingers as three shadows emerged from the glow, transforming into human figures, as tall as giants.

Although three stood, Branimir could only look upon one. Once his eyes fell on the High God, he could not steer them away, nor did he have the desire. Even without introduction, Branimir knew the god to be Svarog, the Grandfather of the Gods, the Lord of Lords. The recognition came from somewhere deep within his being, potentially known before his own creation.

Svarog, his eyes shrouded in a golden blindfold, cocked his head at them as they knelt. His white beard shamed the long beard of Strega, folded and tied so many times that the hair may have reached across the expanse of Aenar. In his right hand, he clutched a fistful of flaming spears, burning as bright as the blaze silhouetting his white and yellow robes.

His imperious, orotund timbre fell from his lips—unlike the lesser gods, who shared their thoughts in the minds of mortals—and crashed against the walls of *Koranitsa* as though the very stone could have bled his word and will. "The *Hall of Iredale* is devoid of mortals bearing witness, and the hour has passed. Svathevit the Red has implored for Kowin the Deathless to return to Aenar to stay the balance. Alas, I can see the charge of Dorofej Kaligula has yet to be fulfilled. Will it be so, Branimir Baran, son of Hrani?"

Branimir shook on his knees. In the distance, he thought he could hear the cracking of stone, thunder felling, and wind rustling as strong as the northern gale. Svarog shadowed over him, even at a distance. The sound in Branimir's ear amplified as though the sanctuary let loose the din from the columns holding it sturdy. Branimir felt disoriented, still unable to see those who stood with Svarog, and completely incapable of looking to Dorofej and Marheena. He stammered incoherent words, scarcely understanding what was being asked of him.

As though Svarog saw his confusion, he clarified the task to Branimir. "The magic of *kaelandur* will not allow Dorofej Kaligula to die by his own hand. Will you rid him of it, Branimir Baran, son of Hrani?"

Branimir squeezed *kaelandur* in his hand, realizing Svarog never wanted him to bear witness with his words, but by his actions. "No!" Branimir bawled. "No, I will not! I will not kill him."

Svarog's tone flattened, gazing blindly at the ceiling through the golden wrapping over his eyes, "Kowin the Deathless will remain in Thrice Ten Kingdom until Dorofej Kaligula's soul resides in the Netherworld with his brethren in the afterlife."

Branimir suddenly could turn his eyes from the Grandfather of the Gods, to see the corpse of a half-dead man, skin rotted and peeling, chained on Svarog's left. The eyes were sunken into his skull; his cheeks had decayed to the degree that Branimir could see the putrefied teeth in his enflamed, bloodied gums. The chains rattled around his wrists and ankles as he shifted, sneering at Branimir. Kowin the Deathless, adorned in his faded, crimson armor and dual-side swords with decorated hilts, billowed smoke from his mouth as Svarog raised his hand with his ordinance. Without warning, Kowin turned to ashes, disappearing from the temple.

"Be certain the Deathless stays caged until the appointed time," Svarog directed the man on his right. The God with Four Heads, Svathevit the Red, showed as bright as a morning sunrise. He made no motion to indicate he heard Svarog, keeping the same emotionless expression on all four faces on each side of his head. His fierce gaze missed nothing. His blood-red cloak draped over his shoulders, swirling in an untamed breeze, from some distant world beyond the temple. His magnificence was only lessened by Svarog's overshadowing glory.

Svathevit disappeared in a flash of light, taking Marheena with him from Branimir's side.

Svarog folded his arms in what Branimir believed to be displeasure. "The sacredness of *Iriy* wanes in the presence of *kaelandur* and the Likhyi within, diminishing the protective wards. The power of the *old-dark* grows stronger as the Ash Tree fades." Branimir attempted to debate Svarog, but found his mouth would not open. Svarog went on, disregarding him, "although, the Ash Tree cannot be fully abolished without *kaelandur*, the chains holding the Likhyi will fracture, giving them a greater bearing on the mortal world."

"I will not kill Dorofej," Branimir finally forced between his clenched teeth.

Svarog turned away. A blue light deepened around him to pull him back to the Beyond, to Thrice Ten Kingdom. "*Iriy* is no longer a haven. Eisliev Kluk has come."

The High God of Wisdom and Fire was swallowed whole by the divine light, leaving Dorofej and Branimir kneeling against the stone of *Koranitsa*.

The gods had abandoned them.

Chapter XXIII

The paved streets under Branimir's feet quaked as they sped from the Great Hall of the Gods. The entire mountain shook with such intensity, Branimir wondered if the city of *Iriy* would collapse to the dale below. In the distance, he could hear the crack of lightning and the fracturing of rock. Along with the clamour sounded the low-rumbling roar of demons rasping and growling on the lower levels as they marched up the mountain. The beginnings of a war had reached the gates.

"I don't understand." Branimir faced Dorofej in the arching shadow of *Koranitsa*. "*Iriy* should have been safe from Eisliev and the demons. Why have the gods forsaken us?"

"*Kaelandur's* magic and the power of the Likhyi have weakened the city, yes? And causes to battle against this inescapable doom, the gods have not. The Likhyi and the gods are cut from the same cloth, yes? I say, the *old-dark* already have begun to destroy the fabric of this world, even when partially caged," Dorofej said, the irritability unmistakable on the edge of his tongue, "and they begin with the destruction of *Iriy*. Hear nothing from the gods' wisdom, did you? Men invited this calamity, and men must either remedy the mistake or embrace it."

Branimir ran his hands through his hair, pulling at the thin strands with aggravation. The city around him, in all its magnificence, would crumble, because he brought *kaelandur* to its gates with the Likhyi trapped inside. The gods were supposed to help him. "You and I were not the ones who killed Wolos. Why should we pay for another's mistake?" he asked.

"Every action is worthy of consequence, yes?" Dorofej rhetorically asked. "Speak of good and evil, or right and wrong, I do not; but about what naturally occurs. The fields, forests, and streams are upset for centuries by a nation's cultivation, yes? Our children and our children's children are impacted by the wars of their fathers, yes? Can one man's hate not squelch the love of another? For eternity, the faults of one man can become the burdens of another." The city of *Iriy* pitched, nearly knocking Branimir to his knees. Dorofej grabbed him by the shoulders, jerking him close. His words were as water dousing flames. "The question is not *why you and I*, but *why are more not* seized at knife's edge? For, in every choice we make, we should think of ourselves as pressing a dagger to our brother's chest, and then see whether our selfishness has wounded the heart."

"I will not wound you, Dorofej," Branimir said, his words garbled. "I would give my last breath before I would see it done."

Dorofej sighed with exasperation, letting go of him. The black mage looked over his shoulder, listening to the demons marching toward the eighth gate. "I say, Eisliev will no longer be kept from *kaelandur*. Re-balanced, the scales of the world must be. You must take my life, Branimir, and destroy *kaelandur*, yes? Give mortals another chance to find their way. Win this battle, we cannot."

Anger flared—more than anger—but he hammered it down. He wanted to scream until his throat bled so Dorofej might hear his resounding response to the harrowing solution. He forced breath through his nostrils in attempt to release steam from his inner ire. His answer emerged as a choked whisper. "No."

Dorofej tried again. "Branimir—"

"We will flee *Iriy* and find another solution, even if I have to travel back to the Netherworld and kill Eisliev with my own hands," Branimir said hastily. "We need you, Dorofej. I need you."

"Branimir! Dorofej!" Alyona shouted, running toward them from further up the road. She appeared to be coming down from the highest spire, appearing as young as she had when they first met at Gaetana months ago. She had clearly taken the vial of the Water of Life that Dorofej had given her.

Tyr trailed right behind her, his eyes wide with concern as the sound of the approaching army grew louder.

Alyona stuttered to a halt feet from them. "Eisliev is attacking the city and has brought half the Netherworld with him. How is this possible?" She looked at Dorofej for an explanation. "*Iriy* is sacred ground. This city should be untouchable by the hand of death."

"Enfeebled the consecrated wards, the primal Likhyi in *kaelandur* has," Dorofej explained. A deafening crack sounded from the gate behind them, the iron and stone splintering.

"That is impossible," Alyona said disbelievingly. "No one has ever marched on the City of the Gods."

"Nine Lands," Branimir muttered, turning to face the walls. He suddenly realized an inescapable truth. "Sulanna and Alden are still down below. We must—"

Tyr halted his words. He could not keep the sadness from his deep tone. "Nothing is left down there but demons, Branimir. We could see the entire dale from the summit above. It is lost."

"They may have escaped," Branimir said, taking a step backward as though he might leap over the mountain's edge to search for his friends. He looked at Tyr and Alyona for any sign of hope. The shared looked between the two plumbed the depths of despair.

"Only one road leads in and out of *Iriy*," Alyona replied.

Branimir gritted his teeth and turned away. How crude would the gods be to give Alden and Sulanna the blessing of a child, only to have them hacked apart by the undead hours later.

"It cannot be," Branimir said stubbornly, pointing to the top of the summit. "How did you two get up there without a flower from Lada to open the gates?"

Tyr answered, "Lada came and took us to the *Hall of Iredale*. The ninth gate was not sealed when we returned just now. But, Branimir, we did not see Alden and Sulanna here or there."

"Maybe Lada took them somewhere else," Branimir said in a brittle voice. "She must have."

The gateway behind them split, pieces falling away as something struck it repeatedly. The unmistakable layer-upon-layer of frozen skin reaching through the crevice was clearly the giant, demonic Bukavac tearing through. Tyr reached for his two-handed axe on his back only to remember he had left it below with Alden and Sulanna.

Dorofej redirected them. "Weapons, we do not have."

"But we can wield *Koldovstvo* with the weakening wards," Alyona said.

"Wield *Koldovstvo*, I will not." Dorofej scowled, shaking his head. "We only have a single route to end Eisliev's assault, yes?"

"No," Branimir glared at the black mage. He could not believe that Dorofej would refuse to fight.

"What is he talking about?" Tyr asked.

"He wants us to kill him so *kaelandur* will be destroyed," Branimir said with frustration. Tyr reeled back in disgust at the proposition. Branimir was glad to see the gut response from the Ispolini. The roars of the demons were growing louder. "We must find another way. We can defeat Eisliev."

Dorofej's eyes pleaded for understanding.

"We cannot kill you, Dorofej," Tyr said in agreement, turning to Alyona who shuffled her feet, considering Branimir's words. Tyr hesitated. The gate behind them would not last much longer. The giant winced at his own words, "If you are certain, why do you not kill yourself?"

"He cannot," Alyona answered for him. "For *kaelandur* to be destroyed, he must be killed by the blade, but the magic of *kaelandur* will not let him."

"By the Nine Lands," Tyr groaned, looking at his own hands. "I have killed before…"

"No. I will do it. It should be me," Alyona said, acknowledging Dorofej with respect. She rubbed her hands against her pant legs and then reached for Branimir. "Give me *kaelandur*."

Branimir shook his head. "I said *no*." He stepped away from the *Kadari*. Behind her, stone fell from the gate in several large chunks, crashing to the ground. It burst into smaller pieces, scattering across the street.

Bukavac squeezed through the gate. Branimir had almost forgotten the massive size of the beasts, standing twice as tall as any human with brawny arms equally thick as his own lithe body. The bodies were colored like snowfall with blue-grey eyes brightly lit like gems. A smaller army had taken Melkorka against the Highborn twelve-hundred-years ago; Branimir could not fathom how the four of them could defend *Iriy*.

"Kill them!" he heard Eisliev shout from somewhere beyond the gate. "Bring me the dagger!"

The first to surge from the opening clutched an iron sword between its three fingers and thumb, roaring with fanged teeth. More emerged from behind the Bukavac, carrying axes and maces, forged in the Netherworld.

"Run," Tyr ordered. Before Branimir could say a word, the Ispolini turned to meet the monstrous demon. Springing forward, he raced to intercept the Bulkavac.

Despite the Bukavac's larger size, Tyr was built for war even when he held no weapon; his physique glistened in the sun's light. The demon swept the sword blade in an upward arc with aim to cut Tyr in two, but the Ispolini was light on his feet, spinning at the last second to dodge the attack. He then hooked his arm under the Bukavac's leg and pulled up with a growl. The demon roared, flailing the weapon wildly before crashing onto his back.

Tyr rolled over the demon, crushing the demon's arm to the stone, and ripping the sword free from its grasp. The giant maintained the momentum, rolling completely to his feet in a fluid motion, crouched at the ready. The Bukavac hastily reached over to slash at Tyr with its clawed hand, only to catch the sword's edge. The bluish-blood spurted with the severed hand. The Bukavac's cry turned to a gurgle as the demon's own sword plummeted through the mouth, the iron point chinking against the paved stone on the opposite side of the Bukavac's skull.

Alyona joined Tyr in the fight, flinging fire and ice at the demons who rushed from the gate. Their screeches and howls echoed through the city streets.

Branimir stepped back as another crashed into Tyr, using its body as a weapon. The giant stumbled back a step, ducking the secondary attack as the Bukavac swung an axe for Tyr's head. With his own battle cry, Tyr kicked with his bare foot into the demon's stomach, and then spun on his heel to slice the sword across the beast's chest. The Bukavac screeched its death cry and collapsed.

"We have to help him," Branimir said, reaching for *kaelandur*. He had no other weapon to wield. Tyr was already lifting the sword against another Bukavac.

"No, Branimir," Dorofej said. "*Kaelandur* has only one life left to take, yes? Kill these demons, or Eisliev with it, you must not." The weapons clanged with as much ferocity as two armies fighting instead of one against hundreds.

Alyona shouted at them. "This place was not meant to withstand a siege. We will die here."

"Then we need to go somewhere else," Branimir urged.

Metal on metal rang as more Bukavac advanced from the gate. Tyr had slain another demon or two, but the numbers would soon be overwhelming. Almost twenty beasts pushed through the gates with hundreds more at their back. Tyr Og swatted at them, barely deflecting their attacks with the sword.

Alyona cried out, dropping fire from above the horde of Bukavac. The flames threatened the space near Tyr. "Where can we go?" Alyona asked.

Branimir looked around with frustration. "Sorod!" he lastly exclaimed. "Sorod can be our escape."

"Beyond the demon army, the gateway to Sorod stands," Dorofej said, pointing at the Bukavac pushing through the gate.

Alyona agreed. "He is right. We would have to miraculously push through them to even reach the gate. But you might escape if you are not to be seen."

He could hear Tyr snarling in the backdrop among the Bukavac. Alyona shouted, throwing stone. Already, she had wrinkles forming near her eyes.

Branimir shook his head, recalling his encounter with Eisliev at *Harrowhal*. "If I am holding *kaelandur*, Eisliev can see me, regardless of whether I am invisible."

"Again, only the one option stands, yes?" Dorofej pressed. "Kill me, and then flee from *Iriy*."

Branimir's roar of frustration melded with Tyr's sudden cry of pain as an axe caught him in the lower thigh. He fell to the ground, swinging the sword riotously at the oncoming demon horde. The Bukavac with the axe circled him, avoiding his flailing sword. Blood flowed from the leggings he wore; the gash cut to the bone. As he swung his sword at the Bukavac, another demon plunged a sword into his side.

"No!" Alyona screamed, flinging fire at the first, only to have another take its place.

"We must hurry," Dorofej cried.

"Give me *kaelandur*, Branimir," Alyona whispered. She reached for him. The marching footsteps were as loud as thunder. The Bukavac were coming for the dagger.

"No." Branimir pulled back.

"Give it to me, Brani—" Alyona was silenced, ripped through the air by the unseen magic, and flung into the statue of Perom guarding *Koranitsa*. The sickening crack of her head hitting the stone could not be missed.

Branimir gasped.

"No," came the voice of Eisliev Kluk, stepping from the throng of demons, his red cloak flowing at his heels. Eisliev's light blue eyes blazed with intensity. He raised a finger, devoid of color, grey as death, at Branimir. "I will take *kaelandur.*"

Tyr cried out at the sight of his old friend, swinging his weapon to catch the still attacking Bukavac in the knees. The demon fell to the ground and Tyr scrambled over him to jam his sword into the monster's chest.

Another Bukavac with an axe advanced.

"Tyr!" Branimir cried out.

The giant spun around soon enough to catch the blade in his chest. He immediately spurted blood, swinging his sword aimlessly at the Bukavac. The demon backed away, leaving the axe lodged in Tyr's torso.

With a grunt, he pulled his sword behind his head and flung it with both hands. The blade ripped through the frozen chest of the retreating Bukavac. The demon screeched in surprise, descending to its knees. No doubt, the monster would die, but Tyr had left himself vulnerable. He tugged at the axe in his chest as more Bukavac advanced.

Branimir tried to rush forward but was caught by Alyona's hand. The first Bukavac loomed over the giant, pulling back his iron sword. Tyr, bloodied and already dying, yelled with defiance. The sword's end ripped through Tyr's throat, silencing his protest.

Branimir turned from the sight, tucking his head into Dorofej's shirt, as the blade was pulled free and the giant slumped over.

"No other choice, do we have. I am sorry, Branimir Baran." Dorofej backed up the steps to the sanctuary.

Branimir saw Alyona fall limp on the ground behind him. Everyone he knew was dying.

"My sincerest apologies, Dorofej Kaligula," Eisliev said, his blood-stained lips twisting into a smile. "I appreciate you and this *Kadari* killing Falmagon. He will be a fine addition to my demon horde. But I am afraid there will be no place for you in the next world as we had agreed." He laughed to himself. "Though, I promise to keep you alive until the Likhyi have been freed from the Ash Tree. I believe that is a fair trade considering the horror your bloodline has not only set on my own, but now, the world."

The black veins beneath Eisliev's grey skin darkened, lifting Alyona's drooping figure from the stone steps. He twisted her with a sneer, while the Bukavac at his back waited for their command.

"Stop," Branimir weakly begged. Fear gripped his heart. The world would break.

"I cannot say Alyona will last, Dorofej," Eisliev smirked, drawing out his words, dropping his gaze to the black mage.

Dorofej took a breath, falling back to his haunches, sitting on the steps in defeat. Never had the face of the Stuhian been etched in such shade. He gulped, pulling up the dark sleeves of his robe. *Faegrim* caught Branimir's eye. "I am sorry, Branimir. When it is done, you disappear. You run."

Branimir had not the time to make a sound, and all the foreboding ridding his heart of courage fled from him. The world became a dream, unrecognizable to Branimir. Something deep within him stirred, screaming at him that nothing was real. Yet he could not help but embrace the state of sentience, brimming with light and love.

A mirage of all who knowingly forewent their own paths to follow Branimir overlapped in his mind like pages being flipped through in a book. The countless benevolent words and kind embraces; the many gentle smiles and altruistic passions. Thousands of words spoken, and battles won, and moments shared overwhelmed him. He could think of nothing else. Laughter occupied his ears. Admiration filled his thoughts.

Eisliev's voluble screams rocked Branimir back to reality, the pleasantries of his hallucinations evaporated. The temple of *Koranitsa* faded into focus. The statues of the powerful gods overseeing the perfectly-spaced, stone steps, brushed with the ever-brooding blood. The crimson shade matched the color dribbling from the end of *kaelandur*, grasped securely in Branimir's hand.

Dorofej's lifeless eyes stared past Branimir at the cloudless sky. The black mage was dead.

"No!" Branimir's shriek was prolonged, echoing off the stone, forever meant to linger across *Iriy*. His voice cracked painfully in his throat. The salted tears burned from the corner of his eyes to the depths of his nostrils. He was drowning in his own sorrow. "No! By the gods, no!" Pain trickled against his temples, forcing him to his knees. *Kaelandur* slipped from his fingers, falling to Dorofej's bloodied robes.

Branimir could not believe Dorofej would have been so cruel. He used *Faegrim* to force Branimir's hand.

"What have you done?" Eisliev bellowed, dropping Alyona, and storming forward. He whipped Branimir around by the jacket. Bran crashed against Dorofej's body with Eisliev looming over him. Fire furiously flared behind his eyes. "You have fated the world to endless death without reprieve. Never again will there be peace!"

Branimir could not make a sound, his soul shattered by the evil he had done. Dorofej's blood soaked into the back of his thin shirt. Feeling the inevitable warmth, his vision blurred with tears.

The din of the Bukavac growling and snarling gave a clear warning of Branimir's imminent death. No doubt, Eisliev would be certain he followed Dorofej to the afterlife to be warped into Marheena's demonic army.

Eisliev fumbled around Branimir, finally pulling the copper dagger from the stone steps where it had toppled. As though he hoped against hope, he held the blade in his open palm studiously watching Branimir from the corner of his undead eye. At first, his face etched with confusion, but then the inevitable happened as foretold.

Kaelandur dissolved into ashes, flowing from his hand into nothingness. The remaining slags fluttered across the stone of the temple as though it had never been.

The black, billowing fog surfacing with *kaelandur's* destruction was unexpected. An unholy darkness spread over the expanse above Eisliev and Branimir with gale-force, stretching as far as the first ranks of the Bukavac, violent and untamed. Branimir struggled against the unfathomable force, noticing the demons milling in the streets, several withdrawing through the eighth gate. He wiped his eyes with his sleeve, staring helplessly at the mass collecting above him.

Finding his strength, Branimir cricked his neck to see Alyona stirring near the statue of Perom. He rolled off Dorofej to his stomach, shielding his eyes from the swirling darkness above him. With what he could muster, he crawled for the *Kadari*.

Eisliev cried out, stooping back from the ethereal form. He shouted as though he were speaking to a voice only he could hear. "I have not failed. Do not renounce me!"

A blast of energy, along with the strident thunderclap, propelled Branimir face first into the stone steps, cracking his forehead open. He groaned, blood straightway gushing down into his eye.

He swayed, lightheaded, swiping the blood down and across his cheek. "Alyona," he forced the name from his mouth. His throat swelled as though he had not spoken for days.

"The Ash Tree will perish!" Eisliev screamed in desperation. "I promise you! You will be freed!"

Eisliev's words turned to wails as the darkness corkscrewed into a downward spiral into his wide-open mouth. The red mage's petitions fell to distorted sobbing as his body convulsed under the power of the profane shade. In a breath, the skin molded into the remnants of a corpse a thousand years old, reduced to nothing but rotten remains. Eisliev Kluk had been defeated.

The Likhyi had come.

Chapter XXIV

Branimir shook the *Kadari* woman with both hands, praying she was not dead. "Come on, Alyona. Wake up. Wake up, please."

Eisliev's decrepit carcass had become little more than a pile of brittle bones and corroded flesh. Branimir could not ignore the smell of the decay, more rotten than all the demons in the streets of *Iriy*. He repeatedly looked over his shoulder to ensure Eisliev did not return from death while attempting to rouse Alyona.

"Alonya." He shook her again.

The Likhyi above him, a pool of darkness hovering over the streets, blocked out the sunlight meant to forever shine over the City of the Gods. Branimir could still see well enough down the streets—enough to see the Bukavac swaying hesitantly behind their now dead commander—but the Likhyi's bleakness reminded Branimir how terrifying it had been in the tombs of *Garain'l* when he first encountered the *old-dark*. His heart raced in remembrance of the fear. The Likhyi had stolen his sight with the impenetrable pitch of its ethereal form. He did not want to experience blindness again, nor did he want to experience the same fate as Eisliev—and Falmagon.

Branimir wanted to flee *Iriy*, but he did not want to disappear and leave Alyona behind.

He hit her across the cheek, feeling the sting against his own fingertips. "Alyona!"

She stirred slightly but gave no sign of waking. The blood on the back of her head had dried. He could feel the soft flesh rising from where she had struck the statue of Perom with her skull.

He needed her to be okay.

The Likhyi's darkness broadened and descended, roiling over the stone, sifting through the demon ranks. The Bukavac gnashed their fangs at the empty air as the mist consumed them. Their ice-blue eyes darkened as though they were possessed by some irrefutable force. Branimir shuffled closer to Alyona horror-struck. The beasts turned to him at unspoken command and raised their weapons at the ready. The clinking of their weapons chilled his blood.

"Alyona," he hissed.

The mist of the Likhyi continue to expand, unyielding, reaching over Eisliev's body toward Branimir. He swore he could see ghastly fingertips forming from the swelling vapor.

He backed away until he practically sat on Alyona's chest, his back pressed against the stone foot of Perom's statue. As the Likhyi neared the tip of Branimir's hooked nose, a blooming radiance vented from the doorway of the temple as luminous as the first light of dawn. The rays struck the *old-dark's* ghastly hands, causing it to recoil from Branimir.

Branimir jerked to the strange light, half-covering his eyes, to see a silver horse appear in the doorway with a rider on its back. The animal was led unconcernedly from the doorway, halting just above the steps to oversee the demon army and Likhyi. As the yellowish glow gently subsided, Branimir saw Svathevit the Red, the God of War and Glory, sitting atop the hoary mount. The four faces on either side of his head remained expressionless, as they had in the temple earlier. His blood-red cloak fluttered behind him, draped over the haunches of the horse. The esteemed god of the Svet, pulled a glimmering blade from the sheath on his back, and held it out to the side.

At first, Branimir thought Svathevit intended to hand him the master-blade. But then the undead warrior exited from the temple behind him. Kowin marched to the stairs, the blue dots of his sunken eyes barely visible, snatching the weapon from Svathevit's hand. He slipped the blade into the empty scabbard on the right side of his belt as though it were a key being inserted into its lock. Then he cocked his neck and reached for the two scabbards on his left, pulling loose two straight-edged blades. He twirled the left blade to hold it upright in his hand, while testing the weight of the other in his right.

The chains at his wrists and ankles unfastened and fell away from his decaying skin. Smoke roiled from his lips. With satisfaction, he lifted his hateful gaze to the Likhyi eddying above them as a storm cloud might.

Svathevit spoke in Branimir's mind with the dominance of the divine. *'Svarog has given way for Kowin the Deathless to stay the hand of the Likhyi until mortals have revealed whether balance can be regained. He shall return to Thrice Ten Kingdom once their failure or triumph has been determined.'*

A roar spewed from the hundreds of demons in defiance, signifying the displeasure of the *old-dark*, their new imperious master. Kowin shortened their battle cry, waving his hand, using *Koldovstvo*, flinging the frontline Bukavac a hundred paces back into their own kind.

The demons wrestled over one another in a fitful attempt to hurriedly return to their feet, to wage war against the unforeseen threat.

Branimir had nowhere left to scoot, but he still shirked back against the statue as Kowin stomped down the steps with purpose. The crimson-colored, steel breastplate seemed to deepen in its redness.

He did not pay any attention to Branimir, engrossed on the reassembling Bukavac. He was uncertain if the man was alive or dead, god or mortal, friend or enemy, but he carried himself as though he were unstoppable.

Branimir grabbed at Alyona's face, pulling at her desperately, while his eyes stayed forever fixed on Kowin the Deathless.

Like a snowstorm, the Bukavac collided with Kowin, fanatically devoted to the Likhyi hissing with irritation in the sky. Nothing could have prepared Branimir for the heroic battle which ensued before him. Iron and steel clashed, sword against axe and spear tip. Kowin moved with trained proficiency, unaffected by his old age or decomposing skin. He ducked under blades, and stepped over polearms, using his two whirling swords to parry and then pierce when an opening broke in the demon's attack. Skin was cut away and guts spilled; blue-tinted gore gushed and sprayed. The Bukavac, standing a head and a half taller than Kowin, soon began to amass at his feet.

The death count was incalculable. And, yet, more demons rushed from the eighth gate to attack Kowin. The rumble of the Likhyi intensified as the *old-dark* beckoned his newfound army to eliminate the warrior who had been sent to deny its emergence. Branimir could not hear the Likhyi's grating tone any longer—now separated from *kaelandur*—but the swollen, curling fog cast a shadow darker than all the Shade Fells.

"Branimir…" Alyona coughed, pulling at his leg. "Get off me. I cannot breathe."

Branimir sprang from the *Kadari*, falling on his knees next to her. "You are alive. Nine Lands, you are alive." He grabbed her by the shoulders to move her, ignoring the death cries screeching around them.

"How am I alive?" She lifted her neck to see the battle raging in front of them. She pulled herself up. "Is that Kowin the Deathless? That means…" She gasped, seeing

Dorofej's body sprawled across the stairs. "Oh, Branimir…No…"

Branimir did not follow her gaze. He could not look at Dorofej's corpse.

She weakly looked up at Svathevit, who remained seated on the silver horse. He watched everything around them with his four faces. The face on the right side of his head, skimmed Alyona on Branimir, but he said nothing.

Kowin stole Branimir's attention, bellowing with fury, running his sword through a Bukavac's chest. Kicking the demon from his blade, he then lifted his hand and released a stream of fire into the demons. Orange and red flames lashed through the ranks of the beasts. The skin of the demons ignited in an infinite blaze, causing them to thrash back with screeches of agony.

Branimir gaped in shock, noticing the festering skin stretching from his cheekbone to his jawbone begin to patch itself together. Threads of flesh stitched up and down the side of his face, while the fire burned and the lives of the demons were stifled.

With a gritty grumble, Kowin unleashed a greater inferno with *Koldovstvo*, crying out the louder. And then, as if showing the extent of his power, he used his magic to rip the statue of Wolos from the front of the temple. With little effort, the thirty-foot tall statue was hurled into the demon legion. The stone shattered against the bodies of the Bukavac. The curled horns, and hooves, and the stone spear of Wolos, wrecked into the horde, breaking bones and crushing skulls.

Branimir also noticed the statue pummeled into the wall and the gate, sealing the entrance and their exit. The Bukavac on the opposite side could be heard crashing into the stone in attempt to break through and pursue Kowin at the behest of the Likhyi.

Kowin roared with power. With every demon life taken, Kowin's body regained the time taken from its essence. The rot and decay disintegrated from his skin, replaced with the thriving color of life and vivacity.

His eyes no longer sunk. His skin no longer hung loose from its bones. His muscles swelled to reflect their impressive strength. Kowin the Deathless was being renewed.

"Branimir, we have to get out of here," Alyona said, struggling to her feet. "Kowin cannot be trusted. We cannot be here when he has finished with the *old-dark*. There is a reason he was held prisoner by the gods."

He looked at Alyona in confusion, but dipped his head in agreement. He thought Kowin fought for goodness and righteousness. He eyed Kowin uneasily, standing upright with her.

Kowin surged forward, cutting his sword through the remaining Bukavac in the street. The demons screeched and bawled, defenseless against his swords.

"How will we pass by him? Where will we go?" Branimir asked, reaching for Alyona's shirttail.

The Likhyi rumbled loud enough to deafen his words, declining toward Kowin. The swelling, black cloud only made it a few inches before Kowin spun on his heel and lifted his hand. A blue, shimmering field of force rapidly formed beneath the Likhyi, spreading a distance great enough to envelop the darkness. Like water trapped in a bottle, the Likhyi sloshed around inside the magical shield, attempting to break free. Kowin gritted his teeth, his dark hair and blue eyes reconstructing with his flush skin until he nearly looked fully human. He appeared to be an Anshedar male, never to have known death.

"Branimir," Alyona murmured, pulling at his shoulder.

He turned around and stopped, facing the thigh of Svathevit. The God of War climbed down from his horse and approached them without word. He now hovered over Branimir and Alyona with his eternal, silent expression. His horse neighed behind him like a meek warning.

Svathevit grabbed them.

The flash of light was dazzling, and suddenly Branimir found himself clear of Kowin and the dead. He blinked several times, identifying the perfected carved stone beneath the shining light of the sun. Svathevit had taken them to another level in *Iriy*.

Bran steadied his feet, feeling Svathevit's hand holding fast to his shirt behind him. He chose not to struggle. The God of War's voice echoed in his head.

'Your share in this tale has expired, Branimir Baran, son of Hrani, and Alyona Gounari, daughter of Meimer. Here, you will find safe passage to Sorod. Beware the path of honor and glory; death awaits. For glory. For Rujan.'

With a shudder, Branimir twisted on his heel to face Svathevit, but the god vanished with his last words.

"Where are we?" he turned to Sulanna. The sounds of battle echoed close by.

Alyona pointed at a shimmering stone wall ahead of them, shaking her head. "Svathevit has brought us to the seventh level. This is the ingress to Sorod."

Alyona ran a hand through her dark hair, looking in the direction of the eighth gate. "The world has not been saved; if anything, it has only become more dangerous with Kowin the Deathless venturing back from the Beyond. His power is only stayed by Svarog stowing away his soul. If he were ever to discover its resting place, he would wield more havoc than the Likhyi combined."

"The Likhyi have not been stopped either," Branimir said with frustration. "The demons at Melkorka will keep hacking away at the Ash Tree until another weapon is forged to break it completely. The *old-dark* have only been hamstrung by Kowin." Branimir irritably clenched his hands into fists. "What have we truly done? Has this all been for nothing?"

"No. *Kaelandur* is destroyed," Alyona assured. "This tale started with Wolos's death, and will end with his rebirth. Our journey is but the pages between the covers of a book. We have given the brothers at Anaerfell the chance to save Aenar."

Branimir took a breath and scratched at the thin hair on his head. "You are right. Erzebeth will see the dragon-men to the Netherworld and Wolos reborn."

"Do not worry, Branimir. I do not think our tale is over," she said.

"Far from it," he agreed.

Alyona stared at the gateway with concern. "Though, the Svet will not be pleased to find us in Sorod. If we are seen, the centaurs will likely string us up for their evening meal."

"Best we are not seen then, yes?' Branimir asked slyly.

Alonya grinned. "A bat then?"

Branimir returned the smile, and disappeared.

ABOUT THE AUTHOR

Joshua Robertson was born in Kingman, Kansas on May 23, 1984. A graduate of Norwich High School, Robertson attended Wichita State University where he received his Masters in Social Work with minors in Psychology and Sociology. His bestselling novel, Melkorka, the first in The Kaelandur Series, was released in 2015. Known most for his Thrice Nine Legends Saga, Robertson enjoys an ever-expanding and extremely loyal following of readers. He counts R.A. Salvatore and J.R.R. Tolkien among his literary influences.